MW00576870

REUNION
IN HELL

REUNION IN HELL

The Selected Stories of

John H. Knox

Volume 1

Edited and with an Introduction by

John Pelan

RAMBLE HOUSE

DANCING TUATARA PRESS #9

REUNION

IN HELL

CONTENTS

JOHN H. KNOX:
POET LAUREATE OF THE PERVERSE

Among all the writers of weird fiction in the 1930s two authors shared the rather unique background of being accomplished poets with solid reputations established in the little magazines and limited editions of the time.

The two men were Clark Ashton Smith and John H. Knox. Oddly enough, their reputations are quite dissimilar today ... While both men brought a lyrical quality to their depictions of the horrific and grotesque, Smith, due in large part to his association with H.P. Lovecraft and August Derleth has had at least one volume of poetry or prose in print since the publication of *Out of Space and Time* in 1942. Most recently Night Shade Books has embarked on publishing Smith's complete short fiction in a six-volume set.

John H. Knox on the other hand was featured only in a slim chapbook published in 1972 and a handful of stories that have appeared in various facsimile editions such as Girasol Collectables' reprints of *Terror Tales* and anthologies edited by the late Sheldon Jaffrey and more recently Ron Hanna's excellent anthology *Weird Wonder Tales*. Other than these few appearances, aficionados of the horror story have overlooked the work of John H. Knox.

This volume is the first in a series that aims to rectify this oversight and preserve the weird tales of John H. Knox in a permanent format such as these stories deserve.

So who was this talented poet and how did he come to make the transition from bard to the author of such bone-chilling tales as "Mates for the Murder Girls" and "Court of the Grave Creatures"?

Born the son of a preacher in New Mexico moving to Abilene as a boy, Knox was encouraged by his father to read Shakespeare and other classic authors. By his late teens he was captivated by more contemporary authors such as Jim Tully, whose tales of the vagabond lifestyle had a profound effect on the young man.

Knox went off to see America first hand via hopping freight trains and doing odd jobs that ranged from manual labor to work-

ing as a cameraman in Hollywood. After two years on the road
Knox returned home to Abilene and where he began writing poetry while furthering his education at McMurray College.

Knox's poetry was well received, appearing in *The Prickly
Pear* and other "little magazines". In 1924 Knox founded *The Gal-
leon* and began his career in earnest and by 1930 Knox found himself in the center of a literary group that included authors such as
Edward Anderson, Files Bledsoe, and William Curry Holden.

Despite being surrounded by such literary types and his own
passion for such serious authors as Thomas Mann and Marcel
Proust, Knox's own fiction was of a much more fanciful and
darker nature.

When *Dime Mystery Magazine* made the switch from tiresome
reprints and mundane mysteries to the new genre of "weird menace" the young author tested the waters by submitting a short piece
entitled "Frozen Energy"; it was accepted and published in the
December, 1933 issue, thus making Knox one of the earliest of the
"weird menace" authors; and a member of an illustrious fraternity
which included Hugh B. Cave. Wyatt Blassingame, and Arthur J.
Burks.

While most of his contemporaries wrote a wide variety of stories ranging from aerial combat to westerns, Knox was far more
single-minded in his approach, concentrating his energies on
Popular Publications' trio of terror: *Dime Mystery Magazine, Horror Stories* and *Terror Tales* with an occasional foray to their
competitor, *Thrilling Mystery*.

The formula of the "weird menace" pulps was that of the "ra-
tionalized supernatural" tale. Generally a series of horrific murders
would occur with all signs pointing to a supernatural agency, with
the implications that a vampire, werewolf, or even a demon from
the pit was to blame. The fiends would demonstrate a penchant for
disrobing and torturing nubile young ladies and would be revealed
on the final page to be all too human usually involved in some lar-
cenous scheme that was dependent on terrifying the local citi-
zenry.

At its worst this formula resulted in tales that resembled a typi-
cal episode of the Hanna-Barbara cartoon *Scooby-Doo* (lacking the
talking dog and hippie van, of course). However in the hands of an
accomplished and inventive author like Knox the stories tran-
scended the limits of the genre and became true masterpieces of
the macabre.

Knox, being widely read, tended to incorporate the folklore of his native Southwest and Northern Mexico into his stories that lent them a verisimilitude matched only by the widely-traveled Arthur J. Burks and the scholarly Chandler H. Whipple.

Throughout the glory days of the genre (1934-1939) Knox was practically omnipresent with a short story or novelette appearing somewhere nearly every month. Sadly, by the end of the decade politicians (who are always on the lookout for something to feign moral indignation over) targeted the "weird menace" pulps as corrupters of young minds and caused *Terror Tales* and *Horror Stories* to fold and *Dime Mystery* and *Thrilling Mystery* to alter their format to somewhat more conventional detective stories.

Knox made the switch and began a series of tales involving the diminutive Colonel Crum. While these stories are fine examples of their type the inventiveness and vigor of his earlier work seemed to be missing. Whether or not this was a result of the stress of his first marriage breaking up or a growing disinterest in a market that was becoming progressively more restrictive, his fiction output slowed dramatically.

By the 1950s Knox had re-married and moved to Alabama, turning his attentions to newspaper work and real estate sales. Again, like his contemporary Clark Ashton Smith, Knox had turned out a career's worth of top quality work in less than a decade, and like Smith did find time to write the occasional tale, but for all practical purposes his writing career ended with the passing of the "weird menace" pulps.

This book and subsequent volumes will collect all the known weird fiction of John H. Knox. For those readers previously unfamiliar with the work of this unjustly forgotten master of the macabre I've included in this volume some of the stories which first introduced me to his work. It's my hope that you experience the same thrill that I did discovering the work of this remarkable author.

John Pelan
Midnight House
Tohatchi, NM
April, 2010

MEN WITHOUT BLOOD

CHAPTER ONE

GRAVES THAT SHOULD NEVER BE OPENED

FOG, LIKE A BLIND AMORPHOUS MONSTER, imposed its tenuous bulk upon the city. A great grey-bellied beast, it brooded above the skyline, pushed down its clammy filaments into the canyon of the street, strangling the bleary street lamps, puffing convulsed wraiths into the dank, black alleys of the slums.

The man who sat in the sickly light from the globe above the flop-house door spoke in an alcoholic wheeze. Fear, like the imponderable pressure of the fog, had settled over this mean and evil district, and this man, for the moment, was its spokesman.

He said, sniffing as he knuckled his bulbous nose, "The p'lice don't know nothin' that goes on here, and people don't give explanations that wouldn't be believed. P'lice couldn't do nothin' anyhow; fightin' things that ain't really men, things that got no blood in their veins."

"That's a rather wild statement," Dwight commented.

"You ain't seen one of them things," the man muttered. "I have—two of 'em. There's more, Lame Lena that sells papers on the corner seen one last night. Knock sounds at her door. She opens it. This thing is standin' there, ugly as a dead monkey. 'What you want?' Lena asks, bitin' her gums. 'Blood,' the thing says. Lena slams the door and bolts it."

"Lena may have gone a little too heavy on the sheep-dip," Dwight suggested.

The man sucked at his greasy stub of a pipe; his rheum-clogged eyes rolled furtively over the gaseous billows of mist that choked the street. "But that ain't all," he said. "Curley Lennox seen one bite a dog's throat in an alley one mornin' 'bout sunup. The mutt howled and fought, but the Thing didn't seem to mind. It run off though, when Curley come up. The dog was dead."

"That's news," Dwight said, "when a man bites a dog."

The jest went unapplauded. In spite of himself it gave Dwight a queer feeling. You couldn't laugh about these matters, apparently.

"Another one bust into an opium dive," the man went on. "I won't say where. But the Chink had a corpse to get rid of later. The rest of 'em run off and left this feller—after they seen the Thing wouldn't bleed no matter how much they cut him."

"Good God!" Dwight exclaimed. "You mean, seriously . . .?"

"Didn't I tell you?" the man growled irately. "Didn't I say there ain't no blood in 'em?"

"A figure of speech, I supposed . . .?"

"Figger of speech, hell! Listen, I seen that fight in Hongkong Charlie's place myself."

"Let's hear about that."

The man rocked forward in his chair which leaned against the fog-sweaty building, and knocked the dottle from his pipe. "Three nights ago, it was," he rumbled. "I'd dropped in fer a spread of chowmein and a little snifter. I sees this Thing with the dead-pan sittin' there an' it gives me the creeps to look at him. But I goes on eatin'.

"Next thing I know there's a howl, an' this Thing has grabbed a Chink kid an' started to run out with him. Up jumps Emilio the Spick, who's sittin' by the door, and out comes Emilio's knife. As slick a knife-fighter as ever cut a Gringo's guts, that Mex. But does it do him any good? The Thing drops the kid, and they fight. The Thing's got no weapon, so it fights with its hands clawed. Emilio cuts him to ribbons, so to speak. Face, arms, throat slashed.

"Then of a sudden Emilio jumps back, goes white, crosses himself and begins to gibber in Mexican. That was when he seen the Thing wouldn't bleed. I seen it, too. There was a gash you could see the raw edges of—like a piece of bled beef."

"And no blood?"

"No blood. And mister, that Thing went out, and nobody follered it, neither . . ."

His words trailed off. Light footsteps sounded on the clammy pavement.

Dwight turned in the direction of the man's bleary glance. The slender figure of a girl was materializing from the mist. She walked with lowered head and face half hidden by the collar of her smartly tailored coat, but Dwight caught a brief glimpse of black, mysterious eyes, that sent a curious glow tingling in his veins, and he noticed how the wan light from the smoky globe lay softly on the perfect texture of her skin. No harpy of the pavements, that girl!

He was wondering what could bring her into this evil district, when, to his surprise, the girl with a sort of furtive duck turned in at the flop-house doorway and mounted the stairs. He saw her trim ankles vanish in the sickly light, heard the click of her heels in the hallway above and turned back bewildered.

The man grinned. His puffy; stubble-rough jowls spread in fat folds over the frayed collar of his coat. "Surprises you, eh—to see a doll like that in here?"

"Rather," Dwight said. "Who is she?"

The sagging shoulders shrugged.

"You're askin' me. Took me by surprise, too, when she come in this evening and paid fer a room. But should I ask questions? She paid; I reckon she knows her business.'

"Yes," Dwight said abstractedly. "Still, with all due respect for your establishment . . . But look here, what's your opinion about these monsters?"

The man screwed his flabby face into a grimace and spat. "Ugh! I don't know. Only they ain't human."

"Why do you say that?"

"Somethin'—a look about 'em. Faces with a greenish gleam on the skin, like you might see on a Chinese vase, eyes so cold and empty it makes you shiver, like when you look over a high cliff . . ." He paused, his brow creased intently. "I tell you they look like them figures of dead murderers from Paley's Waxworks come to life!"

Dwight looked sharply at him, but did not pursue his inquiries in that direction. "I'd give something to see one of your monsters," he said.

The man looked at him narrowly; sudden suspicion gleamed in his rheumy eyes. "You ain't a reporter?"

"No," Dwight said, "I'm a capitalist."

The man laughed. Dwight, too, smiled. Queerly, it happened to be the truth. He didn't add that conducting a private detective agency was his way of escaping the boredom of an idle existence.

"You'd really like to see one of them buzzards?"

"Five dollars' worth," Dwight said.

Greed gleamed rawly in the man's face. "All right." he agreed. "But just a peek. I don't want no disturbance—from him."

"You've got one—in here?"

The man nodded, dragged his shapeless bulk upright. "Came in this afternoon. Face all muffled. But I seen the eyes—the skin. I reckon he's sleepin' now, if they sleep. You can take a peek at him."

Dwight slapped a bill into the grimy palm and followed the scrape of the ragged shoes up the stairway. A dim, fly-specked bulb lighted the upper hall. It was bare of carpet and oily grime stained the floor and cracked plaster walls. The smell was the immemorial reek of such a place. Dwight stared about warily. It might be a trap; you never knew in a dive like this.

The slithering shoes paused. The landlord gripped his arm, shoved his head so close that the smell of sour alcohol was sickening. "He's in Twenty-two," he hissed. "We'll go easy, mister."

He slunk softly to the door and Dwight crept behind him. The transom was dark; there was no sound from within. The man's warty hand was on the knob; he gave the door a little push.

"Hmm!" This time aloud. He shoved the door wide. "Empty!"

"What's this," Dwight growled, "a game?"

The squat man's face was puckered with real surprise.

"So help me . . ." he began, "He ain't come down the stairs."

"Since he's not human," Dwight muttered sourly, "I suppose—"

"Don't laugh!" the man said grimly. "He's here—somewhere."

Then it dawned on Dwight what was in the man's mind.

"Damn!" he swore. "That girl! Where's her room?"

"Twenty-six," the man sputtered, and started forward.

Dwight followed, taking long strides on tiptoe. But they didn't reach the door. It was Dwight who grabbed the other's arm and drew him suddenly back. He had stopped at the closed door of Twenty-five. Feeling the iron grip on his arm, the landlord sputtered, rolled his eyes.

"Jeez! What is it?"

Dwight's features had clouded: the grip of his lean fingers tightened on the pudgy arm, "Look!" he said between gritted teeth.

"What . . . where?" The man raised his frightened eyes, stared.

The transom hung ajar, forming a dark and hazy mirror, and in the moist, distorted depths something was swimming, something like a human body which seemed to move gently with a curious volition not its own.

The man looked helplessly at Dwight; his jaw dropped, but instead of speech a flood of saliva ran out of his mouth and drooled from his pendulous under-lip. Dwight's face was a corded brown mask; the brows dipped severely over eyes gone black and hard as lumps of basalt. A revolver had appeared in one hand; with the other he was pushing the door slowly open. Then he stopped. He felt the shaking body of the landlord, now pressed against him, stiffen with a jerk. The hair on Dwight's neck bristled as he stared.

Between him and the open window, past which the grey and ghostly fog was boiling, the body of a man was hanging in mid-air. Headless and half naked, it dangled by its feet from a rusty iron chandelier, swaying with the gentle momentum of a dying pendulum. Directly beneath the bloody stub of a neck was a white wash-basin, and with each grotesque motion of the swinging corpse, fresh drops of the viscous, ruddy fluid were shaken down into the half-filled bowl.

There was no one else in the room.

Dwight turned. His companion, who had been gaping in speechless vertigo, now began to blubber his innocence in a terrified whimper.

"Shut up!" Dwight ordered hoarsely, and pushed past into the hall. Three long strides brought him to the door of Twenty-six. He twisted the knob. Locked. He rattled it, yelled, "Open it up!"

The hurried scrape of feet and a low muttering reached his ears. He backed away to the opposite wall, braced his thick shoulders and lunged. With a crack the flimsy lock gave, and Dwight's body hurtled like a projectile into the room. His shins struck a chair. He sprawled, cursing his luck, snatching for the revolver which had been jarred from his hand.

Then he froze, his hand poised in mid-reach, staring. In the embrasure of the open window three heads were visible. One of them was the head of the dark-eyed girl who now held in one tense hand a black automatic. Beside, and slightly behind her, wreathed like a goblin in the swirling fog, was something which might have been a man, something which wore human garments, but whose gaping mouth was literally split from jaw to jaw, so that a purplish tongue lolled between tiers of yellow teeth dropped wide apart. And in this creature's hand was the third head—a gory, nauseous thing, with bugging eyes and coarse red hair now twisted between the fiend's wax-yellow fingers.

For a moment, a curious sort of horror, detached and impersonal, swallowed up all physical fear in Dwight's mind. Then his hand moved toward the revolver a few inches away. But almost touching it, he jerked stiff again.

"Do you think I won't shoot?" the girl asked.

Dwight thought she would. He saw the barely perceptible tightening of her finger on the trigger, and froze into immobility.

"Back to the door!" the girl ordered. "Then face about!"

Dwight obeyed. The gun crashed behind him; the light globe shattered and fell in fragments as darkness swallowed the room.

Dwight ducked, ran to the window. It opened on a fire escape landing, and below he could make out dimly two figures descending the iron ladder into the alley. He whirled about, retrieved his revolver and climbed out. But already a car with wet top glistening through the fog was slinking out into the street.

He climbed back into the room, swung out into the hall and almost collided with the craven landlord who was creeping toward the door.

"God!" the latter swore hoarsely. "God! Wot'll I do?"

"Call the police, you fool!" Dwight growled and shoved him aside.

A moment later he was in the mist dreary street, legging it with swift strides toward his office, a definite plan in his mind.

Self-schooled in a dangerous calling, Stanley Dwight had two antidotes for nerves—action and more action. He also had a system of mental discipline which served him well in circumstances like the present. And as he strode, like a tall determined phantom, through the frothing billows of fog, he brushed from his mind the morbid, disconcerting horror which clung like a foul miasma about the night's events, and attacked the problem in a cold and analytical fashion. So by the time he had climbed the stairs, navigated the hall and swung open the door of his office he had already made lip his mind as to his next move. Then he picked lip the note on the desk marked "Urgent," and frowned. It was from his office boy and sales assistant, and it read:

Old Prof. Collins has kept the phone jangling all afternoon. Is he high behind? He says are you going to let them cut his throat or aren't you? If he's not already croaked, you better call him.

Jimmy.

Dwight tossed the note back and swore. "Croak him!" he fumed. "What that old egotist needs is a blind bridle to keep him from breaking his neck every time a paper blows across his path!"

He turned away toward an inner door with the firm intention of going on with his other plans. "But no," he said reflectively, and stopped. "No, he may scare himself to death. But I won't waste much time on him!"

He went out, closed the door, clumped back into the street and hailed a taxi. The car ploughed through the sodden murk of the streets and came to a halt before a cottage on the fringes of the university campus. Dwight told the driver to wait.

Professor Collins, wearing a dressing-gown and carrying a revolver in one slightly tremulous hand, answered the door. He was a small, dumpy man, with scraggly hair fringing a pate as white and ponderous as a roc's egg. His pink face was clean shaven and its cherubic cast belied the erratic temper and the intellect for which the eccentric scientist was noted. Dwight saw at once that the professor was at present as swollen as a toad with indignation and uneasiness. He followed the professor into his bachelor study, prepared for the outburst.

There the dumpy scientist squared off and faced him. And the outburst came.

"Well!" he exploded. "My well-being, I suppose, is a matter of small moment to the world. Still, since I have employed you to protect—"

"So they've written again?" Dwight inquired laconically. "Let's see the note."

He watched the professor as he fumbled among his papers. Pompous and egotistical! Ignorant people often took him for an ass. Better informed people, of course, knew that the man who had startled the scientific world with his discoveries in the fields of biology and organic chemistry, could scarcely be that. Dwight had been in one of his classes and was accustomed to the professor's tantrums.

"It's signed this time," Professor Collins said indignantly as he thrust the sheet toward Dwight.

Dwight took it, glanced at it abstractedly, then stiffened abruptly with interest and alarm. It wasn't the substance of the

note that excited him. The order to leave his laboratory unlocked
was natural enough in view of the fact that valuable supplies had
already been stolen. It was the signature that caught Dwight's eye.
   The note read:

   Last warning. Vacate your house for the night and leave
your laboratory unlocked.
   What we need we will get. Disregard this order and a fate
worse than death will be yours.
                                   The Six Without Blood.

Dwight looked up sharply. It had been his intention to mini-
mize the seriousness of the thing. His real opinion had been that
mischievous students had taken advantage of the professor's nerv-
ousness since the recent robbery to play a joke on him. Now, matters had assumed a different aspect. Was it possible—this grotesquely horrible conjecture which had dawned, nebulous and
half-formed, in his mind?
   "Look here," he said bluntly, "you haven't come entirely clean
with me in this business. What were the chemicals which were
stolen?"
   The professor paled, moistened dry lips nervously. "Why do
you ask that?" His manner now was considerably subdued.
   "Maybe you know," Dwight countered.
   The professor fidgeted; then, as with an effort, he brought his
eyes level with the detective's. "I see I'll have to tell you," he said.
"I had two reasons for holding that back. First, the habit of a lifetime of guarding my incomplete experiments from a prying world.
And second—" Here he paused, and a grim look hardened his mo-
bile features—"and second, the possible consequences to society
of a discovery of the properties of that compound."
   Dwight leaned forward, the muscles of his face tensing. "Be
plainer," he said curtly. "Just what do you mean?"
   "I mean," said Collins, "that if the properties of those drugs
were discovered by evil minds, the very fabric of civilization
would be unsafe!"
   Dwight sprang to his feet scowling. "Then your damned secrecy," he growled, "may cost a ghastly price! I don't know what
your stuff was, but I begin to suspect a connection between it and
an unspeakable horror. Did it have something to do with blood?"

Professor Collins paled; his mouth popped open in astonishment. "It does indeed," he stammered, "but how could you have known?"

"I don't," Dwight said, "but I imagine there are others who do. Tell me quickly what effect the stuff has."

Professor Collins nodded, swallowed with difficulty, got up. "Great God!" he breathed, "What have I done? I knew that there were graves that should never be opened!" His words trailed off in a sort of sob. Then he straightened, clenched his hands, blinked at Dwight. "But perhaps it isn't too late! You shall know all, the whole incredible secret. I have it all written down—a paper I was preparing. I'll bring it." He trotted toward a half-open door which gave on his laboratory.

The door closed behind him. Dwight took a deep breath. His head was throbbing. Thank God he had come here after all! Now he would know. Certainly Providence must have brought him here, brought him to the only man perhaps with the power to devise an antidote for the horror he had unwittingly unleashed.

What did it all mean? *Blood . . . graves opened . . .* Dwight could only guess, and his brain whirled with the chaotic vision of monsters reanimated, monsters with some frightful hell-brew in their veins, monsters more hideous and appalling than beasts, soulless, pitiless, conscienceless! He saw them in a multiplying horde boil up from the dank dens and alleys, swarm through the fetid gutters, gibbering insanely, shrieking like the damned, driven perhaps by a loathsome thirst for what their bodies lacked, howling for blood, blood, blood. . . .

The vision swirled and vanished; reality thundered back as a sound from the laboratory sent an electric current rippling through Dwight's veins. A crash, a muttered oath, and then the scream—a shrill ululation of fear and agony which rose until the walls seemed to shiver before its impact—then died in a convulsed, blubbering sob snapped sharply off!

CHAPTER TWO

WHERE CORPSES WALKED

DWIGHT HURLED HIS BODY toward the door. He tried the knob, beat on it with his fists. It was locked—an automatic spring lock on the inside, he supposed. Damn the man's absent-mindedness!

"Professor! Professor!"

There was no reply. More than fear, Dwight realized now, had been in that wail. He threw his weight against the door, battered it until the bones of his shoulders ached. But it would not yield.

He crouched, applied his eye to the keyhole. His knee-joints went watery at what he saw. Horror like a slimy thing crawled into his throat and choked him.

In the small area of visibility which the keyhole afforded, two figures could be seen. One was the headless body of Professor Collins, sprawled hideously in a welter of blood upon the floor! The other was the grisly Thing lifting its lean, cadaverous body over the sill of the window. In one harpy-like claw, it carried a flagon of some dark liquid, in the other a sheaf of papers.

For an instant the Thing turned its head. Dwight would never forget that brief glimpse of its face. For it was the face of a revenant, a ghoul, a *thing without blood!*

The stunned paralysis which held Dwight lasted for only a moment. He sprang to a side door, gun in hand, and dived out into the black and vaporous night. Groping his way through the sodden murk, he reached the open laboratory window. But the specter had vanished, swallowed up by the humid, incorporeal fog which seemed its proper element. Except for the ghastly, decapitated body, the laboratory was empty.

Then, in the alley behind the place, an automobile motor roared its hoarse vibrations through the smoking mist. Dwight stumbled toward the front of the house, saw that his taxi was still there.

"Get started!" he yelled. "Follow the car that leaves the alley!"

The driver nodded. As the car shot forth, he swung swiftly in pursuit.

But it was hopeless. The fog, that clammy monster who fights for crime, spread the shadow of his tenuous wings about the ghostly fugitives. Somewhere, soon, they made a quick turn and were lost in the greyness.

Dwight saw then that it was useless to attempt to pick them up again. He had seen the car out dimly. He settled back and gave the driver his downtown address. No use in going back to the place. Professor Collins was beyond all help now, and the papers had been stolen. He would phone a report of the murder to the police and then follow the faint and bloody trail alone.

He got out at his office and hurried in. And the first thing he did was to take a stiff drink of whiskey, a very stiff one . . .

Thirty minutes later, Stanley Dwight, unrecognizable in his shabby topcoat and flop-brimmed hat, and with his face considerably the worse for a little deftly applied make-up, shuffled his sagging shoes along a fog-muggy street of pawnshops, penny arcades and cheap clothing stores. Ahead of him, in the middle of the block, a spot of light stood out under the grey nimbus of the fog. Colored globes, which winked like evil eyes, formed an arc over the foyer of an old theater and lit up the cracking sign: *Paley's Wax Museum,* past which the fog in pink and green wraiths was drifting.

A thinning crowd of grey, nondescript figures stood hunched and half interested before the painted box where a gold-toothed spieler with a scenic necktie was talking hoarsely and gesturing with a cane toward the sample exhibits,

"There he is, ladies and gentlemen," said the spieler, pointing toward the waxen image of a burly young giant who stood on a pine plank gallows surrounded by a wide assortment of lethal weapons. "There he is—a man who loved his feller man! Yes sir, why he loved his feller man so much that he ate him!"

Even the unresponsive crowd stirred a little at this ghastly pronouncement. A murmur like a challenge rose from the seedy ranks.

"You don't believe it? It's a matter of police records. And the man boasted of it himself. He ate his pal when the two of 'em was starvin', hemmed up by the law in a Florida swamp. Bysshe Guttman was his name—the only authenticated modern American cannibal! He saved a million bucks from his crimes, hid it away. But the law finally got him. He was drowned a month ago while trying to escape from Alcatraz Island. His body was never recovered from the swift current. So the fishes ate the great lover of human-ity!"

He cleared his throat, spat discreetly within his box and turned to another figure. This was of a small man, incredibly hairy, with a thick black beard muffling his features, and smoked glasses over his eyes. He wore an Inverness cape and there was something monstrous and evil about the soft, almost dainty hands which were outstretched as if for inspection.

"See them hands, ladies and gentlemen?" the spieler barked. "The hands of a sorcerer! Dr. Magwood was this soft-speakin' little feller's name—a skilled surgeon, a madman, a pleasure-killer. In the dark of night he done his bloody deeds for pleasure, cuttin' his victims in pieces an' arrangin' them in neat piles. Foxy as a devil, he claimed he could do magic, even raise the dead. He was supposed to have been killed by a mob, but it ain't certain. Now, ladies and gentlemen, inside you will see . . ."

Dwight heard no more. He shuffled to the curtained entrance, asked to see the manager and was directed to a narrow flight of steps that led him up to a cubbyhole office. The man behind the battered desk lifted a thin, crafty face to regard his visitor.

"You're the manager?"

"Yes."

"I want to collect that ten dollars you offer to anyone who'll spend the night in your Gallery of Ghosts."

The manager studied him shrewdly, rolled a smoking cigar be-tween thin fingers. "We've had a little trouble with that stunt," he said. "Several men got so scared they ran out in the middle of the night."

"I don't care. I need the ten bucks. I'm broke, out of a job. It's good publicity . . ."

"Sure, it's good publicity." A pause. "Got a family?"

"No. What difference does that make?"

"We got to know these things. How's your health—nerves good?"

"Nothing wrong with me. Just not eatin' enough."

"Well, I suppose—if you want to try . . ."

"Thanks," Dwight said. "When do I start?"

"It's about closin' time now," the manager said. "I'll have 'em put a cot in there for you."

Fifteen minutes later Stanley Dwight sat alone on a narrow balcony which overlooked a huge and dimly lighted room. Around and below him, like a vast congregation of the unhallowed dead which the very grave had rejected, the pallid effigies of evil were grouped. Dwight was watching the door which had just closed. The man who had brought him here might still be spying, so for a time he sat perfectly still on his cot.

Three colored ceiling lights threw out a faint and greenish luminescence of a brightness about the equivalent of moonlight. Under this weird unearthly glow, the silent and ghostly place took on the look and atmosphere of a morgue—but a morgue in which no veil or covering softened the icy contours of death's horror, a morgue in which the unhallowed dead had risen with stiff, corroded limbs to mock in a motionless pantomime whatever black and bestial deed had won them this posthumous infamy.

Reaching into his pocket, Dwight took out a folded piece of paper which he had been carrying about for several days. It was one of those anonymous tips, some worthless, some valuable, which drift to the office of every detective. It had come to him unsigned through the mail. It read:

> Have a look in on Paleys Waxworks. The police are too dumb. Men go in there and dont come out. Somebody dressed like them runs out yellin to fool people. Tramps and drifters are all theyll take, so nobody wont know the difference.
> A strate tip.

Dwight pondered the queer message.

Until tonight he had given it little thought. Now, with only a blank void like the fog confronting him, it seemed a clue worth following. It was little enough, but it was something. The flophouse keeper's mention of the resemblance between the monsters and the wax-effigies had brought the note back into his mind. Then too, this place was located in the very heart of the district which the execrable creatures seemed to have chosen for their hunting ground.

Added to this were the words of Professor Collins which, together with his ghastly end, had engendered that appalling hypothesis in Dwight's mind—and now he seemed to see a possible connection between the scattered pieces of the jigsaw puzzle. He meant to wait now, see if anything happened. If not, he would make a thorough search of the place. He wanted particularly to

examine some of the effigies, to see if, as rumor had it, there were
real corpses among them.

Dwight put the note away, stood up and looked about him.
"The Six Without Blood!" Here at least were men without blood.
Their frozen attitudes, their gruesome postures, their staring lifeless eyes seemed to mock his thoughts, jeer at him horribly. The
figure nearest to him, that of a sallow young man who had murdered his father-in-law by thrusting his head into a gas stove, was
seated beside the replica of his fiendishness, staring at it with an
expression almost of pride.

Feeling that by now he should be safe from the manager's eyes,
Dwight stepped to the figure. He stripped the baggy clothes from
the stiff frame, wrapped his own topcoat about it and threw it on
its side upon the cot. He laid his hat over the thing's eyes. At a
little distance it might have been his own body, peacefully asleep.

He then took up his position in the chair by the stove. He ad-
justed his limbs in the very attitude of the effigy, and sat very still
with his revolver on the edge of the chair beside him.

Silence and forced inaction are the immemorial allies of fear.
Dwight, who prided himself on the steadiness of his own nerves,
thought of how an ordinary man might feel in this place alone. He
thought of it with a certain amusement but also with a certain
vague flutter of uneasiness. The imagination is a powerful and terrible instrument. For instance, with very little encouragement from
excited nerves, Dwight could imagine that he had seen a figure—
the figure of a murderess in a group below—move slightly as if
tired of the posture. Well, that was patently absurd. He expected
something to happen, but no such fantastic business as that. He
laughed it aside and waited.

The place was deathly still. A jittery man might positively lose
his mind staring too long at the horrible, frozen immobility of
these grisly figures. With the thin green light over it, it was like
some ghastly tableau frozen in ice. It was like something a man
might see if he came upon some village where a sudden catastrophe had left the whole population frozen in their tracks, standing
hideously in their familiar attitudes with a frightful, timeless pa-
tience, as if for ages unnumbered they had stood thus, and for
other ages would so stand. He imagined how such a man might
wander for days among staring dead faces, until his mind cracked
and he shrieked for them to move or speak.

A totally unexpected throb of cold shot through Dwight's veins.
At first he thought that it was the idea itself which had excited it—

then he realized that in reality it had been an impression that the wax figure slightly behind him had moved. But he did not turn. If anyone were watching now it would be fatal to betray the fact that he had substituted the wax figure for his own upon the bed. As for that wax likeness of a dead murderer, well . . .

His thoughts scattered like leaves before a puff of cold wind. He did not move or start, but now his eyes narrowed in earnest. It was the slight figure of the hirsute Dr. Magwood which had been brought inside at closing time and which now stood here on the balcony just under the dangling noose of the portable gallows. It had seemed to him that this figure had bent slightly as if to peer at the thing that lay upon his cot.

Now, without making a movement, Dwight studied the figure's face. Something like a gleam of life showed in the eyes behind the smoked spectacles. He hadn't noticed it before. The figure was perfectly still now. Why did it give such a curious impression of life and intelligence? It was looking at the cot, looking with a sort of rapt gloating, like an obscene fat spider leering at a captured fly.

Dwight stiffened, stiffened into a cold rigidity that rivaled the frightful statues themselves. For from somewhere in the room below, the rusty mechanism of a clock began to purr and chime. The sound was somehow ghastly in that tomblike chamber.

Then, on the stroke of twelve, the short figure of the evil Dr. Magwood bent forward with a movement slow and mechanical! While Dwight watched with a strange breathlessness and a slow, clammy crawling of his skin, the bearded ogre reached up, caught the noose of the gallows rope and began to draw it slowly down!

Dwight fought to keep his muscles steady. An hallucination had been his first thought. Now, as a flash of reason told him that the thing was really taking place, the horror of that creeping, ghostly pantomime held him with a dreadful fascination. For the feet of the bearded doctor made no sound, yet they were moving nearer and nearer to the cot. And the fiend's grisly lips, which showed like bloodless slabs of flesh between the beard, were parted in a smile of insane gloating!

Dwight held himself ready to spring up, gun in hand. He now understood what sort of hellishness had been going on in here! And at the thought of the unsuspecting men who had awakened at midnight to find this creeping demon with his noose bending above them, his blood ran cold. For the squat figure in the cape was now bending above the cot, was reaching out his pudgy, ob-

scene hands with a sort of hideous gentleness to place the noose
over his victim's head.

Now! Now was the moment! And while the hair bristled on his
scalp, Dwight slid one hand across his lap to seize the revolver at
his side.

Then abruptly cold horror like strangling fingers of ice closed
on his throat. For where the pistol had been, the fingers of his
groping hand encountered something as repulsive as the touch of
rotting flesh. At the same moment he lunged away. Lunged but
could not move—for fingers like the jaws of a vise were on his
shoulders, dragging him back!

He struggled to his feet, still unable to turn and face the nameless horror which had fastened itself upon his back, for the
strength of the thing which held him was like that of a boa con-
strictor. A cold and hairy arm had encircled his throat in a deadly
strangle-hold which held the air in his bursting lungs and seemed
to be forcing his eyes from their sockets with the torturous pressure.

Still he fought with his waning strength, for the horrid little
monster of a doctor was moving toward him now, a low chuckle
quivering in his throat.

A choked cry of fear and defiance rattled from Dwight's lungs
and he made a desperate lunge at the fiend. Something stung his
arm, something like the jab of a hypodermic. His senses began to
swim. Giddily he reeled, felt himself released to stagger forward
blindly.

Blackness passed for a moment over Stanley Dwight's mind,
blackness which he felt, in that awful moment of awakening consciousness, had been something sweet and merciful. For now his
hands were bound to his sides, the noose was about his neck, and
he was being dragged up, up from the floor. He saw the green
lights spinning; he saw the bearded face of the doctor, floating
hazily like the head of a demon. Then the dark flowed back, grate-
fully swallowing mind and senses.

CHAPTER THREE

HOSTAGE OF THE DEAD

D WIGHT OPENED HIS EYES. For a long time, it seemed, he had lain there in a semi-conscious stupor. Now his nerves jerked thoroughly alive. Instinct warned him of the nearness of some living presence.

He blinked into the eerie twilight of the tunnel-like passage in which he lay, realized that he was lying upon a clammy floor of stone, his hands and arms still bound. He flung his body over. Pain shot through him at the first movement of his wrenched and swollen neck. But in the shock which now smote his cringing nerves, the pain was forgotten.

A silent figure was bending above him. It was a woman. Pink tights ruffled at the waist—the outmoded chorus-girl costume of the murderess he had seen move in the waxworks! Next his eye fell on the point of light that gleamed dully on the blade of the knife she held, striking the weird attitude of some sacrificial priestess.

Then he saw the face, and a queer sob of mingled incredulity and despair forced itself between his gritted teeth. For it was the face of the girl with the dark eyes and hair whom he had seen in the flophouse! The black eyes bored into his now with a strange fanatical gleam that gave to her face a mingled beauty and horror. The knife seemed on the point of descending. . . . Dwight's jaw set; he steeled himself for the blow.

And then the frozen look on the girl's face changed. Human feeling betrayed itself, a sort of startled anxiety, "Oh!" she sobbed. Then in a suppressed whisper, "I almost killed you—I thought you were one of *them!*"

"The first break I've had," Dwight grunted. "Cut these ropes quick! Who are you!"

"My name doesn't matter," she said. With quick fingers she slit the ropes and released him. "I came here to kill. You're going to help me."

Dwight got to his feet. "I'm going to get out!" he said.

"But you can't!" the girl whispered. "We're prisoners. The trap-door that leads into the waxworks is guarded, and it's the only exit. They caught me hiding in there, just as they did you. But they didn't search me; I had the knife hidden under my sash. I pretended to be unconscious and they left me in this passage. Now I'm going on. I'm going to kill *him* anyhow!"

"*Him?* Who do you mean?"

"Dr. Magwood."

"Then," Dwight stammered, "it *is* Magwood—here, alive?"

She nodded.

"And what's that got to do with you?"

"You remember," she said, "that man with me there in the rooming-house—the poor creature with the mutilated face? He's Fred, my brother. He *was* Fred, I mean. Now he's a maniac with a broken mind, one of this fiendish doctor's victims."

"Tell me about him—Magwood," Dwight said. "What's he doing?"

"Bringing dead murderers back to life!" she sobbed. "He's stolen the formula for some sort of synthetic blood to revive them. But he has to have fresh human blood for his work. He traps his victims in the waxworks, just as Fred was trapped. He drains the blood from these victims, then revives them with his chemicals and they become monsters.

"Those he can't revive are embalmed and put in this museum. Fred and two others managed to escape. But they couldn't become men again. The stuff in their veins made them thirst for blood. You saw—there—there in that room. It was dreadful. I had searched for Fred, found him there. But he had killed a man, was trying to drink—God! I can't say it.

"You see, that's why I couldn't go to the police. I managed to get him away, take him home, lock him up. He swore he would get the two other victims and come here, kill them all. But—" she sobbed fiercely, "that's what I'm going to do!"

"Rot!" Dwight snapped. "With a knife? We'll go back, fight our way out, then come back with the police—"

Dwight broke off to follow the girl's tense gaze. She was staring toward a ruffled ribbon of light which showed beneath a curtain at the end of the passage. Sounds came from beyond that curtain—a murmur of voices, a rhythmic creak, creak, like the noise of a rusty pendulum. A medley of strange chemical smells drifted to their nostrils, and a persistent reek like the sickening, bloody smell of a slaughterhouse.

A voice rose above the murmur: "A little more blood, Brutus, a little more blood."

Dwight seized the girl's arm. "Come!" he whispered.

She pulled away. "No!" she said. "I'm going in!" And she ran stumbling toward the curtain, the knife in her hand.

With an oath, Dwight raced after her. But he was too late. She flung the curtain aside and went staggering into the room. Dwight followed—and as the thick velvet curtains rippled past his body, talon-like hands clawed at him from either side, gripping his arms and shoulders. He fought, but his body was dragged back, held as in a straitjacket.

Further struggle was useless. The two powerful creatures, with the bloodless. dead faces and cold, empty eyes, pressed their loathsome bodies against him, pinioned his arms securely. Another of the beasts was holding the sobbing girl.

The blood throbbed hotly in Dwight's temples. His throat seemed dry, scaly. He stared helplessly about the strange long room—something between a laboratory and an abattoir. Long tables held test-tubes and retorts and all the gleaming apparatus of the chemist. There were shelves of chemicals and curious looking machines.

In one earner a weird contrivance caught Dwight's wildly gazing eyes. It was something like a child's seesaw, mounted on a frame of gleaming steel. Strapped to it was the naked body of a man, and at each end one of the grisly, grey man-monsters was keeping the contraption in motion, bending and straightening his gaunt, repulsive body with the stiff and rigid movements of an automaton. This accounted for the creaking sound which Dwight had heard in the passage.

His captors had made no move; they seemed to be awaiting orders. Here and there about the walls of the room, numbers of the repellent creatures were squatting on their haunches like apes, their lean, hairy arms dangling, their bloodless faces stamped with a listless and dismal despair. And worse—hunger, stark hunger was in their insane eyes as they watched him through the red, uncanny mist of light which fell from globes in the ceiling. Dwight shuddered.

"Prepare the girl!" The words came from somewhere behind, in a lisping voice that was somehow vile and unnatural.

Dwight jerked his head about. Beyond a nearby laboratory table, the shaggy head of Dr. Magwood was visible, thrusting up
from the hunched shoulders, caped in black like the body of some
loathsome bat. He was moving about briskly with tubes and phials.

The fiend who held the girl moved away with her. Dwight held
himself in check, trying to formulate some plan. With a morbid
fascination he watched the frightful doctor's hands, thought of the
man's unspeakable practices. Those were the hands that cut human
beings to pieces—for pleasure! God! It would be better if he and
the girl were dead and in decent graves!

Magwood was holding a test-tube in each hand. He poured liquid from one to the other. *Pfff!* A small explosion shattered the
tube and sent billows of acrid smoke into the air. The doctor
sprang back, neither injured nor alarmed, and began wiping his
hands on a towel. Now he looked at Dwight, fingering him with
his eyes as a butcher might a calf brought in for slaughtering.

"Strip him and bind him," Magwood lisped, "and take him to
the meat room."

The meat room! Dwight fought again, straining and snarling
like a trapped animal. But other monsters sprang to the assistance
of those who held him. Their rasplike hands tied him and lifted
him and carried him, still struggling, to that place of unspeakable
dread.

They went through a narrow doorway, and Dwight was flung
without ceremony upon the floor. He heard the door close; he
lifted his eyes, and an almost intolerable impulse to retch and
vomit seized him. The reek of the place was frightful, and what he
saw was indescribably worse. For from the walls of this small abattoir, there hung by meat hooks, like so much beef in a market,
four hideous bodies, headless, naked, with small glass bowls beneath each gory neck to catch the dripping blood!

There was a small, round hole in the door at about eye level, a
peen-hole apparently, where the captors could stare in at their victims. Dwight staggered to his feet, inched his way to the door and
stared out.

He gasped, grinding his teeth together and digging the nails of
his fingers into his palms. For two of the nauseous revenants were
carrying the body of the girl toward the seesaw contraption. Limp
and inert, her slender body lay in their clutches like a wilted
flower, her dark hair trailing back from the pallid face.

Horror and a sickened fascination glued Dwight's eyes to the scene. He saw the ghouls halt the motion of the seesaw, narrowed his eyes to stare at the great muscular body that lay upon it. Panic swept over him as he recognized in the square, brutal features the face of the murderer, Bysshe Guttman, the man who had been drowned a month before in the swift currents off Alcatraz!

Disgust, loathing, and a vertigo of incredulous terror gripped him then, held him in its frozen talons as he watched the inert body of the girl being placed upon the machine, saw her strapped there at the side of the dead cannibal, while a strange contrivance of tubes with a dial and siphon was fastened to her numb wrists. He went berserk then, writhing at his bonds, beating his helpless body against the door which would not yield.

Gradually he sobered, took a desperate grip on his throbbing nerves and tried to think. The opening of a door behind him caused him to swing his body clumsily about. A man had come into the room and stood confronting him, and for a wild instant Dwight thought that his reason had cracked. For the man who stood in the doorway was Professor Collins!

After a moment the professor spoke. "It seems," he said calmly, "that we are in the same boat."

Dwight found his voice. "Good God! What—? I thought—"

"It might have occurred to you," said the professor, "that I would be more valuable to them alive than dead. That headless wax figure on the floor in a pool of blood was a thing easily contrived. It served to establish my death and they stole it out of there later."

"Good God!" Dwight burst out. "They'll use you in this business too, then?"

"Perhaps . . ." Collins seemed resigned now, all trace of his erratic temper vanished. "And you too—if you'll permit a rather grisly jest."

"What do they intend to do with us—the girl and me?"

"The girl is being used now," Professor Collins said, "in the process of resurrecting Guttman."

"Then Guttman is . . .?"

"Technically alive now. Magwood tells me that he had planned the thing before Guttman's escape. Guttman expected to be drowned, but Magwood had promised to revive him, and he thought it worth the chance. For almost thirty days the man's heart has been beating. There are moments, he says, when a flicker of consciousness is evident. In the end, I have no doubt, he will live."

"With your chemicals in his veins—like these others?"

Collins shook his head; there was the hint of a smile on his lips now.

"I'm afraid I exaggerated a bit in my excitement," he said. "Frankly, there is no magical chemical, as you believe—only a system. I have used it with considerable success on animals and it consists in the use of artificial respiration, artificial heating of the body, injections of defibrinated blood, physiological salts and *epinephrine,* or adrenalin. Even my seesaw plan, which you see them using, has been experimented with before. It forces the blood to circulate by constantly shifting the center of gravity."

"But these monsters," Dwight protested. "What is it that flows in their veins—surely not blood? They won't bleed."

Not after Magwood has dosed them with a newly developed hemostatic, the work of a Canadian doctor who perfected it to the extent that it will instantly stop bleeding from even a major blood vessel.

"These creatures you see are not reanimated corpses. They did not die. When they were weakened by pain and fear and loss of blood, which Magwood extracted for his use, they were dosed with the hemostatic and told that they were no longer human. Magwood's hypnotic suggestion and the fact that they would not bleed has convinced them that they are nothing but walking cadavers. It also awakened an insane craving for blood. He feeds them small doses and keeps them in a state of docile slavery."

"And these?" Dwight jerked his head toward the hanging bodies.

"They were too unruly, Magwood informs me. He finds other uses for them."

Dwight's face twisted into a sickened scowl; a crawling nausea turned and twisted in the pit of his stomach. The tense silence of the place was punctuated by the creaking of the machine on which the body of the girl was strapped like a human sacrifice, while the blood in her veins was being sapped by the loathsome thing beside her. In the end she would be another of these repulsive ghouls!

Some emotion deeper than fear stirred in Dwight then, something primeval, inherent in his blood. His black eyes blazed with a new fire as he lifted them now to Professor Collins' face.

"Look here," he said, "you're not in the same fix as we are. He won't kill you; he needs you. But with your help, I'll destroy this monster, even if it costs my life, which it probably will. It'll likely cost yours too. But you won't stand back on that account, will you, Professor?"

Collins did not answer at once. As Dwight stared at him, he felt the blood draining from his own cheeks, felt a more appalling horror than any which had gripped him. For Collins had looked away, was staring abstractedly at the wall.

"Speak, man!" Dwight half screamed. "Are you a fiend too, or just a coward?"

Collins' glance swung back; the eyes were cold, emotionless, "You cannot understand, perhaps," he said, "but neither life nor death nor any human value means anything to me—nothing but science. Science is my life, my god!"

"You're a coward!" Dwight snarled. "You're yellow to the quivering marrow of your bones!"

He stopped, biting off his words sharply. A queer alarming light had sprung into the professor's eyes. It was the lurid glimmer of monomania, the flame that hides in darkness, unseen by normal eyes except when betrayed by a moment's passion!

"My God!" The words forced themselves in a half groan from Dwight's throat. "My God! I see it now. There is no Magwood; there is only Collins!"

No flicker of emotion showed in the professor's face, but strange yellow lights were crawling in his eyeballs. "Have it your way," he said quietly. "What of it? Society has dogged me with its taboos, refused me living men for my experiments. But science will not be thwarted. I wondered how long the wig and whiskers and cape would fool you. It doesn't matter. In a few hours you will be hanging on the wall here like any other dog." A look of deep-rooted cruelty betrayed itself in the immobile features as he added, "But first I'll let you see the girl, let you see what we do to her!"

That was the last straw. Dwight's nerves cracked. Reason was swamped; only the blind and driving impetus of outraged instincts remained as he threw his shackled body toward the fiend.

Heels against the wall, he thrust out his lowered head like a battering ram, drove with all his power. It caught the professor in the belly, jarred him back against the opposite wall. Dwight toppled to the floor, writhing and kicking like a tied cat.

Rage, suddenly unleashed, burned like an angry fire in the professor's face. A knife leaped into his hand and he sprang like an insane, gibbering monkey upon the helpless body of his victim. Dwight kicked, butted with his head, rolled over and over, threshing his bound body from right to left, while the little monster clung to him like a catamount. He seemed determined to cut Dwight's throat without injuring the rest of the body. And it was this intent which gave Dwight his few minutes' respite from death.

But Dwight was weakening. At last, with burning lungs racked by the unequal struggle, he found himself flat on his back, saw the blade of the knife inexorably descending toward his jugular vein.

The knife stopped in mid-air. From the main room had come the staccato sound of gunfire! Pandemonium seemed to break loose then. There were cries and curses, the crash of objects thrown and broken, the slap of running feet!

Collins sprang to his feet, dropped the knife, dived through the door.

Flinging his body about, Dwight seized the knife with savage eagerness. While out there the sounds of battle heightened, he struggled with his bonds. He managed at last to free his wrists and ankles. Then he peered out the door. His mouth widened in amazement.

Already the place was a shambles of corpses and milling bodies. The grey-faced monsters were fighting in a pack, like wolves. Urging them on was Collins, with an automatic in each hand, firing at the three men in the curtained entrance.

Those three, automatics in their hands, were spraying the room with a murderous fire! Shoulder to shoulder they stood, shouting cries and jeers at the cornered ghouls, and their faces were like the faces of their foes. They were, Dwight realized now, the three who had sworn to come back and wipe out this place of torment. One of them he recognized, by his split mouth and hanging lower jaw, as the brother of the dark-haired girl. They had arrived just in time.

But the relief which had flared in Dwight's breast was smothered a moment later by mounting despair. He had turned toward the now motionless seesaw. Bullets were whistling through the air, spattering the plastered wall behind it. The half-alive murderer and the living girl were equally exposed to that annihilating gunfire— and it was evident, as men tumbled from the grey and howling ranks of the ghouls, that the crazed gunmen had failed to see or recognize the girl, and would not stop until all life was wiped out of the place.

Dwight measured the distance between him and the girl. He might reach and free her—but they could never escape. They would never survive that fire.

Then inspiration dawned upon his brain with a wild surge of joy. It was a single picture, flashed from his memory—the doctor, the two chemicals which when mixed had caused the small explosion!

Dwight dropped to his hands and knees. He darted out the door and scuttled like a rabbit for the shelter of the nearby laboratory table. One of the ghouls loomed up before him, with up-raised knife. He tackled the hideous shape by the legs. It fell heavily to the floor and he raced on. Bullets sang past him; a slug tore a bite from his heel. but he did not stop.

A moment later the two bottles were in his trembling hands. He placed one of them against the wall, then darted back a few yards and hurled the other at it.

A dull concussion thundered in the air. A sheet of fire leaped out like a spreading stain across the room. Abruptly the atmosphere was choked by a thick and soggy smoke; acrid and stifling, that rolled and boiled its blinding vapor over the scene of carnage.

The cries redoubled. For a moment bullets ceased to fly.

Knife in hand, Dwight plunged through the smoke, fought his way through the struggling, blinded ghouls to the girl. He found her struggling weakly into consciousness, slashed the bonds that held her, threw her across his shoulder. Then, following the wall, he groped toward the entrance. Now the maniacs had come to grips in the blinding fog of smoke with knife and tooth and claw. Heaving bodies were all about him; a knife slashed his shoulder. But he fought his way to the entrance, plunged down the now deserted passage. He climbed painfully through the trap-door that opened in the floor of the waxworks. There he laid the girl aside and heaped a pile of heavy furniture over the basement's only exit, locking the battling fiends in their smoky hell.

Then he called the police.

An hour later Dwight, with the weak but otherwise uninjured girl, sat cozily in the back seat of a police car which was whisking them to their respective homes.

Still a little dazed, the girl had listened to his explanation in silence. Now she asked: "But why did he do it? Why would a respected scientist stoop to such a thing?"

"As he boasted," Dwight said, "science was his god. Anything, even the use of humans in his experiments, was justified in his mind. Society, of course, would not permit it, and that irked him. He wanted to raise the dead, to be a sort of god himself.

"Then the idea of getting Guttman to escape and take a chance on a revival after he was drowned must have occurred to him. He had a special reason for that. Guttman was reputed to have a million dollars hidden, and with that money Collins could have financed his dangerous experiments to the end of his days. And that was what he desired most in life.

"The reason he brought me into it is obvious. He wanted a reliable report of his death to be circulated. That would leave him to work unhindered in his secret slaughter-house, and it would also leave his reputation unstained."

"It's horrible, horrible," the girl muttered. "I—I'm glad, now, that my poor brother was killed. It—it's better for him. But I can't forget the horror of it all."

"You can try," Dwight said. "And if you'll let me, I'll try to help you. I think I can. There are so many things I want to talk to you about. You might begin by telling me your name."

Smiling wanly, she told him. They nestled a little closer together on the seat. Outside the window of the car the fog swirled and billowed, but it was no longer sinister. It seemed soft and somehow comforting, like a pleasant veil that shut out all fearful memories, and walled them in an intimate world of their own.

CHILDREN OF
THE BLACK GOD

AS SOON AS SHE STEPPED OUT of the bus station in the little border town of La Joya, Arizona, Stell Carlson felt the horror return to her—knew that she had not escaped it. She knew, now, that she would never escape it.

"Drew," she gasped, pulling at her husband's sleeve, "Drew, don't leave me!"

"What is it darling?" He looked down at her a little anxiously; then his square face beamed in a boyish grin.

"One of those nervous spells, eh? Well, don't let it bother you, sweet. I'll go down the street and rent a car to drive us out to the ranch. Be right back. Walk around a bit. It isn't every day you get to see a *fiesta* like this."

Stell stood on the flagged walk, hugging to her heart the warm little bundle in her arms, staring down into the tiny pink face peeping from between the blankets, the moist small mouth, the wide, wondering blue eyes. A dry sob choked in her throat. God, it was horrible!

To know, in this dreadful, psychic way, that the horror had something to do with the baby, yet to be unable to tell Drew—unable to explain it!

"No, no," she muttered fiercely to the little face that looked up into her, "No, no! God wouldn't permit that . . ."

But Blanche had told her that such things had happened, here in this very place, among the superstitious Mexicans. Blanche had told her that, trying to shame her out of her fears. Well, she would be glad to see Blanche again, to hear her comforting words. Tomorrow, in a ceremony at Drew's father's ranch, Blanche was to marry Drew's brother, Ben. It was for this that Stell and Drew had made the trip from Dallas. But Stell was wishing now that they hadn't arrived ahead of schedule—so that there was no one there to meet them. She longed to escape at once from this place which had so suddenly become colored with the pigments of her nightmares.

She stared down the noisy street. Twilight was already smudging the last tinge of saffron from the evening sky, but there was a stir in the town tonight. The Mexicans, who comprised almost the total population, were preparing for the Day of the Dead—an ancient *fiesta*. Dolorous tunes drifted from the squat adobe shops and bars where men were toasting death, drinking wine and *pulque* goblets carved like skulls. And past the lighted windows where butterfly cakes were displayed among the yellow "flowers of the dead" revelers drifted, in shawls and *serapes* and huge hats, laughing in tones that carried a note of repressed hysteria. Quaint? Stell might have thought so once. But she remembered the legends of the horrors that took place at these ancient seasons of evil, and now it seemed hectic, ghastly!

Suddenly she stopped. She was scarcely aware that she had been walking until she was abruptly conscious of the woman standing before her, blocking her way. She had stepped out of a greasy looking tent with a fortune teller's sign over the door, and Stell found herself staring with alarm into a seamed and leathery face, half hidden by lank strands of grey hair straggling from beneath the black shawl—staring into small glittering eyes fixed intently on her.

"Leetle *senora!*" The woman's voice came in a low mumble from between the stumps of yellowed teeth. "I see you come from the station. You should not bring the leetle one to thees place!"

Anger flared in Stell for a moment, and she started to push past, but something in the woman's face stopped her—a queer look of pity, of sympathy that gave genuineness to the withered hag's concern.

"But what—" Stell began.

The crone stared at her with shrewd, narrowed eyes. "You have troubles—you are seek maybe? You come, bring baby, to sanatorium—no?" Her voice fell to a thin, shrill hiss. "But I tell you: go away, go away queek!"

Stell gave a start. She hadn't expected that. The hag was of course referring to Dr. Gambit's sanatorium where Blanche worked as a nurse. It was an expensive desert hospital for "nervous" patients. Founded a year ago by the famous specialist, it was located near the Carlson headquarters, and it had proved a profitable venture, not only to its owner, but to Drew's father as well, since it had attracted health-seekers to his dude ranch. Suddenly Stell wanted to laugh. The superstitious Mexicans were of course afraid of all innovations, afraid of the *gringo* doctors and their strange ways!

"But I'm not going to the sanatorium," she explained.

"No?" the hag's eyelids flickered with doubt. "But you are seek," she said.

Stell paled. Yes, she was sick—sick with fear. It was written plainly on her face. And this ancient, bedraggled creature was trying to help her, warn her. "Tell me," Stell suddenly blurted. "what is meant by the *haunting mothers?* Is it true that at these seasons, like the *Day* of *Death*—?"

She stopped. The hag, as if she had been struck, drew away from her with the hiss of a frightened cat. "Do not say that!" she hissed. "You know—?" Her sunken eyes were pools of fear as she stared into Stell's face. Then the fear faded, pity supplanted it. "Poor leetle *senora!*" she muttered throatily. "Ah, but I know. I understand. You wake in night, you want to geeve baby to somebody, maybe to keel baby—?"

"No, no!" The frantic denial came from Stell's lips in a horrified shriek. It was as if a hot iron had been laid against a raw sore. She turned as if to flee, but the hag grasped her arm, held her with horny talons. "Wait!" she husked. "Do not go to thees sanatorium! Do not go to thees Doctor *Matagente. . .*"

But Stell jerked away, staggered dazedly back in the direction from which she had come.

Drew drove up with the car just as she reached the bus station. But Stell's brain was still reeling and her body was numb. Even after they had left the town and were jolting along the rough road that thrust its dim parallels toward the dark hills, she scarcely heard Drew's words as he chatted cheerfully.

God in Heaven! Was it Possible? Could mothers of children do the things they were said to do when the weird madness attacked them? Yes, it must have happened. And was her own case to be another of those horrors? God! If she could only tell Drew, bury her face and blurt out to him the whole agony of her fears. But she couldn't! Before she had been unable to explain. Now—now she was afraid to!

Her mind groped back to the beginning of the obsession. Her mother had died years ago and she had been reared by her father. Stell had always been a bit nervous. But it was not until after she and Drew had adopted the baby that the dreadful dreams—or spells—had taken hold of her. At first it had been a sudden seizure in the night, a freezing sense of terror, a gust of sick nausea surging up into her chest, clutching at her heart, causing her to sit up in bed, staring with nameless horror into the dark until Drew awakened her. Then, gradually, she had begun to feel the *presence* in the darkness. Finally she had seen it. And since then it had never ceased to haunt her brain—that vague and indefinable blur in the darkness which had with each succeeding appearance become more plain—a face, a woman's face! A woman's face covered with streaming rivulets of blood. A face that spoke, that tried to say something to her which she could not understand!

After a few attempts to tell Drew about it, Stell had seen that she could never make him understand. She had held the secret torment in her heart until a month ago when Blanche Morrow had come to Dallas to buy her trousseau, and had stayed with them for a week. Blanche had listened to her without the fear and alarm she dreaded. And Blanche had cheered and comforted her. The recurrent dream, she had said, was simply the result of some repressed memory. Blanche had questioned her, using the methods of psycho-analysis. But the cure had not come. Blanche had promised that they would try again when Stell came to the ranch. If she herself could not cure her, some of the doctors at the sanatorium could.

Now Stell wondered fearfully about the old hag's warning.

"Drew," she asked suddenly, "have you ever heard of the *Haunting Mothers?*"

The car lurched a little as he swung his square good-looking face toward her.

"Are you worrying about such rot as that?" he asked. "It's just a silly Mexican myth. They say that at certain seasons—like this Day of the Dead—that the dead mothers of living children come back as witch-ghosts to haunt living mothers and try to steal their children away from them. Isn't that idiotic? But darling! You're shaking!"

She was shaking. But she managed to stammer. "It's a little chilly—the breeze."

It wasn't, though. It was oppressively warm. The last tinge of color had long since faded from the sky, and a dry hot darkness mantled the wooded hills into which the car was now crawling.

Presently Stell asked: "But Drew, hasn't it happened? I mean, don't the Mexican women sometimes become crazed and—"

"Oh nonsense!" he said quickly. "Of course there have always been women who destroyed their children. You know that. But as for using some fool myth as an excuse . . .!'"

Stell felt cold inside. That hard matter-of-factness of his! She could never tell him. "Drew," she asked. "Who is Doctor Matagente?"

"What on earth!" he laughed, "Doctor *Matagente* means, 'Doctor Kills-folk'. It's just a term the Mexicans use to describe any doctor they don't like. I hear they've been calling Gambit that. Why do you ask?

But Stell had turned in the seat, was arranging the covers with a loving hand about the warm little form that lay asleep in the canvas basket fitted to the back of the front seat. Love and terror struggled in her heart. God in heaven! Was it possible that she—?

Stell whirled back at a sudden screech of the brakes. The car shuddered to a stop. Drew had lurched forward, was hunched over the wheel, rigid, intent, while out of the darkness a weird heart freezing sound was drifting—the sick wail of a child!

"A baby!" Stell gasped. "Oh, my God, Drew, a baby!"

She had opened the car door, crawled out. The white ribbon of the road, with cliffs to the left and a canyon to the right, stretched away to a sudden turn. And now, from the shadows beyond the bend a strange figure was emerging—a Mexican woman, walking slowly, mechanically, carrying a child. The woman paid no attention to the car lights, did not seem to see them. With the slow, automaton-like steps of the somnambulist, she was walking on the road's very rim. And she was not holding the child in her arms. The squirming, crying little creature was held in her hands, extended in front of her!

"Oh, my God!" Stell gasped under her breath, "she's walking in her sleep. We can't startle her, we can't—"

The breath caught in her throat. Drew crawled out of the car, was moving slowly, in a half crouch, toward the woman. Needles of icy fear stabbed Stell's quivering heart then. For the woman left the road, moved out upon a jutting tongue of rock thrust like a thin peninsula into the blackness of the abyss, was moving toward its very end!

Stell started forward, halted with sudden horror. The woman had stopped on the chasm's brink, and with a hoarse cry had thrust the baby out as if to place it in unseen hands!

But there were no hands to take it! Stell threw her arms over her eyes as the small brown figure dropped, and the pitiful cry came wailing up from the darkness below . . .

Then she was staggering after Drew, whose feet were pounding ahead of her. She saw him stoop and seize the woman who had dropped in a heap, saw him drag her shoulders upright. Then she stopped, swaying, fighting back the sick nausea that was smothering her consciousness. For as the woman's head was lifted into the glare of the lights, an insane cry burst from her lips, and she lifted her hands, clawed at her face, digging her nails into the flesh while the blood flowed in crimson streams, and hysterical laughter bubbled from her lips. Stell's brain reeled then and she toppled with a cry.

Drew was carrying her back to the car. She slumped limply in the seat, heard him muttering as he started the engine. She sat up.

"Drew, what became of the woman?"

"She got away from me," he growled. "When you fainted I jumped to catch you, and she got away. And she'd murdered that child!"

"Murdered—?" Stell began weakly. "Yes, she must have been crazed, or asleep, poor creature."

Drew turned a scowling face upon her. "Poor creature, hell!" he snorted. "She ought to be drawn and quartered for it!"

Stell's whole body was suddenly shaking. Her heart sank dizzily into black depths of despair.

CHAPTER TWO

MAD HERITAGE

STELL'S SICK. We'd better get her to bed at once."
Drew's voice booming out roused Stell from the feverish stupor which had gripped her. The car had stopped and Drew was talking to his brother, Ben, who had come out to greet them. Other figures wavered in the light from the ornamental iron lantern hung above the floor of the hacienda.

"Blanche!" Stell's voice was a sick sob of despair.

The door beside her opened and Blanche's strong, competent arms were around her. "My poor darling! Why, you are sick. I believe you have fever."

Yes, Stell was sure she had fever. That horrible hot throbbing in her temples, her dry throat and tongue, the giddy weakness. Blanche helped her out. Drew was telling the others about the Mexican woman.

"I'm going right back after her at once," Stell heard him say.

Drew's father, old Grover Carlson, lean, tall, grizzled, had taken Stell's other arm. She nodded briefly to Ben, and leaning heavily on the supporting arms, went on into the house.

In the wide white bed, in the cool dim room with its beamed ceiling and heavy Spanish furniture, Stell felt better, relaxed a little. Blanche hovered over her, anxiety stamped on her firm. well-moulded features.

"It's just the shock," she was saying. "I'll give you something for the fever and then you must rest. Drew has gone back to see if he can find the woman and the child, or what's left of it."

In the tiny bed beside Stell's big one, the baby lay sleeping. Stell's haunted eyes clung with love and terror to the chubby innocent face—to the little figure, so doll-like in sleep.

"Oh, Blanche," she sobbed. "but it's more than that—it's the horror, it's still with me. It's worse!"

"Yes," Blanche said. "I was afraid of that. I've talked to the doctors about it."

"Isn't there some doctor that can help me—now?" Stell asked huskily. "I can't let Drew know, but couldn't I see one of the doctors at once?"

Blanche frowned. "Dr. Gambit is here now," she said, "In the library talking to Mr. Carlson. But in your present condition, I don't know whether you should . . ."

"But can't you see," Stell said in a desperate, pleading voice, "that I can't go through other night like this—that I don't dare?"

Blanche considered gravely a moment, then nodded and went out. A few moments later she came back, and Dr. Gambit was with her.

He was a tall man, stooped and extremely frail looking. His head was enormous, almost bald, and hung forward as if the thin neck could scarcely support it. And there was ugliness and intellect in the long flabby face, with its big bulbous nose, its deadly pallor, its piercing eyes sunken deep under bristling brows.

He shuffled into the room ahead of Blanche with the abstracted manner of a man who takes no account of his surroundings or of individuals. He nodded to Stell vaguely, then came and sat down in a chair beside her bed and stared at her with an intent, impersonal scrutiny.

"Miss Morrow has told me of your trouble, Mrs. Carlson," he said in his colorless tones. "I assure you that your case is altogether commonplace. You must speak frankly to me of your troubles and we shall soon get to the root of it."

He was holding her hand now and Stell was breathing jerkily. His hand was strangely cold, pulseless. The fingers were long and waxy, and bluish veins stood out sharply under the thick black hair that sprouted to the knuckles. "Dr. *Matagente!*" Stell thought, and was suddenly afraid of the man.

"Just begin at the first," he said, "and tell me all about it."

Stell swallowed, hesitated. Blanche smiled at her, and the ruddy healthful face above the white nurse's uniform was cheering. Stell began to talk, haltingly at first, and then eagerly. She told him everything—how the dream had first come, how it had increased in horror, how the face in the dark had become more distinct until she could almost understand the urgent words it was speaking to her, how she had got the impression that the command had something to do with the baby.

"And then," she finished, "when I heard of this belief of the Mexicans—this legend of the haunting mothers . . . I seemed to understand it all. At the orphanage, where we got the baby, we learned that she was a foundling, that they knew nothing of her parents. But I know, Doctor! The baby's mother must have died, died in some dreadful way. And she has come back to haunt me, to steal the child, to make me destroy it!"

Her voice at the last had risen to a hysterical cry and she felt the doctor's cold grip tighten on her band. "Now, now, Mrs. Carlson," he said, "enough of that rubbish! We are no longer in the dark ages, you know. Your trouble is purely mental. I cannot say definitely yet, but I do not think it is of physiological origin—that is, springing from some physical sickness. And if I am right, the recurrent dream will be easily traced to its source. The fact that the attacks began when you adopted the child suggests to me that the sudden assumption of the duties and cares of motherhood awakened in your unconscious mind some repressed memory—something painful and unpleasant from long ago. Suppose, Mrs. Carlson, that you tell me something about your own mother?"

Stell gave a little gasp. "But I don't even remember her, doctor," she said. "She died when I was only two years old, she—Stell stopped. It had occurred to her how little she knew about her mother, about the manner of her death, even. Her father had always been reluctant to speak of it. A fearful conjecture gripped her now. "So I really can't recall a thing, Doctor," she finished.

She saw his eyes light with a gleam of interest. "In that case," he said, "I think perhaps we had better try hypnotism. We may ferret it out in that way. Do you feel equal to it now?"

Hypnotism! There was something fearful about the word, something fearful, too, about this strange gaunt man who was proposing to take her mind in his hands like a yielding mass of putty. No, she didn't want that now, not yet, not until Drew could be with her! But her heart grew cold at that thought. She couldn't let Drew know! What dreadful things might she not say while the doctor probed her unconscious mind? And she could not wait, could not risk another night with the horror hanging over her!

"Yes, Doctor," she said breathlessly, "yes, I'd rather—now."

Dr. Gambit turned to Blanche. "Miss Morrow." he said, "I'll have to ask you to leave us, if you please."

It was a simple thing after all. At first there was the terror, amounting almost to panic. Then as Stell listened to the soft suggestions of the doctor's voice, uttered in a gentle undertone, a peaceful lassitude stole over her. Then sleep . . .

She came out of it, it seemed, scarcely a moment later. But she saw by the clock on the dresser that it had lasted thirty minutes.

Dr. Gambit still sat in the chair beside her. "You are awake now?" he asked gently. "Good. I think we have accomplished something tonight. Tomorrow we will continue, and soon . . ."

He left the sentence unfinished as he got up and bade her good-night.

"But doctor," she called after him as he moved toward the door, "can't you tell me something now? Will it come again tonight?"

"It is possible," he replied, "but it will not be serious. You must try to forget it now and sleep."

Forget! Sleep! Didn't he know that she could not forget, that she was afraid to sleep? She tried to calm herself and quiet the hammering of her heart. The doctor closed the door behind him and all was still. What had he discovered? A cold tremor shook her. Was it something too terrible to mention—was that why he wouldn't talk about it now?"

Suddenly Stell's body was trembling under the covers. She couldn't lie here alone, thinking, thinking. Where was Blanche? She must have Blanche with her. Sliding quickly out of bed, she fumbled in her handbag for slippers and a dressing gown. Slipping the gown over her pajamas, she stole to the door.

Why, she asked herself, was she so furtive? But she knew. It was the feeling that something was wrong with her, that the others all knew it, that they were watching her, hiding the truth from her. Even Blanche, perhaps.

She opened the door and stepped out into the hall. It was unlighted, but at its far end a luminous puddle from the open library door lay on the dark carpet. A murmur of voices drifted to her ears. Were they talking of her, was Dr. Gambit telling them . . .?

She crept nearer softly. She recognized the droning voice as that of Drew's brother, Ben. It was an unpleasant voice and she could tell that it was now thick with drink. She had never been able to like Ben Carlson, a lazy, neurotic fellow who drank to excess. She couldn't understand what Blanche could see in him.

Suddenly she jerked to a halt. A phrase had drifted to her ears, a sentence, and she froze, incredulous, with a sudden sense of stark insanity churning in her brain as the droning words became clear:

". . . that a young, healthy child," Ben Carlson was saying, "well nursed, is at a year a most delicious, nourishing, wholesome food."

"Shut up, you damned fool!" Drew's father's gruff voice broke in. "That morbid mind of yours . . .?

Ben laughed stridently. A book slammed shut. "Not my morbid mind," Ben said, "I was just quoting Swift. What I'm suggesting is that maybe someone is putting the Dean's idea into practice. You, for instance, Gambit—you look like a little red flesh and blood wouldn't hurt you." He laughed again.

"Be careful of your words, young man," Dr. Gambit said. "I've heard about enough of your ugly talk. I understand you have some sort of theory you're spreading that I'm trying in some underhand way to get control of this ranch property, to add it to my sanatorium."

"Well," Ben interrupted, "you wouldn't mind having it, would you? Aside from the value of the dozen guest houses we've built, the ranch itself is worth a cool hundred thousand. Though, of course, we might take less if things got unpleasant and the natives began to raise hell."

"And how would I profit by ruining my own reputation?" Gambit growled.

"Don't ask me, *Matagente.*" Ben replied insolently. "The Mexicans, though, say you've bewitched some of their women . . ."

"Shut up, Ben!" old Carlson stormed, "or get out of here? Why didn't you go with Drew to see about that crazed woman?"

"Not me," Ben said. "I told him to get Chris Manheim at the sanatorium. They ought to be back . . ."

The sound of a car pulling up before the hacienda cut off his words. Stell, in sudden panic, began to back away. Steps were approaching the door at the end of the hall. Quickly she opened a door behind her, slipped into a darkened room and closed the door, all but a crack through which she peered.

Drew, his face flushed and sweating, came into the hall. He was followed by Chris Manheim, a swarthy young man of about Drew's build, who was a doctor on Gambit's staff. They passed on into the library. Stell opened the door a little wider, heard Drew saying:

"We found her, yes. But it was horrible, She's either stark mad or a fiend. We carried her to town and the sheriff locked her up. Glad I happened to run into Chris as I was passing the sanatorium, or I couldn't have handled her."

"And the child?" old Carlson asked querulously.

"Ugh!" Drew grunted. "That's the horror of it, Dad. And Chris tells me its the second time it has happened around here. Do you know where we found that fiend-woman—" his voice faltered and he caught his breath— "We found her with the child's body at the foot of the cliff. She was crouched, bending above the mangled corpse. When we dragged her off, we saw that its throat had been bitten—by human teeth."

Stell grabbed the doorknob, clutched it, clung to it, while the darkness swam and swirled about her in dizzy currents. "God," she prayed, "God, don't let me faint, not now, not here . . ."

"How's Stell?" she heard Drew asking.

"Calmer, I think," Dr. Gambit replied. "I was with her only a few moments ago. We've been trying to get to the bottom of these—er—nervous attacks she's been having. And by the way, there are a few questions I'd like to ask you. Will you step into the hall with me for a moment?"

As they came out into the hall, Stell closed the door to a tiny crack. The doctor had lowered his voice to a whisper, but by straining her ears, Stell caught the words: ". . . about her mother?"

Drew was frowning, blinking into the Doctor's face. "Yes," she heard him reply, "a painful subject . . . her father told me . . . cautioned me not ever to let her know . . ."

Stell couldn't catch the rest of it, but the doctor's exclamation made it clear:

"Really? That's tremendously important. Died, you say, in an asylum . . .?"

Stell staggered back into the room. In one blinding flash the horrible truth had become clear. Now, like a hunted creature, she wanted to run, to escape, to hide.

Reaching the open window she steadied herself on the sill. She tried to collect her wits, but her pulse beats seemed to rock her skull. She must get back to her room, hide her guilty knowledge, decide what was best to do . . .

Quickly she climbed through the window and came out on a flagged terrace. Hugging the shadow of the adobe walls, she glided to the window of her own room and scrambled in. She thrust her robe and slippers hastily under the bed and crawled beneath the covers. When Drew came in at the door a moment later, she was lying with her eyes closed as if asleep.

She heard him tiptoe into the room and pause to stare at her. Peeping beneath her lids she saw him bend above the little bed where baby Flo lay sleeping. He touched the tiny hands tenderly with a big finger, then turned to stare at her again.

"My poor little girl," he whispered. Then he tiptoed back to the door again.

Stell bit her tongue to keep from crying out. She wanted to call him back, throw herself in his arms, sob out to him all the gnawing horror that was eating like a cancer at her heart. But she couldn't.

He wouldn't understand. Like a leper, she was unclean, accursed, the slave of a hellish madness. No, she must let him go. Perhaps she would never feel his arms about her again, would never . . .

The door opened. Blanche's voice drifted in to her.

"How is she?"

"Sleeping," Drew told her. "I don't want to awaken her."

"It's better not to," Blanche said. "The doctor said she needed sleep. In the morning—"

The light was snapped off, the door closed. Their voices were shut off.

In the morning! No! There must be no "in the morning" for her, no dawn or day, no light breaking bleakly through the window to lay bare some unspeakable horror!

Stell hugged her pillow, buried her face to stifle the swelling cries that throbbed in her throat, gritted her teeth and lay alone with horror which like a scaly reptile shared her bed.

CHAPTER THREE

MANIAC MOTHER

S HE WAS MAD—that was clear now. Her mother had been mad and they had tried to hide it from her, they had hoped to be able to cure her. But they did not know how far the madness had gone, did not guess that it was already too late.

Stell rolled her shivering body to the edge of the bed, reached out a trembling hand and touched the sleeping form in the little bed beside her. "Precious, precious, little Flo . . ." she muttered feverishly. I'll never . . ."

Stinging tears were in her eyes; there was a painful ache in her throat as she choked back the wild sobs that racked her. Thank God, it was not too late to save Flo! She could go away before it happened. She would get up, slip away, run—run—hide herself like some hunted creature of the wilds.

But with numb despair she realized that it wouldn't do. They would catch her, drag her back, to a maniac's cell, perhaps—a place of horror where even the merciful means of self-destruction would be denied her.

Wasn't there some remote chance that Dr. Gambit might cure her? He had seemed so sure. Couldn't she wait until tomorrow? But to wait was to gamble with the life of the baby. Once she was asleep, once the vision came—!

"But if I don't sleep." she told herself, "if I lie here and fight off sleep, and stay awake until morning, maybe . . ."

She lay flat on her back and stared up into the darkness. She kept her eyes open with a fearful effort, until they were dry and burning. She closed them for a moment and the drowsy waves of fever seemed to roll over her like a warm tide.

She opened them again, began to talk to herself, to count. In the thousands, she drowsed . . . She jerked out of it, stifling a scream. She got out of bed, poured a basin of cold water from the pitcher on the dresser, and bathed her hot face. Then she began to pace the floor of her room in her bare feet.

She paced until she was exhausted. The fever seemed worse, too. She crawled back into bed and lay there praying in an undertone. Then she began to repeat over and over. "It won't come tonight, it won't come tonight . . ." Auto-suggestion, she remembered, could be used to combat an obsession.

But the very words were monotonous. Her lips kept on forming them, even after her eyes had closed. Sleep crept upon her, soft footed as a thief . . .

It came suddenly—the sense of suffocation, the violent oppression in her breast, as of some tremendous weight, the swift, painful palpitation of her heart, echoing in her ears like a drum-throb. Then she was aware of having jerked upright to a sitting position, with swollen eyes throbbing, burning, staring into the semi-darkness for the image of that frightful face still stamped vividly on the sensitive film of her brain. And there, as she knew it would be, limned faintly by the moonlight seeping through the open window—was the hellish apparition!

Terror, unutterable despair, froze Stell's blood. Never before had the face been so tangible, so plain in its awful aspect of unspeakable agony. White it was, and cadaverous, with long hair hanging wild about it, and sunken eyes burning with a feverish light. It was like some ghastly painting of a crucifixion by one of those old German masters of the macabre—and suddenly, with a wrenching throb of her heart, Stell was conscious of a new emotion—pity, pity for the agony of a suffering, dying creature.

The face hung motionless in the dark—down the pain-drawn mask of its face, slow dark streams were trickling—blood!

"It will pass," Stell's brain was shrieking, "in a moment it will go."

But it didn't. And then, with a shock that seemed to shatter every brittle nerve in her body, Stell heard the whisper. And now, for the first, the words were clear:

"My baby . . . I want my baby . . . In God's merciful name, my child!"

Stell's mouth opened for a protesting scream, but her constricted diaphragm could not force up the sound, and the terrible gasping, dying whisper went on:

"My baby . . . she's not your baby, she's mine! I cannot rest, I cannot sleep. In the night I am always around you, will always be around you . . . Let me hold my baby, let me hold her in my arms, then I will go . . ."

Again Stell tried to scream, but the terrific effort seemed to suffocate her, and with the sensation of a drowning person, drifting
down into warm, dark depth, consciousness floated off in an unreal and hazy dream.

She was moving, walking, her bare feet crushing briars and
grass without feeling. And before her, moving backward at a
ghostly, drifting pace, was a shape that seemed shrouded in billowing veils, and a face—a terrible face whose haunted eyes never
left her own, a face with supernal agony shining through the dripping rivulets of blood.

And the agony of that face, the pain of its terrible, starved
yearning, the torment throbbing in that death-muffled whisper, had
entered into Stell's soul.

The baby! The baby was still in her arms, snuggling close to
her beating heart. Her breast ached with love at the pulse of its tiny
life, until she felt in her own heart all the ghastly, soul-crushing
despair of a dead mother, struggling up from the grave's grisly
clutches for a sight, a touch of the living child left behind.

The phantom had stopped. Arms were reaching out from the
veiled and formless body: the torment-shaken whisper was pleading:

"Only a moment . . . only a moment to touch her, hold her . . .
She will be yours, then . . . I will go back into the darkness . . ."

Stell's hands were tightening about the child's small body. A
moment, only a moment, she would let the mother touch her. Only
a moment to still the awful heartache, the starved, tormenting
yearning. Her arms were reaching out, thrusting the little bundle
toward the phantom's reaching hands. They fluttered, pale and
bloodless, touched the tiny form—then snatched it!

A voice was screaming, shrilling wild peals of terror into the
still night. And Stell was suddenly conscious that it was her own
voice, dinning the demoniac shrieks into her own ears.

She was fully awake now; the shadow-splotched landscape
swam into focus around her—a hillside, the huddled shapes of junipers, a cliff overhanging a gully, on the brink of which she was
standing.

Had it been real, or a dream? For only an instant the question
hung suspended in her mind. Then she was aware of the little
blanket still in her hands, the blanket still warm with the heat of a
tiny body. Merciful God! it was real! Whatever that phantom face,
that phantom figure might have been, one part of the horror was

certainly real—the little body hurtling down into the dark with a cry!

Like the maddened Mexican woman, she had murdered her baby!

Stell's taloned hand raked, claw-like, across the frozen mask of her face. Down there in the gloom-shrouded depths of the gulch, the little body must be lying. Stell's body surged forward, sucked toward the brink of the cliff by an impulse to throw herself down and die too. Then she drew back. Perhaps it was not so deep; perhaps Flo was lying there still alive, stunned.

She knew it was a mad hope, but her brain was a chaos of crazed terror. Turning, she began to stagger blindly along the gully's rim, looking for a place to descend. She fought through thickets and cactus beds, unconscious of the pain of tearing thorns, wild sobs bubbling incoherently from her throat. Then she jerked up with a start. A tall, lumbering figure was plunging toward her out of the trees!

"Stop! Stay where you are!"

Dazedly, she recognized the hoarse tones of Dr. Gambit's voice, stood paralyzed a his gaunt body hurtled toward her. Then, out of the fog that clouded her brain, a sudden memory flashed. Gambit had hypnotized her tonight, Gambit had—!

With a shriek she threw herself to one side as his body floundered by. He had been watching her, waiting to see his hellish work consummated!

He had recovered his balance, swung about; his lean arms were flung around her, his hoarse voice was husking hoarse commands in her ears. Stell was struggling, screaming:

"You fiend, you monster! You made me kill my baby, you—"

With a sudden wrench she had dragged herself free. She lurched forward, fell, began scrambling up. One hand clawed at the rocky soil, grasped a jagged shard of flint.

"Drop it!" he shrilled, "Don't—!"

He was on her again. He stopped, and his cold pulseless fingers closed about her wrist, jerked her upright. His long pallid face loomed out of the darkness as he pulled her toward him, reached out with his other hand to pinion her arms. But Stell was too quick for him. Her right arm swung back and up; her fist clutched the jagged flint. With all the power remaining in her body, she smashed the rock into his face. His grip on her arm relaxed. With a choked-off gasp he lurched back, crumpled in a heap at her feet. In the thin moonlight she saw his pale face staring up, a trickle of dark blood running down from his forehead into his eyes.

Stell was panting, swaying crazily on legs that shook and trembled. Had she killed him? She didn't care. Whirling about, she began staggering back toward the gully.

She found a place where sloping rocks afforded a foothold, and stumbled down into the depths. She groped through darkness along the rocky channel, and stopped beneath the jutting cliff on which she had stood. Wildly her eyes probed the gloom. But she could see nothing. She got down on hands and knees, crawled, sobbing, over the uneven floor of stones, groping with numb, bruised fingers that shook with a palsy of sick terror, shook with the awful anticipation of the clammy touch of blood, of a small mangled body . . .

"I'll find her," she whimpered between chattering teeth, "I'll find her and make sure that she's dead. Then: I'll kill myself!"

Knees and knuckles were bleeding when she finally straightened, dazed and incredulous. The body wasn't there. She had felt with her fingers over the whole area beneath the cliff some twenty feet above her. What could it mean? There was no doubt in her mind that she had held Flo in her arms, there on the cliff. There was no doubt that she had seen the little body drop, had heard the pitiful cry. Then what—?

"They've stolen it!" she gasped aloud. "They've carried her body away. And that means that others beside Dr. Gambit are in it!"

She stood, swaying unsteadily, trying to digest the meaning of it. But then, what difference did it make now? Flo was dead, killed by her own hands. There was only one thing left for her now— death. Death, swift and merciful, to shut out the agony that was gnawing at her heart—death, before they dragged her back to face Drew with the blood of their child on her hands!

She looked up at the cliff again. She would climb up there, throw herself down upon the rocks. She made a move, then stopped. A sudden fierce rage surged up in her. Kill herself and leave the other fiends unpunished?

"I won't!" she sobbed out wildly. "Not yet. I'm already a murderess. I'll kill the fiends who have done this before I die!"

She started back along the gully in a half run. There was a gun in Drew's bag—a small automatic. Armed with that, and the desperation of one already doomed, she would ferret out the fiends, kill them with the ruthlessness of the crazed savage thing they had made of her. Then she would turn the deadly weapon on herself!

She was clawing her way blindly up the slope when a sound from behind caused her to turn—the swift slither of padded feet on stone. She lost her hold, slid in a small avalanche of loose rock, scrambled up, dazed and half blinded, to face the rush of a dark, shapeless form that was swooping down upon her like some monstrous black vulture.

Wildly she threw herself to one side; but the sweep of a powerful arm threw her back against the rocks. The black-robed shape closed in. Fingers of iron tangled in her loose hair, yanked her forward. Clawing, beating with her small fists at the monster's body, she was pulled toward it, hugged tight in arms like a python's coils. Then, out of the gloom, another shape was surging up—the phantom woman, the hideous, agony-distorted face, framed in its wild streaming hair.

A shrill cry broke from Stell's throat, was smothered off as a damp wad of gauze was slapped against her face, held there. The sickening sweetish reek of chloroform stung her eyes, flowed in through mouth and nostrils, mounting in a stupefying cloud to her brain. She kicked, struggled, writhed, but strong arms held her. She was growing weak, limp; her mind was drifting off on a slow current into a blind, smothering fog.

CHAPTER FOUR

STELL CHOOSES DEATH

"I MUST HAVE DIED," Stell thought as she opened her dazed eyes, tried to focus them, "I must have died to awaken in hell!"

The light was dim, a faint, wavering glow against which the shadows, monstrous and imponderable, pushed and retreated. And there was the face—the loathsome, pallid, pain-twisted face which had lured her to murder, that face which she knew would haunt her through all eternity. Immobile, frozen, twisted as with the torment of a violent death, it was staring at her now from feverish, sunken eyes.

Stell jerked up her lolling head, and the motion cleared another film of fog from her hazed mind. She was seated in a chair, tied securely to its heavy frame. At her left was a small table, and on it a candle that burned with a weak, sickly flame. Solid walls of concrete lay behind the billowing shadows. She seemed to be in a small basement room.

Stell looked at the face again, noted the bent form beneath it, concealed by yards of carelessly draped black cheesecloth. A tangible phantom anyhow, for all the deathly horror of that face!

"Who are you?" Stell sobbed hoarsely. "Why have you done this to me? Where is my baby?"

A long arm was reaching out, pointing silently. Stell swung her eyes in the direction it indicated—and grinding horror crushed her heart. There on the floor near one wall lay the body of her baby. It lay on a pallet of burlap, stiff and still, its little nightdress torn and smeared with ugly stains, a frightful clot of blood on the doll-like forehead with ugly streamers of dark red running down across the pale chubby cheek.

Stell screamed then, surged against the ropes that held her body, rocked forward in the heavy chair, while her raw throat throbbed and strained with incoherent sobs.

"God—Oh, my God! I've murdered her! I've murdered my little Flo! Why, why in God's name . . .?"

"Yes, you *have* murdered her!" The words boomed out above Stell's cries.

She flung herself back, shaking in every limb as she stared with hot, dry eyes at the tall figure which had stepped into the room—a black-robed figure with narrowed eyes staring at her through slits in the hood that covered the head. "You have murdered her!" the deep, disguised, bitterly accusing voice repeated.

"But I didn't!" Stell shrieked. "I only—" she checked herself. How could she deny it? Just as the Mexican woman had done, she had held the child out in her extended hands, had allowed it to drop. "I was mad!" she finished in a broken wail.

"Yes, mad! And you are mad now." The tall shape was approaching her. "You should have killed yourself as you started to do. What is left for you in life now?"

Stell's teeth clamped tight. Wild hate hardened her features in a rigid mask. "Vengeance!" she hissed. "I live for that, only that—to see you punished—punished horribly for this frightful thing you've done!"

A low fiendish laugh mocked her words. "You could never see that," the cold voice replied, "not even if we released you, as we shall not do. What would you do if we did—go back to your husband with your incredible story? You can imagine his reaction to that. A madhouse would be the best thing you could hope for then."

"But what do you want with me?" Stell stammered.

"Nothing," the fiend replied, "but to have you out of the way. We thought that you would kill yourself after you had discovered what you had done. You didn't—but that can be easily remedied."

With black gloved hands he had reached beneath his robe and brought out a white sheet of paper and a pencil. He laid them on the table, then pulled it closer to Stell's chair. "You will now write," he directed, "a suicide note. You may excuse yourself in any way you care to, soften the blow of what you have done. Say that you were crazed, did not know what you were doing. But you have decided that there is nothing left for you now but suicide, and you are asking your husband's forgiveness. When you have finished we will take you to the cliff—"

"No!" Stell screamed. It wasn't that she cared for her life any longer. She didn't. But she wouldn't play into their hand. "I'll never write it," she said, fighting to make her voice firm. "You'll have to murder me instead. You can do that—torture me, burn me, flay me—but you'll never force me to write that note!"

Again her tormentor laughed. "We are not thinking of physical torture," he said. "It is scarcely refined enough for our purpose. I will tell you something. Let your mind dwell on it, and perhaps you will change your decision." His voice fell suddenly to a brittle whisper. "Listen. If you do not do as we tell you, we will push you off the cliff just the same. We won't write that note, but we will make it plain enough why you killed yourself. You remember the Mexican woman—what she did? We will tear chunks of flesh from your child's body, force them into your dead mouth, between your teeth and smear your face with the blood. It will be plain enough then what sort of shame drove you to self destruction!"

For a moment, incredulous horror robbed Stell of speech, of thought. Was it possible that a scheme so monstrous could have been spawned by any brain not born in hell? Whose was the face beneath that hood? Who was the death-faced hag? Stell's frantic eyes fell on her again. The gauze draped figure had come nearer to the light, and Stell could now see that the torture-twisted face was a cleverly made mask, covered with dried blood which had been smeared on it. Probably not a woman at all. But who—?

Was she doomed to die without knowing that?

"Well, are you ready to write?"

The cold voice jerked Stell's crazed mind back to the horror of her situation, and suddenly she was picturing the scene when her body would be found. They would find her dead, and somewhere nearby, the mutilated body of her child. And in her mouth, clutched in her teeth, would be the torn flesh from the baby's body! A vampire, they would call her—werewolf!

The torment of that picture sent Stell's rain reeling off into shrieking chaos. Cold sweat burst out on her brow, and a rigor gripped her body. She closed her eyes and tried to pray, but the words wouldn't come. She could not disentangle her fear-crazed thoughts from the awful picture burned on her brain. Now she understood that no physical torture can approximate the agonies of mental pain, and suddenly the thought of death became sweet and desirable—oblivion, sleep, peace!

"Give me the paper," she whispered. "Free my hand."

It was swiftly done. She wrote jerkily, quickly, keeping her eyes glued to the paper as she scrawled the pitiful message and signed it. Then she closed her eyes to shut out the sight of the baby.

"Do it quickly now," she begged brokenly. "For God's sake, take me to the cliff, let me have it over with!"

They blindfolded her, and after a little while they led her out. One on each side they supported her slumped body, guided her stumbling feet. She dared not scream, dared not risk a fulfillment of her captor's ghastly threat. They had thrust the scrawled note into the bosom of her pajamas. They had promised that the baby's body would not be mutilated. She prayed that Drew would somehow understand and forgive her.

The night was still; the light wind fanned coolly against her burning brow. "They've given up the search, I suppose," she heard the robed fiend remark. "Everything's quiet now."

"God, God,—" Stell was praying,—"let it soon be over!"

They stopped. "We're here."

The voice seemed to reach her from far away. The blindfold was being removed from her eyes. She stared, blinking. The moon was about to set. In the faint light drifting over the trees, she saw the dark gulch yawning at her feet. She would plunge down head first—it would be quicker that way. She didn't want to be simply crippled.

Her body was lumped, trembling. The robed fiend held one of her arms, drew her nearer to the brink of the death leap. He paused. "Now—" he began.

Then something clicked in Stell's brain—that sudden flash of clarity which is said to precede death, and all her hate leaped up like a smothered flame. He was holding her loosely, and he was standing a little nearer the cliff's brink than she, was pulling her toward it. Suddenly Stell acted.

With a swift jerk she straightened, freed her arm, shoved out with all her strength. It was the utter unexpectedness of the thing that made it possible. She had only hoped to drag him with her into the abyss. But his foot slipped as he tried to lurch back. Then his arms were waving grotesquely like flapping wings, and with a hoarse cry he toppled, plunged down into the yawning darkness.

Stell didn't hear his body strike. Like a thing moved by steel springs, she whirled on the second fiend, sprang toward her with her head lowered, ducked under the reaching hands, flung her own arms about the other's waist. If she went down into the gulch, she would not go alone!

But—God in heaven!—what was this? Instead of the folds of black gauze which had covered the phantom-like figure, Stell now felt her face pressed against a starched white dress; and the body that struggled against hers in a deadly embrace, was not the body of some ancient hag. It was young, lithe, strong!

Snarling and spitting like a cat, the woman fought to free herself from Stell's desperate clutches. Fists beat at Stell's head, fingers pulled and tore at her hair. But she clung, shoved, butted, and the two of them fell in a writhing tangle. The woman was on top of her now, pinioning her shoulders to the ground, snarling down at her with a rage-twisted face—the face of Blanche Morrow!

"Blanche!" The cry came in a rasping gasp from Stell's exhausted lungs. She lay still, staring in amazed horror at the face of her erstwhile friend.

"Yes—Blanche!" the other mocked her. "And I've still the upper hand, my dear. In a moment I'll drag you to the cliff, shove you off."

"But Blanche, how could you, why—?"

Blanche Morrow laughed. "For a hundred thousand dollars' worth of property!" she snarled. "Do you think I intend to share it with you and Drew, and that brat?"

"Oh my God!" Stell moaned. "Then you and Ben—?"

"Never mind!" Blanche snapped. "You didn't kill him. The gully's not deep. He'll probably be up in a moment, then we'll—"

"And if I scream for help?" Stell asked.

"Scream!" Blanche taunted. "I'll say you were attacking me—that fits in with the rest of it. Luckily I took off my mask and disguise."

Stell started to scream, but a sound from behind choked off the swelling shriek in her throat. Feet were pounding over the rocky ground. Ben coming back? Stell jerked her head up, began to fight again Then it was Blanche who was screaming! "Help, help! She's killing me!"

And Blanche was falling back, allowing Stell to get the upper hand. And Stell, still crazed by anger and fear, was beating and clawing at Blanche's face . . .

The grip of strong hands on her shoulders dragged Stell back and up. She swung about, panting, dazed. Dr. Gambit was gripping her by one arm. The other was held by—Ben Carlson!

"You!" Stell screamed, "You?" and like a wildcat she flung herself on him.

He stumbled back, shielding his face from her clawing hands. Then Gambit had grabbed her again. A hypodermic syringe flashed in one of his hands; the needle jabbed into her arm.

Stell turned on him, but her limbs went being drained of strength. "Beast—fiend!" she cried, struggling weakly against the arms that held her. Then her brain clouded, and she muttered, "Drew . . . Drew, don't believe them. They've fooled me . . . cheated me . . ."

A white plaster ceiling confronted her opening eyes—the ceiling of a hospital room. She was lying in a hospital bed. What had happened? Suddenly she realized that her body was securely tied by sheets wound around it. She remembered then. Blanche's ruse must have succeeded! God in heaven! Blanche, the fiend, was free, while she was held here—maniac!

Stell lifted her head a little, started. In a chair in one corner of the room, his long, dissipated face looking worn and haggard, sat Ben Carlson. He got up now, started toward her.

"Get away from me!" Stell shrilled in anger and fear.

Ben stopped, stared at her, then turned and went out.

An instant later he was back, bringing with him Dr. Gambit. The latter seemed to have aged ten years. His face was puffy, bloodless; and there was a discolored lump on his forehead. He came toward her now, frowning gravely.

Suddenly Stell was trembling, sobbing. "Are you one of them?" she whimpered.

"Tell me, tell me the truth! Are you one of them, or have they just fooled you with their lies?"

A faint weary smile curled the doctor's thin lips. "No," he said softly, "I am not one of them. And they have not fooled me, though the woman—to give the devil her due—did put on a convincing piece of acting. Unfortunately for her, her accomplice was badly injured when you shoved him into the gulch. He recovered consciousness before he died and made a complete confession."

"Then Ben—?" Stell gasped. She was staring toward him now. He had slumped back into his chair, sat there with his face buried in his hands.

"Ben," said Dr. Gambit slowly, "was as innocent as you are, my dear. He was to be a victim too." He sat down on the edge of the bed and took Stell's hand in his. "The Morrow woman's accomplice was Chris Manheim who, I'm ashamed to say, I was fool enough to employ on my staff. The two of them, it develops, had operated together in all sorts of confidence swindles, and had come here, it seems, with the vague idea of victimizing some of my wealthy patients. Manheim was a shrewd psychologist, and his schemes were amazing in their ingenuity. But once here, Blanche

Morrow saw a chance to get Ben Carlson in her clutches, and get possession of the ranch property. Once they were married, he would have been put out of the way, and Drew's father as well. But that would have left you and Drew and the baby in their way, so they shrewdly planned to eliminate you first . . ."

"But doctor," Stell interrupted, "I don't understand how they did it . . . Am I really mad, or did they drug me?"

Dr. Gambit was slowly shaking his head. "It was the most devilishly cunning thing I ever heard of," he said. "They were too clever to madden you with drugs, since they knew that an autopsy would have been demanded. The scheme involved a new principle in crime, developed by a diabolically cunning psychologist. The Morrow girl got the idea for it when you told her of your troublesome recurrent dream. She planted the seeds of fear in your mind, and later the two of them worked out the details."

"But I must have been really mad!" Stell said wonderingly. "My mother—Oh, I heard you there in the hall, heard Drew say she died in an asylum!"

"She did," said Dr. Gambit, "and as I told him, the clue to your trouble was there. But your mother was not mad in the sense you are thinking. The tragedy which has been hidden from you all your life is the fact that when you were a baby of two, your mother was injured in a railway accident. The brain injury, and the horror, left her permanently crazed. But the significance of the incident, as far as you are concerned, is the fact that you were with her in the accident. While you were under hypnosis I probed your hidden memories; then, after what your husband told me, I understood the whole thing . . ."

"But I still don't see—"

"Let me explain," said the doctor gently. "A neurosis is nearly always the result of a repressed memory—often from remote childhood—which has been pushed back into the unconscious. Your dream, the blood-smeared face, the whispered words, are unquestionably hidden memories of your mother—when she came to her senses among the wreckage, crying for you, for her baby. You saw her then, and though you were only a baby, your unconscious mind retained the fearful impression. It lay there, latent, through your girlhood and early married life. But then, when you adopted a baby of your own, the instinct of motherhood, with its cares and anxieties, was suddenly aroused in you, and they in turn stirred up the distressing memory to haunt your dreams."

"But Blanche," Stell gasped, "how could she have—?"

"Blanche Morrow," Dr. Gambit replied, "discovered the truth at once. When she visited you and you confided in her, she discovered by psycho-analysis, the source of the trouble. She planted terrifying ideas in your mind and arranged to have you here for her wedding during this season of the Mexican 'Day of the Dead'. She realized, that when the dream attacked you, you were in a condition peculiarly susceptible to any suggestion concerning your fears. She realized that by impersonating the woman of your dream, she could prolong that state, could control your will and actions just as a hypnotist controls his subject. That is what she did. They had victimized the Mexican women by the use of drugs, which together with the natives' natural superstition made them easy prey.

"I had suspected foul play, but didn't guess the guilty parties. I was out doing a little snooping tonight when I encountered you. But that blow you gave me put me out for some time. After I recovered and resumed the search, I never thought of looking in that basement room where you were hidden. It was certainly fortunate that we found you when we did."

Stell lay back and closed her eyes. The black darkness felt good. The mystery was solved, but it seemed that the horror was only beginning for her. She knew that she had not been responsible for what she did, and yet—

"Where's Drew?" she asked.

"I'll call him," Dr. Gambit said.

Stell grasped his arm. "No, no," she begged, "Don't! I can't face him. He would try to be kind, but I can't face him now—ever! The baby . . ."

"But the baby's all right," Dr. Gambit said.

"What?' Stell jerked up, straining against the sheet bound tightly across her chest. "No, no. I saw—"

"Here, here," the doctor soothed. "The baby, I repeat, is all right. I just succeeded in arousing her from the chloroform."

"Chloroform!"

"Yes. There was nothing else wrong with her. You see, when Blanche snatched her from you and dropped her, Manheim was standing below and caught her. The other was a set-up, calculated to drive you to suicide. The baby was simply chloroformed and smeared with blood—"

He paused, turned. The door was opening and Drew was striding into the room—Drew, tall and strong with a glad smile of relief on his lips, and in his arms the bright-eyed form of baby Flo!

"Drew, darling! Bring her to me!"

The little form was nestled beside her on the bed, one tiny hand
was reaching out to stroke her face playfully. Drew was bending
above her. The door closed softly behind Ben and Dr. Gambit.
Drew's arm slid under her head, lifted her face to meet his lips . . .

After a while Stell asked: "What did they do with Blanche?"

"She's dead," Drew said in a low tone. "We had her locked in a
room, but she got some bi-chloride tablets somewhere. We found
her too late."

"It's better that way."

Drew nodded. "Pretend it was all a bad dream, honey," he said.
"It was—really. And from now on there won't be any more of
them."

THE SEA OF FEAR

CHAPTER I

DROWNED IN A DESERT

I'M A HARDHEADED, PRACTICAL MAN. You've got to be to hold the office of Sheriff of Colima County, Arizona.

I could sleep in a dank graveyard without a quiver, and a corpse is just a dead body to me. But I'm ready to admit that the first time I ever heard Haas Glanvil talk about his pet obsession it set me tingling with the strangest and weirdest thrill of fear that ever traveled through my usually rawhide nerves.

It was a perfectly still, calm evening, and the setting sun had vanished on the desert horizon like a closed furnace door, and the moon had brightened until the still air swam with silver waves of light.

We were gathered in his study, sitting before the huge circular window that looked out over the mesa's edge, and there were no lights on yet. I was just thinking how it was like staring through the porthole of some monster submarine into the still blue ocean depths when Haas Glanvil began to speak in that queer hushed tone that marked his mania.

"I often sit here," he said, "and watch them pass—trireme Galleys with gilded rams, and the chained slaves plying the oars, and the whip lashing across their straining backs. They pass so close at times that I can see the salt spray on their faces, and I want to call out to them in their forgotten tongue, and ask them a thousand questions."

I swallowed. I was glad it was so dark in the room that he couldn't see my face. "Yes sir," I said, making a grab at sanity, "moonlight like this can make a man imagine all sorts of things."

The aged explorer eyed me sharply and the rapt look on his face softened to a pitying tolerance. "Imagine?" he asked. "Oh, no, I don't imagine it. I've been a scientist all my life—an explorer. If I say there's an inland sea there, and men and boats passing in the night, they're there, whether you see them or not!"

The silence was uncomfortable, damned uncomfortable, and I got away as quickly as I decently could. I'd heard about his mania—his belief that this mesa on which he had build his home had once been an island inhabited by a remnant of the mythical people of Atlantis. But that he believed the ancient sea was still there, and the spirits of the dead as well, was new to me.

Before I'd thought him only a crank, a world famed explorer, too old to go to the far places of the earth anymore, amusing himself with wild theories. Now I knew differently. Now I knew that the frail old man, with the imperious manner of an emperor, was for all his quiet and self-contained manner, a stark, raving madman.

I think there was fear in my heart that night for Theda Glanvil as I rode home across the barren wasteland. Not that I ever expected a woman so beautiful, so patrician, to ever care for a mere desert sheriff. And I certainly never dreamed that our next meeting would see us with the roles reversed—she a suppliant before me, or rather, before my vested authority.

It was weeks later, and just such an evening as had ushered in Haas Glanvil's strange talk. I had finished the day's work and was yanking down the top of my desk when I turned and saw her standing in the doorway.

Little waves of warmth ran through my body and my heart took a jump. She was lovelier than any woman's got a right to be. Slender and tall, she stood against the sunset that flamed round her like an aureole. Her dark mysterious eyes were fixed on me with the strangest look of pleading. I thought I must be dreaming at first, and then she was moving into the room. I saw the pallor of her face which was usually the flushed golden color of a ripe peach. And I finally had the sense to jump up and snatch off my hat.

"Mr. Langtry," she said, "you must come with me at once, please!"

"Of course, Miss Glanvil," I said, "if you'll just tell me—"

"No, no," she interrupted impatiently. "There's no time now. My car's outside. You see," she hesitated, fighting to preserve a semblance of calm, "there's been a—a death."

"A death!" I echoed. "Your—?"

"It's none of the family,' she cut me short, "just—a visitor. But will you come now?"

"Of course," I answered, trying to puzzle out the look of suppressed terror on her face. "But you said *death*. Do you mean murder?"

The fear flared then, stark and terrible. "No, no," she stammered, "not murder. But, well, I can't explain—please come!"

No one else could have pulled such a stunt on me, but there was something about that woman that influenced me against my will. So I phoned Doc Parker, the coroner, and told him to come out to Half Moon Mesa at once. Then I followed Theda Glanvil to her car.

It was a long, sleek job, trim and swift, and it leaped into the desert dusk like a greyhound. "Now," I said, as the motor fell into a steady drone, "we'll have an understanding. Who's dead?"

"Hugo Wadley," she replied.

"Wadley," I repeated, and my brain set to work. My visit to the Glanvil place two weeks before had concerned this man. He and his partner, Graham Hoag, were manufacturing chemists from somewhere in the east. They had been trying to buy the dry lake bottom from old Glanvil for its salt deposits. They had remained in spite of the fact that Haas Glanvil hated and feared them and had even got the idea in his twisted mind that they were plotting to murder him. I had satisfied myself and tried to prove to him that there was nothing in that.

But now this—

Suddenly it clicked—the explanation of her fear. I looked at her. Against the faint saffron flush still lingering in the sky, her dark profile was a lovely thing to see. But her lips were tight now, her eyes glued to the gushing stream of the road.

I waited. A side road slewed off from the highway and we slid into brown dunes dotted with cactus and yucca and greasewood. Then we dipped into the white caked basin of the dry salt lake, in the center of which stood Half Moon Mesa, an island rising from a dead sea. Rudely shaped like a half moon, its craggy base jutted abruptly, rose in cathedral-like surges to a flat top where, like a fantastic mud-dauber's nest, the pueblo-style house of Haas Glanvil stood. The car slowed as the shadow of the mesa crept toward us and suddenly I asked:

"What makes you think your father killed him?"

If I'd struck her, her reaction couldn't have been violent. The car lurched sideways, the back wheels spinning in loose sand. Brakes slammed it to a stop and Theda turned, facing me, her eyes ablaze.

"But he didn't!" she husked. "You can't say—"

"How did Wadley die?" I snapped.

"In his bed," she answered. "He'd been feeling bad, we found him—"

"You're making matters worse by lying," I said.

Her hands, still gripping the steering wheel, were trembling; her face seemed utterly bloodless. "Mr. Langtry," she said, "we're not rich, but I have, well, about five thousand dollars of my own—"

"Do I look like I could be bribed?" I grated.

A faint smile tugged at the corners of her sensuous lips and was gone. "No," she answered, "not with money. But you see, I'm, well, desperate. Father didn't kill Wadley; nothing human killed him. But he'll be accused; they'll send him to a madhouse—" She moved nearer to me and abruptly her soft fingers were on my arms, crawling up in a slow caress. "Mr. Langtry, Steve," her voice was a throaty, musical sob, "am I beautiful, desirable—to you? If I should offer you myself, ask you only to save my father—"

I'm no Horatio Alger hero and she had leaned against me now. Her face was close to mine, her lips pouted, pleading, her eyes were dark pools of invitation. And there was a warm perfume that came from her. My blood churned; I was giddy, with a strange wild singing in my veins.

"Steve, it would be so easy, a little oversight on your part—"

A moment more and I don't know what I'd have promised. But suddenly my stampeded emotions ran jam against some flinty substratum, and I pulled away, snapped open the door behind me, dragged myself from her arms. "This is scarcely fair—to either of us," I told her unsteadily. "Get over here on this side. I'll drive the rest of the way."

Weakly she obeyed. Her head slumped forward in her hands; there were muffled sobs.

I walked around the car. A round white moon hung like a silver bangle in the grey veil of the sky. Stars were peeping out. I reached in, snapped on the headlights, started to crawl under the wheel.

But I didn't, I froze stiff. Ahead, where the lights plowed gleaming tunnels through the purple dusk, a huddled shape lay prone to the left of the road. It lay on a bed of wind rippled sand that had drifted against the long bare ridge of rocks running down like a monstrous seam from the mesa's craggy base. At the start I noticed its peculiar position—hands out thrown, palms cupped like a strangled swimmer.

I turned at Theda's scream. She had seen it too, had stumbled out of the car, was running toward it. I ran after her, caught her as she swayed unsteadily above the ominous shape.

"It's Hoag," she sobbed hysterically, "Wadley's partner. And he's, he's—like Wadley was—"

Then I noticed it, released Theda to bend forward, touch the corpse with my hand. My flesh crawled and the short hairs on my neck bristled. "Great God!" I swore, and a wave of insanity swept through my brain as I remembered Haas Glanvil's strange words:

"If I say there's a sea here—it's here, whether you can see it or not—"

My hand jerked sharply away. My eyes had not deceived me. The clothing of the corpse was dripping wet, smelt of brine, was outlined by a wet line in the sand where water had dripped. Shakily I reached out again, moved the man's head. A stream of water trickled from between his bluish lips!

"I told you no human killed Wadley," Theda was sobbing. "And Wadley was like this—lying on the sand. We carried him in and we knew we couldn't tell the truth because no one would believe us—not after Dr. Farn told us how he died."

I stepped back, surveyed the unbroken, unmarked ridges of the encircling sand; marred by no footprint. The cold and nameless terror of those mysteries beyond man's ken clutched at my heart. I knew what she meant, knew even before Doc Parker verified it, knew that something utterly impossible had taken place here. I knew how this short, fat man, lying on warm desert sand with no footprint near him had died.

He had been drowned!

CHAPTER II

"BRIDE OF THE SEA, COME BACK . . ."

FEAR SOMETIMES AFFECTS ME in a peculiar way, particularly if there's a hint of the supernatural to challenge and baffle and enrage me. In this case I got cold and hardboiled and machine-like. Gripping Theda's wrist to keep her from running on to the mesa, I made her wait with me until Doc Parker's flivver drove up. I'll never forget the look of dazed horror on the little doctor's face as he straightened up from above the fat, cold body of Graham Hoag.

"Steve," he said, "I scarcely know what to say—" He paused and I saw his eyes wander over the unbroken sand. "The man's lungs are full of water, salty brackish water. He died of drowning."

"I guessed as much," I growled. "How long has he been dead?"

"An hour at least," he answered.

I made a mental note of the fact that if he had been here an hour he must have been here when Theda left; she must have passed him.

"Well," I told Parker, "there's another stiff at the house, Doc. We'd better go see it too."

We left Hoag where he lay and started back to our cars.

The road followed the bare seam of wind exposed rock to a point at the mesa's base where a four-car garage of adobe stood within a sort of cove formed by the half-moon shaped butte itself. Here we left our cars and climbed up stone steps to the top of the mesa, an uneven plateau comprising three or four acres, with Haas Glanvil's terraced adobe villa standing at one half-moon tip.

"Not a word to anyone about Hoag," I whispered to Theda as we entered the house.

We found the whole group—household and guests—gathered in a long living room with paneled walls, beamed ceilings and heavy furniture. The servants, an aged Mexican couple, hovered in one doorway.

Walsh Glanvil, lean, leathery, grey, the rancher brother of the mad explorer, came toward me, extending a muscular hand. "Good of you to come, Langtry," he said, "not that I feel there's anything suspicious about Wadley's death, but then, it's better, you know—"

He left the sentence unfinished. I was looking at Dr. Farn who stood at the far end of the room. A trim, slender man, with an iron-grey goatee and pince-nez glasses perched on a sharp nose. He was Haas Glanvil's personal physician and friend.

"What was the cause of Wadley's death, Doctor?" I asked.

Farn had a poker face if I ever saw one. Without batting an eyelid, he answered, "My examination was superficial; I preferred to wait for the coroner. He can see for himself. Wadley is in his bed."

"Where you found him?" I asked sharply.

Farn's thin shoulders shrugged. "I did not find him," he said.

"Well," I told him, "you're a damned fool to lend your support to an attempt to mislead the law even if it was agreed that Miss Glanvil was to misrepresent things to me. Unfortunately there's been another murder. Hoag is dead out there on the sand."

"Hoag?" "Murder?" Startled voices echoed my words.

Barton Wedell, Theda's fiancé, a tall athletic young man with a tanned handsome face came over and placed an arm about her.

"This is damnable!" he said. "But we may as well be frank—now. Theda was afraid, on account of her father's condition, that he—"

"I understand," I cut him short. "Where is Haas Glanvil now?"

"In his study," Wendell answered. "He won't open the door."

I turned to Doc Parker who had been standing quietly behind me. "Better go and look Wadley over," I told him "Dr. Farn will go with you. I've got some questions to ask these others."

Farn scowled but obediently led Parker out. "Now," I said to the others, "I want to know why each one of you is here at this particular time. We'll start with you, Wendell. You're Miss Glanvil's fiancé, I understand, and you were teaching in a university until two months ago when you came out here. Just why have you stayed here?"

He didn't like it. I knew he wouldn't but I wanted to ruffle him.

He flushed, cleared his throat. "Two months ago," he said, "I was not acquainted with either Mr. Glanvil or his daughter. But I knew Miss Rosa Glanvil, Mr. Walsh Glanvil's daughter, at the university. She brought me an interesting archeological specimen which her uncle had asked her to submit to some authority on ancient pottery—"

"What was this specimen?" I asked.

"A cake of salt," he replied, "cut out of this dry lake bed. It contained the preserved imprint of an ancient vase—a vase that only remotely resembled anything left by the Indians. It bore, in fact, a design much like the Grecian bas relief of Atlas upholding the world. And since Atlas was the fabled king of lost Atlantis—"

"I get you," I interrupted, "that gave weight to Haas Glanvil's theory that a remnant of the lost race once lived here. So you left the university and came here—"

"And I stayed," he finished, "at Mr. Haas Glanvil's insistence. We've made other important finds. Also, Miss Glanvil and I—" His glance toward her expressed the rest.

I nodded, turned to the explorer's brother. "You've been staying here constantly for a month or more, haven't you, Glanvil?" I asked. "Yet your ranch is only about fifteen miles away. How is it that you've deserted your own home and your business to stay here?"

Walsh Glanvil smiled. "I'm under suspicion too, eh, Langtry?" he asked easily. "Well, the truth is that I'm afraid to leave Haas for an hour, in his present condition. My daughter is away at school. I have an able Mexican foreman, so I'm able to stay near my unfortunate brother."

"You consider him insane?"

"No doubt of it."

"And what about Wadley and Hoag?" I asked. "Haas Glanvil certainly didn't like them. Yet they stayed."

"That was my doing," Walsh Glanvil replied promptly, "and another reason I stayed here. It was a wonderful chance for Haas to sell this worthless land for its salt deposits. Though he refused, I hoped that in time I'd be able to persuade him to change his mind."

"Do you think," I asked pointblank, "that your brother contrived in some way to murder Hoag and Wadley?"

It startled him and he dropped his glance. "No, no, of course not," he protested. But as he raised his eyes they rested for a moment—a moment too long, I thought—on a man in the farthest corner of the room.

He was a small man, wizened, dark, with something of the look of a crouching spider about him. He was dressed in somber black that matched his tousled hair and large hypnotic eyes.

"Mr. Le Quex," I addressed him, "they tell me you're a noted psychic, a famous ghost hunter. Just what is your status here?"

Le Quex stood glowering, his black eyes roving defiantly from face to face. It was obvious that the man was not popular. "I am here," he said finally, "as Mr. Haas Glanvil's guest. I am the only real friend he has. These others call him crazy. It is infamous. He has discovered things that will startle science. His great mind, confined to a body which cannot carry it to the ends of the earth any longer, has found other lands to explore."

"What lands?" I asked.

Le Quex's eyes narrowed and his voice came in a hiss. "The land of the dead! Who knows where the boundaries lie? Here in this spot the two worlds overlap—the worlds of life and death—"

"Rot!" Walsh Glanvil suddenly growled. "Muddy the water with your rubbish will you, you scoundrel?"

Le Quex caught his breath, glaring at Walsh Glanvil like a spitting cat. "You'd like him declared insane, wouldn't you?" he grated. "Then you'd get your hands on his property maybe. Where were you when Hoag and Wadley died? And you, Wendell?"

Walsh Glanvil made a lunge at him, his big hands fisted. But I grabbed his arm. "A good question," I said.

Walsh got a grip on himself, turning his glaring eyes from Le Quex to me. "Hoag and Wadley had both been gone since dinner," he told me shortly, "nosing around the salt flats. I was tinkering with my car in the garage. Haas, so far as I know was locked in his study. Farn says he was here at the house. You'll have to ask the others."

I turned to Wendell. His face had set like cement, and I caught a flicker of something like fear in his eyes as he stared at Theda's face. It was queer, because it seemed somehow rather a fear *of* her than *for* her. "I was off hunting for more pottery," he said, "in the caves around the mesa's base. Miss Glanvil, I think, was in her room—"

"I wasn't!" she turned on him angrily. "You needn't try to shield me. I don't mind admitting I was out walking with Mr. Le Quex."

Wendell bit his lip; Walsh Glanvil's face went livid.

"You want to tell it all, then?" he growled. "It's an abomination—insane, monstrous. This dammed Le Quex with his sorcery—"

He stopped, and above the tense electric silence came a sound that curdled the air with its overtones of terror—a shrill voice, edged with hysterical passion, chanting in the toneless rhythm of an incantation:

"Cleito, Cleito—queen of the sea-girt isle, Bride of the Ocean—two you have taken, my enemies. Come again, Cleito, come—"

Haas Glanvil's voice, chanting behind the locked door of his study!

I suddenly looked at Theda. She had straightened, gone rigid, staring through the doorway with a wild unseeing look in her eyes. Then her hands clenched, a tremor ran through her body, and she slumped.

Barton Wendell caught her, carried her gently to a divan and began fanning her pallid face. Presently she opened her eyes, and as she did so Wendell straightened, whirled toward Le Quex. His face was a mask of rage, his fist clenched. "Now," he said through gritted teeth, "I'm going to strangle you, you damned snake!"

I caught his arm. "Just a minute," I said. "What's all this?"

He stared at me a moment, then at Theda, and the strange look of fear came over his face again. "Ask Le Quex," he said throatily.

Le Quex said nothing.

Walsh Glanvil snorted. "I'll tell you," he said, "—briefly. Haas, and this damned Le Quex are trying to make a devil of her!"

"A devil—!"

"Sure," he said, "you heard Haas calling Cleito, didn't you? Well, she was supposed to be the goddess of the Atlanteans. Haas not only believes that the ancient sea still exists, he believes the dead are here too. And he believes that the dead goddess-queen comes back to life through the body of his daughter!"

It floored me for a moment. Now I understood the look of fear on Wendell's face when he stared at the woman he loved, the woman he could not be sure was herself or that other—that dead thing, that corpse-queen who lured men to a ghostly death.

"What about this business, Le Quex?" I demanded.

"All pioneers of thought," he said sententiously, "all explorers of new worlds, have been called sorcerers, have been martyred by human ignorance. Let them speak. It is true that the spirit of Cleito comes back to earth." He paused and a slow smile spread over his crafty features as he added. "But if Cleito has lured these men to their death, you may have some trouble, my friend, in pinning the crimes on a ghost."

"But if I happened to pin them on you?" I growled.

The glitter of his beady eyes seemed to hurl back my challenge. "You will do best," he said, "to let the dead bury the dead. Cleito," and here he swerved his glance to Barton Wendell's face, "may come back!"

The threat was plain enough. Wendell's face went a shade paler, and something like an internal shiver passed through me too as I gazed at the slender voluptuous figure on the divan.

She lay now with eyes half closed, her full ripe breasts under the tight fitting bodice rising and falling with her gentle breathing. With a pang of fear stabbing my heart, I realized that Wendall was not the only one who had reason to fear the maddening spell of her beauty.

I jerked my mind back to normal with an effort, tried to laugh at myself. Why I had actually been half believing this rubbish about a dried sea that still existed and a dead queen who came back to sate her bloodlust on the living. Was it possible that Le Quex believed it, or was it a cunning hoax to cover his own black crimes? Again I glanced at Theda. Was she his victim—or his accomplice?

"All right," I jerked out abruptly, "one of you will come along with Doc Parker and me to get Hoag's body. For the time being we'll lay off the subject of phantom seas and siren queens."

I turned. The two doctors were just coming back into the room. Farn, erect and composed as usual, betrayed no emotion on his mask like face. But Dr. Parker was visibly upset. As he came toward me I noticed that his right hand was holding something and that it shook.

"Wadley was drowned too?" I asked, matter-of-factly.

He nodded. "No question about it, Steve, and yet—"

"Of course," I cut him short, "it's incredible. But if it's true we'll find some rational explanation. There are certainly no salt tides washing over these dry flats now—"

"But there's something else I might mention," he interrupted.

"What?"

"This," he said, extending his hand. "I found it tangled in Wadley's hair."

I took the small greenish-brown thing from his hand and stared at it. My scalp crawled queerly. It was damp and a faint brackish smell came from it. It was a sprig of seaweed!

CHAPTER III

THE DEATH SHIP COMES

D R. FARN AND BARTON WENDELL helped Theda to her room and presently returned. "She's suffering from fright and nervous shock," the doctor said. "A little rest and she'll be all right."

Wendell volunteered to go with us to get Hoag's body.

We walked in silence, single file, down the stone steps that led from the mesa's base to the salt flats below. I was trying to keep a sane attitude, but it wasn't easy. The moon was high in the sky now and the air swam with limpid light. Again and again the impression came over me that I was walking down through invisible water to the weird depths of a ghostly sea. It didn't help matters any either when we reached the body of Hoag, lying in that horrid sprawl that suggested a stranded swimmer.

We stopped, staring down at the body, and Doc Parker licked dry lips. "It's bad enough," he said in a thick half whisper, "to know that the man was drowned. But even so, how in God's name did he get here?"

I didn't answer at once. The intense moonlight had made me a little giddy. A faint breeze washed against my face like a warm tide and for a mad instant I seemed to see the white crest of breakers shattering on the rock ridge beyond the shingle where the dead man lay. My fingers touched the still damp sprig of seaweed in my pocket and an insane panic claimed me—a feeling that I had to run or be suffocated.

I mastered it, got a grip on my nerves again. "He was carried here," I said through gritted teeth.

Wendell laughed nervously. "Carried?" His nod indicated the unbroken drifts between the body and the rock ridge.

I stared too. Yes, it was impossible. There were no footprints anywhere save our own. Nor could he have been thrown there, even if we could imagine a man strong enough to do it, without suffering bruises and broken bones. With long strides I crossed the belt of sand to the rock ridge. Like the rib of a half buried skeleton, it ran in a curving line to the mesa's base. A man carrying the body might have run along this rock ridge without leaving a track, but he couldn't have got the body to its position in the midst of the sand.

I walked back. "Let's take him in," I said.

We hefted Hoag's plump body by feet and shoulders, and my flesh crawled at the touch of his cold and clammy flesh. Slowly, in a tense, constricted silence, we carried our grisly burden to the mesa's top. Here we paused, panting. It was queer how we breathed more freely here. I caught Wendell staring back into the shimmering depths of air with an expression such as a diver might wear after he has plunged down to drag a bloated body from the wreck of some sunken ship.

We carried Hoag to his room and I started back to the living room. A low buzz of conversation drifted to my ears, and I went on tiptoe, paused in the hall listening. But I was disappointed in the conversation. Farn and Walsh Glanvil appeared to be arguing world politics.

"But Germany," I heard the doctor say, "could gain a decided advantage by withholding her potash. In a few years many crops would fail, the wheat and cotton rust—"

"Oh, yes," Walsh Glanvil interrupted, "but our scientists would solve the problem. Potash compounds are everywhere."

"But to separate it from the feldspar and silica—"

With a shrug I started on into the room, but stopped as Walsh Glanvil suddenly exclaimed, "Hell! Where did that damned Le Quex go? A minute ago—"

"He was in that corner," the doctor finished.

"He gives me the creeps. He's like, like a damned shadow—a shadow of something bad. Look here, Farn, are you so entirely skeptical about the supernatural? I sometimes think Haas is more than half right. Do you think this sheriff will ever find out how these men died?"

"Maybe," said Farn slowly, "you could answer that."

The pause was electric. I held my breath, waiting for Walsh Glanvil's answer. But it never came. From the left wing of the house came Barton Wendell's voice calling, "Theda! Theda!"

The next instant I had whirled as his feet came pounding into the hall. "Theda's gone!" he yelled. "Her room's empty. She's—"

I can't describe the feeling that came over me then. I had forced upon myself an utterly detached attitude toward the woman, had even toyed with the thought that she might be an accomplice in the crimes. Yet now, at the sound of Wendell's distracted cry, a casque of ice seemed to freeze about my limbs and cold brine ran through my veins. Theda gone! That lovely face, that splendid, lithe-limbed body fallen prey to nameless powers of evil, lying now perhaps cold and dank and dead on the moon-washed sand—

I guess I knew it then—that I was madly, insanely, in love with her. But I didn't pause for reflections. Grabbing Wendell's arm I jerked him to a halt, rasped senselessly, "What do you mean?"

"But she's gone!" he shrilled. "Her room's empty!"

Farn and Walsh Glanvil had come into the hall and now the four of us followed Wendell to Theda's room. It was as he said. There was the empty bed, there the faint indentation where her lovely form had rested!

Wendell ran to the window, began yelling her name. The rest of us ran through the house. She was nowhere to be found. In the kitchen the sleepy faced servants swore that they had not seen her. And Le Quex was gone too!

Running back I met the others congregated in the hall. Doc Parker had joined them. Farn seemed the least excited. "It's likely," he said, "that she simply went out for a breath of air. We mustn't let panic—"

"Panic hell!" I grated. "We've got to find her—and Le Quex. Scatter out and look for her, you four. This thing has gone far enough. I've got to have it out with Haas Glanvil, find out what he and this damned spiritualist have done to her!"

Dr. Farn frowned. "I doubt," he said, "if he'll let you in."

"He'll play hell keeping me out," I told him, "I can damned soon shoot the lock off his door."

However, I didn't have to. As I rapped at the door of the explorer's study, a thin, reedy voice demanded, "Who's there?"

"Langtry," I rasped. "Open up. Theda's disappeared!"

"Ah," the voice said, and that was all.

"Open that door," I ordered, "or I'll shoot the lock off."

A key grated, the door came open, and Haas Glanvil, a frail but erect shape in his green silk dressing gown, was confronting me.

I pushed into the room and closed the door, stood a moment staring about the strange interior of the study. Cases of books lined the walls and the furniture was mostly antique—heavy desks and tables and chairs. Dark, musty draperies on which the dim light lay with a sullen gleam. For though the rest of the house was modern, with electricity from Glanvil's own power unit, the aged explorer used nothing but candles himself. They stood now like long dead fingers, pushing the dark back with their flaming tips, spreading a yellow smudge over the brass sextant and compass and huge globe of the world which stood on a carved oak table.

My eyes came back to the figure of Haas Glanvil himself. He stood silent, his lean face with the yellow skin stretched like a film of silk over his high cheekbones, betraying no emotion at all.

"Did you understand me," I asked, "when I said that your daughter had vanished?"

He smiled and a faint light kindled in his cold, pale eyes.

"To be sure," he replied. "She is doubtless with Cleito, roaming the marches of that lost continent which Plato describes. You do not believe? But listen—" Here his speech came fast, with a nervous rush like a child reciting a piece by heart. "The historicity of Atlantis has been established. Moreover it is known that a fragment of the race migrated to Mexico. Do you know that the pyramid of Xochicalco in Mexico is of almost identical dimensions as the sacred hill of Atlantis. It was Cleito who presided over that sacred hill; while in Mexico it was Coatlicue. The similarity of those names is no accident. And that is not all—"

"That may all be true," I interrupted him, "and a part of the race may have come here. But I'm talking about your daughter now. What have you and this fiend Le Quex been doing to her?"

"Doing to her?" he asked. "Why nothing—only by the use of gentle suggestion preparing her soul for a communion with the dead."

"Hypnotism, in other words," I snorted.

"No, no," he denied, "nothing of the kind. Only talk, gentle suggestion. Think of the possibilities. If the soul of Cleito enters into her I may be able to recapture even the language of lost Atlantis. By merging the soul of my daughter with the soul of Cleito I may be able—"

"Merged with Cleito!" I suddenly snarled, my face twisted with disgust. "Are you a devil yourself? Do you mean that you want the spirit of a dead she-devil to take possession of Theda? Do you mean you want to make of her a vampire-thing, a ghoul who lured men to their deaths? Do you realize she may have lured Hoag and Wadley—"

"My enemies!" he said. "They would have stolen this land—"

I snatched at that. "And who else," I asked, "do you consider your enemy. Who else might Cleito lure?"

He frowned. "I think," he said slowly, "that Walsh has always been jealous of me, jealous because of his daughter who hasn't had the opportunities I've been able to give Theda."

My eyes narrowed. Was this the key? Was Haas really mad, or had he devised a hellish plot to murder his brother too?

"Look here," I said grimly, "let's drop this pose, this hoax of the dead returning, this talk of—"

I paused. Haas Glanvil had turned away from me, seemed no longer to hear. A rapt, faraway look had come over his gaunt features and he was staring toward the huge circular window that looked out over the mesa's rim.

I turned too. The sight was indescribably weird. The candles in the room were so dim that the great window shone with moonlight like a massive shield of silver. Haas Glanvil, half crouching, was moving slowly toward it. I followed, and for some reason the very air seemed to crawl with invisible vermin of terror.

We paused, he crouching, I standing over him. The half-moon shaped cliffs of the mesa curled out before us like a sort of harbor. Far below the salt flats lay, a pale desolation. Directly across from us the opposite cliffs loomed through the layers of moonlight like the submerged foundations of an island.

All was still. The swimming moonlight made me dizzy and weird fancies began to float through my brain.

"They are coming!" A grating whisper came from Haas Glanvil's lips. "The galleys of Cleito! Look!"

I looked—and froze. Terror tore at the roots of my hair, shrieked against my eardrums with the accents of madness. For suddenly in the shimmering tides of light that lay between us and the opposite cliffs, a shape was moving. It was a nebulous thing, a phantom craft of grey and silver—a galley! But I saw it distinctly.

As the air gusted from my lungs in a sick heave, I saw white-crested waves lap about its prow, saw oarsmen straining naked arms, saw the bearded slave-master with his strange high head-dress lash out with his whip as the ghostly craft shot through the air, straight into the black shadows of the rocks, where it melted—

How long I stood there half insensible, with the room rocking and revolving about me, I do not know. But horror held me, stupe-fied me, and I knew now that I too was insane, that some ghastly madness in the very air of the place had clamped its talons on my brain.

It was the screaming that aroused me. It came through an open window in the left wall of the room, and it was a man's voice, pleading, bleating with terror and pain:

"Theda," the voice screamed, "Theda, don't—in God's name, don't—spare me—"

Somehow volition returned. I had whirled, was plunging through the door, pounding down the hall, lurching out into the moonlight—

CHAPTER IV

THE KISS OF DEATH

THE COOL WIND THAT FANNED against my hot brow sobered me a little. I stared about. No one was in sight on the mesa's top. The bleating cries had ceased. A fearful silence brooded over the terraced house, the moon-splashed mesa, the shimmering depths of air below. I shivered. That voice had been Barton Wendell's and he had been screaming, pleading with Theda in an agony of pain and terror, pleading for mercy!

Suddenly it came again, but more distant, and choked, as if from lungs already suffocating; it came from the depths below the mesa's rim.

"Theda, Cleito—mercy—I'm dying—"

A hideous gurgle cut it short.

With long leaps I reached the mesa's rim, sprinted for the stone steps that led down. Dizzily I began to descend, fighting the frightful picture that swam in my brain—Theda leading her lover toward the cliff. His staggering figure, following blindly in the coils of a diabolic spell, his toppling fall—No, not falling. That would have been less horrible, more natural. What I seemed to see was his floundering body threshing the air, fighting madly against the ghostly waves of a sea that did not exist.

Terror rocked me. For as I stumbled down, I, too, seemed to feel phantasmal tides reach up and envelop me—brackish water pouring into my lungs, my senses reeling in agony.

Then, almost to the bottom, I saw him. He was moving across the stretch of salt flats that lay between me and the rock ridge that ran out from the mesa's base. But he wasn't running. I cannot describe the frightful movements of his body except to say that they were like the unreal motion of a figure in a slow-action film.

Floundering, flailing his arms slowly like a swimmer, he seemed to push against invisible tides that spun his body around, rocked it and tossed it. Then he began to sink on collapsing knees, his head rolling grotesquely, his arms beating weakly, folding finally as he slumped with a hideous slowness and lay still.

Even before I reached him I knew what I would find. And I was right. He had managed to reach the rock ledge, and his clawed fingers were fastened on it in a pitiful grip. His clothes, like the clothes of Hoag, were dripping wet, and as I rolled him over, brackish water ran in a thin trickle from his already stiff and distorted lips.

Straightening up, I stared wildly about. I thought of artificial respiration. But I didn't know much about that, I'm ashamed to say. Better find Doc Parker. I started back, stopped. In the shadows where the seam of rock joined the mesa, a shadow moved.

I started toward it along the ridge. But it had vanished. Maybe I had imagined it. Where were the others anyhow? Suddenly in a cleft of the rock near my feet I caught the gleam of moonlight on some shining object. I halted, stooped, fished the thing out and stood holding it foolishly in my hands. It was nothing more than a tin flour sifter.

I wanted to laugh. In the state of nerves I was in, there seemed something ludicrous about my find. I started to throw it down. But the faint germ of an idea was stirring. A flour sifter. And it wasn't broken. What was it doing—obviously hidden—here?

I reached into the cleft again and this time drew out a canvas cement sack. Something clicked in my skull.

With quick excited strides I stepped from the rocks to the sand dunes. At the edge I filled the sack. I took a few steps into the sand, then, carefully stepping back into the tracks behind me, I stooped and began to pour sand from the sack into the imprints in front of me. When they were almost filled, I scooped a sifter of sand from the sack and sprinkled it gently over the remaining unevenness. The result was astonishing. No trace of a footprint remained!

I straightened up, the tremendous significance of discovery buzzing in my head like a swarm of bees. How the fiends behind these horrors had managed to drown the men, I could not say, but I knew now how they had managed to leave them lying in the midst of a plot unmarked sand. They had carried them out, then simply walked backward, filling their tracks as they went. Human hands and human brains were behind the atrocities after all!

Dropping the sifter and the sack, I began legging it along the rock ridge toward the mesa's base. This was the path the murderers had used. Somewhere among those caves and crannies at the butte's base there must be—

I halted. Beyond a projecting angle of rock, there was a puddle of clear moonlight, and in it a shadow moved—a shadow crouched above a blacker blot on the white salt crust. I crouched, crept nearer, flattened myself against the rocks and peered round the edge. Horror like a bony fist slammed into my stomach, knocking the breath from me.

The black blot that lay sprawled on the ground was Le Quex; the figure bending above him was Theda! She wore the same dark dress in which I had last seen her, but a strap had come loose at one shoulder so that a half of one white breast was exposed; and her black hair, unbound and wind tossed now, rippled about her face in an ebon cataract shot with silver moonrays.

Standing there in frozen indecision, I felt waves of ice and fire run through my veins. For like some evil and incredibly lovely witch-thing out of folklore, she was crouching above the body of the man whom I had no doubt she had lured to a hideous death. Then she lifted her eyes—and saw me!

She sprang up. "It's you—Steve?"

Her voice was low, throaty, vibrant with a savage melody. "Music of Death," I thought, and I did not answer. Instead I stepped slowly out, my teeth gritted against the spell of her beauty. For already she was moving toward me, slowly, with a sensuous floating grace. The soft wind outlined every delicious curve of her superb ripe body, and fear, stark and abysmal, mingled with the wild wave of passion that swamped me.

"Stop!" I grated when she was a yard away. "Stand where you are. I'm arresting you for murder!"

"Me? Murder?"

It came in a soft gasp; yet even with its note of startled alarm there seemed mingled a taunting elfin laughter—a mockery of me and my authority. Unconsciously my hand had touched the butt of my revolver and now I felt strangely foolish under the steady gaze of her violet eyes. But there was an echo in my ears, Barton Wendell's dying cry: "Theda—mercy—"

I said: "We won't talk here. March toward the house. I'll follow."

"But Steve, you're joking. Why, I was just coming to look for you, to show you him—and something else, back there among the rocks. Come with me a moment, Steve—"

"Stop it," I grated between set teeth. "It's no go. Probably it's what you told the others, but I—"

Her sudden rush checked further words.

"Steve," she cried, "Steve!" and suddenly she was against me, all the warmth of her pressed to my breast, all the melting softness of her ivory arms pinioning my own arms to my sides, all the dazzling beauty of her face uplifted to mine, while the words tumbled in a passionate torrent from her lips:

"Steve, you can't believe that—not now. Not now, when there's no one else on earth I can trust, no one to trust me. Say you trust me, Steve. You love me, I know you do. It's in your eyes, in your voice, in the way your heart hammers when I touch you. You must trust me, come with me now and question later."

I tried to shove her away. The feel of her, the wild-flower odor that came from her hair, the warmth of her breath against my face, the wild passionate rush of her words were melting my will and strength.

"Don't!" I gasped lamely. "It won't work, you can't—"

And I could get no further. My blood was singing in my veins; my joints had turned to jelly. Yet even in the instant of surrender I made some foolish excuse to myself. To hold her only a moment in my arms, to crush her against me for a brief intoxicating instant, to feel her lips like crushed rose petals against my mouth! That would be all, and then—

My arms went round her; my senses swarm as I drew her to me. Briefly the thought of Barton Wendell with the salt water choking his dying lungs flashed through my mind. But it was too late now—

And then it came.

The crunch of a shoe on loose rock behind me was the warning. I tried to pull from her clutches, tried to turn. But suddenly my skull seemed to cave under the impact of some tremendous crushing weight that struck with the soft *sug!* of a sandbag. There was one terrible instant of vivid consciousness in which I realized her treachery. Then I was sinking, sinking into blackness.

CHAPTER V

THE PIT OF BRINE

I WAS FLOUNDERING IN AN ICY SEA, slapped and buffeted by waves of black brine, and hands were reaching down, grasping me, dragging me to the deck of a galley. It was a ghost-ship, and the dead oarsmen sang as they plied the oars. I knew that they were bearing me to some nether world of horror. I jerked with a spasm of terror—and awoke.

Sweat was dripping in cold beads from my face; the moonlight was dazzlingly white. I was lying on the salt crust, propped against the black rocks of the mesa's base. There was a gag in my mouth and my hands and feet were tied.

"Theda—Cleito—my darling—"

The thin quavering cry cut through the desert silence and I suddenly realized that it was what had awakened me. Then I saw her—a dream, a vision under the shimmering moon.

From beyond the shadow of the rock outcropping where I had been slugged, she came, her lithe limbs flashing, her black hair tossing as she danced. She was almost nude, with only a little skirt of glittering sequins about her slim thighs and gleaming cups of bronze over her swelling breasts. And while she paused in her backward dance, the staggering shape that followed her came into view.

It was Haas Glanvil. The dressing gown flopped about his bony legs. His white hair tossed. His gaunt face in the moonlight was wild with madness.

"Cleito—wait—come near, speak to me—"

He had paused, panting, leaning against the rocks. His voice was a flutey quaver, and now she was moving toward him. I tried to yell then, but the gag choked me. I knew what was coming, and it did—

There was a dull and scarcely audible crunch of the sandbag against his skull, a wild choked cry. The old man pitched forward, while from the shadows behind him a black shape sprang.

It was sickening, revolting, horrifying. The temptress had claimed another victim, this time her father!

But suddenly I was tense, watching the swift denouement of the frightful drama. The shape that had sprung from behind the rocks seemed only the shadow of a man, a thing of two dimensions. But he swiftly scooped up the old man's body, flung it over his shoulder, and following the girl, came toward me with long strides.

I slumped back, closed my eyes to a slit, lay as if dead. The woman passed me, so close that I could have touched the gleaming flesh of nude limbs. The man with his grisly burden followed. I saw that his body was encased in black tights and that his face and head were covered by a mask that shone bronze in the moonlight. They passed me with scarcely a glance, moved straight into the shadows of the rocks and vanished.

I sat up, staring. The base of the mesa, I knew, was honeycombed with crevices and caves, carved there ages ago by the waters. It was into one of these openings that they had gone. I was lying at the mouth of their lair!

My brain was working in a white heat now. No time for idle speculation. They certainly wouldn't leave me here long. Presently they would be back to carry me into the murder den where the other victims had doubtless already taken.

I tugged at the bonds that held my wrists. They were so tight that the thongs cut into my flesh and they drew my arms tight behind me. I might escape by rolling my body along, but it would be slow, and they could trail me easily.

My revolver was gone: I couldn't reach the knife in my pants pocket, even if it was still there. Then I thought of my watch.

I whirled about, and standing on my knees, pressed breast and belly against the cliff wall. I scraped along it until a projecting splinter of rock caught my watch pocket in my vest. Then I reared up. The pocket tore away; the watch fell out, and an instant later I had slumped down and seized it with my bound hands.

It took me only a moment to shatter the crystal, grasp a fragment in tense fingers and double my knees back under me. Then I went cold with despair. My ankles, I found, were tightly tied with picture wire!

Almost at the same instant I heard a distant mumble of voices from the shadows, knew that they were returning.

The idea that popped into my panic-stricken brain then was the straw at which a drowning man clutches. Not much—but something. With the sharp fragment of glass held between my thumb and middle finger, I ran my index finger along its razor edge. Gritting my teeth, I cut deep, and the blood gushed.

Reaching back behind me, I ran the burning bleeding finger along the salt crust in a straight line, pointing toward the crevice where the fiends had gone in. I tipped the line with the angle points of an arrow and crudely drew a childish skull and crossbones under it.

Now I could hear their feet. I dropped the glass, heaved up and forward, went down on my belly and wriggled toward the crevice. If they didn't see the crude marker I had drawn, it was barely possible that a searching party might find it. I flopped forward and lay still.

They came out, the beam of a flash crawled over me, a guttural voice which I could not recognize because of the mask's distortion, spoke: "Must have come to his senses and then passed out again."

The collar of my coat was seized in a viselike grip and I was dragged into the darkness.

The crevice turned and twisted. I lay limp, my toes and knees dragging. Light showed ahead. I was pulled through a narrow aperture where piled rocks indicated how the opening had been hidden, and was flung rudely to the floor of a small cavern. Its walls were encrusted with salt crystals on which the light from a carbide miner's lamp played with diamond gleams.

I lay inert, not daring to move, but probing the part of the cavern that I could see with slitted eyes. There was a long table at one end filled with chemical apparatus, bottles and tubes and burners. But the thing that caught my eye was the jagged three-foot hole in the center of the salt crust that formed the floor. Over it a wig-wamlike derrick of rough timbers had been erected to support the pulleys of a block-and-tackle, and there was a rope running down into the shaft.

Suddenly the man in the black tights stepped into my field of vision. Briskly he seized the end of the rope which was tied to an iron spike in the floor, and began to heave. The air gusted sickly from my lungs at the horrid thing that came into view. Scrawny legs first, it rose out of the hole—the dead, brine-dripping body of Haas Glanvil!

The drownings were clear now. Down under the salt crust was a subterranean stream or lake of brine, and the fiend had dug through to it. But who, and why—?

The bronze painted mask hid the fiend's features. In stature he might have been one of three tall men in the Glanvil household. Now he seized the swinging body and dragged it out upon the floor. Stepping next to the long table he reached into a glass tank and fished out a sprig of seaweed, started back toward the body, but stopped.

My breath caught in my lungs. In my excitement I must have lifted my head a trifle. With a snarl the fiend sprang toward me.

"Playing unconscious, eh?" he snarled, and one gloved hand reached out and snatched off the gag tied around my head. Then he kicked me square on the jaw. Well, if you're conscious I'll give you a little treat before we immerse you in the briny bath. I'll let you watch us while we give Theda her last baptism."

Theda! The word was like a spike piercing my brain. Theda? My head jerked up, my eyes rolled round the chamber, came to rest on the figure in the opening. The woman was standing there, the woman in the skirt of glittering sequins. But she wasn't—

She laughed, harshly, cruelly. "Startled?" her cold voice questioned. "Don't recognize Rosa Glanvil, Walsh Glanvil's little daughter, eh? But of course it's been four years since I went off to school, and my blond hair's dyed black now, and I've made a careful copy of Theda's makeup."

It was true. With the natural family resemblance, the similarity of ages and sizes, and the clever make-up, she might easily have been taken for Theda in a dim light.

"Good God!" I swore. "So you're after Haas Glanvil's estate, though I thought it was little enough. And your father here—"

I didn't finish. Brute terror froze the words in my throat. The tall, black sheathed fiend had come out of a branching crevice bearing in his arms a still, white burden, the sight of which sent an agonized rigor through my frame. With the black dress half torn from her body, she lay inert and unconscious in his arms—Theda!

I tried to struggle up, but a cold voice from behind the mask snapped, "One move and I'll drop her into the hole."

I froze, watched with bugging, pain stabbed eyes while the monster fastened the rope about her ankles, swung her lovely body, head down, above the yawning pit, and stood holding the rope in his gloved hands.

The hair rose on my scalp. Sweat burst in tortured globules from my pores. My voice broke through the paralysis: "In God's name, Walsh Glanvil, not that—not Theda! Listen to me. I'm beaten, but I can still be valuable to you. I'm the sheriff of this county and I'll do for you what torture and death couldn't force me to do—I'll help you cover your crimes. You'll need it. But free her, let Theda go, and I'll do anything, write a false report, then let you kill me if you want to!"

His harsh laugh mocked me. "No need of that," he cackled, "even if I trusted you. This place will be blasted to hell when we're through, and there'll never be a shred of proof to pin it on us!"

The pulleys creaked, each rusty squeal cutting like a knife into my heart as Theda's lovely body slipped slowly into the fearful depths. Madly I flung myself toward the monster, reared up, fell at his feet. He laughed as I lay there, quivering like a tied and maddened beast.

"Attack me, will you?" he asked. "And what will happen to her if you make me drop the rope?"

He was only too horribly right. I couldn't have touched him even if I had been free. I crouched in a paralysis of horror and again the pulleys creaked faintly, the rope began to crawl slowly along the floor behind him like a sluggish snake.

I'm not much of a praying man, but my brain was yammering prayers then. "God in heaven, save her, do something before I go mad, before I throw myself on him—"

A sharp hiss from across the chamber broke in upon my agony.

"Listen!" it was the girl. In two nimble leaps she stood beside the black clad fiend. "Can you hear—someone coming?"

He stiffened. My heart leaped. A low mumble of voices came from the depths of the tunnel that led out. "My gun!" the killer snapped.

Mechanically she sprang to the table, snatched up a revolver and came back.

How the one thing that could possibly save Theda flashed into my brain then I do not know, unless it was an answer to my frenzied prayers. But suddenly, almost before I knew what I was doing, I had lunged forward. As Rosa stood beside the man, holding out the gun, she suddenly drew it away.

"Wait—that voice. I think it's father. You can't shoot him!"

The fiend's answer was a rasped oath. With his left hand still holding the rope, he snatched the pistol from her. "The hell I can't. And if you try to stop me—"

She sprang at him like a wildcat. "You can't, you promised—"

The monster whirled; his hand on the rope loosened, it began to slip—I caught the rope between my teeth. My head went down then in a blind dive to tighten the slack before the sudden pull tore it from my grip. I felt the weight of Theda's body tear at the corded muscles of my neck, but I held with the grip of madness, held even when the crash of gunfire broke out, volleyed and reverberated.

With cold brutality the fiend was swinging his gun at Rosa. It crashed against her skull and she toppled back; her foot slipped on the edge of the hole and with a shrill cry she went down. There was a dull splash, drowned by a yell from the tunnel opening. Then the gunfire increased. I felt my senses reeling from the strain on my jaw and neck muscles—then silence—

It was only when I felt a hand grasping the rope firmly, releasing the strain against my locked teeth that I raised my head, looked up into the grim and anxious face of Walsh Glanvil.

I guess I must have fainted like a woman then.

I opened my eyes. I was lying on my side on the cavern floor. Theda was lying a few feet away. Her eyes were still closed, but she was breathing easily. Walsh Glanvil was standing over us, and behind him was Doc Parker, gun in hand. Glanvil's lean face was the most terrible mask of pain and tragedy I had ever seen.

"Rosa," he faltered. "She's—down there?" He was nodding toward the hole.

"Yes," I said. "She died trying to keep him from shooting you."

"That's something," he said, "a little comfort. She was in with him though. I suspected it toward the last. But even now—" his voice choked; he wiped his sleeve across his watery eyes. "God! How that beast must have warped my poor girl's mind!"

I nodded. "Being a doctor," I said, "he probably used drugs."

"Doctor?" he gasped.

"Sure, Farn."

I suddenly jerked upright, whirled about. Standing by the long table, a test tube in his hand, stood Dr. Farn. The lean body of the black clad fiend lay on the floor. The mask had fallen away from his head and blood now stained his twisted face—the face of Barton Wendell!

"Good Lord!" I gulped, "I thought —" Then the mists began to clear up. "So he was faking it all the time—that drowning. He just wet his clothes and filled his mouth with water and staggered around calling Theda's name! Then while I was talking to Theda he slipped up behind me and—" I checked myself, looking at the others. "But why?"

Farn came slowly forward. "I think I can explain it all," he said. "I had suspected it, but I wasn't sure. This place is more valuable than a gold mine."

"But what?"

"Potash!" he said. "More priceless to humankind than all the gold on earth. You may have overheard me talking to Walsh Glanvil tonight about potash. I was feeling him out to see if he was mixed up in the plot too. I satisfied myself that he wasn't. Later I told him my suspicions and the two of us came out with Doctor Parker to search. It was Parker who saw your blood sketched arrow and—"

"But the potash," I said.

"Oh, yes. Without potash in fertilizer the crops of the world would starve. Yet no deposits of any size have been found before except at Strassfurt in Germany, where a receding and returning sea deposited it over a period of thousands of years. Something similar must have happened here, for this salt crust contains it, and that brine down there contains it in the form of potassium chloride of a percentage so high that I'm afraid to estimate it. This place is worth more that a diamond mine."

"I begin to see," I said. Hoag and Wadley had probably found that out too, and that's why they were put out of the way. But how did Wendell get onto it?"

"That cake of salt with the imprint of the ancient vase," Farn said. "After Rosa Glanvil had taken it to Wendell at the university, he must have accidentally discovered its chemical content and realized its value. Then he and Rosa, who was in love with him, framed the whole thing. Wendell came here, made love to Theda, and got into Haas' good graces. Maybe he planned to marry Theda and later murder her, I don't know. But Hoag and Wadley brought things to a crisis.

"He had to act fast, though of course he had already perfected the build-up, with Rosa's help. She, of course had been impersonating the mythical Cleito to encourage Haas' madness; now he used her to lure his victims into his clutches. With the others out of the way, Rosa would be the sole remaining heir to the properties and—"

"But look here," I interrupted. "You speak of Haas Glanvil's madness. I saw that damned galley myself, floating in the air."

Farn smiled. "I saw it too," he said. "That's how I happened to search Wendell's room tonight and find there the small projector and the roll of old film from some historical movie in his trunk.

You see, his room was just above Haas' study. With the projector he could throw the pictures on the opposite cliffs, then hide the machine quickly. When you rushed out of the study tonight, Wendell must have already escaped from his room and started yelling to lead you off."

He paused; we both turned toward Theda. She lay with open eyes now, had apparently been listening for some time. "I suspected Barton too," she said, "when I learned from a servant that Rosa had come back to the ranch without Uncle Walsh's knowledge and was hiding there and coming here to meet Barton secretly. But I was so terrified for father's sake that I said nothing.

"Tonight I slipped away from you all to investigate alone. I found this cave, but there was no one in it, and coming out again, I stumbled on poor Le Quex's body. He must have come looking for me and accidentally found something which made it necessary for them to murder him too." She paused, staring at me. "And I didn't have time to tell you Steve, though I had decided to tell you everything then. But he slipped up and slugged you, and a moment later knocked me out too."

"I hope you'll forgive me," I said, "for ever doubting you a moment."

"How can you ask me to forgive you," she questioned, "when I owe you my life?"

Sometime later I met Theda.

"Did you mean it," I asked, "that about your knowing that I was in love with you all along?"

"What do you think?" she asked with a tantalizing smile.

I let her know plenty quick.

THE THING THAT DINED ON DEATH

CHAPTER I

BUTCHERY

CLIFF SLADE LAY FLAT ON HIS BELLY, his muscles stiff as jerked beef, and cursed the dry leaves that crackled with each movement of his body. His breath was an imprisoned weight in his chest; it trickled out in slow wraiths of steam from between his parted lips; the beating of his heart was like a heavy fist slugging his ribs.

There it was again! The rustle of feet in dry grass, and another sound—horrid, indescribable—the soggy ripping of a blade in tough tissues of flesh!

In the dark blot of shadows beyond the intervening band of yellow hill grass, a fiend was about his execrable business—dark sadistic butchery that had changed the peaceful hillsides and byways about the village of Midvale to heathen abattoirs, where the bleeding cadavers of animals were found night after night, mutilated in a peculiar and abhorrent way.

Slade's elbows, supporting his weight, began to tremble. On the chill, clear moonlit air that layover tree and hillside like a film of silver, the odor of blood drifted to his nostrils—warm blood that flowed and steamed. What sort of hands were those that were digging into a dead beast's intestines? Slade shivered.

The sheep had bleated only once—a shrill and almost human cry of agony. He had heard it from the little road that skirted the hillside and he had left his car and crept up toward the source of that awful cry. Now he lay within a few yards of the nameless ogre; yet he dared not go nearer the black shadows that masked that awful mystery.

Slade wasn't a coward, but he was unarmed, and he knew that the monster, whatever or whoever he was, carried a blade of deathly sharpness for his swift incisions, incisions that might have been made by some mad surgeon. Slade quivered hotly at that thought. He was a doctor himself, a new doctor in a narrow, suspicious little village. He had heard that malicious gossip was hinting that he himself might be the fiend!

Rage boiled in Slade's veins, pumping new energy into his frozen limbs. Slowly he rose to his knees. His numb fingers clawed at a crumbling rock outcropping, yanked loose a jagged fragment. He straightened cautiously to his feet, braced himself, and like a discus thrower, hurled the rock into the massed shadows of the cedar clump.

Crash!

The rock hurtled through splintered branches, struck the stony ground with a thud.

Breathless, Slade listened. There was no further sound, no outcry. He picked up another rock and dived into the moonlight. Three bounds carried him across the patch of hill grass. He ducked under low, thick-tufted branches, paused, staring into gloom.

Slade fumbled for a match, clicked it against his thumbnail, held the weak flame in cupped palms. An invisible hand seemed to clutch at his vitals, twist his stomach into a knot.

Almost at his feet it lay—the bloody corpse of a sheep. The throat had been slit first; the head was twisted grotesquely awry. One glance at the wound in the abdomen was enough. He knew what had happened there. Monster hands had plunged into the bloody welter, had fished out one bleeding organ, the sole object, apparently, of each gory debauch—the liver, the liver of a sheep!

Slade dropped the glowing match. It fell sizzling in a scarlet puddle. A sort of slick dizziness seized him and he backed quickly out of the carnage-scented gloom. Why was it always the liver which the ghoul tore from its bleeding victim? There was something faintly familiar about the sound of that.

Standing on the hillside, Slade stared up toward the tree-tufted ridges above him. Beyond the graveyard, whose white palings shone a hundred yards away, was a bright diadem of lights among the trees. Slade thought of the man who owned that place, the sleek, tall Asiatic, Merro Daak, who had bought the old stone house from Peter Marsden and rebuilt it for a country home. Merro Daak, the fashionable radio astrologer, whose name was on every woman's tongue. Slade had seen him often, passing through the village in his big foreign-made car, with his jaded and debauched companions, on whose neurotic faces Slade's eye had read the imprint of sickening abnormalities. Did the orgies which were said to go on in Merro Daak's house have any bearing on these bestial atrocities?

Slade plodded back to his car. His brain was a whirling chaos. For there were yet other pieces to be fitted into the weird jigsaw puzzle. Above all, there was the question of what was happening to Esther Corman.

Something tugged at Slade's heart as he thought of Esther with her dark hair and violet eyes. A few weeks ago they had been on the verge of marriage. Then Esther had changed, had begun to avoid him, had become strange and secretive. Where, particularly, had she been going at night? Two things troubled Slade in this connection.

Three weeks ago, Esther's best friend, Mary Wycliffe, had disappeared, had left a rather ambiguous note saying that she was going to the city and would not be back. And shortly after that, Esther had met Merro Daak, had seemed strangely fascinated by him. It was then that she had begun to change. One of those two things had done something to Esther!

Slade crawled into his roadster and kicked the engine into life. One thing was certain; tonight he would untangle a part of the mystery at least. For that afternoon, after a heated argument, Esther had told him that she had been going out with Len Marsden, Slade's best friend. Slade didn't believe it. Tonight he was going to find out from Len himself.

The car followed the winding road that skirted Graveyard Hill and began to climb the stiff grade to the slopes above it. Here, on a gloomy hummock, stood the sagging frame house where Len lived with his father, old Peter Marsden, a man once wealthy, now ruined in health and mind and fortune. Slade drew up before the dilapidated gate, yanked his emergency brake tight and got out. A dim light burned in the front window of the old house. Slade mounted the rickety front steps and rapped at the door.

"Come!" a cracked voice called.

Slade opened the door and stepped in. A billow of warm air enfolded him. The gloom of the bare room was partially dissipated by the yellow glow from an oil lamp and the red embers of a coal fire in the grate.

Old Peter Marsden, his wheelchair pulled up close to the fire, his paralyzed legs wrapped in a blanket, sat, as he always sat, with a Bible on his lap, a Bible open, Slade was sure, on the terrible poetic chapters of the Apocalypse. For Marsden, since the day when dark tragedy had numbed his mind and paralyzed his limbs, had become a religious fanatic, predicting the corning end of the world.

"You look," said Peter Marsden, as Slade came toward the fire, rubbing his cold hands together, "like you'd seen a ghost."

Slade tried to laugh. "No, just dropped in to see Len."

"He ain't come in yet," the old man's mournful voice croaked. "But look here, you ain't shakin' jest from the cold. What's happened?"

Slade looked at old Marsden sharply. Under the thatch of greying hair, the square wrinkled face, chiseled in strong lines, showed the ravages of a crumbling brain. Yet a certain shrewdness lingered. Like a child, the old man sensed things, was not easily lied to.

"Another butchered sheep," Slade told him, frowning. "I can't imagine what sort of hellish—"

"Can't ye?" the old man interrupted. "If ye read the Scriptures ye could. It's the signs of the end. The slaves of the Anti-Christ is about their evil business—sacrificin' flesh to the Dragon!"

"Anti-Christ?" Slade asked

"The false prophet that in the latter days seduces the world, the evil prophet from Babylon who leads the people to idolatry!"

"And who—?" Slade began.

"Who? Who indeed!" old Marsden cackled. "Who but that Asiatic Babylonian, Merro Daak? Ain't his false prophecies heard from ocean to ocean—his heathenish soothsayin' over the radio? Listen at this—" His lean brown finger traced a passage on the open page, and he quoted: ". . . 'and there was given unto him a mouth speaking great things and blasphemies, and power was given unto him to continue forty and two months.' "

Slade turned quickly to stare into the fire. Strange how the old man had echoed his own suspicions, though in a different way. "You think he's to blame for these butcheries?" he asked.

"Listen to me," Peter Marsden said. "I ain't so crazy as people say. Why'd Merro Daak buy that old house from me, away off here in the hills? How come he brings them flocks of people out here, keepin' lights burnin' all night? I tell you they're a-worshipin' the gods of Babylon in that place, worshipin' him with strange an' evil orgies!"

Slade cleared his throat, looked away. There were plenty of rumors of pagan orgies in the place alright. *And the livers of sheep* . . . There was a connection, if he could only get it. He said, changing the subject deliberately, "Len's usually home by now, isn't he?"

"Usually," the old man agreed.

"Then I'll just wait for him in his room," Slade said. "I wanted to borrow a book from him; I'll look for it."

He went out into the dark hall and closed the door behind him.

Slade went into Len's room, lighted the lamp and the oil stove that stood beside the book-littered desk where Len studied. Len, who worked by day in a machine shop, was studying civil engineering at night. Poor Len, a young man with a brilliant mind, fighting to overcome the handicap of poverty!

Slade began to pace the floor. Len Marsden was the only close friend he had found in the village. True, he had always suspected that Len was in love with Esther. But that didn't prove . . .

A sudden ugly thought broke in upon his mind. There was a crazy streak in Len's family! What was this tragedy that hovered in the background? Something about an elder brother who had mistreated a girl of the village and had been lynched for it. The shock had caused old Peter Marsden's mind to crack, had caused *astasiaabasia* to paralyze his limbs. That had happened five years ago. Yet, if there were madness in the blood . . .

Slade suddenly realized that he had stopped before a bookshelf. His eyes had been scanning the titles without really seeing them. Now one double tier of faded letters struck his brain with a shock:

The Magic of Ancient Babylon.

Slade's heart took a violent jump. With shaking hands he took the book from the shelf and carried it to the table. As he laid it down it fell open of its own accord. Breathless, Slade bent forward, stared at the heading above the page. "Hepatoscopy" was the queer word he read there. On the margins of the text he saw

notations in Len Marsden's hand. Eagerly his eyes seized on the
print, began to read:

> *The favorite method of augury among the Babylonians was
> by examination of the liver of a slaughtered animal or human.
> The soul was supposed by primitive people to reside in the
> liver. More blood, too, is secreted by the liver than by any other
> organ of the body, and upon opening the carcass it appears the
> most striking, the most central and most sanguinary of the vital
> parts. This rite was called Hepatoscopy. The liver of a sheep
> was commonly used, though in certain esoteric ceremonies
> connected with the pagan mysteries, this organ, taken fresh
> from the body of a virgin was required. In reading the hepato-
> scopic signs, the chief appearance of the liver was noted, as,
> shade of color of the gall, lengths of the ducts, etc. The lobes
> were divided into sections, lower, medial and higher, and the
> omens of the future varied from the phenomena there ob-
> served . . .*

Slade straightened with his brain reeling, trying to digest the
ghastly significance of his find. Undoubtedly Len Marsden had
been studying this awful and forgotten science. Why? Slade
clenched his hands, closed his eyes as if to shut out the black vi-
sions that swirled in the smoke of the lamp. It was absurd to suspect Len.

Suddenly he stiffened, closed the book, whirled about. A sound
from across the hall had reached his ears—the sound of a door
being opened softly, of stealthy steps on a creaking board. Slade
blew out the light, sneaked to the door, opened it softly and stared
across the hall into the kitchen.

A giddy nausea seized Slade then, froze the breath in his lungs,
congealed his blood. By the wagging light from a candle he saw
the pale, emaciated face of Len Marsden, who had just entered the
back door. Len tiptoed to the kitchen sink, rested the candle on the
drain board and turned on the water tap. Then Slade saw something which he had not noticed before. Len's hands were stained
with blood!

CHAPTER II

THE FACELESS THING

INCREDULOUS DISMAY held Slade rooted in his tracks. Even now, with the guilty picture before his eyes, the thing seemed an abomination too terrible to be true. But it wasn't just the blood, it was Len's whole manner—his chalky, haunted face, his air of furtive stealth. Hot unreasoning rage flared through Slade then. He swung the door wide, stepped out.

Len Marsden whirled. "Cliff Slade!"

"Yes," Slade said, grimly, hollowly. "Where's Esther?"

"Esther?" A dazed look came over Len's face.

Slade advanced a few steps, his fists knotted in hard lumps. "Yes, Esther," he growled. "And why the blood?"

Len's hands dropped limply to his sides. "You can't believe— You don't understand! I couldn't let father see that blood. His poor brain's tormented enough already. I was walking out from town, cutting across Graveyard Hill when I stumbled right into one of those bloody butcheries in a cedar grove—got the gore on my hands." He paused, gasping for breath. "But why are you asking me about Esther, Cliff?"

"Because," Slade said, "something's happened to Esther. She goes off at night and no one knows where. This afternoon she told me she's been going out with you!"

"With me?" Len gulped. "But that's not true. I think the world and all of Esther; you know that. But I wouldn't come between you two. I've noticed There's something wrong with Esther too— ever since Mary Wycliffe disappeared. But I haven't been out with her, Cliff—not once, I swear it!"

Slade hesitated. Despite Len's pallid, twitching face, there was the ring of truth in his words. "All right," he said, "but I want to know why you've been studying up on hepatoscopy?"

Len dropped his eyes. "You saw that book?" he asked. "I should have told you, I guess. But I was afraid you'd think it was just wild talk like father's, afraid you might think my mind was touched, too. But the fact is, Cliff, I think I've got a clue to the monster behind these outrages. He may be at the bottom of Esther's trouble, too."

"You mean Merro Daak, I suppose?"

"Don't laugh, Cliff. I know what you think about father's wild talk. But the old man is about half right. Merro Daak is behind these outrages. Here's something you may not have thought of: the chief god of the Babylonians was Merodach—the phonetic equivalent of Merro Daak. Get it? The astrologer is the head of a cult which is reviving the ancient practices of Babylon, and—" He broke off short, whirled toward the outer door.

"What is it?" Slade asked. Then he heard. At the front a car had come to a stop with screaming brakes. Men's gruff voices could be heard in hoarse murmurs. They were getting out, corning toward the house.

Len Marsden snatched up a towel, began drying his hands. Then he blew out the candle quickly.

"What's the—?" Slade began.

"Shhh!" Len hissed in the darkness. "I heard your name mentioned. You know there's been talk—"

Slade had tiptoed to the door that led into the hall. The bang of heavy fists was sounding on the front door of the house. Old Marsden's cracked voice called out, "Come." Then a billow of sound surged in—the scrape of booted feet, a confused babble, above which sounded the deep bass of Sheriff Corman, Esther's father.

"That young Doctor Slade," Cliff heard him say, "we're lookin' for him. His car's parked in front here."

Slade held his breath, heard old Marsden reply, "He ain't here. What you want with him; what's he done?"

"Plenty!" Corman's gruff voice boomed. "He's gone off with my girl. There's been another animal slaughtered, too, and Lafe Braze saw him leave the place in his car."

"You're blamin' that on Cliff?" old Marsden asked. "You're blind fools! I know who kills them critters in the dark of night!"

"It's that young doctor," someone in the group growled. "I reckon he's up to some sort of crazy experiments—"

"Experiments!" Peter Marsden shrilled. "It's the experiments of hell, an' Merro Daak is the fiend!"

"We've questioned him," Corman said. "He's got a group of friends with him, and they've all accounted for themselves. Now if Slade ain't here, what's his car doing out in front?"

Holding his breath, Slade suddenly started forward. But Len Marsden's tense hand on his arm drew him back. "They'll mob you!" Len hissed. "You can't go in there. Slip out the back way. I'll tell them I drove your car here. As soon as I get away from them I'll meet you in the orchard by Merro Daak's place, and we'll find out—"

His sucked in breath, cut the words off short. In the front room a Babel of angry growls had drowned out old Marsden's shrill protests.

"Search the place! We'll find the butcher!"

Heavy feet thudded on creaking floors, moved toward the hallway. With his heart hammering a staccato undertone to the wild tumult of his thoughts, Slade felt himself being pushed toward the back door. A gust of cold air sobered him. Len was right; you couldn't argue with men whose minds were deranged by excitement.

"Hurry!" Len whispered. His hand was gripping Slade's. Slade returned the pressure briefly, then turned, was running through the white waves of moonlight like a frantic swimmer.

He passed the dark barn and outbuildings, swept on by panic. A burst of voices sounded behind him; one rose shrilly above the hubbub: "Get bloodhounds after him . . ."

Slade jerked himself alive again; the terror of the hunted fugitive sent him plunging into the dense gloom of the trees. Shadows dripped from the thick foliage, seemed to cling to him like tentacles retarding his flight. Esther gone! And they believed that he had kidnapped her, believed that he was the mad butcher who disemboweled animals in the dead of night! He pictured himself in the hands of those crazed villagers and shuddered.

Abruptly Slade stopped, clutched at a limb for support, leaned there panting. He stared down along the slope below him. He had reached a point directly above the graveyard. Below him the pale white shapes of the tombstones gleamed like the scattered teeth of a giant. To his right, less than half a mile along the slope shone the lights of Merro Daak's stone house. Slade made a start in that direction, then paused.

The bloodhounds! If they picked up his trail at the Marsden place, they would follow him directly to his destination!

Out of the enveloping silence the faint gurgle of water drifted to his ears. He moved nearer the sound, came to the brink of the narrow ravine through which a shallow stream rushed down from the dark ridges above. The stream would save him.

Clinging to stunted junipers and tough grass, he clambered down into the arroyo, splashed out into the icy sheet of silver. Needles of cold stung the calves of his legs, sent frigid currents through his veins. He would follow the stream down, hide in the graveyard, and see which direction the chase took. The chances were they would follow the stream up into the hills, once the dogs lost the trail. If they did, it would leave him free to hurry on to his rendezvous with Len.

He stumbled on through the icy current, slipping on mossy rocks and regaining his balance, moving down with the current. Suddenly he halted, shivering with a cold not born of the water. From the dark slopes behind and to his left a faint and eerie ululation drifted to his ears, stabbed him with daggers of dread. The bloodcurdling bay of the bloodhounds!

Slade dived for the steep bank on his right, floundered against it clumsily, clawed for a hold on the jagged rocks. His feet were awkward frozen weights; his fingers were stiff with cold. Painfully he hefted himself up, crawled out on the dry grass, panting. Before him the graveyard spread out its sepulchral forest of white marble. He stared behind him.

On the hillside above the now dark house of the Marsdens, the faint pinpoints of lanterns bobbed grotesquely among the trees. Again the dismal baying of the dogs vibrated against his ears. He staggered up, dragging his leaden feet, stamped them on the dead grass turf as he plunged in among the gibbous shadows of the tombs.

At the crest of Graveyard Hill he came to the little arbor used in summer for a chapel. Dry vines covered the latticed sides, and its roof was thatched with straw. Slade climbed up, threw himself down on the straw roof, began to burrow in. With all but his head covered, he lay shivering, staring out toward the slopes beyond the ravine.

Back and forth among the fringe of trees the lanterns bobbed, drawing nearer to the stream gradually as the baying hounds lost the trail, circled, picked it up again. A feverish impatience smoldered in Slade's veins.

He looked at the luminous dial of his watch. He had been here twenty minutes—twenty precious, wasted minutes! But now they had reached the ravine. The hounds had redoubled their baying.

Round and round they dashed, dragging shadowy figures on taut leashes as they tried to pick up the lost trail. The spots of lights gathered in a group. Now they were moving off, moving up toward the hills.

Slade sucked cold air into his lungs with relief. Now he was free—for hours at least—free to find Esther, to snatch her from whatever dark peril threatened her.

He straightened, began kicking the straw from his limbs. "They won't dare harm her," he muttered savagely; "they won't dare—"

His jaws snapped together, teeth clicking on the chopped off syllable. He leaned forward, muscles tense, chills prickling the flesh between his shoulder blades, his eyes glued to the square white blot of a burial vault that stood between two cypress trees a dozen yards or so away.

Had something moved there, or had he imagined it? Moonlight, filtering through the trees, lay in livid streaks across the vault's stone front. All was still now. Yet he was certain something had moved there!

Whose vault was that anyhow? He had been in the cemetery only a few times, but he seemed to remember it. Wasn't it—Great God, it was! It was the vault of Banker Trainor, and that very day it had yawned for a new occupant—the banker's daughter, a frail, slender girl of twenty.

Slade found himself shaking; cold sweat beaded his brow as he writhed in the clutch of grisly premonitions. He made a move to lower himself to the ground, then abruptly flung himself flat on the straw roof again with spectral fingers of horror clawing at his throat. He wasn't imagining this, this thin strip of black that had suddenly stretched in a line across the white front of the tomb, this strip of black that was gradually widening. Slowly, silently, as if propelled by the invisible hands of an incorporeal phantom, the door of the vault was swinging open.

Now it was wide, an empty rectangle of black—a black mouth that had swallowed dead things, that was now preparing to disgorge—what?

It came so suddenly that Slade could not say whether it had stepped into the black frame or materialized before his eyes. But it was there, a shape of abysmal terror, white, tall, clothed in something that clung in loose folds about it like rotting cerements, seemed draped like a loose cowl over the head. Slade stared, straining his eyes to pick out the lineaments of that face beneath the cowl. But under the hood was a blot of black, a spot of empty darkness that matched exactly the hue of the surrounding gloom. Under the cowl there was no face, no face at all, only a yawning, empty void!

Slade abruptly pushed himself back, slid his body feet first from the low roof. Dry grass turf thudded against him as he landed in a huddle and began to pick himself up unsteadily. The grass had muffled the sound of his fall. Now he straightened weakly. He crept to the edge of the arbor and peered around it. The thing was gone.

He stepped out into the moonlight, probing the shadows with his eyes. Then he saw it. Already yards away, it was moving as no living thing ever moved. A shapeless, fluttering white blur against a background of dark trees, it moved with swift leaps like a kite jerked by wild wind currents—moved a good two feet above the ground, which it did not seem to touch at all.

With a hoarse cry rasping between his teeth, Slade jerked loose from the rigor that held him and plunged forward after the fleeing phantom. But he went less than a dozen strides, for suddenly the pale horror fluttered out in a shapeless flash of white, swirled like a spreading smoke puff, then seemed to bunch itself and dissolve in the inky shadows.

Shade jerked to a halt, drawing one hand across his startled eyes. What was the Thing, and what had it been doing in the sepulcher of the newly dead? It had fled in the direction of Merro Daak's house. Had the astrologer by black sorcery loosed the bodiless demons of ancient times to walk the earth again?

He whirled about, stared at the yawning door of the vault. Unearthly dread clutched at him then. It took courage, but he went in, striding doggedly toward the ominous portals. Straight into the crypt he walked, and the match already in his hand rasped against the door, sputtered into yellow flame.

He stopped then, but only for an instant. The match fell from his fingers. He whirled wildly, came reeling out into the moonlight again. And he ran—leaping graves, dodging headstones, unwilling to pause for his brain to digest the awful thing he had seen—the coffin dragged from its shelf, the lid wrenched open, the ghastly thing within. For the unembalmed body of the girl had been mutilated like the bodies of the sheep, mutilated by inhuman hands that had sliced a wide incision through grave-clothes and flesh to reach the awful object of its sacrilege!

Slade's feet were winged things now, driven on by the hot tumult of a brain that shrieked, "Esther! Esther!" If there existed things so loathsome that even the dead were not immune to their ravages, what would they do to the helpless body of a living woman?

What might they not be doing even now to Esther Corman?

CHAPTER III

THE SLAVES OF ISHTAR

A T THE EDGE OF THE CLEARING in which stood the old stone house with its gardens and orchard, Slade halted. He had been running as a man runs in a nightmare, wildly oblivious to his surroundings. Now he sobered. Clear wits would be needed to grapple with the evil entrenched in this ancient mansion.

Crouching, he crept into the orchard, moved furtively from tree to tree like a shadow. The lights in the upper part of the house had gone out. A few lower windows glowed dimly. Along the graveled driveway cars were parked; moonlight gleamed on sleek, shiny hoods and fenders. There was a crowd here tonight—wealthy neurotics, thrill-seekers. Slade pictured their flabby faces and shuddered.

Should he try to get in, or should he wait for Len Marsden to join him? Len would know the lay of the land, the arrangement of the house. The place had once been his home, before the ruined fortunes of Peter Marsden had forced him to sell it to the astrologer. Why had Merro Daak wanted this place in particular? That question seemed to trouble old Peter Marsden, too.

Slade stopped, peering at a huge grey wedge-shaped structure that reared its bulk among the garden shrubs. It was the ancient mausoleum of the Marsden family, dating back to a time when people buried their dead on their own estates. Two ideas had flashed into Slade's mind at once.

This old place was close to a graveyard, and it also contained within its grounds a burial vault. If a man were bent on carrying on traffic with the dead, here was an arrangement perfect for his needs, here were sepulchers near at hand to be plundered for the grisly appurtenances of sorcery.

Creeping up behind the vault, Slade crouched in its shadows, staring at the somber walls of the house. A slither of furtive footsteps among dry grass stalks reached his ears; a dark figure crept out from the shadows beyond the crypt.

Slade studied the figure a moment through slitted eyes. Then he hissed sharply, "Len!"

The figure spun like a top, stared, came toward him.

"Cliff?" Len Marsden breathed. "I had a time getting away from them. They knew I'd lied to them about your not having been there. The old man threw a fit and had to be put to bed, but they made me go with them. I slipped away as soon as I could. What kept you?"

Slade told him. Len whistled under his breath. "Lord!" he said, "then it's even worse than I suspected. You're convinced now?"

"I'm convinced," Slade said grimly. "How do we get into the house?"

"They're gathered in the dark basement," Len told him. "Some sort of ceremony seems to be in progress. We'll listen in."

Silent as shadows they stole through the shrubs of the garden, then, on hands and knees, they crawled toward a square, black opening in the foundation of the house.

A droning sound reached their ears as they crept nearer, a mumbling buzz like a hive of angry bees. A small window, hinged like a door, hung open a few inches. Flat on the ground, Len and Slade snaked nearer. Hot air billowed out of the aperture and the buzz of voices resolved itself into a chant, low, somber—a ghostly medley from invisible throats, weird words from the dark mysteries of the past:

> Seven are they, seven are they! Battening in Hades, seven are they!
> Knowing neither mercy nor pity, The Evil Ones of Ea . . .

Slade felt his flesh crawl. "What is it?" he gasped in Len's ear.

Len swallowed; his breath came jerkily as he whispered. "They're getting ready for something awful. That's the chant of the Seven Demons of Babylon—a sort of vampire who stole the sacrifices from the altars of the gods."

"Let's do something!" Slade grated. "If Esther's in there— How can we get inside, Len?"

But Len was already crawling away. Slade followed. Hugging the foundation, they came to the back of the house, stopped at another narrow window.

"This," Len whispered, "opens on a storeroom—or used to; it connects with the main basement. You go in there. I'll climb to a second-story window and come down through the house. One of us will get in there sure!" He gripped Slade's hand a moment, tensely. "Good luck!" Then he was up and gone.

Slade fumbled with the window, located the hinges, pushed gently. With a faint creak it swung open. The interior was pitch dark; the murmur of the chant was still audible, but it was muffled. The door that led into the main basement must be closed. Slade struck a match. The narrow, cement-walled room was empty except for the stacks of old furniture and boxes along the walls. Slade blew out the match, thrust his body feet first through the window.

Breathless, he stood in the thick dark. A weapon—he needed a weapon of some sort! He had nothing but a large clasp-knife in his pocket. He fished it out, opened it, crept to the door. The weird murmur of the chant still droned in his ears. He grasped the knob of the door, turned it softly, gave the door a gentle pull, peered through the crack.

Warm air struck his face, the reek of aromatic fumes. A chanting chorus washed against his ears like a rumbling wave of madness. Then the chanting ceased. In the center of the pit of gloom that yawned before him a globe of greenish light kindled on the dark. It brightened, glowed like a monstrous planet in the gulfs of space, began to shed faint rays of emerald over the eerie room, over the huddled occupants. Then a voice—the oily, evil tones of Merro Daak—was speaking in measured syllables.

"Tonight we celebrate the mysteries of Ishtar, goddess of love and fertility. As Ishtar, Astaroth, Astarte, Aphrodite, she has gleaned the harvest of the hearts of men since the dawn of time . . ."

The green mist of light brightened; the macabre scene swam before Slade's eyes like something seen through depths of murky water. The low-ceilinged room, draped in dark tapestries, the weird figures of the worshipers, kneeling in a semicircle before the long altar, and behind that the raised dais, with its drawn canopies of velvet. It was from behind these curtains that the voice seemed to come.

"In the hanging gardens of Babylon, they sang the praises of Ishtar, and in the secret groves of Ninevah her priests wielded the bright knives, the bright, blood-drinking blades . . ."

At these words, spoken with slow, evil relish, moans of unholy ecstasy broke from the kneeling ranks. Slade stared with crawling revulsion at the dim shapes. Strange garments covered their forms; conical casques were on their heads, and their skirted, half-naked bodies glittered with metal sequins and brilliants. But for their faces they might have been snatched from the terraced fanes of ancient Nippur.

But those faces! Wild with evil passions now shamelessly unmasked, they glowed in the greenish light like the visages of ghouls. Aged faces, most of them; rich, jaded, avid for the final thrill before death claimed them; and young faces, too, loose-mouthed, flabby, revolting.

"Before your eyes shall be enacted Ishtar's descent into Hades, just as it was enacted by the initiates of old. We shall see the goddess go down into Aralu, the Land of No-return. At each of the Seven Gates she is stripped of some of her jewelry and clothing until she stands nude and helpless before the Gods of Darkness. There she must bow in homage while a sacrifice to Allatu is made."

He finished, and on the sudden silence a muffled blare of trumpets sounded from some hidden source and the curtains about the dais parted and drew back. A shudder seemed to pass over the craning devotees. Then while gasps of lewd admiration wheezed from their lungs, a double throne was revealed on the dais. In one seat sat Merro Daak in the robes of a Babylonian king, and in the other seat sat a woman whose slender body was draped in the loose folds of vari-colored veils. Golden sandals were on her tiny feet and a golden crown on her head, and her loose hair fell in ebon ripples about her shoulders.

Now she rose with graceful, mincing steps, began to descend the steps of the dais. Light from the green globe fell suddenly athwart her face, and Slade, standing rigid behind the door, felt his muscles constrict, felt fingers of horror claw at his quivering flesh.

For the veiled woman, parading with shameless poise before the avid eyes of that depraved throng, was Esther Corman! Was it possible? Esther, his Esther, the abandoned priestess of this pagan cult of shame?

It took all the strength of Slade's will to hold himself in check then. But he knew that he must wait, not give himself away too soon.

Esther had reached the floor, was moving toward one end of the semicircle of crouching worshipers. Then from the ranks, dark figures rose—seven of them—draped in flowing robes of black, they stood erect, like sentinels guarding the gates of hell. Esther had faced about, was moving toward the first of the dark seneschals. As she paused beside him, the black-robed figure stepped forth, reached out and snatched the crown from her head.

"Enter," he intoned. "It is the command of Allatu!"

The hidden trumpets sounded two blasts. The kneeling figures bent to the floor and straightened with outstretched arms, and Esther moved on to the next robed figure. Here the ritual was repeated; the dark figure snatched from her shoulders the veil of crimson; the trumpets blared, and Esther moved on.

Hot tears of shame and rage stung Slade's eyes as he watched the progress of that evil rite. As each succeeding veil was stripped from Esther's body the excitement of the repulsive devotees increased. They bowed and straightened, flung their hands, rolled their greedy, glittering eyes, began to mumble and cackle blasphemous prayers to Ishtar and the demon-gods of Babylon.

Then the last portal was reached, and Slade, with hot shudders wringing the sweat from his body, saw the last veil torn from Esther's body amidst the lewd howls of the mob; saw her move like an animated thing of marble toward the white-draped altar and bow meekly before it.

Then something moved from the shadows of the left of the dais. Two huge Negroes dressed in scarlet loincloths paced into the light. On their massive shoulders they bore a catafalque on which lay the nude, bound body of a girl. At the altar they stopped, lowered their burden, laid it out upon the white cloth like an offering and retired into the shadows again.

"The sacrifice to Allatu!" a dozen hysterical voices wailed. "The sacrifice to Allatu. Let the god receive the offering!"

Would they dare? Slade stood frozen in a vertigo of horror, staring at the helpless girl whose body gleamed like polished jade under the eerie light. Then he recognized her. She was Mary Wycliffe, the girl who had vanished from the village three weeks ago!

Merro Daak, a smirk on his thin, cruel face, was coming down from the dais. The green light was growing dim. Was this the signal for the final orgy, for bestialities too shameful for even this unnatural light? Suddenly the kneeling figures rose, their bodies shaking, writhing in wild convulsions.

The next instant the light flared out, and Slade, flinging the door wide, leaped into the room. He shifted the knife to his left hand, held it low against his leg. He wouldn't use it unless he had to. Then, with his right fist flailing and pummeling, he threw himself into the press of milling bodies.

Nausea claimed him at the touch of gelid, unclean flesh, of lewd fingers pawing at him. The reek of sweating, perfumed bodies. Lewd mumblings gave place to shrill, half-animal cries of alarm as Slade floundered among them, fighting his way toward the altar where he had last seen Esther crouched in hideous adoration.

He was almost through the mob when suddenly the whole lust-crazed pack seemed to sense the presence of an alien. Hoarse growls of rage bubbled from their throats, and they threw themselves upon him like the unleashed dogs of hell.

He fought in earnest now. Howls of pain blubbered above the din as his fists flailed into skinny ribs, sunken bellies and lean jaws. But still they came on; like maddened harpies they clutched at him, clawing, spitting, hissing. He hadn't used the knife yet, but now a hot wave of unreason swamped his mind, and with a hoarse curse he dragged up his left arm, fist tight on the handle of the murderous blade . . .

And then it happened—that wild scream of agony shrilling out of the dense gloom like the shriek of a siren, that single scream, knifing its frightful message into startled ears—a woman's scream, and no mere cry of pain, but a wail of mortal agony—of death!

Like wilting phantoms, the unseen clawing hands fell away from Slade's body, and on the air, suddenly frozen to an awful silence, came a peal of ghoulish laughter, and then the heavy thud of a falling body.

Slade was stumbling forward toward the dais. His foot struck something soft, heavy. He stumbled, fell sprawling in a welter of some warm, sticky fluid, straightened, threw out groping fingers and touched the rounded contours of warm naked flesh.

A sob of mad dismay exploded in his throat. Then someone came running with a candle. Yellow light spread a mist in the choked air and the whole unspeakable horror was plain. He saw first the thing on the floor before him—the bound body of the girl who had been laid upon the altar, now lying in a puddle of scarlet from the awful gaping slit in her abdomen. Sickened, Slade looked up, and a new terror claimed him. Beyond the lambent candle glow a ring of ashen faces goggled at him with dumb accusing horror.

Instantly he knew why. Crouching there with blood smeared on his hands and clothes, he was still holding the knife in his hand!

"Murder!" a high-pitched voice shrilled.

Then Slade understood. These jaded thrill-seekers hadn't wanted this. But they had got it anyhow. They had invoked the powers of hell, and now—

Where was Esther? Slade straightened, shifted the knife to his right hand, stared grimly, defiantly into the ring of fear-frozen faces. Quickly he shot a glance over his shoulder. The dais, the thrones, were empty. Esther was gone; Merro Daak was gone, too!

Slade turned back. The ring of sunken-eyed debauchees had drawn closer, mouths agape. Slade stiffened, swung the knife in a swift arc, growled, "The first one who makes a move gets that!" Then he began to back slowly away.

Slowly, step by step, he retreated; and slowly, keeping at a safe distance, they followed. To the left of the dais, in the basement wall, he had seen a door. If he could gain it—

Now the wall was behind him; he inched to the left, felt the door, fumbled for the knob. The door came open. Then the cowering pack lunged.

Swiftly Slade fell back, pushing the door with him. Then his shoulder was against it, slamming it on their baffled cries and beating fists. The next instant fumbling fingers had found the bolt, shot it home.

Slade straightened, turned about, fumbling for a match. He was never very sure of what happened next. There was a vague impression of something vast and white looming before him, and the next instant a terrific weight struck his skull. He pitched back, struck the door, crumpled. The darkness that enveloped him burst in upon his brain, and all was black.

CHAPTER IV

RATIONS FOR THE DEAD

FOR A LONG TIME, IT SEEMED, he had known that the three of them were entombed—he and Esther and the dead thing. He was not sure if he and Esther were dead, too. But it did not seem to matter, for it was certain that they had been here for ages—and would doubtless be here forever. And a strange yellow light filled the place, and there were rats.

It was the red, beady eye of a rat that he focused his attention on now, hitching his mind to it, anchoring his consciousness, so that he would not again be dragged down into the depths of the abyss. The place was certainly a burial vault, for there were the shelves and the ends of rotting coffins protruding. And the dead thing beside which the rat now crouched was certainly a permanent tenant, sitting there on a packing box at one end of the place, unmoved, unworried by the rodents who scampered about him.

But there was light here; light from an ordinary lantern which rested on another box a few feet away.

That thing on the box! He certainly wasn't pleasant to look at. His clothes were rotted; his face was hideous, too; but it wasn't rotted. It was almost black, dried, leathery, shrunken, and the lips were peeled back from yellowed teeth, and there were no eyes to stare from the empty sockets. The rats had doubtless eaten them. Why was he sitting there, that ugly fellow?

Slade twisted his head about, stared at Esther. Like him, she was seated on the floor leaning against the cement wall, her body half-covered by an old blanket. But her head was leaning sideways, and her eyes were closed. Why were they sitting here? Ah, now he knew. It was the iron chain that encircled her throat. It was fastened with a padlock, and ended at a heavy staple in the cement wall. There was one about his own throat, too!

But what did it all mean? Then in a sudden flash he remembered; came back to full sanity with a jerk. A hot flame of terror singed his mind. He pulled himself nearer to Esther. Was she dead? He reached out shaking hands to touch her, grasped her arm, shook her.

"Esther, Esther! In God's name, darling . . ."

She stirred; dazedly she turned toward him dark eyes, wide, dry and dumb with fear and pain. "I've been asleep again," she said. "I couldn't wake you, I—I—" It ended in a sob.

He seized one of her hands, fondled it hungrily. His brain was hammering now like an engine with a broken piston rod. "Brace up, darling. What happened?"

"But I don't know, Cliff. That's the awful part of it. Oh, but I've been through hell, and then—this!" She shuddered, drew the blanket closer about her. "You see, when Mary Wycliffe vanished, I suspected that Daak had lured her away. I wanted to find her. I deliberately made friends with that monster, allowed him to bring me here to this place where he entertained and victimized his awful friends. But I couldn't get a trace of Mary. Then he asked me to take part in one of his horrid pageants. I even did that—tonight—and for the first time I saw Mary. He must have lured her away, doped her, and kept her prisoner here. Anyhow, when the lights went out during the ceremony, I tried to get her untied, tried to rouse her. Then—then, I scarcely know what happened. It seemed that something huge and white was near me; then something struck my skull, and I went out. That's all I knew until I came to my senses here. Where are we, Cliff? Why are you here?"

Slade bit his lip till the blood was salt in his mouth. But what could he tell her?

"My guess is that we're in the old Marsden vault, darling. I imagine Merro Daak has used it before. Why didn't you tell me about Daak, about where you had been going, Esther?"

"I couldn't, Cliff," she sobbed. "I knew that man was a monster. I was afraid that if an alarm was sounded, he'd kill Mary to hide his crime. That's why I lied to you, told you I'd been going out with Len. But what happened to you, Cliff?"

Slade told her briefly, omitting the more terrifying parts. "But don't worry," he added, "if he leaves us alone awhile we'll manage to get out, or to attract someone's attention to us."

He said it, but he didn't believe it himself. He reached back, began fumbling with the padlock that held the chain about his throat. Even as he felt that solid heavy lock he sensed the hopelessness of it. Abruptly he jerked his head up, the blood congealing in his veins, his throbbing, distended eyes glued to the door of the vault. The tumblers of a lock clicked; the door was opening . . .

Terror gripped his body then in a straitjacket of ice; he heard Esther sob brokenly, but he did not look at her. The door swung open, and framed against the pale luminescence of the night was the Thing from the graveyard.

There was a body beneath the folds of that sheet. He could see it now, could understand the awful illusion the thing had produced against a dark background. For the legs, the arms and hands, the face itself, were covered by a skintight sheath of black.

It came in, closed the door, stood peering at them, through the tiny slits where gleaming eyes were visible. Slade swallowed the hard lump in his throat.

"Daak," he flung at the ghoul through gritted teeth, "you can drop the flummery and come out in the open. What's your game?"

The words broke off with a brittle snap on his lips. For a cackle of dry, senile laughter had bubbled from behind the black sheath that hid the head, and a voice which Slade instantly recognized, said:

"Ye don't recognize me, eh, Cliff Slade?"

Surely this was a nightmare! It couldn't be true. But the fiend had now thrown the sheet aside, had reached up and pulled the black hood from his head. The bony, grey-haired head of Peter Marsden!

"It can't be!" Slade hushed. "You're—you're a paralytic—"

"Eh? I was a paralytic," the old man croaked. "But I fooled 'em all. Fer months I set there in that chair a thinkin', an' I fooled 'em all. I heared the doctors a sayin' that there paralysis was a hysterical affliction, a thing of th' mind. So 'twas, I found out, tryin' my legs out on the sly an' a curin' myself. Only I didn't tell nobody. There was too many things I had to do in secret, a lookin' after Emmett, a tryin' to git him well again . . ."

Emmett! Get him well again! Slade's brain was reeling; he lifted horrified eyes to the hideous, mummy-like thing that sat on the packing box. Emmett! That was the old man's elder son who had been killed by the mob five years ago!

"You're a lookin' at Emmett, I see," the old man went on, an insane pride twinkling in his sunken eyes. "Ain't very pretty now, Emmett ain't. But I reckon I kin keep him alive till the resurrection."

"Alive? But he's been dead five years!" Slade blurted out before he could check himself.

"Eh?" old Marsden said, seating himself comfortably on the
box beside the lantern. "Oh, you might call him dead, but I ain't so
sure. There ain't no corruption in Emmett. Right after that there
mob killed him I done somethin' to him. I used to sneak here in
the dead o' night—fore that paralysis hit me—an' I smoked him
an' fixed him up with Indian herbs so's he wouldn't putrefy. I
done a good job, too. He ain't all dead, Emmett ain't. He eats."

"Eats!" The word ripped from Slade's throat in a convulsive
sob. The thing in all its horror was dawning on his mind. This old
man, whom everyone had thought harmlessly insane, was a homi-
cidal maniac of the most dreadful type. Swiftly, wildly, Slade's
brain was gropin' for some way in which to get control over that
deranged mind.

"I don't understand," he said, fighting to keep his voice steady.
"You mean you've been feeding him all these years?"

"Well," the old man said, "I reckon he got awful hungry for a
spell. That was after I sold the place an' while my legs was still
paralyzed. But I was a workin' out my plan, an' little by little I
was knittin' me this here black suit, so's I could slip through the
dark to feed Emmett. First I fed him vittles from the house, but
that didn't seem to do him no good. I knowed what he needed was
meat. Then for a time I fed him on chickens, rabbits an' such-like.
It was after this here Merro Daak bought my place that I seen how
I could git him fresh meat an' make folks thing the astrologer done
it. I know that the olden soothsayers sometimes cut the livers from
animals. Then, too, I thought the livers would be good meat for
Emmett, since I couldn't take time to bother with the whole car-
cass . . ."

"But look here," Slade choked out, "you can see it hasn't done
him any good, you can see—"

"Mebbe not," old Marsden cut him short, "but it sort of kept
him goin'. Still, I reckon there's somethin' in what you say. I fig-
gered myself that what he needed was human flesh an' blood."

The whole shadowy crypt was spinning wildly before Slade's
eyes. He saw the gradual progress of the old man's mania, from
horror to horror, and now—

"But you're wrong!" he gasped wildly. "Emmett's dead. He
can't eat. You know he can't eat!"

A cunning smile bared the old man's yellow teeth. "Oh, yes, he
can," he said. "You jest ain't seen him. He's gonna keep on eatin'
fer many a year, keep on till he's eat the livers of half this town

that tortured an' kilt him. No one won't never suspect me. I've learned to slip about like a shadder. Look how quick I got to the graveyard tonight after they left the house. I seen you there atop that arbor. But I can run like hell. You seen how I managed to slip into that basement tonight, too, in the dark, cut the liver from that girl, slugged Daak an' this here girl with a pipe an' dragged 'em into the furnace room to a secret hidin' place where I left 'em till I could git 'em safely here. I got you, too. I know my way about, I reckon. They won't git me!"

"But now," Slade argued, "they'll be suspecting you."

The old man grinned cunningly. "Ye're wrong again," he chuckled. "They've blamed it all on Daak. Them people confessed that he carried girls off before an' held 'em prisoner. They think he run off with this here girl, after killin' the other one. They got that whole bunch of heathens in jail right now."

Looking into that mad face, Slade felt the last faint spark of hope die to darkness in his heart. Beside him he could hear Esther sobbing softly. Dazedly he saw the old man rise from his seat, begin pulling an ancient coffin from one of the lower shelves. Wild horror choked Slade then, crushed his throat to frozen speechlessness. For old Marsden had dragged the coffin to the floor, swung back the lid, and with a hideous chuckle had reached in and dragged up a body by the hair—the body of Merro Daak!

"I'll show you if Emmett can eat," the crazed man gloated. A razor was in his hands now. He bent over the body of the dead astrologer.

Esther screamed. Twisting about, Slade saw that she had slumped in a faint. He closed his own eyes then, retched with sick convulsions. He was a doctor, but this . . .

When he opened his eyes again the mutilated body of the astrologer lay in its own blood while the old man stood above it, the dark gory liver in his hand. Chuckling, he walked to the box where the mummified body of his son was propped grotesquely and laid his frightful prize beside it like an offering. Then he came back and sat down on the box facing Slade. "He won't eat it if I watch him," he said, "but he'll eat."

Slade watched, but his swollen eyes were dazed with unspeakable horror. His brain was spinning; red madness hovered over him with heavy wings. Then, confusedly, he saw the dark shape creep up from the shadows, blink rapidly with red eyes, and seize the bloody morsel. A rat! The thing's teeth sank into the gory prize, dragged it back into the shadows again.

Old Marsden turned, his mad face lighted with a look of triumph. "See, see?" he chortled. "It's gone. Emmett's shore hungry
tonight!" Then he looked at the slumped figure of Esther, looked
long and significantly.

"My God, Mr. Marsden," Slade choked, "you're not going to
do that—to us?"

"Eh?" the old man asked. "To us? No, I ain't goin' to do it to
you. I don't reckon Emmett would want to eat one of Len's
friends. I ain't goin' to kill you. I'm a-goin' to leave you in here to
keep Emmett company. I reckon Emmett gits awful lonesome.
You can eat with him, too. But that there girl . . ."

His words trailed off, swallowed by the abysmal roaring in Slade's
skull. After he had seen Esther slaughtered, he would be left here;
and when his mind was gone, his body wasted with hunger, he
would be invited to share the ghoulish repast of the dead . . .

Blackness smothered him in recurrent waves; the scene glim-
mered and faded before him. He would make one last struggle—
hopeless, he knew—and then he would beg to be killed first.

Suddenly he sat up, his head swimming, tried to focus his
crazed vision on the door of the vault which again was opening!

Old Marsden sprang to his feet, the bloody razor gripped
tightly. The door opened. Was this the delirium of insanity, or was
that Len Marsden standing in the doorway? It was, it was Len! A
wild cry of crazed joy broke from Slade's lips, broke and dwindled
to a whimper.

"Len, *you* here?" old Marsden sputtered.

Len's face was scarcely human—wax over bones. His shrunken
eyes burned with the fever of madness. "I'm here—I came to warn
you. They're looking for you."

Incredulous dismay stabbed Slade's brain. No word to him, not
even a glance from Len. The breath was whistling harshly between
old Marsden's teeth. He stared at his son uncertainly, fingered the
razor. "Close the door," he growled. "How did you find me?"

"I guessed it," Len said. "I've heard you mumble about Emmett
in your sleep. I've come to help you. I hate this town that tortured
him, too."

Slade's brain was shrieking in a mad delirium. Len, with the
tainted blood in his veins, had cracked under the strain, had become a madman, too. Len closed the door now, shambled in and
stood beside his father.

Peter Marsden turned toward his captives. "What we got to do, we got to do quick," he said. "How about young Slade?"

"Kill them both!" Len snapped. "He stole the girl from me." He made a quick dive toward Esther.

Shrieking a volley of curses, Slade kicked out at him. But Len got on the other side of Esther's unconscious body. "Throw me the keys!" he yelled.

Quick as a leaping rodent old Marsden sprang to a shelf, snatched up a ring with two keys on it and tossed it to Len. Len caught the keys. Slade, paralyzed with crushing terror, saw Len's fingers shake as he snapped the lock open, seized Esther's body and began dragging it with quick jerks to the center of the floor where he crouched above it like a wolf.

Slade threw himself against the wall.

"The razor!" Len Marsden snapped. "Give me the razor. We'll feed Emmett again before we go."

Light from the lantern flashed on the bloody blade as it passed from old Marsden's hand to Len's. Slade shut his eyes then and black madness claimed him.

It was old Marsden's cry that jarred him from his stupor of horror. His head jerked up; his eyes bugged. The razor lay on the floor beside Esther's body, and Len and Peter Marsden were struggling in the center of the crypt.

"Traitor!" the old man was screaming wildly as he fought with maniacal strength against Len's pinioning arms.

Slade held his breath. The old man's crazed strength was enormous. Time after time, he tore himself loose from Len's grip and threw his knotted fists into the younger man's face and body. Once Len stumbled, almost fell. He came back with a rush, and this time his right arm swung up from the floor. There was an audible crack as the blow connected and old Marsden, arms flailing the air, fell back. His head struck the concrete shelf behind him and he crumpled to the floor.

Len staggered back, his mouth agape, staring with glassy fixity at his father's crumpled form. Then he slumped down on the box beside the lantern, buried his face in his arms and shook with bitter sobs.

"The keys!" Slade shouted. "Throw me the keys!"

Len straightened, fished the keys from the pocket into which he had thrust them and flung them to Slade. Then he staggered to his father's body, knelt beside it. "Not dead," he said presently with a gasp. "Thank the Lord, I didn't kill him!"

The chain fell away from Slade's throat and he stumbled to his feet. He threw himself down beside Esther, gathered her cold body in his arms. "You weren't a moment too soon," he told Len. "How did you manage it?"

"After I left you," Len explained, "I got into the house but was caught and tied by a couple of Daak's guards. I lay there unable to get loose until some of that crazed bunch got Corman and his posse to the place. They of course suspected Merro Daak, but they suspected you, too; and they weren't sure about me. They held me in jail until an hour or so ago. I went home then and found Father gone. I began to wonder then—about him. I remembered some wild talking he had done in his sleep, crazy stuff about feeding Emmett. I'd never paid any attention to it before, but now it gave me a clue and I came straight here. When I saw Father with the razor in his hand I knew I'd have to pretend to help him until I could get him under control. Poor Father, it'll be the madhouse for him now."

Slade was lifting Esther from the floor. Len sprang to help him. But a sudden movement caused him to turn back to the huddled body of old Marsden. He had lifted himself, was sitting upright, the razor gripped in his hand. "Madhouse!" he shrilled. "You'll send me to the madhouse?"

Len leaped to seize the razor. But he was too late. With a swift stroke the old man drew the gleaming blade across his throat, fell back with bright blood gushing down upon his chest.

Hugging Esther's cold body to him, Slade staggered out of the crypt of death. The chill air was good against his face. In the east the first faint streaks of dawn were smudging the pale sky. The horror was over! And it was better that the old man had gone as he had, better for Len, too, whose tortured brain had borne enough!

With a surge of delirious joy, Slade pressed his burning lips to Esther's face. Her eyes opened, startled at first, then softening as she saw the brightening sky and Slade's face above hers. She didn't ask any questions then, just snuggled closer in his arms as he bore her with swift strides toward the house.

REUNION IN HELL

CHAPTER ONE

DESPERATION

WHEN A MAN IS DOWN AND OUT, when his money and his clothes are shabby, when his plans are shattered and the last slim hope fades bleak and desolate. The faces surging around him in the street become the faces of cold, unsympathetic strangers; the street itself becomes impersonal and hostile—and the cold tentacles of fear begin to reach into the very depths of his soul.

Dave Powell did not see the sunshine as he and Arthur Kimball came out of the Graybar building. For him the day had suddenly become grey and chillingly depressing. Hope had died back there in the office they had just left—hope to rehabilitate themselves and get back on their feet.

Kimball had been so sure that they would be able to get the backing that was so desperately needed. Dave had counted on it so confidently. This last hope *couldn't* fail them—but it did.

He didn't say anything as they stepped out onto the sidewalk. What was there to say? He hardly knew where he was going as he walked along Forty-second Street. His thoughts were not there on the crowded street; they were in a shabby walk-up flat, facing a situation that baffled and terrified him.

Evelyn was there in that flat—Evelyn, his wife, and the loveliest woman he had ever seen. It was a sacrilege to take any one so sweet and lovely to such cheap and ugly surroundings. But it wasn't the poverty, wasn't the dismal flat, that had affected her. It was something else, something incomprehensible and insidious that had come over her and changed her until he hardly knew her.

Dave had been able to face the loss of his money, his friends, his social position. Those things had been swept away one by one; but they did not matter—he still had Evelyn, and the world was a place of hope and of opportunity that must sooner or later give him a chance to win back the happiness that had once been his.

But now Evelyn was slipping away, slowly but surely; and Dave watched with horrified eyes, like a man in a nightmare, powerless to stop her, though what he saw twisted his soul in agony.

A groan wrenched from his lips—and he looked up, startled and suddenly aware of his surroundings. Then his eyes narrowed and became hard as he gazed at the photographs framed in showcases outside Sam Tabor's theater. Photographs of lovely women in half-naked poses.

Dave felt a chill run down his spine. He could see Evelyn's photograph framed there—could see her standing in the middle of the stage, tantalizingly stripping off her flimsy clothes until she stood stark naked in the glare of a spotlight before hundreds of licentious, lustful eyes!

Evelyn—his Evelyn, who, until a few months past, had been all that was sweet and modest! The dread that had been growing on him for weeks clamped down on him, sapped the strength from his muscles. Now, with this latest failure, his last hope was gone. Now he would not be able to take her away, as he had planned, to get her away from the insidious influence that was changing her, coarsening her—cheapening her!

"You've get to say one thing for Tabor," he heard Arthur Kimball say as they looked up at the alluring photographs; "he does get unusual women. Not the regular run of burlesque babies at all. Girls you'd hardly expect to find in this game. Wonder how he manages it."

The cold grip tightened around Dave's heart. That was Sam Tabor's boast—that he got girls no other burlesque producer could touch. But how did he do it? By hypnotism? Power of suggestion? Or had he mastered some other devilish black art that enabled him to take hold of the mind of a pure, sweet girl and break down her resistance until she was putty in his hands, ready to do as he ordered?

Was that what was happening to Evelyn?

At first the change in her had been hardly noticeable. Just little things, little modest mannerisms that she dropped. Then it was plainer, more unmistakable. She was letting down, relaxing—

finding amusement in things that formerly would have disgusted her.

An indefinable transformation—but its effect was now undeniable, and terrifying. She was becoming hard, callous, cynical—yes, almost brazen! A year ago she would have treated with contempt an offer such as Sam Tabor was now making; now she not only considered it seriously—but her eyes lighted up with anticipation at the prospect!

"I don't know how he manages it," Dave grated, "but he's not going to succeed with Evelyn. I'll kill him before I'll let him drag her out there on his dirty stage!"

"Easy, easy," Kimball soothed. "You're almost shouting, old man. Don't get so worked up; something will turn up for us yet."

That was to cool him off, Dave knew. Arthur knew that they would not get another break. The last hope was gone; they were through, licked.

Little more than a year ago Dave had been wealthy and without a worry in the world. He and his two partners, Arthur Kimball and Len Glancey, owned a copper mine that was coining money. Besides, he was engaged to marry Evelyn Campbell, beauty contest winner and a budding stage star. He had the world in the palm of his hand!

Then a syndicate of Eastern capitalists became interested in the mine. A dozen of them went out to inspect it—and the partners' lucky star set. While the inspection was going on a terrific explosion wrecked the mine, killing or maiming all of the party. Kimball and Glancey had been with them. Kimball was only scratched, but he buried Glancey before hurrying back to New York to help Dave try to salvage something from the wreckage of their fortunes.

The ensuing lawsuits wiped them out entirely, leaving nothing but the wrecked mine. Without ample capital to reopen it the property was worthless—and they were broke.

Even so, Evelyn insisted that Dave go through with their wedding plans. They were married and took a small apartment, but even that had to go when her show closed and Sam Tabor, the producer, switched to burlesque.

It was six months after that before Tabor came around to the squalid flat with his insulting offer and his inviting contract. Had the fellow needed that long to work up his courage, Dave won-

dered—or had he waited patiently until he was sure the time was
ripe and Evelyn would nibble at his rotten bait?

Dave's hands were clenched into white knuckled fists and his
lips were pressed into a tight, hard line as he glowered at Tabor's
display boards. The fellow would never have an opportunity to
flaunt a photograph of Evelyn's veil-draped figure in those showcases for this filthy rabble to smirk at and devour with ravishing
eyes!

At his side he felt Arthur Kimball's hand on his arm, felt Arthur urging him down the block, away from the front of the theater. But as he yielded and started down the street he could fairly
feel penetrating eyes fixed on him.

Was Sam Tabor there, somewhere in the lobby of his theater?
Had he heard that impetuous vow? Dave could catch no glimpse
of the burlesque impresario, but the "feel" of those watching eyes
would not leave him.

Even after he had left Kimball and was riding downtown in the
subway that sensation of being watched, being studied, was with
him. So much so that he glanced around the car and scrutinized his
fellow passengers. They all seemed to be absorbed in their own
affairs—except perhaps that thin, dark little man sitting in the corner on the opposite side. Were those dark eyes studying him cov-
ertly?

Dave watched the little man out of the corner of his eye. Several times he was sure that the dark, flashing eyes were staring
straight at him; that the thin features were alight with interest.
Then he shrugged in disgust.

"I'm letting this thing get me," he warned himself. "This is no
time to start developing nerves."

Nevertheless his nerves were ajangle when he climbed the three
flights of stairs to his flat. He dreaded to face Evelyn—to admit
that he had failed again. The old Evelyn would have understood
and would have been quick with her sympathy. But this new,
changed Evelyn—there was no telling how she would react.

As he put his key onto the lock he paused, listened. That was
the sound of voices inside. Evelyn was talking to someone—to
Sam Tabor!

Grim-lipped, Dave turned the key in the lock and stepped into
the sparsely furnished living room—and his heart sank sickeningly.

"I wouldn't come here if it wasn't the right thing for you," Tabor was saying persuasively. "This is your chance to climb back

up with the headlines. With that figure you'll knock 'em out of their seats."

But it wasn't what Tabor was saying that appalled Dave; it was Evelyn herself. She was leaning back in an easy chair, wearing a negligée that was startlingly low in the neck—and her slim legs were crossed so carelessly that he could feel the warm blood surging up into his cheeks.

Tabor was eyeing her appreciatively, his tongue licking out over his thick lips, his dark eyes bright and eager. Dave had never liked the fellow. He was too oily, too smooth. Now, finding him there in the flat with Evelyn, threw Dave into a blind rage.

"I told you last week that we don't want to have anything to do with your dirty proposition," he shouted, whirling in on the producer. "You're not going to make a cheap strip-artist out of my wife, Tabor; you may as well get that through your head. Now get out! We don't want to hear any more about you or your show."

Tabor's heavy-featured face flushed. Then the set grin was back on his lips as he rose to leave.

"You're being a prudish fool, Powell," he said softly. "I'm offering Evelyn a chance to make some decent money, and you're standing in her way. But I won't be surprise if you change your mind and talk sensible before long; others have before you."

Soft words, but Dave felt that there was steel beneath them—a threat that mocked him. Then Evelyn spoke from behind him.

"Don't mind Dave, Sam," she said easily. "I'll think it over and give you an answer next week."

Those cool words stabbed at Dave and left him alternately cold with nameless fear and hot bubbling rage. As the door closed behind Tabor he turned and confronted this women who was his wife—and who was now almost a complete stranger to him.

The negligée fell back over one shoulder, and he caught his breath at the loveliness of her. She was exquisite, adorable, the woman he had put on a pedestal above all of her kind—but now there was something in her eyes from which he recoiled. Something unfathomable; something evil—wanton!

Was this Tabor's hellish work? Suddenly Dave recalled that the producer had once been very attentive to Evelyn, but she had laughed at him. Did he still have hopes of winning her by undermining her affection for her husband? Was that why he was so persistent in his efforts to lure her into his show? Was that the explanation for his appalling change that had come over her?

Dave looked deep into her lovely eyes—and into his heart crept that sort of terror that leaves a strong man unnerved by the realization that he is utterly helpless!

CHAPTER TWO

THE BROTHERS DENTON

THE RAPPING ON THE DOOR came a second time before Dave Powell realized what it was. Then he turned the latch, opened the door—and stared in surprise into the thin, dark face of the little man he had noticed in the subway.

"Please pardon the irregularity of my introduction," the stranger said as he tipped his hat to Evelyn. "I am Simon French, and I have a proposition which I hope will interest you, Mr. Powell. No, I am not a peddler," he interjected as Dave started to close the door. "I am an attorney, and if I may come inside I can outline my proposal in a few minutes."

Before Dave quite knew what it was about the little man was inside, seated, and looking at him keenly, nodding his head with satisfaction.

"I was not mistaken," he congratulated himself. "You will do very nicely, Mr. Powell. One chance in a million—and I had the good fortune to find you. I am the legal representative for Mr. Herbert Denton, a member of a very wealthy family. There are seven of the Denton cousins, heirs of their grandfather. By the terms of his will they must get together once a year to spend a week-end at the family homestead, at which time they are paid a liberal allowance for the year.

"In case one of them fails to appear he loses his allowance and is cut out of the estate entirely. That is where you come in, Mr. Powell. My client, Herbert Denton, is seriously ill in Europe. He could not possibly get back for the reunion, and by that misfortune faces the loss of his entire inheritance. The situation had me baffled—until I saw you in the subway this afternoon and followed you home. You are almost an exact double for Herbert Denton, Mr. Powell!"

"And you want me to—" Dave floundered puzzledly.

"Exactly," Simon French cut him short. "I want you to impersonate my client. I want you to attend the reunion as Herbert

Denton. There is nothing morally wrong about that; rather you will be doing a good deed in saving his inheritance for a young man who through no fault of his own is unable to help himself—and for that you will be adequately paid. Five thousand dollars for two days' work."

"But—" Dave began.

"I know exactly what you are thinking," interrupted the attorney with a nod. "How will you be able to manage such an impersonation? Quite easily, I assure you. The other six are Herbert Denton's cousins, not his brothers. They meet him only once a year at these reunions and know very little about him—and care less. You bear such a remarkable resemblance to him that, with the coaching I shall give you, you will not raise the slightest doubt in the minds of the others. It was indeed a Godsend for me that I found you!"

It had all come so suddenly that Dave could hardly grasp the details of the amazing proposition. He was skeptical about it—shied away from it instinctively—until he realized what he could do with those five thousand dollars. They would enable him to thwart Sam Tabor—to get Evelyn out of the fellow's reach before he managed to corrupt her any farther.

And that was all that mattered. Evelyn couldn't stay here—couldn't be allowed to walk out onto Sam Tabor's burlesque stage and strip herself shamelessly before those gloating eyes. Everything that was fine and sweet in her would die—would be murdered—if ever she did that.

"Okay," Dave snapped decisively. "Sounds all right to me, if you are satisfied that I can get away with it."

But it didn't sound all right to Evelyn. She half rose from her chair, and fright flickered in her eyes and paled her cheeks.

"I don't like it, Dave," she protested. "Somehow—it sounds dangerous. I won't let you go alone—not unless I go with you."

Dave's heart leaped. Now she was again the girl he had married, fear for his safety sweeping everything else from her mind. She was not yet lost irretrievably; there was still hope for her if he could get her away—out from under the influence of whatever it was that was demoralizing her.

"That is quite permissible," Simon French agreed readily. "There is no reason why Herbert Denton should not have married during the past year and should not take his wife with him. There will be other Denton wives there. Then it is agreed—and I shall come back here tomorrow afternoon to supply you with what information you will need and to coach you in your rôles."

As business like as when he arrived, the attorney rose to leave, but as his hand touched the doorknob there was a slight noise outside in the hallway. Dave sprang to the door and yanked it open, bolted into the narrow corridor.

It was empty, but he could hear the sound of running footsteps on the stairs. He leaned over the banister, but the footsteps were now clattering across the lower hall and then were lost in the street. Probably one of the kids in the house, he decided as he went back into the flat.

If Dave hand any misgivings about Simon French and his proposition he stifled them in his determination to save Evelyn from Tabor and from herself. It was not until Saturday afternoon when they stepped into the limousine that called for them that he began to wonder what strange hazards lay ahead of them.

After all, they knew nothing about this Denton family except what French had told them, and they knew nothing whatever about him. Dave tried to draw the chauffeur into conversation when they stopped for gas, but the fellow seemed to understand little English. Nothing to be learned from him.

As the car sped steadily up the Hudson Valley Dave sat back and took Evelyn's hand in his own. Her fingers were cold, icy, and there was fear in her eyes.

"Yes, I am afraid," she whispered, when he questioned her. "Perhaps it's intuition. Something tells me that we should not have come, Dave."

And Dave Powell was glad! This was the girl he knew and loved. No matter what else Simon French's proposition did, it had given Evelyn back to him!

It was dusk before the limousine turned off the country road it had been following and entered a walled estate, through two big iron gates. The place was way off by itself, seemingly miles from another habitation. There did not seem to be a soul around—

And then Dave suddenly straightened in his seat and peered out into the thickening gloom. He was almost certain that he had seen a face staring at them out of the shrubbery beside the gates—a horrible death's-head of a face that bristled the hair at the back of his neck!

But now there was nothing visible in the shrubbery. As if by their own volition the heavy gates swung together and clanged shut—and then the dismal reverberation of their closing was drowned in the excited yelping of a pack of dogs that closed in around the machine. Huge, savage creatures, with slavering mouths and wicked looking fangs. They sprang up at the windows and howled their rage as the shatterproof glass repelled them.

Not until the car drew up beside a large brownstone building did the howling escort fall back reluctantly.

The Denton family seat was a depressing place in appearance. Architecturally outmoded, it did not look as if it had ever been anything but an eyesore on the landscape. Gloom fairly exuded from it, and Dave found it hard to imagine any one ever laughing or being happy there.

And the tall, grey-haired man who came to the door to welcome them fitted the place perfectly. His expressionless face was thin and cadaverous, and he had the funereal manner and black clothes of an undertaker, This, Dave knew, must be Gregory Denton, oldest of the cousins.

"You have chosen a very charming wife, Cousin Herbert," Gregory complimented when Dave introduced Evelyn. "A very charming wife, indeed." And Dave saw that his grey eyes sparkled; avid desire leaped unchecked in them for a moment—and then they were again as expressionless as the rest of his blank face.

Perhaps it was the disagreeable atmosphere of the place, perhaps that momentary flash of evil desire in Gregory Denton's eyes—something sounded a note of warning in Dave's consciousness. The limousine had turned, was starting back the way it had come. Something subconscious urged him to shout after it, to call it back, to get in and speed away from there while there was still time.

Instinctively he moved toward the open door. Then it swung closed solidly, and the opportunity to turn back was gone.

Gregory led the way into the spacious living-room and introduced Evelyn to the other Dentons who were assembled there. Four of the cousins were brothers—Gregory, Carl, Hubert and Alfred—and a more weird-looking brotherhood Dave had never seen. They were apparently all of middle age, though this was hard to judge, for their faces were perfect blanks, except for their eyes—and in the case of Carl and Alfred one of the eyes was glass. Carl was a horribly deformed cripple who could hardly hold up his head, and Hubert was a hunchback who had to be supported by a metal brace.

Dave shuddered inwardly and turned to the other cousins. These were younger, more presentable looking men—Morgan Denton, with Sylvia, his pretty young wife; and Steven Denton, who was married to Annabelle, a vivacious young blonde.

Quite a different sort, these, from the rest of the family—and yet Dave noticed that Evelyn was staring at one of them as if she had seen a ghost. Her face was even paler than it had been, and as soon as an opportunity presented he drew her aside.

"That Steven Denton—he isn't a Denton at all!" she whispered with fear in her voice. "I know him, Dave. He is Thaddeus Hurleman, second-rate actor who used to work for Sam Tabor. The last I heard of him he was in prison for theft. I felt it all along, Dave—there is something crooked, something terribly dangerous, here!"

Steven Denton was Thaddeus Hurleman. That meant there were at least two impostors among the Denton cousins. And Hurleman had worked for Sam Tabor. The mention of Tabor's name sent a bolt of suspicion searing through Dave. What did Tabor have to do with this set-up?

But before he could consider that possibility he heard Gregory Denton's voice raised above the low hum of conversation.

"As you all know," Gregory was saying, "we do not keep a large staff of domestics here, and so it has always been customary for the Denton women to help prepare and serve the dinner. So, if you young ladies will came with me—"

Evelyn looked at Dave doubtfully, but Annabelle laughed gaily.

"Here we come!" she called. "Lead on to the kitchen!"

There was nothing for Evelyn to do but follow her, but Dave didn't like it. Somehow, he felt that it wasn't safe to let her out at his sight in that house.

Nor could he overcome his uneasiness as he sat in the book-lined study and sipped wine with the other men. Sam Tabor—was he behind this thing in some way? Was that what he had meant with his veiled threat about Dave changing his mind?

Those Denton, brothers, with their mummylike faces, weren't very reassuring either. Dead-pan faces—but with eyes that glittered and shone with barely suppressed excitement.

When they took their places around the long refectory table in the dining room those eyes fairly blazed and the expressionless faces turned expectantly toward the kitchen door. Dave noticed their fingers twitching impatiently; heard their feet scuffling restlessly. They were on edge—waiting—waiting—

Then the kitchen door opened—and Dave's hands clenched down hard on the arms of his chair while sickening terror swept through him!

The girls were bringing in the food, but it was not what they carried that drew every eye in the room. It was the girls themselves. They were dressed in flimsy white gowns, so sheer that every delicate curve of their bodies was revealed as clearly as if they had been entirely unclothed.

The eager eyes of the Denton brothers fastened on those girlish figures, bored through the flimsy gowns as if they did not exist, and reveled in what they saw. Sheer animal lust blazed in their eyes, revealed itself in every attitude of their taut bodies.

And Evelyn was entirely unconcerned! Dave caught her glance as she leaned forward to place a plate before Gregory Denton, and she smiled with that cool smile he had grown to dread!

Impulsively he started to rise from his seat, to protest angrily, but at that moment he caught the piercing grey eyes of Gregory Denton fixed on him—and what he saw in their glowing depths warned and checked him. Evil, covetous lust flamed in those depths and mingled with murderous hatred that needed but a spark to ignite and release it. To start trouble now would be to seal Evelyn's fate.

CHAPTER THREE

OUT OF THE TRAP

THE MOMENT THAT INTERMINABLE MEAL dragged to a close Dave hurried Evelyn to the third-floor room that had been assigned to them. There he took her in his arms and held her close while his eyes looked searchingly into hers. Yes, they were changed; the pupils were smaller than usual. That meant dope! In some incomprehensible way the evil thing that was working a hellish transformation in the girl had reached her even in this remote mansion!

"You're just a stiff-necked old Puritan, Dave," she laughed lightly when he protested against her lack of covering. "You didn't hear any of the other men objecting, did you? Don't be an old killjoy all the time. Come on—let's go down stairs and see what's doing."

The carelessness in her tone and the reckless gleam in her eyes stabbed at Dave, but he planted himself firmly in the doorway.

"You're not going down to those filthy beasts," he told her grimly, "and you're not getting out of my sight again while we're in this house."

She protested strenuously at first, then merely pouted as she began to yawn and blink, Soon she nodded and dropped off to sleep and Dave tucked her into bed.

For a while he sat up, trying hopelessly to figure out what was happening to the girl. Then, baffled and discouraged, he lay down, fully clothed, beside her. Sam Tabor, Gregory Denton, Thaddeus Hurleman—one by one they paraded through his mind until they blended into a composite of villainy that was blotted out into nothingness.

Evelyn was screaming shrilly and all three of the devils were chasing her when Dave sat bolt upright on the bed and tried to get his bearings in the darkness. His hand groped over the bed beside him, touched a covered figure. He bent over it. Of course, it was Evelyn. She was fast asleep.

But the shrill screams were still knifing through the darkness; screams that were palpitating with livid terror!

They were coming from out in the hallway, somewhere on that floor. Dave grabbed his shoes, slipped into them, turned the key in the door, and stepped out into the hallway—just in time to see a hideous death's head burst out of one of the other rooms.

For a fraction of a second the ghastly thing seemed to be suspended there in the air, glaring at him—baleful eyes, a horribly twisted mouth and a great hole where the nose should have been! The sort of frightful creature that should appear only in delirium! But it was there in the hallway, dimly revealed by the reflected moonlight!

Horror froze Dave immobile in the doorway, while a yell of terror welled up into his throat and stuck there.

All in the fraction of a second. Then the thing ducked. The head disappeared.

Footsteps scuffed down the carpeted hall—and Dave caught a glimpse of a dark figure as it darted across a spot of moonlight and scooted down the stairs.

The thing was gone, but the terrified screams rose higher, hovered on the verge of hysteria.

Dave ran across the hall to the doorway through which the thing had come. From his pocket he snatched a package of matches and lighted the lamp that stood on the dresser just inside the doorway, then held it over the bed from which those blood-curdling screams were pouring.

Trembling hands clutched the bedsheet and held it up in front of a wide-eyed, terror-contorted face. Behind that pitiful protection Sylvia Denton cowered and tried desperately to crowd herself even farther back against the unyielding headboards.

Dave glanced around the room, but there was no sign of her husband.

"Where is Morgan?" he shouted so that his voice could be heard above her wild sobbing.

"I don't know! I don't know!" she screamed hysterically. "When I woke up he was gone. He left me here—left me for that awful creature! He left me, I tell you! He's not my husband! Oh, God, I wish I'd never listened to him!"

Patiently, soothingly Dave talked to her, and gradually he convinced her that the danger was past. Then the tears came, and between bursts of weeping she sobbed out her story.

"He isn't Morgan Denton, really," she confessed. "He's John Roeder—a friend of mine. A man gave him a chance to make some easy money by coming up here and pretending to be. Morgan Denton, but he had to have a wife. He knew that I was broke—so he came to me and asked me to go into it with him—to pretend to be his wife. That's all we were doing—just pretending for this week-end. There wasn't anything else to it, really."

"But what makes you think he ran out on you?" Dave prodded.

"Because he got scared—and he's yellow," the girl said bitterly. "He didn't like the looks of those men with the queer looking faces—the Dentons. We decided there was something phoney in the deal, so we were going to slip away in the morning. But he didn't wait—he ran out tonight and left me. When I woke up he was gone—and that thing—that awful skeleton head—was looking down at me—and cold damp hands were tearing my nightgown off and pawing me!"

So "Cousin Morgan" was an impostor, too. That meant that only the four Denton brothers were genuine, Dave considered, as he sat on the edge of the bed and listened to her terrified sobbing. Only the four Dentons were genuine—and the others had been lured to this out-of-the-way place. For what hell-inspired purpose?

As if in answer to his question a blood-chilling bedlam broke loose outside the building. Dave identified that snarling, howling chorus all too easily. The dogs! They sounded like a pack of starved wolves battling over a kill—and in the midst of their savage cacophony he caught a new, nerve-tingling note—a shriek of unbearable human agony!

The tumult seemed to be on the other side of the house, so he ran out into the hallway—and almost collided headlong with a panting, gasping figure that came racing and stumbling up the stairs. Thaddeus Hurleman reeled back from that contact and cowered against the wall, covering his face with his shaking arms from which his coat sleeves hung in tatters.

"Snap out of it and let me know what's happened!" Dave ordered, as he dragged the trembling man over to a hall window.

Then Hurleman recognized him and some of his panic subsided.

"I thought you were one of *them!*" he panted hoarsely. "One of the Dentons. They're murdering fiends! I could see it in their eyes. This place is a trap—and we're caught in it. There's no way out! Roeder—he called himself Morgan Denton—Roeder and I decided we'd slip out tonight while our skins were still whole. We got out all right—but we walked right into the dogs. God Almighty—what beasts! Listen to them out there! Roeder's in the middle of them!"

From the window they could look down onto that ghastly struggle plainly illuminated by the moonlight. A growling, yapping, snarling mound of furry shapes that leaped and tore at one another—and at the bloody horror that was in their middle.

Once Roeder managed to stagger to his feet, and a fragment of a dying scream tore from his bloody lips—to end in a choked gurgle as long white teeth snapped together in his throat. Then he disappeared under that milling, snarling pack for the last time.

Roeder was out of the trap, Dave thought grimly as he stood helplessly watching that bloody carnage—but God alone knew what lay ahead for the rest of them!

CHAPTER FOUR

DENTON DIVORCE

SICK WITH HORROR, Dave and Hurleman turned from the window and faced each other. The actor was trembling and dabbing ineffectually at the ugly wounds on his arms with his blood-soaked handkerchief. His sniffling was the only sound in the house; even the girl Sylvia's sobbing had quieted.

"This place may be a trap," Dave snapped suddenly, "but we're not going to lie down and wait for it to close around us. First of all we're going to check up on the girls and see that they're all right. Then we're going to hunt up these Dentons and force them to get us out of here. Come on, Hurleman; we're not licked yet."

Hurleman seemed to find new strength in the hope of escape. His sniffling stopped and Dave helped him bind up his wounds with strips of cloth torn from his shirt. Then they started down the shadowy hallway together.

First Evelyn's room. She was sleeping just as Dave had left her, undisturbed by the shrieking in the house and the uproar outside. He closed the door quietly and locked it from the outside.

Next they went into Sylvia's roam. She had dozed off to sleep still cramped up against the top of the bed, the tears still wet on her cheeks.

And finally the room that Hurleman had shared with the blonde Annabelle. Like the others, she was sleeping soundly.

"Drugged," Dave muttered as they bent over her. "They would be able to sleep in the middle of a boiler factory tonight."

The remaining rooms on the third floor were empty and showed no signs of having been occupied. Cautiously they made their way down to the floor below and examined each room by flickering match light. These rooms were evidently the bedrooms of the Dentons, but none of the brothers was in them.

Not a soul on the second floor. Nor in any of the rooms on the main floor. That left only the cellar—and as Dave led the way down the creaking stairs it, too, seemed to be deserted. Dusty old furniture, barrels, boxes and piles of rubbish were on every side, but no sign of a living soul.

And then Dave turned to Hurleman and looked the question his lips did not frame.

"I heard it, too," Hurleman whispered. "Sounded like a scream, then a dull moan."

"From over in that direction," Dave nodded, as he led the way to the rear of the cellar.

It took them several minutes to locate a low archway tucked away in a recessed niche of the wall. Behind that a flight of stone steps led downward—downward into the blackness from which the screams and moaning were now coming more plainly.

Groping with his fingers along the damp wall, Dave led the way downward until the steps ended and a black tunnel stretched out before them, twisting and winding, and then opening into a dimly lit subterranean room that was a few steps lower down.

At the head of those steps Dave stopped, with Hurleman pressing close at his back, and gazed down into what seemed to be a combination torture chamber and operating room; a fiendishly conceived laboratory of pain that was fitted out with a hellish combination of ancient and modern torture implements. Racks, forges, stocks, operating tables, bloodstained screws and a wicked looking array of shiny, razor-sharp knives—

But it was the amazing drama going on in the center of the chamber that gripped their attention. At one side there was a gaping black cavity in the brick wall of the place, and huddled miserably before it were three naked women, screaming and moaning.

Dave looked at those women, and his stomach seemed to crawl!

They were actually young—though now they seemed old and haggard. Evidently they had once been beautiful, but now they were frightful looking specters, their bodies torn and hideously mangled by torture, their faces scarred and fiendishly disfigured. Blood ran in crimson trickles from freshly opened wounds, and they seemed barely able to stand up and face the blankfaced tormentors who gloated over them.

"You have served your purpose," Gregory Denton told them brutally. "You are no longer satisfactory wives, so we are about to divorce you so that we shall be free to remarry. Step into that hole!"

The cowering victims drew back and stared at the black hole as if it were the pit of hell!

"Oh, God! Not in there!" one of them shrieked through broken lips. "Don't put me in there! Kill me out here in the light!"

She threw herself frantically at Gregory's feet, but he kicked her out of his way and lashed her savagely until she crawled, whimpering, into the aperture. Then the others were shoved in after her, and the Dentons began to consummate their divorce.

Brick after brick they built up that wall, cementing it tight so that the living tomb would be airtight!

Dave's hands were balled into aching fists as he watched that wall rise, watched the tiers of bricks pile one on the other until only the staring, pleading faces of the entombed victims could be seen. Half a dozen more bricks and the wall would be complete, airtight. Then death would be only a matter of hours.

But that was not according to schedule. In the topmost layer a brick of only three quarter length was cemented into place, leaving just sufficient space to permit air to get in to the prisoners. Not only were the poor wretches to be buried alive—they were to starve to death in their ghastly tomb!

Now their moans and sobs came only mutedly through the narrow air hole, and Gregory dropped a curtain down over the rebuilt wall.

"I knew you would want to know all about our weddings," he mocked, "so I've arranged to have you hear everything that goes on. You can even croon the wedding march as we lead the brides in."

The brides! That meant those sleeping girls upstairs! It meant that Evelyn was to be mated with one of these fiendish monsters, to be maltreated and tortured until her lovely body was a thing of shuddering horror, and finally to be thrust, whimpering and moaning behind that wall of death!

Blind, overpowering rage engulfed Dave Powell as that maddening picture flashed before his mind's eye. A muffled curse grated from his clenched lips and he tensed his body and poised to leap down and close with those devils, to get his clutching fingers around their worthless necks.

But before he could make a move Hurleman jumped on his back and clamped a hand over his mouth.

"No, you don't!" the actor hissed in his ear, but already the scuffle had made sufficient noise to be heard.

Gregory Denton let out a bellow of rage and sprang for a weapon. Then all four of the Dentons were rushing toward the short flight of steps.

Franctically Dave broke Hurleman's grip, threw him off, and whirled to meet the Dentons—but in the next instant Hurleman's fist smashed viciously into his face. That treacherous blow dazed him, and for a moment he staggered helplessly. Dimly he knew that Hurleman was running away, could hear his pounding foot-steps fading down the tunnel—and then the Dentons were upon him.

It was almost dark there at the steps, but even in the semi-darkness Dave could see those blank, expressionless faces closing in on him, could feel the blazing hatred of their evil eyes. Fists struck out at him; knives flashed and bit into his shoulder, his arm; something heavy whistled by his head and almost knocked him off his balance.

But this was the moment he had been waiting for. His fists lashed out with the regularity of pistons and the rage driven force of pile drivers. He felt them sink sickeningly into cold, pasty faces, heard grunts of pain and savage curses.

A dark body loomed up in front of him—and went down as his fist crashed into it. Then another flashed past him. That was bad—now the devil would creep up on him from the rear.

Dave hunched his shoulder and got ready for the blow that might knock him out. But it didn't come—and now the devils in front of him seemed to have had enough. They had backed away; were crouching waiting for him to come at them.

For a moment he stood there panting catching his breath—and the muffled wail of the entombed women came to him and flashed an S O S to his brain. Evelyn was upstairs alone!

Dave cleared that short flight of steps in two jumps and raced blindly, his hands held out before him, along the dark tunnel. As he reached the steps leading up into the cellar he could hear the Dentons running through the tunnel behind him. Across the cellar and up the stairs to the main floor. He slammed the door behind him and turned the key in the lock—stood panting with his back against the panels.

The pursuit seemed to have stopped. Now everything was deathly quiet except the panting of his own breath—and then, again, his blood seemed to congeal in his veins!

Through the stillness came a hoarse shriek of terror—a moan of agony—from somewhere upstairs!

With his heart in his mouth he ran to the stairway and dashed up to the third floor. At the top of the stairs he paused and listened. Evelyn's door seemed to be closed, but a dark figure was just disappearing in another doorway, down the hall.

Had he been in there at Evelyn?

Dave sprang across the corridor to her door—and stumbled over something soft and heavy that sprawled on the floor in front of it. The door was still closed—locked as he had left it!

Then he bent over that heap on the floor. It was a man, stripped to his shirt and underwear. Dave lit a match and bent over the body—and drew back in revulsion. Staring up into the flame was the hideous death's-head he had glimpsed in the hallway earlier in the night. But now it was even more horrible, its gruesome features contorted in the agony of actual death.

What was the creature doing there before Evelyn's door? Had he come for her as he came for Sylvia? And if so, who was it that had killed him and scuttled away down the hall when Dave approached?

He had no answers to those questions, but his hand trembled as he fumbled with the key, trying to get it into the lock. What would he find when he opened that door? A shivery presentiment of evil seemed to stay his hand, to sap the strength from his wrist.

Then he flung the door open and stepped into the room with a lighted match held over his head and a moan of pure anguish broke from his palsied lips.

He did not need that match to tell him that the bed was empty. A moonbeam streaming in through the window fell full upon the crumpled sheets, the drawn back covers. Evelyn was gone!

The match burned down and seared his fingers. Hardly feeling the pain, he dropped it and lighted another, turned dazedly to survey the empty room—and then leaped forward with a wild shout. A whole panel of the sidewall stood open, swung out into the room.

That was the way she had gone!

Dave sprang to the opening and stared into it. Behind that swinging panel a black shaft like those used for dumb waiters ran down through the floor. He leaned out over it but could not reach the other side. Then he got down on his knees at its edge.

"Evelyn! Evelyn!" he shouted down into the darkness, but only the hollow echo of his own voice answered him. Only the echo of his own voice—and a stealthy sound outside in the hallway!

Dave's leap carried him from the edge of the black shaft to the doorway, then catapulted him into the hallway in time to see a dark figure try to scoot past. His flying tackle launched him across the corridor, to twine his arms in a death grip around those running legs. With a crash he and the skulker thudded to the floor.

Then he was all over the fellow, pounding and flailing at him. His fist smashed into a cold, pasty face and felt the repulsive thing ooze away from under it.

Then he struck out again—and his hand encountered a whole gob of that cold substance; as if the fellow's clammy face was falling away like rotten flesh.

Aghast, he struck a match while he kept the fellow securely imprisoned under his knees. The sputtering flame revealed the blank face and black suit of one of the Dentons—but the face seemed to be all askew, twisted all out of shape. Out from under the chin another was jutting!

Dave grabbed that upper chin and yanked—and the thing came away in his hand. It was part of a rubber mask that fit like a glove. With another yank the rest of the contraption tore loose—and he stared down into the scared face of Sam Tabor!

"You don't understand, Powell!" Tabor spluttered. "I'm innocent! I didn't have anything to do with this! You don't understand!"

Stark terror leaped in his bulging eyes as Dave's fingers closed around his throat and squeezed—squeezed. Desperately he tried to tear loose.

"You don't get me right!" he gasped painfully. "I killed that fellow—who was trying to get—Evelyn! I—"

His head fell back limply, and Dave slowly loosened his fingers, started to get to his feet—to look up into three hideous death's heads that surrounded him, that closed in on him as something exploded with a terrific roar inside his skull!

CHAPTER FIVE

WEDDING NIGHT

BILLOWING WAVES OF NAUSEA swept over Dave Powell, carried him dizzily up on their crests, dropped him sickeningly into their troughs, and washed him up onto the shores of Inferno itself. His head ached and throbbed maddeningly, and there was a moaning dirge in his ears.

When he opened his eyes and blinked dazedly around him he knew it was no nightmare; he *was* in hell. Nowhere else would there be such misery; nowhere else would such a fiendish gargoyle of a face be leering down at him. Not only one—there were three of the horrible looking creatures; three living death's-heads—and other faces that he should be able to place.

Of course, that was Evelyn sitting there in an easy chair— Evelyn dressed only in her lacey nightgown—Evelyn smiling up into one of those terrible travesties of a face. And that was Sylvia sitting comfortable in a chair on one side of her—Annabelle laughing gaily on the other.

Annabelle—Sylvia—Evelyn!

Gradually it all came back to him, and he glanced fearfully around him. He was in the subterranean torture room, tied securely to a chair, and a little distance away sat Sam Tabor glaring at his captors and Thaddeus Hurleman whimpering and straining at his bonds with frantic fury.

Those black-suited devils with their indescribably mangled faces seemed to be waiting for something. When the tall, grey-haired Gregory stepped over to Tabor and jammed a long iron rod down his back, inside the ropes that bound him, Dave began to understand.

"You have kept us waiting quite a while, Powell," the leering devil scolded mockingly, "It seemed a shame to start the ceremonies before you were able to appreciate them, but now we are ready to go. First of all. We shall take care of this fellow who murdered our brother Alfred."

As he spoke he fastened chains around Tabor's wrists and ankles, around his middle, secured him helplessly to the sturdy iron bar. Then, at a sign from him, the crippled devils who were his brothers came to his assistance and helped him carry the bar with its human burden to the front of an open furnace where it fit into grooves at the sides.

Gregory touched a button at the side of the contraption and the metal bar began to revolve. He pressed a bellows and the somnolent fire roared into dancing flames. Tabor was going to be roasted alive, like a trussed fowl on a spit!

Dave caught a glimpse of his terror filled eyes and knew that he had given up all hope, but there was courage in the man's big frame. He was no sniveling coward like Hurleman.

"You were wrong, Powell," he grated through clenched teeth, while the flames burned his clothes to cinders and brought streams of sweat out on his purple face.

"I came here to try to save Evelyn. I saw Simon French go into your place—and I knew what a crooked rat he was. So I listened at your door. Followed you out here—and managed to slip into the house when the dogs were busy tearing that other poor devil to pieces."

For a few moments he was silent, and Dave thought that consciousness had left him. Then the tortured eyes opened again, the drooling lips moved.

"I always loved Evelyn," he muttered thickly. "Thought I could win her away from you, Powell—but not—this way. "You were wrong, Powell—wrong—" His voice was rising, becoming delirious. "Evelyn," he called as he turned his writhing face toward her. "Evelyn—I thought you were in danger—I—"

But Evelyn did not even look at him. She was laughing up into Gregory's awful face, and the fiend's hand slipped caressingly around her shoulder. Dave caught a glimpse of her eyes and saw that she had no proper comprehension of what was going on around her; that she had no realization that a man was giving up his life in the agony of hell on earth because he loved her and had tried to save her.

The sickening smell of Tabor's roasting flesh filled the underground chamber; his dying groans mingled with the hopeless keening from behind the newly built wall of death and Evelyn laughed up into the face of the monster who cuddled her in his arm!

Then it was Dave's turn. Gregory and his brothers came over to him, untied him from the chair but kept him helplessly bound as they carried him to the cruel bed of a rack and stretched him out on it. Desperately he tried to break loose as they untied his wrists, but they were too much for him. His wrists were secured in the leather handholds, his ankles fastened to the foot of the diabolical contraption.

"As you are the only one of the three who is married to one of the ladies who are about to become our wives, it is only proper that you be kept alive the longest," Gregory gloated over him. "You will have ample opportunity to enjoy the ceremonies to the full—probably for several days before your strength gives out."

The inhuman devil turned the wheel at the side of the rack and the stretching began. Spasms of agony shot through Dave as his limbs were drawn in four directions until he knew that another half inch of stretching must snap his bones out of their sockets. Rivers of sweat rolled off him as he lay spread-eagled and rolled his head, pounded it against the bed of the rack to try to forget the torture that was screaming in every straining joint and sinew.

"That will be sufficient for now," Gregory leered. "Now for our third guest."

Quaking and begging for mercy, Hurleman was dragged to one of the white- topped operating tables, spread-eagled helplessly and stripped of his clothing. Over him Gregory poised, a horrible caricature of death, with a gleaming scalpel in his hand and the fires of hell burning in his eyes.

Hurleman's shriek, when that sharp blade sliced into him, echoed and reechoed deafeningly through the vaulted chamber. Dave watched with bulging eyes while the fiend worked his bloody knives, cutting, carving, dissecting his victim alive!

The dying wretch's screams drowned out the groans from the spit on which Tabor was roasting to death, drowned out the wails from those lost souls behind the wall—and then grew weaker, to mingle with them in an infernal symphony of agony.

But even that chorus of torment was unable to pierce Evelyn's drugged consciousness.

Dave groaned and rolled his head aside so as not to look at her—not to see what was coming. It would not be long now, he knew. Tabor's moans had almost ceased; his body was a charred, blistered thing that crackled and hissed as the flames licked at it. And Hurleman was silent, practically disemboweled on that frightful table.

The Dentons were losing interest, becoming restless. And then it came. The twisted hunchback deserted the operating table and strode over to the girls.

Dave told himself that he would not look—but his burning eyes swiveled back to Evelyn despite his determination, She was still safe! The hunchback was devoting himself to the blonde Annabelle, mauling her, pawing her, caressing her with his twisted scar of a mouth. And her arms were around his neck, returning his passionate kisses wantonly!

Then he picked her up in his arms and staggered with her to a low doorway that Dave now saw at the far end of the room. The door clicked shut behind them—and clanged in Dave's tortured brain like the door of a tomb.

Now there were only two left—Sylvia and Evelyn. It would be only a question of minutes before one of the fiends picked her up in his foul arms and carried her off. And he was powerless to do a thing to help her!

Frantically his racing brain conjured up wildly impossible hopes of rescue; but there was no chance at all for that, and he knew it. The only one he had told about Simon French's proposition was Arthur Kimball—but Arthur had no idea where the Denton place was located even should some sixth sense warn him of their danger and urge him to the rescue. That hope was futile.

Gregory, too, now was sated with the orgy he had dominated. He stripped the bloody gloves from his hands and tossed them onto the operating table as he strode over to the rack. Again he gripped the wheel and turned, turned—until the streams of perspiration seemed to be spurting out of Dave's pores.

"Enough for now?" the fiend grinned crookedly. "But I'll be back; don't worry about that. I'll not forget you—but now—"

With gloating eyes and twitching face he walked to the chair in which Evelyn sat and slipped into it beside her, drew her onto his lap. Dave watched the horrible face kissing her; watched the lecherous hands pawing her, tearing at the flimsy nightgown, pulling it down over her shoulders!

Then the devil had her in his arms—was carrying her off to one of those doorways at the back of the room!

Something snapped inside Dave at that moment. He lay there too numbed with horror to utter a sound—yet wild yells were issuing from his throat. In that paean of agony and despair he could distinguish words:

"Evelyn! Evelyn, darling! My God, if you ever loved me—if you ever cared at all—do something now before it's too late!"

His whole seal went into that frenzied appeal—and the drug-heavy veil lifted from in front of Evelyn's eyes. Sanity leaped back into them—and then incredible horror as she glanced around that charnel house. Terrified screams burst from her lips, and she beat her little fists into the scarred mask that was Gregory Denton's face.

But what good to bring her back to hellish reality? Gregory laughed at her, gripped her more tightly, and strode to the door—

And then the thing that could not happen happened!

Down the steps that led from the tunnel Arthur Kimball charged, his face convulsed with rage and a blazing revolver in his hand. With the second thunderous report Gregory Denton staggered and sprawled lifeless on the floor. Then deliberately the gun swerved and trained on the groveling cripple who was trying to hide beneath the rack on which Dave lay. It roared again—and a choked gasp bubbled up from the cripple's throat.

Without a glance at the rack Arthur sprang across the room and gathered Evelyn into his arms. Dave yelled to him, but without a backward glance he strode to the doorway for which Gregory had been heading ad went inside.

The door clicked shut, and the torture room was silent except for the moaning undertone that issued from behind its wall. It was strange, Dave thought, that Arthur had not heard him; but probably he was too excited to notice. He would come back as soon as Evelyn had a chance to tell him that be was still alive.

But the silence remained unbroken. Only the low moans—and then a slithering sound on the floor beside the rack.

Something was tugging at it, dragging itself up, clutching at the wheel. It was the repulsive cripple that Arthur had shot. Now his ghastly face was over the edge of the rack; he was tugging at the wheel. Even on the verge of death had this fiend summoned enough strength to revive and come back and torture his helpless victim?

Suddenly the life which he had despaired of saving was very dear to Dave Powell. He shouted Arthur's name, called for Evelyn, yelled until the walls of the underground room rang. They must have heard him!

"Save your breath, Dave," the voice of the cripple husked at his ear. "They won't answer you. Evelyn can't, and Kimball won't."

Dave stared at the deformed creature in amazement. The wheel was loosening, not tightening. The hellish strain on his muscles was relaxing—to be followed by a fearful spasm of pain that was even worse than the rack had been able to do.

"Listen carefully," the husky voice whispered. "There are some things I have to tell you—and I haven't much time left. You don't recognize me, of course, but I'm Len—Len Glancey. Yes, yes,"—as Dave started to interrupt— "I know I'm supposed to be dead and buried, but I didn't die in that explosion. You can see what it did to me—would have been much better if it had killed me. It left me this way—at Kimball's mercy. He buried an unknown laborer under my name, and then took me to a private sanitarium and had me nursed back to life."

Now the wheel was turned back all the way and he was fumbling with the straps that bound Dave's wrists, but his strength was almost spent.

"Kimball brought me here—to this house he owns," the cripple gasped. "The 'Dentons' aren't brothers at all. They are three of the capitalists who were blown up with the mine. When they recovered they were monstrosities, shunned by their friends. They were glad to come here—to Kimball's supposed sanitarium—for treatment. He debauched them, turned them into drug-crazed degenerates, and milked them of their money with these orgies."

One of Dave's hands was free, but now the cripple could do no more. He sank back to the floor, exhausted. Frantically Dave tugged at the other strap himself, while Glancey's amazing confession rang in his ears.

"This was going to be Kimball's last night," the dying man gasped. "I discovered that he has this place planted with enough dynamite to blow it to hell. He didn't need us any more, so he was going to double-cross us. He's gotten enough money from these millionaires to reopen the mine. It's in operation now. That's why he brought you here—to eliminate you so that the entire property would be his. That—and so that he could have Evelyn."

The husking voice had died to a barely audible whisper, but now Dave's arms were free and he was bending forward, tugging at the straps around his ankles. One came loose—and then the doorway through which Kimball had taken Evelyn flew open!

Clutching the tattered nightgown around her and screaming wildly, she ran into the room and stood looking around frantically for a way to escape. Then she saw the rack.

"Dave!" she screamed, and ran toward him.

But Dave was looking beyond her, to the snarling face of Arthur Kimball. With a final tug he freed himself from the torture device and leaped across the room just as Kimball raised his revolver.

The black muzzle yawned, vomited flame—and a burning streak bored through Dave's shoulder. Then his fist smashed at the weapon, knocked it out of Kimball's hand, and they went down in a desperate death grapple.

Dave put every ounce of strength he had into that struggle, but his tortured muscles were weak. They would not respond to his will, and gradually he felt himself giving way, felt Kimball getting the upper hand.

Kimball felt the turn of the tide, too, and his bloodshot eyes seethed with unholy triumph.

"You poor fool!" he spat. "Trying to stand in my way! When I want something, I get it. Even if I have to blow up a mine to manage it! Yes," he jeered, "it wasn't just an accident that the mine blew up. I knew that would wreck you, and if Evelyn had had any sense it would have wrecked your marriage, too. But she had to be a stubborn fool—so now I'll have her without bothering about marriage—and after I'm through with her she'll stay right here with the others, to go the way the mine did!"

Dave shouted at him, pleaded with him, begged him to act like a sane man—but Kimball wasn't sane, he realized as he looked up into those red-rimmed eyes. Avarice and lust had shattered his reason—but in return they had given him phenomenal strength. His steely fingers closed like a vise around Dave's throat, bit into his flesh, and cut off his wind.

Red spots danced before his eyes. The room swam in a red haze. He was falling, falling . . .

And then, as if in a nightmare, he saw an awful death's-head rear up over Arthur Kimball and smash a club down on the madman's skull! One blow was all that Len Glancey had the strength to deliver, but that was all Dave needed. Once that constricting grip loosened from about his throat he flung himself at Kimball with berserk fury.

Before Kimball could clear his dazed head a hard fist smashed into his face, another came up under his jaw, and a third knocked him off his feet. Then Dave was on top of him, hammering him into submission, flailing away at his snarling face until it was a bloody pulp.

Not until he felt a tug at his elbow did he stop that vengeful punishment. Then, dazed and panting, he looked around at Len Glancey. A moment ago the cripple had been gone. Now he crouched there on the floor, and a trail of his blood led to the far end of the room.

"Get out!" he gasped. "Get out—right away! You just have time. I've thrown the switch. We're going to eternity—all of us in this place. Hurry, Dave! The dogs are chained—the way is open. Get out! Any minute now—"

At any moment those walls would come crashing in and bury them in a living tomb! Dave wanted to help Lea, wanted to rescue Annabelle, wanted to tear down that wall and liberate the imprisoned women—but at any moment Evelyn would be crushed under tons of earth and stone!

Frantically be seized her and pushed her toward the tunnel entrance, then grabbed the still dazed Sylvia and dragged her up the steps.

Arthur Kimball saw them going, and realization of his danger percolated into his semi-consciousness. With an animal-like whine he tried to climb to his feet, but the arms of Len Glancey, the man he had maimed and ruined, closed around his legs in a grip that only death could break.

That was the last glimpse Dave Powell had of the torture chamber—the picture that was etched indelibly into his memory as he shepherded two frightened girls out into the cool night air and raced with them to safety.

The shock of the explosion that wrecked the brownstone mansion knocked them off their feet, but as they lay there on the soft turf he found his wife's eager arms around him and her soft lips pressed close to his. He did not need to look into her eyes to know that she was again the girl he adored—now and for the rest of their lives.

MASTER

OF MONSTERS

CHAPTER ONE

STRANGE FRUIT

DOT HAD MANAGED to keep a stiff lip until we had driven past the little village of Montross, and were well up into the hills. The nervous strain of the past few hours had been terrific, and there was certainly nothing in the chill and preternatural stillness of that mountain dusk, that lonely winding road, that cold and faded sky above black mantled hills, to lift the breathless weight of dread which bore down on us. We had avoided speech, as if by mutual consent, and now Dot's first words broke from her with a sob, and for once the pressure of her warm, lovely body, huddled dependently against mine, caused an ache of misery in my throat.

"Gil" she gasped suddenly, "Gil, I know don't want to talk about it, but you must tell me. Just what did Porter Prohawk say? Does he think Father's mad? Does he think he's done something—something awful?"

What could I tell her? Professor Paul Malcolmson was her father. He was the head of the Department of Psychology in the Prohawk Seminary for Girls, and during the five years I had taught there, as an assistant in the History department, I had known him as a very brilliant and very eccentric man. I had heard the scandalous talk which had gone on for years about certain obscure psychological researches which the professor had been conducting with the aid of his best students, but I had been inclined to discredit the wild rumors as exaggerations. This morning, Porter Prohawk himself, the wealthy and philanthropic owner of the private school, had called me into his office and told me in his blunt way of the horrid scandal that threatened both Professor Malcolmson and the school itself. But I was still uncertain about how much of it I should tell Dot.

Finally I told her. "I'll be frank with you if you'll be frank with me, darling. This is just what Prohawk told me: 'Gil,' he said, 'you and Malcolmson's daughter are engaged, so I'm going to make you share the burden of a big responsibility. The old man has got himself into trouble at last, I'm afraid. He disappeared, and he's apparently taken with him Martha Karn, who is the daughter of one of our wealthiest patrons. A young man in the town, Clay English, who's engaged to the girl, stormed into my office this morning to find out what had happened to her. She had left the dormitory last night with Professor Malcolmson. She didn't return and the professor didn't show up at his classes this morning. Now I managed to quiet the young fellow by promising that the girl would be back by tonight. But you and the professor's daughter, Dorothy, are going to have to find the old gentleman, warn him, and get him back here with the girl, at once. If you don't manage to do it by sometime tonight, I'll have to go after him myself."

"But didn't he say—?" Dot broke in.

"Wait till I finish," I said. "I asked him if he knew where your father might have gone and he said he did. He said he was certain your father had gone to the mountain lodge, Stonehenge, which he rents as a quiet place in which to study and work on his book. He said you usually went along with your father, as a chaperon for whatever girl he happened to take along as his assistant, but that this time he had failed to take you. That's why he was worried."

"And that's why I'm worried," Dot put in. "I thought at first he might have stayed all night in his study at the school. But I found out differently. Then I learned that Martha Karn was missing. But I didn't say a thing because—well, because I was afraid—"

"Ah!" I said. 'Now we come to that part of it. You've never told me just what you know about your father's mysterious research work, about those other girls—"

"Oh, but I know so little, Gil!" she sobbed. "He won't tell me a thing. For five years he's been working on some sort of book— something new in psychology. That's why he let Prohawk lure him away from the university to teach in his seminary. He wanted an easy job that would give him more time for his book."

"There are rumors that he came to a girls' school because he always uses girls in his research work," I suggested.

"Oh, that ugly talk!" Dot exclaimed. "He uses girls because their minds are more sensitive. Each year he has chosen his most brilliant pupils to help him. I knew all of them. I know what they say he did to the minds of those girls. But it isn't true. Each of them did have a nervous breakdown, but that was only because of mental strain. Those girls all adored father: none of them ever said a word against him, and none of them would give his secrets away—not even to me."

"Two of them killed themselves," I said.

"Yes," Dot agreed, frowning and biting her lips. "Rosa Warren and Stell Bickley. But it was after they had left the school. It was probably because of something else."

"Maybe," I agreed. "But why does he have to keep his research work so secret?"

"Because he doesn't want his ideas stolen by other scholars," Dot said.

I stared at the slowly darkening landscape with a gloomy gaze. Was Dot still holding something back? I couldn't say. Her answers had been straightforward enough. The old man, I knew, was eccentric and suspicious. No one less gentle than Porter Prohawk would have put up with his high-handed ways. But Prohawk, a self-educated man who, it was said, had laid the foundations of his wealth in a mining camp, was inordinately proud of the scholars he had gathered for his school. And old Malcolmson had always been his special pet.

But this morning Prohawk had seemed apprehensive, had actually hinted that the old man might be mad. I tried to think otherwise, but when I remembered those girls who had "helped" him in his research work—all brilliant girls of cultured, wealthy families—how they had gone away from the school, all nervous wrecks, I gritted my teeth angrily and little shudders quivered between my shoulder blades.

What dark and hellish things had old Malcolmson conjured up to haunt them? What was this strange book he was writing? Might not Dot herself be in danger? I stole a glance at her, felt my heart burn with protective love. Then again I stared moodily at the massed pine trees marching their black battalions past in the fading light.

"We're almost there," Dot said, "and I do hope—"

The sudden scream of the brakes drowned out her words; the violent jerk of the car threw her away from me. My foot shook as I removed it from the brake pedal. With a pounding heart I snapped off the ignition, looked at Dot.

"You didn't see it?"

"See what?"

"I don't know exactly," I stammered dazedly. "I just caught a glimpse of it among the shadows of the trees—something dark against a little patch of sky, something that looked like—"

"Like what, Gil?"

"Like a body," I said, and shuddered, "like the body of a woman, hanging from a limb. I'm going to see . . ."

"Don't, Gil!" She grabbed my arm. But I pulled away, opened the door, slid out from under the wheel.

Silence hung like a thick dust in the bluish twilight. Fearfully I peered into the gloom beneath the pines, took a few cautious steps along the road's edge. Dot had followed me out of the car and was now clinging to my arm. Perhaps I had only imagined that ghastly silhouette of death, perhaps . . .

I jerked to a stop. Above choked underbrush and aspen saplings, the hideous thing was visible again—the body of a girl in a ragged skirt, hanging stiff and rigid against a pale patch of sky.

I felt Dot's fingernails dig into my arm as she clutched convulsively, heard her suck in her breath with a gasp. Then a voice came from the shadows beneath the hanging horror, an old-womanish voice that crackled like a flame among dry leaves.

"Hurry, Aaron," it said, "I be a shiverin' with fear. Hurry before the dark comes. The *things* will come with the dark, to claim her."

With fists clenched, I forced myself forward for a better view. But abruptly I stopped again. For suddenly, as if animated by some unhallowed burst of life, the black corpse swayed to one side, then dropped like a plummet through the limbs and struck the ground with a hideous thud.

Horror was grappling at my heart, but, shoving Dot back, I fought through the underbrush, snapping on my pocket flash as I went on. On the edge of a little clearing, I jerked up short. The corpse of the girl—a barefoot mountain lass of about eighteen—had dropped in a ghastly huddle on the leafy mould, and bending over it was a skinny hag in a black bonnet and shawl. A second figure—that of a man—was climbing down the trunk of a pine tree.

"What's the trouble?" I managed to stammer.

The man slid quickly to the ground, landed on his feet. He was a hulking, bearded hill man, and he held a knife between his teeth. Now he grabbed up a long rifle that had been leaning against the tree and held it hip high as he blinked into the light.

"Trouble enough here," he growled. "What's it you want?"

"I was just passing," I said, "and I saw—"

"Ye'll do well to keep passing," the man warned. "We buries our own dead in the hills. The girl you see is our daughter, Minny. She hanged herself."

"Hanged herself!" I gasped, the horror of that bald statement freezing me. "But why?"

It was the old woman who interrupted me now. Lifting her sunken eyes to the light, she whined: "Ye can ask that of the cursed witch-woman, Febe Megget of Stonehenge. Ye can ask the old professor from the city—him that brings victims to her *coven*. Them two has loosed the *things* in these woods—the *things* that drives mortals to madness and sinful death."

"Things?" I repeated hoarsely, noticing the emphasis she had placed on the word. "What sort of *things?*"

"Nameless things," the old woman croaked. "Things it's a mortal sin to mention, things that ain't neither man nor beast!"

"Hesh—you!" the man suddenly snorted. He turned to me with a suspicious stare. "They's been a passel of cars goin' to Stonehenge lately. Maybe you be headed there, too."

"No, I'm going to Eagle Pass," I lied. Then I switched back to the former topic.

"Why don't you get the law after this witch-woman, if she's to blame?" I asked.

"Law?" the old woman sputtered. "Law won't do no good against devils from hell. What it takes is to have the curse of God put on 'em. And Brutus Pews will do that."

"And who is Brutus Pews?" I asked.

"Ain't you heard of Brutus Pews, the Prophet of the Hills? Him it is that seeks out the devil-invokers and—" She didn't finish; her voice choked off with a hoarse cough; her body jerked convulsively and stiffened. At the same instant I heard Dot scream.

Like something spun about by springs, I whirled, and stark terror sent the breath wheezing between my teeth. I saw the thing for only an instant, yet the memory of it will never leave my brain. One moment it was monstrous blot against the sky, a huge shapeless something, vaguely like a giant bat. It seemed to have dropped from the foliage of a large pine tree. I saw it as it struck the ground, seemed to bounce up and then lunge straight toward the screaming figure of Dot. I sprang forward blindly then, like a maddened animal whose mate is threatened.

Tearing through the tangled underbrush. I heard the crack of the hill man's rifle behind my back. Then I saw that Dot had fallen, that the thing was crouching like some hideous shadow above her prostrate form. Convulsed with terror and rage. I threw myself toward the monstrous shadow with a maniac's cry.

But the creature did not wait for my attack. It suddenly rose like a black pillar of smoke, hovered there for a split instant, and then seemed to melt swiftly into the dense shadows of the trees.

I stumbled to her side, dropped down to my knees and lifted her head and shoulders. She was as limp as the newly dead, but when I pressed my ear to her breast I could hear the beating of her heart. Thank God, I had not been too late. Gathering her up quickly in my arms. I raced for the car.

My brain and all my senses seemed caught in a crazy whirl-pool, as I literally fought my way through the underbrush with that loved form in my arms. But I was not too completely dazed to no-tice one thing which set my nerves quivering with a fearful revul-sion. About the place where the shapeless shadow had descended, there lingered an odor that is indescribable. It was something that faintly resembled the odor of reptiles, blended with the reek of carrion, the fetor of slime. Yet it was neither; it was unearthly.

It was a smell that belonged to no creature known to man!

CHAPTER TWO

EXPERIMENT OF THE DEVIL

I REACHED THE CAR, trembling, covered with cold sweat. I laid Dot carefully on the cushions, loosened the collar of her topcoat and fanned her with my hat. Presently she opened her eyes. For an instant terror was written on her pale face, and then she recognized me.

"Gil!" she sobbed, "Gil!" and threw her arms about me, huddled, trembling against me.

"Easy, darling," I said, trying to keep the frightened tremor from my voice. "It's all over. You're safe."

"But Gil, did you see it—that awful thing?"

I bit my lip, steadied my nerves with a tremendous effort. "I saw something," I managed to say evenly. "I think perhaps it was a big buzzard, or a bird of that sort."

"Buzzard? Oh, Gil, you know it wasn't! No buzzard was ever of such monstrous size, and besides—"

"I know," I put in hurriedly, "it seemed so to me, too. But when we're frightened our eyes play tricks on us." I was disengaging myself from her arms and getting back under the wheel. "We mustn't let our imaginations—"

"Oh, it wasn't imagination, Gil! It was something, something not of this world!"

"Nonsense!" I protested weakly. "You didn't see it closely, did you?"

"Not closely," she said. "I fainted when it came at me. But I saw enough to know . . ."

I started the motor noisily, backed the car fifty yards or so down the road. I wanted to see what had happened to the hill people, to renew my offer of help. Yet I dared not get out of the car, dared not leave Dot alone for an instant. I turned my wheels sharply, so that the headlights shone into the woods. I called to them, but there was no reply.

"They must have run off, after that one shot," I said finally, and I was not sorry. After all, I had Dot to think of and I was anxious to get her away from that fearful place. I meshed gears and sped the car along the lonely road.

The woods, now deepening to a monotonous black sea, swept swiftly past on either hand, and beyond, the stark crags were clothed in ghostly filaments of mist. The night was rising like a swift black tide over the world, and as I swung my small roadster along the winding road, I cursed the delays which had prevented our getting an earlier start.

It had been fully three hours, after my interview with Porter Prohawk, before I had rounded Dot up and got started. I wished now that I had persuaded Prohawk to come with us. But he was no longer at his office when I had stopped there as we were leaving. Could it be that he had already driven out here? I sincerely hoped so!

"How much farther is it?" I asked Dot.

"Around the next turn and up a lane," she said in a voice that was little more than a whisper. "Oh, Gil, I'm terrified. Something may have happened to father."

"Don't think that," I begged. "We've got to keep our heads level. Who is this Megget woman the old crone mentioned? You've never told me of her."

"I never thought of her much," Dot replied. "She's the old woman who owns the place. She lives in the back with her daughter, Carmina, and rents the front to Father. I'd always looked on her as a sort of harmless half-wit, though she does look like a witch."

"And what about this fellow Brutus Pews?"

"He's one of those religious nuts who preaches some new gospel to the mountain folks," she said. "He goes barefoot and wears a cassock like a monk and preaches against witchcraft and devils. He's always coming around to argue with Father. I heard him accuse Father of sorcery once, but Dad just laughed at him."

"And did you think him amusing?" I asked.

"Indeed I didn't," she answered. "He's a sinister looking brute, bearded and with eyes like Rasputin. Oh, I wish we didn't have to go to that awful place, Gil!"

"I'll see that nothing harms you, darling," I promised.

I wish I could have felt as bold as I made that sound, but I didn't. Despite my effort not to show it, an indescribable feeling of dread was closing about me. Fear, like some monstrous invisible spider was enmeshing me in the skeins of its web.

When Dot pointed out the lane that branched off from the road, and I had piloted the car into a rutted tunnel of darkness, I felt an almost irresistible impulse to turn back in spite of everything. I might have actually done it, too, so fearful was I for Dot's safety, but just then the black outline of Stonehenge showed above the trees. I saw the dark, irregular silhouette of a rambling, terraced stone building, which seemed to be shoved flush against the rocky bastions of the hillside, and I felt then, with a deep inner dread, that I had come too far to turn back.

A graveled driveway led into the gloom-shrouded grounds which were like a wild, untended garden choked with shrubs and vines. But I could make out no sign of light in the house.

"Perhaps there's no one here, after all," I said, and prayed that I might be right.

We got out of the car and followed a path that led up mossy steps and over a flagged terrace. There was the dank, unpleasant odor of sunless vegetation about the place which gave it the atmosphere of some vast, crumbling tomb.

I paused before a heavy door of paneled oak, to listen. Suddenly I started. For though no light shone from the windows, I could hear the faint mumble of a voice—or voices.

Instead of knocking, I grasped the knob of the door, turned it softly, and pushed it open about a foot. I heard Dot gasp, and I hissed softly to silence her. I was not above eavesdropping now, if it would give me any clue to the professor's fearful secret. And it appeared that we had arrived while some of his ghostly research work was in progress.

The dark of the doorway was like a velvet curtain before our eyes, but out of the clammy gloom a voice was speaking in low accents. Although it was muffled, there was a queer note of suppressed eagerness in it, and I recognized the peculiar smacking lisp of Professor Malcolmson.

"What do you see?" I heard him ask.

There was a moment's silence, and then the answer came, in a woman's voice. But it wasn't a normal voice; it was little more than a high pitched whisper, toneless, weird, as if the lips of something dead were speaking.

"Vapors," said the voice, "vapors, water, strange trees."

"The same as last night?"

"Yes."

"Nothing moves?"

"Nothing."

"You're sure? Observe closely. Doesn't something creep in the green slime, some-thing huge, dark. Look closely. Eh?"

"Yes, yes." The voice was a little breathless now. "Something dark, a shadow, I think."

"No, not a shadow. Look closer. Describe it."

"It's huge—bigger than an elephant. It's body is a rusty green, splotched with dark like the body of a snake —"

"Go on! Does the thing approach you?"

"Yes. It seems to breathe a whitish vapor," the voice of the woman quavered now.

"Calm, be calm. What else?"

There was a pause. Then softly, but with a note of gathering hysteria: "Oh, my God! You must let me go now!"

"No, no, do not move. Do not turn. Describe! The swamp is heaving perhaps, the slime rushes away. He is rising, rising . . ."

"But I can't! Merciful God! I'm afraid!"

"Splendid! The creature approaches you . . ."

"No! Not that—something else."

"What?"

"Something more terrible. I can't see it. I feel it, hovering over me . . . I smell it . . . Oh, it's awful. It wants me! It's trying to seize me! Oh, it . . .!" The words trailed off in a wild cry that came through the dark like a siren's wail. Then the shrill scream: "In God's name! Mercy! It's got me!"

A blinding flash of light, like an exploding rocket, burst from a nearby doorway that opened into the hall, shattering the dark for an instant with its white flare. Then the blackness surged back. There were sobs, low moans of exhaustion, and the deep bass of a man saying:

"The Incubus. It was the Incubus!"

Mastering the ague of terror that shook me, I pushed Dot back and stepped into the hall.

CHAPTER THREE

WHAT THE CAMERA SAW

TOOK THREE SILENT STEPS and halted. Yellow lamplight flared in the room; I stared through the doorway. A large photographer's studio camera stood directly across the room, its lens focused on a curtain-covered doorway. Standing by the camera were Professor Malcolmson and another man—a huge, burly fellow, with long hair and black beard. He was dressed in a rust-colored cassock and his feet were bare.

"So you think you have photographed a devil, eh?" the professor was asking the other man, with a chuckle.

"You shall see," said the bearded one. "And when you have seen, you will cease this deviltry and pray God's pardon." He was removing a plate from the camera.

"What rot!" the professor laughed. Then he faced the curtained doorway.

The curtains had parted and I stared with revulsion at the ugly figure which appeared. She was short and squatty, and lank strands of matted grey hair hung down over a leathery, wrinkled face which was like a carved gargoyle of sin. And she was half carrying, half pushing, the slender figure of a girl whose half-nude body was shaking with jerky spasms.

"Old Febe Megget and her daughter," Dot whispered from behind me.

The professor was staring at the woman. "How is she, Febe?"

The woman lifted her hideous face, which I now saw had only one eye, and leered as she said: "She's still a-shakin'. She must've seen something sure 'nough that time."

"Put her on the couch," the professor directed briskly. "She'll be all right."

A sort of slow-smouldering rage was burning in me. I stepped out into the light.

The professor whirled with a startled exclamation. Then he recognized me, and his eyes narrow. "You, Gil? What the devil are
doing here? And Dot with you! What does this mean?"

For a moment I said nothing, simply stared at him as be approached with slow strides. He was a tall man, slightly stooped,
with a thin face so waxy pale that not only flesh seemed gone from
it but blood and muscle as well, leaving only dead skin on dead
bone. One of his pale eyes had a peculiar squint, which accentu-
ated the satyr-like expression which a large mouth, large ears, and
a pendulous underlip gave to his face. He was dressed in a wrinkled black suit which set off the paleness of his face, which moved
in restless grimaces as he came toward us.

"Well, well," be snapped. "What's the meaning of this interrup-
tion? Speak up!"

"Oh, Father," Dot gasped, "we were so worried, and—"

"And Porter Prohawk sent us to look for you," I put in.
"There's a nasty scandal brewing. What have you done with Martha Karn?"

"Martha Karn? I don't understand."

"She was seen leaving the dormitory with you last night. She
hasn't come back."

"But I took her back," the professor said. "What's this rot about
a scandal? Prohawk knows I came out here to do my research
work."

"Perhaps," I began. "if we were alone—" I looked significantly
at the others in the room.

The professor turned about frowning. "Of course," he muttered.

To the bearded man who had been watching us with his smouldering black eyes, he said: "Take it on out and develop it, Pews."
Then he turned to the woman. "You can carry Carmina to her
room, Febe. I'm through with her for the night."

The man called Pews turned about and left by a side door. The
hag began tugging at the still quivering body of the girl. I watched
in disgust as she propelled her from the room. The girl, I saw, was
young, with black hair and dark eyes, which now stared with a
horrid, vacuous gaze. She was dressed in a queer, scant costume of
animal pelts. As the woman vanished into the hallway, the professor called after her: "You can fix Dorothy's room up too, and the
other spare bedroom. Since they're here, they'll have to spend the
night."

Then he turned back to me with a frown. "Now," he said, "sit
down and we'll get this nonsense over."

I sat down on the vacated couch and Dot sat beside me. She was strangely silent and the frightened look had not left her eyes. The old man apparently noticed it, too, for he growled: "You can go up to your room, Dorothy. You appear upset, and doubtless need rest."

"But father . . .!"

"Go at once!" the professor said sternly.

Dot flushed, then got up and walked to the doorway. In its embrasure she turned to glance at me, and I read a question in her eyes. If I had told her to stay, she would have stayed then and defied him. But I didn't. I thought it best not to irritate old Malcolmson until I had heard from him the explanation I was determined to hear.

"And now," said Malcolmson, when she had left, "proceed to explain."

I was nettled by his manner, and I stated bluntly why we had come. I told him approximately what Prohawk had said, and added: "You understand that young Clay English may cause trouble about that Karn girl. He may get in touch with her parents— and he may even come here."

For just an instant I saw the old man's eyes flicker with something like alarm. Then he had regained his composure.

"But I told you I did not bring her here," he said. "You must surely realize that all wild talk is groundless."

It was exactly what I wanted him to say. It gave me a lead. I told him point-blank that I wasn't sure at all that it was groundless. And I spoke of the mountain girl who had hanged herself by the roadside, and of the things the hill people had said.

At the mention of the suicide he sprang to his feet. "Great God!" he exclaimed, "that's awful. But you must believe me, Gil. I did not drive the girl to madness. I put her under hypnosis only once. She seemed so frightened afterward that I never used her again."

"You can make excuses," I said, "but you must recall those other suicides—Rosa Warren and Stell Bickley. You must realize that the time for secrecy is over. You're going to have to come out into the light with your researches now!"

"Eh, what's that?" he snapped. But I gave him a level stare and he dropped his eyes. Then, folding his lean hands behind him, he began to pace back and forth across the floor of that gloomy, book-littered study. Presently he stopped squarely before me, his lean fingers twining and untwining nervously, like long bloodless worms.

"You're right, Gil," he said huskily. "I'm going to reveal my whole project to you. You know of course that I am working on a book, have been working on it for years—yet no one, I suppose, except Porter Prohawk and the people who have worked with me, know its subject. You can't guess it, I suppose?"

I shook my head.

The old man grinned, his eyes narrowed. "It will be called," he said, *"The Secret Shapes of Fear.* It will be a treatise on human fear, a history of that emotion. In it I shall define and trace to their sources in the remote past, all of the chimeras that have ever haunted the brain of man!"

"Trace to their sources?" I repeated, questioningly.

"Exactly!" he said. "Nothing like that has been done before, eh? But I shall do it. You see, Gil, we know that every form of fear—the fear of ghosts, of vampires, of dragons, and so on—is rooted in something real and actual in the remote past. We also know that every human brain contains a horde of buried racial memories—the subconscious mind. It is from the subconscious mind that I dig up the prototypes of terror. That's where my assistants come in. I hypnotize my subjects and then, with the proper atmosphere, and the proper suggestions, I send their minds exploring, and their subconscious memories bring up for me those hidden truths."

I pondered. There was a weird and fascinating logic in the old man's words. The idea was daring, intriguing. "But Professor," I asked, "you don't mean that you can dig into these memories and find real dragons, real vampires, real demons?"

He laughed. "Of course not, Gil," he replied. "But what started the dragon idea, for instance? Something real—you may be sure. It isn't hard to guess. The dragon was modeled on the Mesozoic monsters—the giant saurians—the Tyrannosaurus, the Triceratops, the Pterodactyl, and so on. A few of these monsters must still have remained on earth when man was emerging from the sub-creature. They were the prototypes of the dragon."

And that girl tonight—?" I began.

"Exactly," he said. "She was hypnotized, and she was looking into the past through her subconscious, seeing these monsters as they really were, not merely as they were recreated from their bones. The first division of my work will deal with the origin of the dragon, and I have called it, *The Beasts Beyond Eden."*

"The Beasts Beyond Eden!" a deep voice bellowed as if in mockery of Malcolmson's last words, and both of us looked up with a start to see the cassocked figure of Brutus Pews standing in the doorway. He was holding in his hands a photograph, fresh from the developing room.

"You shall see what sort of beasts you have drawn up from the gorges of hell!" he almost roared. "There were no beasts beyond Eden, no beasts except the unregenerate devils of hell, the devils which, according to the Scriptures, looked upon the daughters of men and found them fair. Those are the beasts you summon to prey upon innocent girls—the *incubi* of ancient lore, the ravaging, lustful demons who prey upon the sleeping daughters of men!"

"What rubbish, Pews!" Professor Malcolmson exclaimed, starting toward the fanatic. "I agreed to let you try a photograph, but you're being a nuisance. What have you on the print?"

"Look for yourself," the bearded man replied.

Malcolmson snatched the print from the other's hand, and carried it to the light. I saw him start, stare closely, and then with a muttered oath, wad the wet print and hurl it to the floor.

"What's on it?" I asked.

Malcolmson stared at me a moment almost angrily. "Nothing," he said, "nothing. There was a defect on the film which caused a whitish smear, an absurd thing!" He turned to scowl at Pews.

"You make me sick!" he snapped irritably. "Go home, go to bed. I'm tired. I want to get some sleep."

For a moment the fanatic stared at Malcolmson out of his great wild eyes; then he lifted one huge hand in the air. "The curse of the Almighty be upon you," he intoned, "if you persist in these abominations!" Turning, he stalked out of the room.

I looked at the professor. He was staring at the floor with a queer preoccupation. Suddenly he jerked his head up "The man is an ignorant fool!" he muttered. "But you'd better go to bed. We can discuss matters in the morning. Come, I'll show you to your room."

I agreed, though I had my mind made up ready about what I would do once he had left me. The professor picked up the lamp and preceded me through the door. I followed, but as I passed the spot where he had thrown the wet print, I stooped quickly, snatched it up, and stuck it in my pocket.

We went into the hall and up a flight of stone steps to a room on the second floor. The professor waited for me to light a lamp, then left me, with a brief, "Goodnight."

I closed the door and barred it. Then, with quaking fingers, I fished the wet print from my pocket and spread it out on the table under the light. It showed the girl called Carmina, huddled against the bare wall of a room. Her expression and her attitude were horrible. Her hands were thrust out, her eyes dilated, her mouth gaping with screams. On the print above her was a curious white smear. Unspeakable horror gripped me. For what had seemed at first a shapeless blank, now appeared as the white silhouette of something huge and terrifying which hovered above the woman. There was the vague suggestion of a head, and something that looked as though—My God!—it might have been huge, bat-like wings.

I straightened up my head whirling wildly. The thing on the print bore a horrid likeness to the grisly horror which had attacked Dot. We had not imagined it after all! And Dot was sleeping alone in this awful place!

Suddenly I blew out the light, stepped to the window, and raising it, let the chill breeze from the pines fan my throbbing temples. The moon, a ghostly wisp of silver, floated in a flying froth of clouds, silvering the wild landscape with an eerie light. Then abruptly, out of the silence it came—an awful sound that tore my nerves at the roots—a low, wild sobbing, drifting up from the dark below, and a woman's voice, gasping the blood-curdling plea:

"Harder! Strike harder! Lash me! Beat me! Kill me! In God's name, let me die!"

In an instant I had flung myself over the windowsill, was clambering down a ladder of thick vines to the dark ground below, where those awful moans were rising.

CHAPTER FOUR

THE MADNESS SPREADS

MY FEET HIT THE GROUND with a stinging impact. I straightened, my head spinning dizzily and my blood pulsing like the pound of pistons in my veins. A chill breeze whipped wraiths of fog through the dark trees in a weird, writhing procession, and rustled the shrubs about my feet. The pitiful sobbing had momentarily ceased.

Then I heard it again—from behind me. I spun about, my heart in my throat, and staggered through the shrubs toward the sound. Then I saw the light shining from a barred window in the rock foundation of the building. As I hurled my body through the tangle of umbrage, I heard new sounds, sinister, ominous, punctuating the groans like the beat of metronome—the regular rhythmic crack of a lash on bare flesh . . .!

"Whip me! Kill me!" the tormented voice entreated in shrill accents of hysteria.

Where the barred square of light fell on the frozen leaf mould, I flung myself flat on my belly and thrust my head to the aperture. The sight I saw was horrible beyond words, was like a scene torn from the lurid pages of the *Inferno.*

On the bare stone floor of a cement walled cell lay the writhing body of a woman. Her clothing, half torn from her body, hung in ragged shreds. Her face, haggard and bloodstained, was the twisted visage of a maniac. Wild eyes, burning with a horrid feverish light in red-rimmed sockets, rolled weirdly with each spasmodic jerk of her body, which was writhing under the cracking sting of the lash. Above her stood a young man, disheveled and with the dazed, vacuous look of the insane. He was beating the girl with a belt, in the slow weary rhythm of an automaton.

I recognized the girl as Martha Karn; the youth maltreating her like some jaded and drunken sadist was—Clay English!

"Stop it!" I shrieked above the frightful din of the woman's cries and the whip's tormenting cracks. "Stop it, you damned fiend, or I'll kill you!"

The man jerked up stiffly, lifted haggard, empty eyes to the window, stared with gaping mouth. The black lash dangled limply from one hanging fist, and, relieved for an instant from its burning torture, the maddened girl redoubled her screams:

"Strike, strike!" she shrilled. "Lash me, you fool! Oh, in God's name, don't stop! My eyes are beginning to close. Oh, God, God, God!"

The words dwindled to animal-like gurgles; froth gathered at the corners of her twisted mouth, and she suddenly lifted clawed hands and began to pull the tangled hair from her scalp. Blood ran down her forehead, into her eyes . . .

"Stop her!" I screamed, choking with horror. "Stop her, I say!"

But the young man had turned his idiotic glance back to the writhing, self-tormented figure, and now he lifted the belt again, and this time he brought it down with such force that it left a livid trail of blood across the girl's nearly naked body.

I staggered up then, panting, shaking in a convulsion of nausea. Now I understood that the woman was not the prisoner of the man who was flaying her. They were both prisoners, and they were both stark raving mad, gripped in some ghastly delirium to which their fiendish captor had driven them. And their captor could be but one person. Professor Malcolmson!

Still in the grip of a numbing horror, I went weaving drunkenly toward the front of the house. A man who would coldly drive any human to such depths of shame and agony was less than human. The daughter of such a man would not be safe in her own father's hands. And I had let Dot go meekly away from me, at his command! Where was she now? Was he subjecting her even now to the shameless and unthinkable horrors which had driven Martha Karn into the inferno of madness?

I cursed myself for a double fool, a criminal idiot! And while I cursed myself I knew that I must penetrate the hellish secret of that house of horror and save Dot before it was too late. As for Malcolmson, I would break him in my two hands, pound the life from his body with my fists!

I gained the front terrace of the house and started across it in a crazy lope. Then at the door I paused. A cautious instinct warned me not to dash madly into the fiend's clutches. I steadied myself with an effort, got a grip on my nerves, then opened the door softly and listened.

Not a sound came from the interior of the darkened house. Where should I go first? My immediate impulse was to rush directly to Dot's bedroom. But on second thought I decided against it. If Dot were still in her room, it would be a good indication that she had not yet been molested. If he had intended to make her the next subject of his hellish researches, he would have taken her to the room with the curtained door, from which I had seen the hag bring out the spasm-wracked body of her daughter. It was to that mysterious room that I must go!

Holding my breath, which seemed to rasp audibly from my heaving lungs, and listening fearfully to the hollow thudding of my heart, I stole along the darkened hallway. At the door of the study I paused, listened, and then crept on across the room.

There was not a sound except the faint crunch of my shoes on the rug, As I moved, step by slow step, through that awful blind void, the silence became a torment of suspense, seemed to press like a stifling and viscous fluid against my eardrums. Anything would have seemed better than that awful empty stillness which I imagined alive with frightful implications.

At length I reached the opposite wall, groped along it until my fingers encountered the velvet curtain that hung across that fatal doorway. Here I paused again, parted the curtains and softly opened the door behind them. I stopped then, with sheer terror crawling like frozen scorpions across my flesh. I had heard nothing; I had seen nothing, Yet other senses had quivered to the impact of vague warnings.

The room was cold but still and clammy with the dank air of subterranean tombs. Mingled with that crypt-like reek was another odor—that unearthly reptilian smell that had permeated the air of the woods at the spot where Dot had swooned before the rush of that monstrous and nameless shadow!

I had to take my courage in both hands then. Another moment and I would have rushed from that hellish darkness in blind panic. To prevent that I gritted my teeth, fished my flashlight from my pocket and sent its beam streaking across the clammy darkness, the round spot of light struck the opposite wall of the room, and I sucked in my breath with a start.

It was a very strange room indeed, for it was built against the bare face of the cliff itself, and in this wall, on which my light now played, there was a rudely circular opening about ten feet in di-

ameter, whose ragged mouth of discolored rock showed it to be a
natural cave in the cliff.

With a queer, fearful fascination my eyes fastened on that black
aperture of darkness. What was the meaning of this mysterious
room? Did something unearthly live in the black depths of that
ancient cave—some demoniac slave which Professor Malcolmson,
like King Solomon of old, had bottled up in the bowels of the earth
for his own dark purposes?

With a shudder, I made a half turn to spray the other walls of
the room with light. Suddenly I jerked stiff and immobile, with the
flashlight frozen in a convulsively knotted fist. Feet had moved in
the darkness, to my right—the feet of something which I now
knew had been standing behind that door, watching me. As I
turned my fear-distended eyes toward the sound, a voice spoke in
low and deadly accent.

"If you value your life, don't move an inch."

I didn't. Perhaps I couldn't have if I had tried. A second later
the lank form of Professor Malcolmson had stepped into the glare
of my torch. He held a revolver trained on my breast and his
squinted eyes fixed me with a vulture-like stare.

"What does this snooping mean?" he demanded.

I had recovered my voice by now, and the actual knowledge of my
peril seemed a relief from the grueling suspense. Now I knew the
worst and there was no point in pretending.

"You don't have to ask me that," I said. "You know how I've
found what a hell-hole this place is. It was my hope to save Dot
from the fate of poor Martha Karn."

I saw the professor's mouth clamp tight, watched the muscles
in his lean jaws play beneath the skin. "You saw her then? And the
young man?"

"Of course," I replied. "I heard her mad cries from my window."

"Ah!" he said, and he frowned, appeared to ponder. "And quite
naturally you concluded that I was an inhuman monster?"

"What else could I conclude?" I snorted. "You surely don't feel
it necessary to lie to me any longer?"

"Not any longer," he said slowly. Then a change seemed to
come over him. His face grew more haggard, cadaverous; his lips
trembled. "I'll tell you the plain truth, Gil," he said. "I did bring
the Karn girl here, of course. But in some way I made an awful
mistake, a criminal blunder perhaps. I hypnotized the girl and re-

corded her reactions, as usual. But," he faltered, his voice falling to a whisper, "in this instance I was unable to bring her back out of the hypnosis!"

"She's obviously mad," I said. "She'll be dead soon."

"God help me!" he moaned. "I did everything in my power to quiet her, but neither drugs nor suggestion had any effect. She is under some ghastly delusion of terror. I could do nothing but lock her up and hope that would wear off."

"And Clay English?" I asked.

"Yes," he said. "The young man—he found out in some way where this place was, and came here this afternoon. What could I do? I obviously could not bring the girl to him. But he was armed, threatened to kill me. It was a simple matter of defending my own life. I managed to get the drop on him, and at the point of a gun I disarmed him and locked him up, too."

"And now?" I challenged.

"Now," said Professor Malcolmson, "I don't know what in God's name I shall do. The young man seems to have caught the madness, too. I have almost begun to believe the wild talk of Brutus Pews."

I watched the old man shrewdly through slitted eyes. Was he pretending, acting?

I could not tell. I said: "Whether he's right or not, there's something hellish at work here, and unless you're a fiend yourself, you'll help me get to the bottom of the horror."

"I'll do anything, Gil," he answered, "I'm a broken man. That thing I saw on the photo that Pews made has terrified me beyond words."

"Where's Dot?" I demanded.

"Locked in her room," the old man said fearfully. "God! I've been pacing the floor in that upper hall."

"Then let's do something!" I rasped.

"What *can* we do?"

"Plenty," I answered. "If this thing isn't really something out of hell that you've invoked, then its the work of a human agency. If that's true we'll get to the bottom of it. Tell me first why you use this room built against the cave?"

"A simple matter of atmosphere," old Malcolmson explained. "The subterranean smells, the rocks, and so on, help get the minds of my subjects in the right channels, help to recreate the feeling of ancient times, when all men were cave dwellers."

"All right," I said. "And this is the room where the madness comes on the women. There are only two entrances—the door and the cave. If the monster who preys upon them doesn't come through the door, then he must come through the cave."

"But the cave has no other outlet," the old man protested. "After about a hundred feet it comes to a blank wall."

"Then I want to examine that wall," I said, and started toward the cavern's mouth, with Professor Malcolmson following.

For just a moment, as I stepped into the foul, muggy air of the cavern, I wondered if the old man intended to murder me in the cave's black depths. But I went on.

The ray from my pocket torch, playing head of me along the twisting tunnel, frosted the sweating walls with a macabre light. Great hairy spiders scuttled before the glare, and once a bat floundered squeaking across our path. Then, at a sudden twist, the cavern widened, and came abruptly to an end.

Old Malcolmson had stopped. I stepped head, spraying the ragged walls on all sides with a white mist of light. I could detect nothing that resembled a concealed opening. I didn't neglect the ceiling, either; but it was obviously solid. I turned back toward the professor.

"You were right," I said. "If anything lives in this place, and comes out to haunt your helpers, it's something that can become invisible at will."

"Something that would photograph as a splotch of white, a splotch of *nothingness,* eh?" he mumbled uneasily. "Something that—"

The words seemed to catch in his throat. He whirled about toward the darkness behind him.

Then I heard it too—Dot's voice in a wild, sick whimper of terror. Dot's voice calling like a lost soul from the depths of hell Dot's voice breaking, choked off to hideous silence on the last shrieked repetition of my name.

"Gil! Save me! Gil, Gil, Gil—!"

CHAPTER FIVE

BEAT ME—TO KEEP ME AWAKE!

MALCOLMSON WAS YARDS AHEAD OF ME, and before I could shake off the first awful instant of paralysis following that soul-blasting cry, he had plunged like a leaping manikin into the blackness. I followed, trying to cry out to Dot from a throat choked with hot horror.

Then as I rounded the tunnel's first turn, my foot slipped on the slimy rock. I struck the wall, careened back, and fell sprawling on my side. The flashlight, jarred from my hand, struck the floor with a crash and went out. Stunned, bruised, half mad with rage and terror, I staggered to my feet, and snarling insane curses, groped wildly through the dark.

Dragging a hand along one wall, I found my way to the tunnel's mouth.

"Dot!" I sobbed from bursting lungs. "Dot! Where are you, Dot?"

No reply. No sound at all. No spark of light in the abysmal gloom. "Professor Malcolmson!" I called. And again silence mocked my cry.

I stumbled into the room, lunged toward the door in the opposite wall. The door was closed. Weak with a sick premonition of catastrophe, I seized the knob, twisted, pulled, and released it. The door was locked!

Blind rage throttled my reason for an instant, and I began to pound on the oaken panels with my bare fists and kick savagely at the door with my feet. But it was useless. The portal, I suspected, had been built to resist just such a desperate attack. I turned about and, sagging weakly against the door, faced the blackness of that room of horror.

Then, abruptly, the hair on my scalp bristled. Something which I had not noticed in my first excitement was frightfully manifest to my senses now. That odor—that reek of reptiles and slime—had become stronger in the room!

Was the monster itself, that nameless, bat-like demon, lurking in the darkness of this cursed chamber, waiting to seize me at my first move?

I stood there and I was afraid to breathe. The nails of my fingers were gouging the flesh from my palms; my body seemed to rock under the trip-hammer pounding of my heart. Finally I could stand it no longer; my nerves cracked, and flinging my fists wildly into the empty air, I lunged forward, ready to throw myself on the horny body of the Devil himself.

My feet slithered across the floor with a sibilant scrape, and then suddenly I jerked erect, drew back with a hiss of alarm. One toe had struck something, some soft but heavy body that lay unseen before me on the floor. Weakly, I dropped to my knees, felt out with groping, palsied hands, touched flesh, a shoulder, a throat, a face—touched Dot, lying motionless and cold in the fetid dark . . .

"Dot, Dot!" I called wildly, thrusting an arm beneath her shoulders, trying to lift her. Then I pulled away. An icy wave of despair curdled my blood. Dot's body was still and cold.

With fingers as numb as lumps of wax, I fumbled for a match, struck it, stared with burning eyes at the pallid travesty of her face. It was rigid, a frozen mask of fear, and the eyes, wide, staring, seemed already tinged with the dull patina of death.

She was dead then! And if she were dead I would go mad, here in the clammy darkness with her body! I would be a madman, a raving, senseless think like the Karn woman with her torture-mania.

Then an idea a struck me, sobered me, saved my sanity.

Dot's body could not have stiffened from death in the brief interval since her last cry! She wasn't dead. She was in the grip of some awful spasm.

I didn't know what to do, but I did the only thing I could think of. I massaged her cold limbs, stroked her forehead, and finally the hysterical tension of her muscles loosened, and she came alive with a choked cry.

"Darling, darling," I muttered, gathering her in my arms.

For a long time she lay there, sobbing brokenly. Then she asked: "Where are we, Gil?"

I told her, explained how I had been trapped here, how I had found her in the dark. I did not say that I suspected it was her father who had trapped us. I told her there was nothing to fear. The door, I had noticed, could also be barred on the inside. We would bar it and wait here until morning. Porter Prohawk would surely be here by then.

"But darling," Dot said huskily, "doors and bars won't stop that awful *thing.*"

"What thing?" I asked. "You simply had a nightmare. You ran into this room, and then you fainted."

"A nightmare, yes," she whispered throatily, "but a nightmare that takes on shape and substance, that becomes a real thing. Oh, Gil, I understand it all now, I know what happened to those other girls."

I listened while she told me, and a terrible agony of dread fastened itself on me, like an invisible hand tearing my heart.

She had slept, she said, and the thing had come to her in a dream—the same hideous, nameless shape we had seen in the woods. She had awakened, and the monster had vanished. She had slept again, and once more it had come, and this time it had been harder to shake off the grip of sleep. After that, she had tried not to sleep, had fought it off with agonized prayers. But finally it had claimed her. Then the demon had come, had seized her, dragged her from her bed and carried her off in throttling, leathery arms. She had lost consciousness . . .

For a moment after she had finished, I could say nothing. The ominous words of Brutus Pews were thundering in my brain. "The Incubus! The Incubus!"

"But wasn't it just a dream, sweet? How else can you explain it?"

"I don't know, Gil," Dot answered, "but I know that it was real, as real and tangible as you and I. I think it is something old Febe has brought up by witchcraft and sorcery. That awful Brutus Pews may be helping her, too. I don't know what it is, but I think it seizes our sleeping brains and uses them as a means to materialize, as spirits are said to materialize through the brain and soul of a medium. That's why you must not let me fall asleep. If I do, it will come again. I know it!"

"Try not to think of it," I begged.

"I will; I'll fight the thoughts out of my mind, but you must promise one thing, Gil. Don't let me sleep, don't let me sleep if you have to beat me to keep me awake! Yes! Beat me—to keep me awake!"

I caught my breath. The image of Martha Karn flashed suddenly into my mind. Now I knew the meaning of those pitiful cries, those dreadful pleadings for the sting of the whip, and another frightful picture flashed into my mind: I saw myself standing, like that other man had stood, above Dot's writhing, lovely body, my arm rising and falling . . .

"No, no," I suddenly choked aloud. I would never do that, I swore, anything but that! No matter what!

"Gil, Gil! Oh, God! I dozed for a minute—I saw it!"

"No, no, darling. Where was it?"

"Over there. But it's gone now." She took my hand, pointed with it in the direction of the cave's mouth. "The thing itself is black, but it has a hazy outline like white fire!"

"You imagined it, darling."

"No, I didn't. Don't let me sleep, Gil."

I began to stroke her arms. A cold, unearthly numbness had settled over me. I knew I must not let her sleep.

I shifted my position, gathered her close against my breast and began to slap her gently between the shoulder blades with the flat of my hand. Yet again she dozed, and again awakened with that shrill scream.

"Beat me, harder—harder!"

"Don't let me sleep, Gil!"

I began to strike her harder. She had reached up with one hand and tangled its fingers in her golden hair. I shuddered.

"Let's get up!" I stammered suddenly. "I'll walk you about, keep you moving."

I got her to her feet, and supporting her with my arms, began to walk her back and forth across the floor. Yet even then her head would drop suddenly on her breast, and I would have to shake her, jerk her about, dig my nails into the soft flesh of her arms, to keep her from sleeping.

Then I saw the thing, almost at the instant Dot's head had fallen forward for the sixth time. I had gripped her to shake her, and my eyes had turned in the direction of the cave. My fingers relaxed their hold, and a wild cry of terror burst from my lips as Dot fell to the floor. The fall awakened her. Her scream blended with mine, and as swiftly as it had come, the thing vanished. But I had seen it, had seen the outline of a monstrous, etched in luminous lines, had seen vast wings traced on the darkness, and a hideous horned head in which great burning eyes glowed like pits of fire. And I smelled again the reek of its awful presence.

"Beat me, whip me!" Dot was screaming. "Don't let that thing get me, Gil . . . Don't let it take me in its slimy arms. Quick, quick, I feel myself dozing again, fainting . . ."

I was little more than a madman now.

The hot currents of blood that seemed to surge through my skull, had swept my reason away. Dazedly I unfastened my belt, slid it from its loops, and gripping it by the buckle, stood above her. When she screamed again, I raised my arm, brought down the leather lash. I heard it crack across her flesh, and the hideous sound was like a blow on my eardrums. I suddenly began to shake. I gathered the belt in my hand, flung it to the far corner of the room, and with fists knotted, whirled about in the direction of the cave.

I couldn't do it, I couldn't! Let the monster come! I could grapple with him with my bare hands, die if need be defending Dot, but that other—no!

It came. One moment all was darkness, and then, in that spot which I knew was the cave's mouth, it was standing, in almost unseen, monstrous form fringed with lines of white fire. My throat was dry, my breath was hot in my nostrils as I waited, poised, tense and rigid, above Dot's body. Then, with a rush of fetid air from his great invisible wings, he charged.

I threw myself forward to meet him, with the blind courage of sheer desperation. I struck out with knotted fists, flinging them at the demon's approaching hulk. An awful fetor choked me, the great wings seemed to close around me, suffocate me, and as my knuckles thudded against that hellish body I seemed to feel the bones of my fingers splintering with each futile blow, as they struck, not living flesh, but something horny, leathery, that seemed to ooze a sickening slime.

I ducked my head, butted like a battering ram against the vast weight which was forcing me slowly back. But great arms were flung suddenly about me, gripping me like the coils of a boa.

Wildly I pounded with one free arm until it seemed that my fist was being battered to a pulp. My senses were beginning to swim. With a last desperate jerk I tried to fling myself loose from the crushing embrace. Then something that was like the impact of an exploding shell struck my skull . . .

CHAPTER SIX

NINE DEVILS ARE SUMMONED

I CAME TO MY SENSES with a start. I was lying, belly downward, on the flagged floor. All was dark about me, but in the air I could still smell the reptilian odor of the winged demon.

"Dot!" I called, "Dot!"

There was no answer. I struck a match. Dot was gone; the monster had carried her off in his slimy arms! A wave of sick despair swept over me. Better be dead than face the awful knowledge of her fate. I staggered to my feet. My lungs ached from the terrific pressure of the beast's arms. My head roar and my temples throbbed, as if spikes had been driven into my skull. I ran to the door. It was still locked. I whirled back and faced the empty darkness of the room.

How long had I lain unconscious on the floor? Was there yet any chance to save Dot, even if I could break down the door? I found myself sniffing the loathsome stench that permeated the room. The fact that the smell was still strong in the air indicated that the beast had not been gone long. Another idea followed swiftly on the heels of this thought. The monster had not entered by the door. I knew that. Then he must have come out of the tunnel, through some concealed opening that I had failed to see. The stench of his slime-covered body might lead me to the hidden exit through which he had carried Dot!

I had a few matches left. I struck one of them, to get my bearings, and then plunged toward the opening of the cavern. From there I made my way in the dark, feeling along the clammy walls. The deeper I went into the cave, the stronger became the reptilian odor. I was right; the monster had passed through here. Somewhere, there must be a hidden opening . . .

Reaching the inner crypt where the tunnel widened, I dropped down upon my hands and knees. If there was an opening, I reasoned, it would reach from the floor up, and if the monster had passed through it, he would have left some of his reeking slime about it. Slowly I began crawling about the rudely circular walls, pressing my nose close to the clammy rocks—and sniffing.

I had completed three quarters of my circuit when I stopped, my muscles suddenly stiffening. I had encountered a spot where the reek was frightful. I rubbed the place, and my hand came away smelling too. There could be no doubt that the demon had touched the wall here. I struck a match.

Yellow light flickered out over a large slab of rock half as big as an ordinary door which seemed distinguished in no way from the rest of the walls. I began to run my fingers around it. I came back to the floor again without finding anything. But there my fingers encountered a small crevice half hidden by loose rocks. Thrusting my trembling hand in, I encountered a small knob of iron. I pressed it and stepped back. There was a faint creak of hinges, and when I struck another match I saw that the artificial rock of plaster covered a small wooden door, which had now swung open.

I put the match out quickly. "This fiend from hell," I said to myself, "is no novice at ordinary earthly mechanics." Then silently and with the warmth of fresh hope kindling in my veins, I stooped, passing through the opening, and paused in what was obviously a man-made tunnel.

Quietly, measuring each step with care. I moved along the dark passage. Presently it made a turn, and now ahead of me I detected a narrow wedge of light, as if a door that opened on some lighted chamber were ajar. I began to look for a loose rock which would serve me as a weapon.

I found one and crept on. The acrid smell of incense reached my nostrils now, and I could hear a low buzz of voices.

Slowly, softly, I crept toward the ribbon of light, gripping the jagged rock in one hand. Nearing it, I went down on hands and knees, thrust my head up to the aperture between door and sill. My heart stood still then, hung like a dead weight under my ribs, and I seemed to be hovering on the threshold of another world—the world of witchcraft and black sorcery.

Blue smoke from glowing braziers fogged the hellish scene. Black rocky walls hung with the stuffed bodies of dead creatures—snakes and lizards and bats with membraneous wings—enclosed that pit of infamy. In a chiseled niche in the wall opposite me stood a hideous idol. Its full obscenity is indescribable, but there could be no doubt about the being it represented. With its horned head, fat belly and goat shanks it was horrible in a way that no conventional illustration of Satan can approximate. And kneeling before that ghastly idol in rigid adoration was the girl, Carmina, the daughter of old Febe Megget.

Here was the only figure I could see, but muffled voices drifted to my ears from the parts of the cavern beyond my field of vision. Cautiously I reached out and opened the door a little wider. It was with an effort that I suppressed the cry of sick horror which rose in my throat.

Propped against the opposite wall of the cavern was a huge cross of heavy wood, and bound tightly to its beams was the naked, sagging body of Clay English.

Beneath it on an altar-like slab of rock lay the body of Martha Karn—and bending above it with a gleaming knife in her hand was the horrid witch-woman, Febe Meggett.

I began to stagger up, gripping the jagged rock in a convulsive clutch. Then I stopped, mastering the impulse to rush in and crush the hag's hideous skull. There were others in the cave, and Dot perhaps was in there too. Martha Karn was obviously dead; so was Clay English. Nothing could be done to help them now.

I held my breath. The hag had begun to chant. Waving her arms so that the sleeves of her long black gown flapped like the wings of some obscene bird of prey, she intoned:

"Furies, demons, ghosts of the bloodless dead, I do conjure you by the blasphemed names of Tetramagrammaton and Adonay, Alga and Saday and Planaboth to attend and witness the blood offering of our new daughter, who comes to worship at the ancient shrine. And by the great maledictions of *Sathanas* I summon the devils of the nine orders—*Pseudothei, Mendariorwm, Iniquitatis,* Revengers, Prestidigitators, Ariel powers, Furies, Criminators and Temptors. Arise and drink!"

She finished, and like a striking falcon the knife descended. I saw the smoke from the braziers dart licking tongues over the ghastly sacrifice. I saw the blood run crimson over the gleaming body of the girl. Then I hid my eyes, retching with nausea.

When I lifted my head again, it was to see the hag standing with hands extended over the mutilated corpse. In one hand she held the gory heart, which had been torn from the girl's breast, and in the other a goblet that glittered with the ruby hue of blood.

"Come!" she was saying softly. "Come! You must bear the sacrifice to the Black One's altar!"

To whom was the hag speaking? She seemed to be addressing someone on the opposite side of the cavern, someone who was not visible from where I lay.

"Come!" the hag repeated.

Into my field of vision a figure drifted, the figure of a woman, naked save for a scarlet loincloth. Golden hair streamed over her ivory shoulders. She walked stiffly, her small hands clinching and unclinching, the pale oval of her face distorted to a mask of inexpressible agony.

A red mist of madness swam before my eyes, and the joints of my limbs seemed to dissolve. For that woman, moving with agonizing steps toward the waiting sorceress, was Dot!

I staggered to my feet, stood gripping the edge of the door, while the horrid scene rocked and reeled before me like the images of a nightmare. For moments I did not have the power to move, and locked in that ghastly paralysis I watched that awful rite begin.

Now Dot was taking the horrid objects from the woman's extended hands, and now she was moving back across the cavern, back toward the black idol beneath which the girl, Carmina, was still bending. There she paused, and with a hand that suddenly began to shake she lifted the goblet toward the idol's gaping mouth.

"Steady. Hold it!"

That sharp command, uttered in a man's voice, had come from somewhere near me, from somewhere along the wall of the cavern to my right.

At the words I saw Dot stiffen. Some of the blood from the goblet spilled, fell down upon the gleaming body of the girl kneeling below her, which at once began to twitch with convulsive shudders.

"Steady now—not a move!" the man's voice rang out again. "Turn your head this way. Smile! Smile, damn you! I'm holding a knife to your father's throat, and if you don't . . ."

God in Heaven! I suddenly understood by what fiendish means they were forcing Dot to join in these hellish rites of devil worship. But who was the witch's accomplice, and why—?

The thought was never finished. For suddenly there was a hissing explosion in the room and a blinding flare of light. I heard Dot shriek, I saw her body collapse limply before the unholy altar, and in the next instant I was plunging madly into the smoke-fogged cavern.

Chaos followed. I saw the witch-woman leap toward me with a knife, howling with rage. Ducking to avoid the sweeping arc of the gleaming blade, I struck at her with a rock as she floundered past me. She fell sideways, and I whirled about. Something with the power of a plunging piston struck the side of my head, sent me reeling against the wall. As I straightened, I recognized the monstrous black shape hurtling toward me. It was the bat-creature. With all my strength I hurled a rock at his hideous head.

It missed, and the next instant he was upon me.

I fought with the desperation of madness; I fought with every remaining ounce of my failing strength—but I was beaten from the first. The blows I rained wildly against the armored hulk of the monster's body beat him back momentarily, but injured him not at all. He pressed me back inexorably, clinching with me, throttling me with the pressure of those vice-like arms, Then the hag, who had scrambled up from the floor, threw herself into the fray. She leaped upon my back, clung there like a screeching monkey, while her taloned hands clawed at my throat.

I went down, stunned, crushed, half-strangled, and my brain was shrieking as in a last delirium. "This is the end, the end, the end . . .!"

CHAPTER SEVEN

WHEN THE CROSS FELL

IT WASN'T THE END—not quite. As they dragged me, limp and half conscious, across the cavern floor, lifted my sagging body and bound me with coils of rope to the foot of the cross where the dead man hung, I knew they were reserving me for further tortures.

Lifting my aching head, I stared dully about the cavern. Now that there was no longer any hope, a sort of detached curiosity seized me. What was the bottom of the hellish scheme? For there was certainly a man beneath the weird bat-costume, which I could see was cleverly made of leather and alligator skin, and smeared with luminous paint. A *human* monster lurked beneath that disguise. But there was a method in his madness.

I watched him now. He was standing beside a large photographer's camera—the same one I had seen in Professor Malcolmson's study. The witch-woman and her daughter stood beside him. The batman was removing a plate. "This will be quite enough," he said to the woman. "I'm going to see how it comes out. When I get back I'll finish off the girl's lover and the old man." Carrying the plate, he then turned and left the cavern by the entrance through which I had come.

What did it mean? The fiend had forced Dot through that ghastly ritual, and he had forced her to pose with a smile on her lips in an attitude of worship before the altar of Satan. Then he had photographed her. What would he do with her now?

The witch-woman and her daughter moved aside, and I now saw the bound figure of the old professor lying on the ground beyond the camera. The fiend had promised to come back, to kill him and to kill me. And who was this fiend with the big body and the deep voice? I remembered the man who had stood by the camera in the professor's room, the man who had made the photograph which I now knew was faked. And Malcolmson had let that man dupe him, overcome him, finally murder him—the man he had called a religious fanatic—Brutus Pews!

Suddenly I began to struggle against the ropes. God, God! If I could only manage to escape while the fiend was gone. Dot was still alive, and I noticed another entrance to the tunnel. It yawned in the shadowy all to my left. It probably led out into the open hills. If I could only free myself, I could beat these women off, seize Dot in my arms, and carry her into the sweet, free air of safety!

But the rope was tightly wound about my body. I heaved and struggled until the sweat ran from my burning brow, yet they held me. It was maddening, doubly so because I could see that easy avenue of escape, and yet must know that I would never reach it. I would die here a helpless animal, leaving Dot behind me to the brutal uses of that hideous bearded madman who had planned this hell on earth!

With my head twisted about, I stared at the black hole which was the cave's outer opening, stared at it as a dying man marooned on a desert island must watch a vanishing sail fade on the horizon

Suddenly, with a queer gurgling gasp in my throat, I saw something move in that spot of darkness. Chills prickled my body. Had I imagined it, was this the delirium of approaching death? No! It was the head and shoulders of a man, a man crawling slowly out of the darkness toward the lighted cavern.

My glance was glued to that slowly emerging head with a hypnotic fixity, while a wild hysteria of incredible joy shrieked through the boiling channels of my blood. A ray of light had fallen for a moment on that face—a square jawed face, bronzed, powerful, and on that thatch of greying hair and on the steel-grey eyes that stared intently ahead.

The man was Porter Prohawk! Porter Prohawk had not failed us! He had realized that something must have happened to us and had come himself to save us.

I turned my eyes back into the cavern. The old hag and her daughter were bending over Dot's prostrate form. I realized that I must do something to help our deliverer, must catch the attention of the two witch-women, so they would not see him. I suddenly began to babble. I called out to the women, curse them in the most hideous terms I could imagine.

They looked up at me. The old hag cursed me, ordered me to be silent. I redoubled my abuse. With a snarl, she picked up a knife and came slithering toward me across the cavern.

Had I gone too far? Wild terror gripped me as I saw the approach of the gleaming blade. Would Pro hawk be able to stop her? She was almost upon me now, the knife lifted to plunge with one swift stroke into my breast. And then it happened. The sharp crack of a pistol rang out from the tunnel. With a choked cry the old hag collapsed, fell face downward on the floor.

The girl Carmina shrieked, then started in a wild run for the other exit. But again the report of the pistol rang out, and she fell in a limp huddle, drilled through the head.

I felt no pity for either of them, only a surge of savage joy that fate had at last tripped these two. Prohawk knew how to deal with such creatures.

"Thank God!" I gasped. "You didn't get here a moment too soon. How did you find this place?"

"When I saw that the house was deserted," he replied, "I knew that something foul was afoot. I suspected that Febe Megget and her daughter had a cave somewhere for their witchcraft, so I searched—and found it."

He stalked over to where Dot lay and lifted her in his arms.

"Dot, Dot," he called to her softly.

She opened her eyes and a look of relief flooded her face. "Oh!" she cried. "It's you, Mr. Prohawk! Where's Gil?"

"He's here," Prohawk said.

"Quick!" I called to him. "You'd better free the professor and me, before Pews gets back."

He looked at me, frowning. "Pews?"

"Of course. Brutus Pews. He's the fiend at the bottom of it all."

Prohawk jerked up straight, still holding Dot in his arms. "Right," he snapped. "I'll carry Dot outside to safety and come right back." He left quickly, moving with determination.

I was shaking now, shaking in every limb and muscle. My throat seemed full of hot sand; my eyes burned, my heart pounded like a beaten tom-tom. I was praying, praying wildly that Pews would not return before Prohawk did.

And then, with a black rigor of despair stiffening my body, I saw the door of the inner tunnel begin to open, saw Brutus Pews, dressed now in his cassock, come slowly into the room, a black automatic in his hand.

Swiftly, on whispering bare feet, Pews came toward me. A moment he paused before the cross to which I was tied, and looked at me with his wild black eyes. Then he executed a sudden turn and faced the second tunnel. My heart sank. In the doorway stood Porter Prohawk.

Prohawk fired first, but Pews ducked, and the bullet whistled past him. Then his automatic spoke in a rapid staccato, and I saw Prohawk pitch to the floor, clutching at his left shoulder.

A wave of blackness swallowed me, and when it washed away I saw Pews still standing in the same spot, staring about over the carnage in the cavern. An inspiration came to me then. There was yet a chance to save Dot. It would probably mean the loss of my own life, but I did not care so long as I would be able to carry Pews down with me to death. If I could summon the strength to lunge forward, to tilt this heavy cross away from the wall, to let it fall forward, it would strike Pews on the head . . .

Almost simultaneously with this very thought, I acted. Heaving out with bunched muscles, I felt the cross lift, move away from the wall.

Pews made a wild half turn, and for an instant I saw the look of fear on his face. Then the shock of the cross as it fell knocked me out . . .

I opened my eyes, startled to discover that I was not dead. The cross was above me now, and as I twisted my head up and about, I saw the reason that I had not been killed. The falling cross had borne Pews down to the floor, and it was his motionless body which supported the weight of the huge beam and had prevented its crushing me to death.

Suddenly I noticed the knife which had fallen from the witch-woman's hand. With an effort, I forced my hands farther out from the ropes that encircled me and grasped it. Then frantically I began to cut at the encircling bonds.

Where was Prohawk? I stared toward the tunnel as I worked, and saw that he was no longer where he had lain.

The ropes fell away; I dragged my aching body out from beneath the beam, straightened, staring with horror.

Porter Prohawk was still in the cavern; he was standing above the trussed body of old Professor Malcolmson. But the thing that sent tremors of madness through my brain was that he was pointing the revolver at my heart!

"Stand where you are!" he ordered. Prohawk laughed then. "You fool," he said. "Haven't you guessed it yet? Well, I suppose I'll have to tell you, before I kill you, as your reward for getting that meddling hillbilly out of the way."

He told me then, told me coldly and with pride, the whole hideous scheme which his twisted mind had evolved, and I saw how incipient madness had gradually ruined the man's fine brain.

He had earned his wealth by the sweat of his brow, and lost it in the Wall Street collapse. He had swallowed his defeat and sworn vengeance on the financiers who, he believed, had robbed him. With what he could salvage from the wreck of his fortune, he had founded the girls' seminary as the basis of a blackmail scheme of gigantic proportions. His school would cater only to the daughters of the cultured and the wealthy. He hired the most celebrated teachers and then, when he engaged Professor Malcolmson and learned of the strange book he was working on, he had seen a practical plan for his villainy.

In his mining days Prohawk had known the witch-woman, Febe Megget. Now he brought her into his scheme, purchased Stonehenge and gave it to her. Then he brought Professor Malcolmson, persuaded him that it would be a good place for his researches. The rest had been easy. The old Professor had acted as the innocent tool of Prohawk's fiendishness, luring the girls here, upsetting their minds. Then he, Prohawk, in the bat costume, smeared with snake oil, would seize them in the night, bring them to the witch's cave and force them to indulge in the most hideous orgies, of which he would preserve photographs. With these awful photographs, he kept his hold on the nervously wrecked girls, insured their silence, and black-mailed them until, like Rosa Warren and Stell Bickley, they took the easiest way out.

"But," I pointed out, "you certainly can't go on with it any longer."

"No," he told me, "I have decided now to marry and settle down. I went a little too far with the Karn girl, you see. She was completely crazed. I knew I couldn't release her, and murder would halt my plans. So I decided to end the whole thing and wipe the slate clean. I hurried. back to town and sent you and Dorothy out here. I determined to kill every one of you but Dorothy and make it look like Malcolmson had done it."

"As soon as you left my office this morning, I hurried out here by a shortcut. I murdered the mountaineer's daughter because she had learned too much. I hung her body from the pine limb and waited for you to motor by."

Then, he jerked the pistol about and shot Professor Malcolmson through the head.

Before I could move the gun was trained on me again.

I looked into the face of death then, began grabbing frantically for any straw to hold him off a few more moments.

"But look here," I stammered, "you can't get by with it. Dot will brand you as a fiend."

"Oh no," said Prohawk with a laugh, "that's the beauty of my plan. Dorothy is now safe in the house. She believes that I rescued her from the fiend Pews. I deliberately planned that rescue. She will be grateful to me, and with you out of the way, she will learn to love me. I will go back to her now and tell her that Pews killed both you and her father, and then I then killed him."

It was the end! But I was still holding the knife, and I was determined to die fighting. I stared wildly about the room. Then a movement caught my eye. It was Brutus Pews. One of his hands was snaking slowly out to reach the pistol which he had dropped. But I looked at him too long. Prohawk saw me and understood. He took a swift step toward Pews and trained the gun on his head.

I knew then that this was the only chance I would ever have, so I sprang.

That fight taught me that a pistol has its disadvantages in a hand-to-hand struggle. I didn't know it before, and I was just taking a chance when I made that attack. But Prohawk was startled and before he could whirl the pistol muzzle from Pews to me, I was inside his reach.

The pistol went off but it went off over my shoulder. I was already within arm's length of Prohawk then, and the knife in my hand was busy.

As soon as I knew that he was dead, I turned quickly away from the horror of his bloody corpse and began helping Pews from the cave.

We found Dot safe and sound, waiting at the house. It was a terrible task explaining to her, but with Pews' help I got it over and we drove to the city.

Pews was a help, too, when it came to explaining things to the police. Though suffering from a broken shoulder, he had been conscious all the time in the cave, and had been waiting for his chance. He had heard Prohawk's confession in full. He said that rumors of witchcraft had attracted him to that part of the hills months before, and he had been trying to track down the culprits. He had of course suspected Malcolmson at first, just as I had done. He had faked the "spirit photo" to see the old man's reaction to it, and had then decided that Malcolmson was not guilty. The fact that I had left the secret door in the cave open had enabled him to come to us.

That's all, except that Dot and I are supremely happy. That awful night is, of course, a black spot in our memories, and we avoid thinking of it. But sometimes I believe that the horrors we experienced there together in those dreadful hours welded the links of our love even stronger, forged bands of steel about our hearts that nothing in all the world will ever break.

GALLERY

OF THE

DAMNED

CHAPTER ONE

THIRTY PIECES OF SILVER

THERE WERE SIX OF US IN THE ROOM—six men and the dead thing that had been a man. There was something else in that room too—terror! *Terror*—no longer an abstraction, but a live thing that coiled under the diaphragm and sucked the heart and courage from a man. We didn't look at each other's eyes.

Herman Tyrone was there. He was the City Librarian, and my boss, and they had called him in on the case for reasons which weren't yet entirely clear. Chief of Police Lee Teed was there, and Mayor Blythe, and Police Commissioner Gregg Savage, and a big hulking figure in the doorway—Sergeant Veal—whom you'd have thought a massacre wouldn't shock, but who now looked like a fat kid who's eaten too many green apples.

The dusk hung like a fuzzy blanket against the window, and a few discouraged snowflakes fluttered past against the greyness. I looked out over the soot-fouled roofs of tenements, over mucky courtyards splotched with leprous patches of dirty snow, and I saw the long chalk smudge of the viaduct with its fleet sparks of light flashing and vanishing. And I seemed to see the intangible some-thing that brooded in the room become huge and monstrous, ex-tending the shadow of its vulture wings over a whole city, where from behind locked doors men scuttled furtively at a newsboy's wailing cry. *"Mutilated Body Found. . . . Death Fiends Invent New Horror. . . ."* And there was wonder and terror on stricken, bewil-dered faces.

These things went through my mind because I had turned away, leaned on the sill, stared out. There had been a convulsive jerking of the muscles of my abdomen that reached to my throat, and I hadn't wanted to be sick in front of the others. Now I turned back.

Nobody had changed his position and nobody had said any-thing. They looked at the thing on the door. The man's body was naked, lean. The nails had been driven through his wrists, and tongues of dry brownish blood ran down the forearms. The head hung sideways, resting against one shoulder bone. Pressed down tightly over the forehead was a curious wreath that seemed to be made of the thorny stems of a rose bush, and in one side of the lank body there was a hole with blackened edges, and dry gore, like candle drippings under it. A blunt pointed-poker lay on the floor beneath the dangling feet, and it had made the hole.

Chief Teed turned slowly about, swept the sordid room with his eyes. Then he reached up and turned off the light.

"Let's go," he said in a husky undertone.

Two policemen were pacing up and down in the hall. We passed them, clumped down the steps, got into a police car at the front and were whisked swiftly through the shuttling currents of traffic to police headquarters. We got out and went into the big grey building with its warm, depot smell. We went into the Chief's private office and slumped into chairs, and some of us lighted cigarettes. And still nobody talked.

Lee Teed didn't sit down. He paced the room, his hands knot-ted behind him. Police Commissioner Gregg Savage, fat-jowled, fishy-eyed, sat slumped across the table working a thick, blunt cigar from one corner of his mouth to the other. The tall, thin mayor drummed the table with his fingers. Only Herman Tyrone's long, wrinkled, intellectual face showed any composure. He puffed a cigarette and eyed the others with sardonic detachment.

"Well," Chief Teed said, with a sudden hoarse grunt, "go bring him in, Veal."

Veal left the room.

"I suppose," Herman Tyrone said in his dry, scholarly voice, "that you're now going to show me the author of this charming fantasy we've just seen."

Teed stopped. "For God's sake, Tyrone," he growled, "this is no time to joke. It's for the sake of the city that I'm asking you to help us. We should forget political animosities at a time like this."

"I'm no detective," Tyrone said.

"I've got detectives," Teed moaned, "plenty of them. But this isn't routine stuff. It's bigger than individual cases; it's something hellish. A special sort of knowledge is required to grasp the clue to these horrors. You know something about abnormal psychology, about history. You're a scholar, a—"

"A librarian," Tyrone said with mellow bitterness.

Teed only scowled: Savage cleared his throat.

"But if you've caught the fiend—" Tyrone began.

"The fiend! Great God in heaven! There are I don't know how many fiends! And they're not men, they're robots. Why this rat, this poor demented shell of a man we caught—" He seemed unable to finish.

"What about him?" Tyrone prompted matter-of-factly.

"Why, he was trying to hang himself," Teed sputtered. "We ran him down in East Blenden cemetery. He was trying to hang himself to a tree limb, and," he added in a husky whisper, "in one hand he was clutching thirty dimes!"

"Thirty dimes—thirty pieces of silver!" I blurted the words unintentionally. My scalp was crawling, stung by little needles of ice.

Herman Tyrone sat forward with sudden interest. "Why did he do it?" he asked.

"How do I know?" Teed moaned. "You've got to help us find out. The psychiatrists say he's not crazy—not in the usual sense. It's something—something more like devil-possession!"

Just then the door opened and we all turned. I think if the man Veal was pushing into the room had been a big ape-like creature the shock would have been less. There was something horrible about the man's insignificance. He was ragged and rat-like, with a huge nose dominating a wizened swarthy face that now had the pale cast of a cadaver. His hair was crinkled and reddish and a ragged fringe of the same color ran along his jaw and chin. He seemed afraid and yet not afraid. It was queer. It was as if the man felt his own insignificance and yet at the same time was conscious of some inner power that made him gigantic and monstrous and beyond the reach of mere men. I couldn't puzzle it out.

Veal shoved the man into a chair, and he sat there and goggled at us as if he were only half conscious.

"What's your name?" Tweed barked at him.

"Issicar—J. Issicar," the rat-like creature said throatily.

"You never did anything like this before?"

"No."

"Why did you kill John Cranston—crucify him?"

"I had to. It was my destiny."

"He was your friend wasn't he? Lived with you? What did you have against him?"

"Nothing. He was my friend. But I had to kill him."

"Who told you to do it?"

"Nobody told me to."

Teed stepped toward him with a growl, shook a knotted fist before his eyes. "You're lying! Somebody told you to do it. If you don't want the hell shellacked out of you, you'd better talk. Who told you to do it?"

The derelict dropped his eyes. "Nobody told me to do it; but I was paid."

"You were paid? What do you mean? Who paid you?"

"The old man with the black beard," Issicar croaked.

"What about him?"

"It was last night," Issicar said, frowning as one who remembers something half forgotten. "I had been thinking for several days that I was going to have to kill Cranston. I don't know why; I just knew it. Then, as I was going up to our room the old man with the black beard came shuffling along. He didn't say a thing, just handed me a little package and shuffled off. I opened it; it had thirty dimes in it. Thirty pieces of silver, you see. I went up to the room. I knew what I had to do. Cranston was sick, in bed. I sat by the bed and looked at him. I had one hand in my pocket, feeling the thirty dimes. Sudden like, he looked at me with a scared look. Then he said, just like he'd read my mind: 'Well if you're going to do it, do it quick.' I leaped on top of him then, got my fingers around his throat. After he was dead I nailed him to the door."

For a full minute I think no one in the room breathed. Then Gregg Savage, puffing out his fat cheeks, exploded, "Jesus Christ?"

The words had a strange effect. Issicar rose from his chair as if jerked by invisible wires, and a scream—the most bloodcurdling scream I had ever heard—jangled from his loose lips where foam had suddenly gathered. The scream knifed into our ears, swallowing up the dull rumble of traffic, swallowing up everything in a hot explosion of horror. Then, before Veal could catch him, Issicar fell face forward to the floor and lay there in a stiff spasm. When Veal rolled him over his eyes were open and he was breathing, but he was as stiff as a corpse. Blood from a bitten tongue ran out one corner of his mouth and mingled with the froth of foam. They had to carry him from the room.

CHAPTER TWO

FIGURES OF HELL'S HISTORY

My hands on the arms of my chair were shaking. I'd never had anything effect me quite like that before. There was something about it that my mind shrank from, as if the meaning behind the incident was so awful that a man wouldn't want to learn it, wouldn't want to guess even.

Herman Tyrone was on his feet now, frowning soberly. "J. Issicar," he said softly. "The very name is horribly significant. Judas Iscariot. The man believes he *is* Judas Iscariot!"

"I figured that," Teed said. "But the others—"

"You've caught others?" Tyrone asked.

"One other," Teed said. "But he's in the morgue—stabbed himself. I've tried to keep it quiet; there's enough panic already. And the people blame *us* because we can't give them an explanation . . ."

"What about this suicide?" Tyrone asked.

Teed swallowed. "It's crazier even than Issicar's case," he said. "This fellow was a fruit-truck driver. Nothing peculiar about him before. About a week ago he started going crazy. First he tortured animals. Then he tried to kill his old mother, but she escaped him, went away. His wife was afraid to tell the police because he threatened to kill her if she did. Well, he got the idea that he'd really killed his mother, boasted about it to his wife. Next he set fire to his house and danced and sang and tried to keep his wife from putting the blaze out. But she managed to do it anyhow. Then Luigi Domitius—that was his name—began to talk of killing himself. He'd awake shrieking in the night that swarms of flying ants were on him, and other crazy things. Finally he ran out to a shed behind the place and hid there, thinking the police were after him. His wife followed him and he pulled out his knife and forced her to dig a grave in the floor. While she was doing it, he sobbed and cried, 'What an artist is about to die!' and told her to bury him there and keep the grave a secret. The wife says he started to stab himself several times but didn't seem to have the nerve. It wasn't until the police, called by the neighbors, beat on the doors of the shed that he finally stabbed himself in the throat. Now what in God's name do you make of that?"

Tyrone had been listening intently. Now he cleared his throat. "I think I can tell you what obsession was preying on the man's mind," he replied. "The details give it away to anyone familiar with Roman history. The man's attempted murder of his mother, his trying to burn the building, the dreams of ant swarms, the flight and hiding and forcing another to dig his grave, the very words of his cry, his cowardly hesitancy and his final stabbing himself in the throat, are all exact details from the life and death of Nero! I might mention too that Nero's original name was L. Domitius Ahenobarus."

Teed turned a wan smile on the sour face of the police commissioner. "Didn't I tell you, Savage? Didn't I say Tyrone was the man we needed?"

Savage grunted. "But how in the hell," he asked, "would an ignorant truck driver know those facts about Nero?"

"That's the point!" Teed said, turning to Tyrone. "There's a detail I left out. The man's wife said that he had been reading a lot lately—something he had never done before. She didn't know where the books came from, and since he had burned them, we couldn't tell. But that's where you can help us, Tyrone. That sort of people don't have money to buy books. They get them from the public library. Now it's up to you to watch for that type of people who come in and get books on some particular historical character. See?"

"I see," Tyrone said. "It may be worth trying. But has it ever occurred to you that if there's a connection between these cases it would indicate some master mind behind it all. And if that's true, *he* would furnish the books without resorting to the library."

"Mind behind it all!" Teed echoed with annoyance. "Sure there's a mind behind it—the devil in hell!"

"Perhaps," Tyrone said quietly. "Is that all for tonight?"

"That's all," Teed answered gruffly.

Tyrone bowed shortly, picked up his hat and topcoat, and we left.

A biting wind blew down the canyons of the street and thin snowflakes danced in the bleary glare of the street lamps. There was a haunted look on the faces of passers-by. My thoughts were heavy clotted things, moving slowly in a cold vacuum of dread.

For no reason at all I had begun to worry about Frances— Frances Mormar, the girl I loved, the girl I hoped to marry soon if the new city administration didn't blight our plans by kicking us all out of jobs. Frances was Tyrone's secretary, and when we had left her in the warm lighted office on the top floor of the big public library building she had promised to wait there for me. Yet the dread of what I had seen and heard had crawled like a poisonous worm into my vitals. I was worried about Frances and I couldn't say why.

Tyrone's words broke in upon my thoughts in a hoarse heavy growl. Alone with me he had dropped his scholarly reserve. "Why," he muttered, "have that bunch of crooks called me in on this? They know I hate them, know I fought their election with all the influence I have. They're going to kick me out just as soon as they can. Why have they asked me to help them?"

"Because," I suggested, "Teed and Savage and the rest are incompetent and they know it. They're new in office and afraid of public opinion. They're scared to death they won't get this murder epidemic stopped before the people are up in arms against them. They *need* your help!"

"I wonder," Tyrone grumbled. "I wonder if some of than are not mixed up in it themselves. Maybe Sam Wembly can figure it out."

Sam Wembly was the editor of *The Clarion,* a small newspaper which had fought bitterly to prevent the election of the present city administration. He and Tyrone were close friends, and Tyrone had written many of the paper's editorials anonymously. I wasn't surprised then, when we came into Tyrone's outer office, to find Sam Wembly waiting there.

Tyrone greeted him laconically and slumped down in a chair. I hurried into the inner office. The light was burning, but Frances wasn't there. It scared me a little, but then I was sure that she must have stepped downstairs to the book rooms. I went back through the room where Tyrone and Wembly were talking and hurried downstairs. But none of the girls at the desks had seen Frances. I searched the whole building, and a crazy wave of hysteria was mounting to my head. No one had seen Frances. She must have gone out by the side door from the offices, they told me with wondering looks at my haggard face.

I went back to the office. "Frances is gone!" I blurted, breaking in on Tyrone's conversation.

"Well," he said, looking up, "she's not paid to stay here all night."

"But she promised—" I began. Then I dived into the inner office again. My breathing seemed curiously constricted. I stared about vacuously. Then, in her chair, I saw the envelope with my name written on it. I snatched it up and tore it open almost with one gesture. Then I gasped. The note read:

Dear Guy:

Thanks for the book? But what a queer way to give me a present, and what a queer subject to choose! I'm both puzzled and interested, so I'm going home to read. You can drop by there if you like.

Frances

I stared at the thing like an idiot, and suddenly noticed that the paper was fluttering in my shaking hand. What in God's name did it mean? Books—present? I hadn't sent or given her any books. Books! God in heaven! Books had come mysteriously into the hands of that madman too!

Still holding the note I dashed back through the door into the outer office. I stood there dazed, dumb as a stunned ox, waiting for a break in the conversation. Tyrone was saying:

". . . so it wouldn't surprise me, Sam, if the whole thing is a frame-up—a clay pigeon for the new officials to shoot at. Teed, of course, wouldn't have the imagination for such a scheme, but Blythe has and Savage has. The idea would be first to start a panic and then show off the efficiency of the police department in squashing it. At the same time they'll get the public attention away from the gambling racket they're probably mixed up in, and which they've had to make a pretense of fighting."

"Mr. Tyrone!" I sputtered. What did I care about the damned administration and its schemes now? What was important except that Frances was in danger?

"What is it, Guy?" Tyrone asked, looking up with annoyance.

"Look here," I choked. I was beside him in two steps, shoving the fluttering paper into his hands.

He read it. "Well?" he asked, puzzled.

"But I didn't give her any books!" I stammered wildly. "I didn't . . . don't you see, she's got a bunch of books . . . like that maniac got. Somebody's . . ." the words choked off in a throat dry with the dust of terror.

Tyrone stiffened, frowned, stared at the paper again. "By God!" he swore, "if that damned bunch is trying to mix that girl up in this hellish—" he checked himself. Something in my terrified face must have excited his pity, and he finished, "But maybe we're wrong, Guy. Better hurry out to her place at once, though, and make sure."

I grabbed up my hat and was gone.

I got my roadster out of the parking lot behind the library building and swung it into the slippery, fast-freezing slush of the street. I managed to navigate the choked traffic lanes without accident, and once beyond the district of signal lights, swerved west over the viaduct and roared at a criminal speed up Brant Avenue to the old red brick apartment house where Frances lived. Slamming on my brakes in front of the place, I skidded the car to a stop and clambered out.

Pounding up the steps at a half run, I chanted wild prayers in an undertone. Surely she's here; she's got to be here! I reached her door, knocked, then hammered frantically, already sending something ominous in the silence that was the only response.

"Frances!" I called hoarsely. "Frances!"

No answer. But down the hall a door opened, a woman's scowling fat face was thrust out. It was Mrs. Polk, the landlady.

"Oh, it's you," she said. "Miss Frances just went out."

"Then she *was* here?" I asked fatuously.

"Yes. She's just been gone about fifteen minutes."

"And she didn't leave any message for me?"

"Not that I know of."

"Thanks," I muttered hollowly. Then, with a sudden idea: "I want your pass key. I've got to get into her room. It's important."

Mrs. Polk was doubtful about the propriety of this, but she finally acceded. She knew how things stood between Frances and me and I guess she too was a little alarmed at my anxiety. She gave me the key and I went into the room.

I closed the door behind me, switched on the light and stood there with my heart pounding. How awful, how empty, how terrifying even, the place seemed without Frances. I went into the bedroom and the kitchenette, just to make sure. Then I came back into the front room and bit my lip in silent agony.

Something must certainly be wrong; Frances wouldn't have acted this way unless something was wrong! Then I caught sight of the pile of books on one end of the divan.

I stepped over and snatched up the first one in my hand. It was a new book, obviously fresh from the shelves of a shop, and the title burned itself into my fogged mind:

"The Life of Madame de Montespan."

Madame de Montespan! . . . the courtesan mistress of Louis XIV, that passionate, unbalanced woman whom jealousy had driven to mad and secret depths of depravity! That lovely she-devil about whose life dark traditions cluster, initiate of the shameful secrets of sorcery and Satanism!

I snatched up the other books, glanced at each and flung it to the floor with a curse. They were all on the same subject, and all, I noticed, were books that stressed the evil and erotic side of the enigmatical woman's character.

These were the books I was supposed to have given Frances! Who had sent them; what did it mean? My brain reeled before the awful and inescapable answer to that question. Some fiend, some monster whose powers were more than human, had snatched an awful secret from the arcana of hell, and was twisting in his dark hands the helpless souls of men and women. And this devil, this *abomination,* had picked Frances for a victim, had begun the awful process which would transform her into something not human, into a mindless robot parading in the borrowed garments of a dead personality!

It sounded wild, it sounded crazy, but I knew that it was true. Rage misted my eyes with a red fog; the wolves of horror gnawed my entrails.

Teeth gritted, fists knotted, I started to turn away. Then I stopped. A small square of paper which had fallen from between the leaves of one of the books attracted my eye. I stooped and picked it up. The thing was a printed circular. "Peace Out of Chaos," read the heading, and underneath was the message:

"In the midst of doubts, seek the peace offered by the ancient religions of the East. Seek the true path of Knowledge as embodied in the teachings of Swami Atmananad at THE SHRINE OF KARMA—2164 Railroad Street."

An oath whistled drily between my teeth. Light had dawned on my mind like a bursting bombshell. Through sheer accident I had stumbled on a clue which all the others had missed. The Shrine of Karma! Why hadn't I thought of that place? That old crumbling warehouse by the railroad tracks where a turbaned Hindu spoke nightly to a throng of ill-smelling bums, gathered there to escape the cold and forced to listen to the doctrines of that strange cult of reincarnation—the transmigration of the soul!

Suddenly I whirled about, crumpling the circular in my hand. I switched off the light, slammed the door and went down the steps three at a time. If Frances had gone there I would find her, and I would break the lean Swami in my two hands, force the truth from him! Yet fear, gaunt and grisly, ran at my heels.

Was I already too late to save Frances?

CHAPTER THREE

OFFERING OF THE SABBAT

THE PAVEMENT OF THE AVENUE was as slick as greased skids and through the fogged windshield the clustered lights of the city danced like drunken fireflies as the car skidded and lurched precariously through the dark.

I remember it, but I scarcely noticed it at the time. It seemed that I couldn't think of anything but Frances, of the crazy, unbelievable peril that hung over her. Frances, with her soft grey eyes that were always shining bravely, her hair that was the color of honey with sunlight in it, her trim little figure that I watched for eagerly every morning of the world from the window of my office. I thought of a thousand little insignificant things, like the way a shadow would lie in the hollow of her throat and the way she cocked her head to one side when she laughed.

Then I got a hold on myself, forced myself to think. I remembered Tyrone's words that I'd overheard there in the office, and I wondered if he could be right. Mayor Ely I knew for one of those adventurous, imaginative politicians who can get by with murder, and Commissioner Savage and the rest of his crew were a cunning and enterprising bunch. Would they go this far? Why not? And calling Tyrone in on the case would be a clever way of blinding a dangerous foe.

And what about Frances? In the back of my brain that thought kept hammering like a plunging piston. I'll pull her out of their clutches, I told myself. You can't kill a soul in an hour and replace it with another, for all the vaunted secrets of the East. It takes time. They took time with those broken wretches they made monsters of.

I swung the car into a dank street of soot-smudged buildings and headed toward the railroad yards. The old warehouse loomed ahead now, its dirty windows gleaming a sickly yellow through the frosted windshield. A few cars were parked in front. I nosed up among them and got out.

The big double doors were closed tight against the cold, and as I pushed in, waves of foul, sweat-scented warmth swam around me and a vast murmur of voices buzzed against my ears. The place was crowded. The grey, nondescript man-swarm filled the rows of pine benches, squatted in the aisles, leaned against the walls, huddled around the two big-bellied coal stoves on either side of the hall. The glare from a few weak electric bulbs made a pale pretense of light, smeared ashy stubble-dark faces with a yellow sheen, pooled shadows in cavernous eye hollows. At the far end of the hall was a raised section of flooring with the remains of a broken rail, which had probably once been used for office space. Two sides of it were curtained off, leaving an open stage in the center. I moved nearer, stood near the back row of benches. Suddenly, with a queer, uncomfortable feeling, I sensed watching eyes. Not the casual glances thrown at me as I moved forward, but some secret and intent scrutiny. I glanced quickly to the left. A head turned swiftly away from my glance, a thickset heavy head, resting like a bucket on square shoulders.

The man was on the back seat. Coarse black hair covered his head and thick whiskers masked the lower part of his face. But I studied his profile—the nose, the ear, the peculiar up-flare of the left eyebrow, and in a flash recognition dawned. Under the too-luxuriant whiskers was the face of Gregg Savage, the Police Commissioner!

Why was he here? Investigating? Maybe. And maybe for some other reason, some darker purpose.

I looked up. The buzz of voices had subsided abruptly, dwindled to silence. A figure had appeared on the stage, a figure dressed in a long orange-colored tunic. Bare brown legs terminated in flat sandals, and the lean figure moved out from the wings with an elastic, pantherish stride that bespoke power. On his head was a turban of the same flame-colored stuff, and as he turned and faced the audience I noticed on his brown forehead two horizontal stripes of white, and I happened to know what they meant.

It was the mark of Siva the Destroyer!

A silence, almost reverent, fell over the motley assemblage. You felt that the audience was in his hands from then on. He began to speak. I listened idly while my eyes searched the audience. But nowhere could I see Frances. The words of the Swami drifted to my ears in an undertone. I recognized his patter as a nebulous blending of Buddhistic and Yoga ideas, and I didn't pay much attention to it until the speaker launched into the doctrine of the transmigration of the soul. Then a phrase caught my attention, and I listened.

"The undying soul of man," said the Swami in his sibilant tones, "passes from body to body, from tenement to tenement through the dark ages of its history. Life dies in the individual but the soul is reborn in a new body. Yet there is no memory of past lives. Only when Karma is reached is the true identity of the soul revealed—only then does the soul look upon itself as in a mirror, feel the disguise of its temporary body fall away, and know itself for what it is!"

A tense hush brooded over the listeners now; heads leaned forward, horny hands gripped bench backs as they hung on the Swarm's words. And then it happened.

I saw the man rise. He was in the left wing of benches, near the wall, and there was something in his manner—deliberate, calculating, that caught my eye. Then he swung about, surveyed the audience, and I saw his face. If ever a face wore the look of devil-possession, that man's did. It was gaunt, rigid as if frozen, and his eyes were not the eyes of a man, but the yellow orbs of a panther about to spring. My muscles tensed; I knew instinctively that something terrible was going to happen, and it did. With a sudden hoarse scream of, "Blood, blood, blood!" the man whipped a revolver from beneath the folds of his coat and began to fire wildly, indiscriminately into the crowd!

Panic claimed the crowd then, rose and swept over it like a breaking wave. Shrill screams of agony rose, crescendoed, faded in the wild cacophony of mad fear. The aisles between the benches were packed in an instant with a fighting stampede. They clamored and fought, fell, crawled under benches. Then the sharp scream of a police whistle, and three bluecoats, clubs flailing, had burst in at the door, were ploughing a path toward the center of panic.

It seemed an age that I stood there, paralyzed, gripping the back of the pine bench. But it was really only an instant. The last pistol shot had just faded in my ears when I saw the woman rise and begin struggling with the madman. That sobered me, sobered me with the stunning impact of a new terror. For that woman was wearing a camel's hair sport coat and a jaunty little black felt hat perched on a head of golden hair. Unless I was mad myself, that woman was Frances Mormar!

I went into action then with shoulders and elbows. As I passed the packed center aisle I saw the end of the mad farce. The maniac had suddenly collapsed, and the woman in the tan coat was pushing her way wildly toward the side exit. The stunned crowd parted for her. She reached the side door, plunged out, vanished, a flying smudge in the outer dark. An instant later the police had reached the man.

I fought my way to the spot, pushed up on the fringe of the circle the police had cleared. A burly patrolman was bending above the man. He lay on a bench, his gaunt, inflamed face staring up, a dagger buried to the hilt in the bloody welter of his shirt front. But his eyes were open, his mouth wide, and though blood was running from its corners he continued to gasp in the rattling voice of the dying: "Blood . . . blood . . . blood . . ."

"What's your name?" the big policeman barked.

"Jean Paul Marat!" the man croaked.

"Who stabbed you?"

"Charlotte Corday. To the guillotine with her . . ."

The strange words produced a magical hush. The policeman was jotting notes. Then, from the fringe of the crowd, a small withered Chinese pushed his way forward. Globules of saliva sputtered from his cracked mouth as he jabbered:

"No, no. I know these man. He clazy. He go clazy two, three week . . . He blake out on skin, sit in bathtub alla day . . . lite clazy stuff 'bout kill everybody, chop off head, make stleets flow by blood . . ."

The police jerked the Chinese forward, began to fire questions at him. Another policeman growled: "Anybody know that woman?"

I suddenly felt sick and weak. I dropped my eyes, afraid that the man might see my face, read there the secret fear and the awful knowledge that tormented me. Then I saw something else—something that sent a flash of heat and a flash of cold zigzagging through my thumping veins. On the floor near my feet lay a handkerchief—a woman's handkerchief with black embroidered initials in one corner.

God! I knew who had dropped that damning square of white cloth!

"Awright, get back! Get back there!" One of the policemen was shoving at the crowd. Terror froze me. I felt big hands thrust against my chest, caught a glimpse of blue uniform and brass buttons. Would he see the handkerchief, would he . . .?

Blind instinct prompted my next move. I took a shuffling step back, deliberately tripped myself, and fell sprawling to the floor. Quickly one hand, thrust under me, grasped the handkerchief, shoved it into a pocket of my vest. Then I stumbled up, waited until the policeman had turned away, and then began pushing my way through the crowd.

Just as I reached the side door one of the policemen noticed me, yelled: "Hey, come back here!"

He was too late. Wild horses couldn't have dragged me back. I dived out upon the loading platform, leaped to the ground, staggered up and began to run.

Finally I paused, came to my senses.

I was under the viaduct. I had left my car, but I didn't care. I couldn't risk going back for it now. I had to find Frances at once. I walked three blocks to a lighted street, hailed a taxi and gave him the address of Frances' apartment house.

Only then did I fish out the handkerchief and look at it. A faint shred of hope had held me back from the abyss of utter panic. Maybe the handkerchief wasn't Frances' after all. Now my last doubt vanished under an avalanche of dismay. The letters embroidered in one corner were, "F. M."

I leaned back against the cushions, closed my eyes. Outside the cab window

I had noticed the newsboys with frosty breaths, scuttling wildly, pink papers waving.

"Aaaxtra! Read all about it! Jack the Ripper Prowls Again! Women's bodies found in alley . . ."

Horror, like a black bog, sucked me down into its vortex; weird nightmare bobbed in the churning currents of my brain. I saw the legions of the mad swarm through the city, damned souls propelling the stolen bodies of their victims. Judas the crucifier, Nero the torturer, Marat with his wolfish bloodlust, Jack the Ripper, gloating obscenely over the dismembered bodies of women! There was no end to them! The fiends of history lived again. And Frances had become one of this army of the damned!

No, not yet, not yet! If Frances had stabbed that fiend there in the crowded hall, she had done it to protect herself. It was like killing a mad dog! But where had the dagger come from? Why was she there? Frances, with her gentle, tender heart, stabbing a man? Not the Frances I had known! No, I couldn't lie to myself. Frances was not the same; the alchemy of hell was already at work . . .

The taxi slithered to a halt. I was jerked upright, opened my eyes, clutched at the door handle. "Wait," I told the taxi driver, and hurried into the apartment house.

I had had enough foresight to keep the pass key and as my feet thudded a swift staccato on the stairs I fished it from my pocket. My hand shook as I fitted the key in the lock of Frances' door, shoved it open. I closed the door softly behind me. My heart sank. The place was dark.

I flipped on the light. The room looked just as I had left it except that the door into the kitchenette was closed. I could see into the bedroom and it was empty. Maybe she was in the kitchenette, hiding there, frightened. For she surely must have come here after her flight from the police in the hall!

I stepped to the door quickly, opened it, then staggered back with a harsh gasp of sick alarm, clutched at the door to steady myself and stared with swollen eyes of terror. I couldn't see anything at first through the thick oily smoke that seemed to fill the room, but I was dizzy with an awful stench that clotted my nostrils.

It was the odor of burning flesh!

Then I saw the reddish glow among the dispersing fumes, and I groped for the light switch, snapped it on and turned to confront the fearful sight. There was a white porcelain table in the center of the small kitchen. At one end of it, on an inverted bowl, squatted a hideous little black idol with a horned head and fat belly. Propped against the bowl was an inverted crucifix smeared with blood that was not yet dry. And in front of that was the silver bread tray on which something was burning.

I drew nearer, holding my breath against the frightful reek, and stared. Dry twigs had been piled in the silver tray, and among the smouldering ashes lay something small and black and withered, something that emitted the noisome smell, something that—Great God! was it possible? It was; there could be no mistake. I knew it as I turned away, weak and nauseated.

The thing that had been burned on that pyre before the image of Satan was the severed hand of a child!

CHAPTER FOUR

THE DREAM OF BLUEBEARD

I DON'T KNOW HOW I got the strength to act after that. But I did, though I moved like one in a dream. Shocked and horrified as I was, it was my protective love for Frances that kept me going. I didn't care what she had done, I knew she was the helpless tool of hellish powers, and I must save her.

First I must get the hideous evidence of the ghastly sacrilege from sight. I emptied the smoking tray into the sink and ran water over it. Then, mastering my revulsion, I fished out the charred sticks and the pitiful fragment of burned flesh and bone, wrapped them in a bundle with the idol and the crucifix, and hid them in the bottom of a wastebasket. Then I opened the outer window to let the fumes out, and went down the hall to see Mrs. Polk.

From her I learned that someone had come into Frances' apartment a few minutes before. She had not seen who it was but supposed it was Frances. She had not heard her leave. She promised to phone my apartment at once if anyone went in again at Frances' door.

I went back down the hall, closed the door of Frances' room, and hurried back to the taxi. I gave the driver the number of the block in which I lived.

I was still nursing one tiny flare of hope. If anything had happened to Frances, I reasoned, she would certainly come to me. Even if she felt some strange madness claiming her she would fly to my arms, knowing that I would shield and protect her. Maybe, I told myself desperately, she has gone to my rooms, or has left some message there for me.

I got out at the corner, some cautious instinct prompting me not to give my address to the cab driver. I waited until he had driven off, and then, wrapping my topcoat about me, plowed into the stiff wind that swept down the avenue in icy currents.

My head was bent low against the blast, and at first I didn't notice either the car parked at the front or the figure that was moving toward it. I was almost on him when I halted, and looked up suddenly into a black bearded face with small bright eyes shining from beneath the shadow of a black flop hat. Then the man had shuffled past me and was climbing into a car.

It took me a moment to collect my thoughts. The man had been coming out of my apartment house. He was a stranger, and a very sinister looking stranger—stooped, dressed in a long black coat, and with those peculiar shiny eyes! Instantaneously the words of the maniac, Issicar, flashed through my mind: "The old man with the black beard . . ."

I whirled with a cry on my lips. But the car was already speeding away into the night.

I hurried inside. My apartment was on the first floor. I unlocked the door and rushed into the room. I stood a moment, then snapped on the light. There was no sign of Frances. But there was something else—a brown bundle on an end table by the divan. I picked it up, tore the wrappings away. Books—a half dozen of them! Then I glanced at the title of the one on top of the stack and my blood congealed.

"Bluebeard—The Life and Crimes of Giles de Rais."

I continued to hold the book in my hand, staring at it stupidly. The old man with the beard had been in this room and had left the books! And that meant that I too had been selected, that I—Great God! . . . Bluebeard! Giles de Rais, that sinister sadist and mass murderer whose very name is a stench in the nostrils of mankind! And I had been chosen . . .

Feverishly I pawed at the other books. "Bluebeard—A portrait of the Original," "A Gallery of Monsters," and so on. All dealing wholly or in part with that same abysmal Satanist of medieval France!

I flung the last book down with a hoarse curse. As I did so a typewritten sheet fell out and lay face up on the divan. I snatched it and with horrified amazement, read:

"Genealogical Note."

"On October 27, 1789, the ship *Fleur de Lis* landed a load of French immigrants in New York. Among them was one, Henri Paul de Rais, a lineal descendent of Giles de Rais. Settling in New York, Henri Paul de Rais, in order to escape the odium which still clung to his once illustrious name, changed it to the Anglicized equivalent, 'Deray'."

That was all. I let the paper flutter to the floor. Through the fog that hung thick over my stunned mind a ghastly conjecture was thrusting its hideous shape. "No, no," I muttered aloud, "it's absurd!" Yet, as little as I knew of my ancestry, I did know that they were French, that they had come from France in the latter part of the eighteenth century and had settled in New York. And I did know that my name was Deray, and that my father's name was Paul!

I sat down and felt the panic gathering in me, a slow swelling sensation through my whole body. I felt it particularly in my throat. "This is idiotic!" I said quietly—too quietly. I could hear my temples throbbing. "This is absurd!" I reiterated.

Then I remembered the others, realized that they must have thought it absurd too. And I thought of them later, thought of Issicar, standing pale and ghostly before that awful mockery of the crucifixion, saw Domitius, the knife at his throat, saw the others in a grisly and multiplying horde, and amongst them Frances—and me! And finally I saw the thick head and shoulders of Gregg Savage, hunched in his disguise, watching the ghastly show.

I sprang to my feet then, my fingernails digging into the flesh of my palms. "Damn him to hell!" I shrieked. "I'll kill him— tonight!"

Then I was horrified at my outburst, clapped my palm over my mouth. Had anyone heard? I turned around, walked to my telephone and dialed Herman Tyrone's house. Tyrone himself answered. His voice over the wire sounded comforting, but far away.

"Mr. Tyrone," I choked, "this is Guy Deray. Gregg Savage is mixed up in this hellish business. I'm going to see him tonight; I'm going to kill him! I just wanted to tell you why—"

"What in God's name?" came Tyrone's excited voice, "Are you mad?"

"Not quite," I said, "not yet." Then the whole thing tumbled from my lips. When I had finished, Tyrone said:

"Now listen to me, Guy. You'll do nothing wild and rash tonight. That would be playing into their hands. And the thing is getting worse, the madness is multiplying to an epidemic. You may be quite right about Savage, but in your case, I imagine, they're only trying to scare you. You don't think a mere set of books can derange your mind?"

"No," I stammered, "but I'm afraid it's just the first step. Then there's Frances—"

"You may be mistaken about her," Tyrone said. "Anyhow I don't think they'd do more than frighten her badly. The thing in her room was probably a set-up. But at any rate I'll get a man from the D.A.'s office to get on her trail, and I'll keep in touch with you. Now you're worn out, your nerves are ragged, and you'd better go to bed and get a few hours sleep. You hear? Get some rest, so you'll be able to carry on. Will you do that?"

I promised. I was too exhausted to protest. He was probably right, and my nerves were certainly frayed. But I didn't believe that I could do what he suggested anyhow—not with Frances unaccounted for.

I went over and sat down on the divan and began looking at the books. I stared at the weird illustrations. Tyrone was right, I told myself doggedly. No mere set of books can derange a man's mind —not mine anyhow. I began to read, just to show myself that I wasn't afraid of the damned books. And my mind was so weary, so tormented with worry, that I found the reading relaxed me. I read on and on . . .

Suddenly I jerked up. My head had fallen forward; I had dozed. I shook off the drowsiness and went on reading; the book had absorbed my interest with a horrid fascination. I dozed again, jerked myself awake. This time I got up. I was definitely sleepy now. Well, I would set my alarm clock and get two or three hours rest— three would be enough. Then I would go on with my plan to find Gregg Savage and choke the truth from him. In the kitchen I mixed a toddy and then went to bed.

I dozed, awakened with a start. Something had scratched against the window screen. Without even moving my head, I rolled my eyes to one side, stared out. The cold air was like a luminous poison; all was still. Silhouetted against the pale light were the bare branches of a box elder by the window. A branch must have brushed the screen!

My eyes rolled back against the darkness of the room. Against that screen of gloom the weird shadow shapes paraded again— scenes from the life of Bluebeard, scenes of dark carnage and unholy lust. I couldn't banish them.

Then, out of the corner of my eye, I saw something, and suddenly with a shock of terror, I realized that it was no tree limb this time. It was a shadow on the screen, black against the pallor of the night—the shadow of a human head.

With a dreadful slowness I rolled my eyes toward the apparition. It was real! Under a black flop hat there was a dim and ghastly face, a black beard, strange inhuman eyes! It was the face of the old man I had seen in front of the apartment house!

I felt the impulse to rise, to throw myself out of bed. Then suddenly with unutterable horror I realized that I couldn't move, couldn't speak!

I thought of an insect impaled on a pin, of a rabbit paralyzed with terror before the hunter's gun. I was like that. And those terrible eyes were boring into me like heated pistons, stunning me, sending into me the evil and irresistible currents of an alien will.

And then I saw that the lips were speaking, saw them move slowly, and the words, meaningless to my conscious mind, seemed nevertheless to speak to some other part of me, some part that was deep beneath the surface of thought. Like a sweetish syrup those words flowed over me, poisoning and killing consciousness with the painless, stifling nepenthe of ether fumes.

And then I was slipping away, slipping slowly into a vast black hole that had no bottom—sinking, sinking . . .

It was a strange and horrible awakening. My head ached; there was a dopey, lifeless feeling, a disinclination to move, and an awful gnawing sense of remorse. Then I remembered the dreams. I had dreamed that I was Giles de Rais—Bluebeard—and I had lived and acted the awful crimes which are laid at his door!

Now the scenes tumbled back to me in wild confusion, scenes laid in olden Prance. I had been a man of consequence, a Marshal of France, an imposing man with a stern wolfish face and a beard so black that it looked blue. I remembered battlefields with the hooves of the horses trampling on dead and dying bodies, and the smell of blood in the hot air had been spicy and sweet. That was strange. For the smell of blood has always been unpleasant, even repugnant to me!

And there were other scenes of blood too, scenes not ennobled by the clangour of battle, scenes dark and shadowy in which grey confining walls, and eerie yellow torch flames, and silence and the flash of knives figured prominently. Solitary scenes these, in which I was a lone and hooded figure, creeping in clammy dungeons, driven on by a terrible and unnatural hunger. And there was a certain dark room where cadavers multiplied like the carcasses of flies in a spider's web. And I had gone there often, sometimes alone, sometimes with a companion—a woman, a child, whose trembling uneasy looks and frightened questions had delighted me. And I remembered the clang of a heavy door, a scream muffled by stone walls. And later, I would go creeping from that unhallowed place—alone!

How could such things have run through my mind? I was sickened at the memory of them. Then I remembered something else—something that caused cold daggers of ice to stab through my quivering body. There had been other dreams in which the modern had mingled with the ancient. There was a child I had lured into a sinister room to murder, and strangely that child's face had been the face of the newsboy on my corner. And this time I had done the thing with a knife, a butcher knife, and I had washed my bloody hands in a porcelain sink!

I sat up abruptly in bed. This was madness! Why was my whole body trembling? Dreams are that way—confusing, fantastic. I must put these morbid fancies out of my mind! They were nothing but dreams!

I jumped out of bed, started to the closet where I had hung my clothes. Then I saw them hanging over a chair near the bed. I stopped, puzzled. I was certain I had hung them in the closet! Must have been a bit foggy in the head last night! Hadn't I imagined that face at the window, too?

I slipped into my underwear and pants and started through the kitchen to the bathroom. Grey light filtered weakly through the window and at first I didn't notice anything wrong. Then, almost at the door, I halted with a jerk. Something lay on the floor there. What—?

I sprang to the wall switch, snapped on the light, drew nearer, stiff legged, staring. Newspapers! A whole thick stack of newspapers. I saw the black headlines that screamed: "Jack the Ripper Still at Large . . ." I saw, but the message scarcely registered. I was thinking of something else . . .

I kicked the papers aside savagely, grasped the knob of the bathroom door. Then the strength seemed to fade from me like snow in the sun. My whole body wilted as if every bone socket in my skeleton had crumbled and my muscles were fighting to keep the limp shell of my body erect. I had opened the door—only a few inches, but wide enough. Now I clung to it, gasping, fighting for air while the world rocked and reeled before my eyes.

What I had expected to see in that room was there. The boy was there—the newsboy! He was in the bathtub, in a pool of blood. There was a butcher knife on the bathroom floor and it had come from my kitchen. And my shirt was lying over the sink, and it was splashed with scarlet stains!

I won't speak more of that. Even now I can't write it down without a swimming of the senses, a sick convulsion beneath my ribs. As for my condition at that moment when the realization of what I had done, of what I was, swept over me, I can only say that it was a yammering madman who turned and went reeling out of that place.

CHAPTER FIVE

ARMY OF THE ACCURSED

WHEN I CAME TO MY SENSES I was I on the divan. I don't know how long I had been there. But my horror-stricken mind had been digging back into confused memories, reconstructing piece by piece the shadowy picture of my loathsome crime. Yes, I had done it!

I was a monster then, I was no longer myself! The awful burning eyes of that accursed apparition at the window had done something to my soul. And this, this was only the beginning!

I staggered to my feet, seized by the sudden wild panic of one trapped in a burning building. I wasn't afraid of the police, I wasn't afraid of the consequences of a discovery of my crime. *I was afraid of myself!*

Conflicting impulses struggled in my fevered brain. I wanted to scream, to run into the street shouting my crime to the world, begging to be killed. I even snatched up the telephone, intending to call the police, confess. But I set the phone down again. I couldn't do that—I couldn't! It was the thought of being dragged before the accusing eyes of my fellow men, branded as a monster, a loathsome fiend, a thing no longer human! I couldn't bear that. Better be my own executioner!

I stumbled into the bedroom, fished my revolver from the dresser drawer and came back. I made sure that it was loaded. I stood in the center of the room and closed my eyes. I muttered a prayer, felt the cold muzzle of the gun against my temple, felt my finger tight on the trigger. Then, as abruptly as I had raised it, I lowered the weapon.

"Coward!" my brain was shrieking, "You're taking the easiest way out. And you're leaving Frances. If you're going to die, why not give your life in a final desperate struggle with the fiend?"

God! how that helped me. I still wanted to die, but now I could die like a man, and if I could drag down into the abyss with me the loathsome monster-maker who had made the city a shambles, I would ask nothing else of God or man!

I thrust the pistol into my pocket, went back into the kitchen and flung the pile of newspapers into the bathroom—being careful not to look at the thing in the tub—and then locked the door. I was ready for the fight. I went to the telephone and called a taxi.

When the cab deposited me a half hour later on a dark corner in the wholesale district I had already worked out my plan of action. First I would go to the Shrine of Karma, search the place. If I found the source of evil there, I would sell my life dearly. If I should escape with my life, or if I should not find there what I expected, I would go on to Gregg Savage, the other officials, and at the point of a gun I would discover the truth!

With my coat collar turned up against the chill air I went skulking in the shadows through the odorous market district, now stark and sordid in the greyness of approaching dawn. Across from the dilapidated building which housed the Swami's cult, I stopped to stare. My car was still parked at the building's front. Apparently the police had overlooked it. No lights showed in the dirty windows of the hall.

I crossed the street, circled the place stealthily. Still I saw no light. I crept up on the loading platform and tried the side door. It was locked. I crept to the back of the building and in a pile of debris and broken machinery I found a leaf from an automobile spring. Then I went from window to window until I found one on the far side which had one of its bars torn loose. With the spring leaf I managed to pry the window open. I paused then, staring into the dark interior of the building, listening. But there was no sound. I crawled inside.

The wide hall was silent, appeared to be empty. The wan light from the windows made a grey twilight. With my revolver in one hand I started back toward the curtained space behind the stage. It was dark beyond the curtains. To the left I made out walled off rooms. The place seemed utterly deserted. I went to the first door, opened it softly and stepped back. No sound. I stepped inside, then stopped with a jerk.

Light seeping faintly through the drawn blind of a window revealed an iron bedstead, and on it a motionless figure. I held my breath, peering. The figure did not move. The sound of gentle breathing now reached my ears. Holding my gun trained on the recumbent shape, I struck a match with my left hand.

I let it fall. God in Heaven! The figure lying on that squalid bed, covered only with her topcoat, was Frances Mormar!

In an instant I was beside her. "Frances—Frances!" I whispered huskily.

She raised with a start; her hand flew to her mouth as if to stifle a scream, and then she recognized me. "Guy!" she sobbed, "Guy!" and flung herself with wild abandon into my arms.

"Darling," I breathed, holding her close to me, feeling an awful, gnawing bitterness at the thought that the hands that caressed her were the hands of a murderer, "why didn't you come to me, darling? What are you doing here . . .?"

Stifling her sobs, she told me. The books, as I suspected, had been accompanied by a note saying that they were from me. She had gone home and had been reading there when a Western Union boy had brought a typewritten note, also supposed to be from me, and asking her to meet me at this place. She had thought it was some joke connected with the books and had come. Mystified, she had looked for me and had then found a seat and waited. When the man sitting next to her had jumped up and started firing, she had tried to wrest the pistol from his hand.

"But that dagger," I stammered, where did you get that dagger?"

"Dagger? But I didn't have any dagger!"

"You didn't stab him then?"

She drew back, stared at me. "Oh, my God, Guy! You thought that too? I knew the crowd thought so; that's why I was so terrified and ran away. But I didn't stab him. I was struggling with him for the gun when he whipped out the dagger with his left hand and stabbed himself. I knew they thought I'd done it, and in a wild panic I ran. I hid outside, shivering with cold and terror. They looked for me but couldn't find me. I was afraid they'd trace me to my apartment and I didn't know what to do. When they had all gone and the place was dark I crept out from my hiding place and ran square into the Swami. He had been hiding too, afraid that the police would blame the thing on him. He told me that I could hide here until I thought it safe to go home."

"And where is he now?" I asked.

"I don't know," she said. "He left me here and I haven't seen him since."

"Then you didn't go back to your apartment after leaving it the first time?" I stammered.

"No," she said, "I stayed right here. I intended to get up and go in a few hours, but I must have fallen asleep."

I hugged her fiercely to me now. Hot tears were stinging my eyes. In a few moments I must send her away to safety, and I might never see her again! "Darling," I choked, "I want to ask you about those books. They didn't affect you, did they—upset your mind?"

Why did she hesitate then? Why did that little shiver run through her frame? "I, I don't know, Guy," she stammered. "It's rather queer about that. I did read some from the books, but it was a typewritten paper in one of them that affected me most," she paused, laughed nervously. "It's rather silly, but it said that I was descended from the family of Madame de Montespan. Her maiden name, you know was Mortemart!"

My muscles jerked with a quick spasm; then, to cover it I forced a laugh. "That's absurd, of course," I said. "You didn't let it prey on your mind, did you?"

Again she hesitated. "No," she said, "not at the time. But now that I think of it, that must have had something to do with those crazy things I've been dreaming . . . ."

"Dreaming!" I blurted. "What did you dream?"

A little breathless gasp escaped her. "They were rather awful," she said throatily. "It seemed that I *was* Madame de Montespan, that I did ghastly things. Let's don't talk of them. But I wonder—?"

"Wonder what, darling?" I husked.

"Why how in the world I ever knew the details of such loathsome things—such things as the Black Mass . . .?"

I stiffened. The room had begun to rock giddily before my eyes. I did not want to question her any more—not now. "Frances," I said hoarsely, "you must get up now and get your coat on. My car's in front of this place. I want you to get into it and drive straight to Herman Tyrone. Tell him to keep you in hiding until he hears from me. And whatever you do, don't go to your apartment!"

"But Guy—" she began.

"Please, darling," I said, "let me wait until later to explain. If you love me you'll do exactly as I say."

I bundled her into her coat. She was shivering now as I piloted her from the room. We stopped in the center of the stage and I gathered her in my arms for a final embrace. I could scarcely trust myself to speak. I pushed her away from me finally, mumbled between gritted teeth, "The front door—hurry, darling!"

She nodded, turned away. She took a half dozen faltering steps and then stopped.

I didn't see at first what had stopped her—not until she screamed. Then I plunged toward her, caught her in my arms as she stumbled back and toppled. At the same instant the *things* came out of the shadows.

They didn't come with a rush; they didn't move like anything human or animal that I had ever seen. They moved like robots, or like dead things that neither feel nor hear nor see. There must have been a dozen of them in front of me—revenant shapes in baggy garments that seemed stiff with grave mould, revenant faces with gaping mouths and dead staring eyes—soulless, mindless monsters, moved by the currents of an alien will.

Shambling slowly, unsteadily, like automatons they came toward us. Frances was a limp weight in the crook of my left ann. Dragging her with me, I backed away, then spun about. But there was no opening for escape. They were behind us too, around us, converging slowly in a, tight circle.

For an instant I stood paralyzed, staring into those ash-grey expressionless faces while my muscles twitched impotently with spasms of horror. I seemed to know that guns and bullets would not stop these monsters. Then the madness that lay in their dead-fish eyes seemed to invade my own brain. I leveled my pistol at the nearest shapes, emptied it in their faces. The swift concussions blasted the silence and three of the shapes pitched to the floor. But the others paid no attention. On they came trampling over the bleeding bodies of the fallen.

I let Frances slip to the floor then. I fisted my hand around the empty pistol and using it as a club sprang into the ranks of the creeping horrors.

It was a nightmarish thing, that fight against those numb, soulless ghouls. For they fought in silence, without savagery, without spirit of any kind. It was like battling a horde of corpses that keep hurtling down upon you from some abysmal chute. Yet I was fighting like a panther, beating at their flabby bodies, raking, jabbing, hammering with the pistol at their slime drooling, cadaver-faces. I saw flesh ripped by the gunsight, saw eyes jabbed into bony skulls, saw them fall before my plunging savagely, only to rise and lumber hideously toward me again.

And nowhere could I beat an opening through the ring of death that hemmed me in, that was gradually pounding and dragging me down with the slow heavy hammering of insensate club-like fists, the dragging tearing weight of taloned, pawing hands. Like the cold, gelid tentacles of an octopus they sucked me down into the reeking whirlpool of their bodies, crushed the breath from my lungs, crushed life and light from my terror maddened brain.

Then the darkness was sweeping over me in rhythmic waves and I was shrieking Frances' name, telling her to run, to escape. And then I could not even shriek any longer, could only struggle like a dying worm beneath a black ant swarm. After that it was over, and the dark merciful currents closed over me, swallowed me in grateful oblivion.

CHAPTER SIX

DARK BONDAGE

I CAN'T REMEMBER any particular point at which my senses returned to me. There were periods of darkness and periods of semi-darkness in which my consciousness was like that of an infant who sees and hears without comprehending, and a weird pageant of shadow shapes passed before me and around me and left no definite impression on my mind.

Then there was a pain—and a memory of greater pain—and I began to be aware of my existence. I moved weakly, but my limbs, my whole body seemed to be encased in a straight-jacket. I was sitting upright but I could move neither forward nor backward, and there was a frightful aching pain in my left leg. I tried to move it— making only a weak effort—yet it sent a searing flame of agony through my entire body until it seemed to tear at my scalp, blind my eyes.

I didn't try to move again. I sat with a sick throbbing in my stomach and stared at the scene which I seemed to have been watching for ages.

The room which I was in was dark. But through an open door in front of me I could see into a low-ceiled room, lighted by the dim reddish glare from hidden lamps, and there was a buzz of activity there. Grotesque shadow shapes like the ghouls who had beat me down were moving about; there was a buzz of low voices, cries of agony at intervals, and cold commands in a certain voice which affected me strangely. From time to time I heard this voice call out names. But it was incredible that those names should be linked together, for ages in history separated them, and they were names of infamy: Tamerlane, and Cesare Borgia, and Caligula, and Catherine de Medici and Messalina were jumbled together with names of monsters of the modern world. For a wild instant it seemed to me that I must have died and awakened in hell, a damned soul among the damned.

Then I noticed that the dungeon-like room beyond the door was crowded with grisly engines of torture. There were the racks on which a body could be stretched with ropes and pulleys; there was the Iron Virgin, that oaken cylinder with hinged doors and an interior studded with spikes. On the floor lay a wretch whose body was being crushed slowly beneath the weight of flat stones. And there was the *strappado.*

I watched it operate. The naked body of a man was hanging by his wrists. Weights were attached to his ankles. A pulley creaked and he was hoisted to the ceiling. Then he was allowed to drop with a jerk. The rending shock tore a shriek of agony from his throat, and he hung there, moaning and blubbering, and I knew that his shoulders had been dislocated. And while he whimpered in torment a voice spoke to him, that awful voice which I remembered as a part of my dreams of pain, and the voice was saying:

"You are Ivan the Fourth, Czar of Russia. Your wife is Maria Nagaya, You have murdered your son in a fit of rage and with your own hands have strangled your enemies. You are now going to massacre the citizens of Novgorod."

I saw the thing repeated, not once but many times. And then I saw them bring out a girl, a girl with wide terrified eyes, and a disheveled mass of golden hair. Thumb screws were tightened on her wrists, and as they tormented her she screamed. And those screams jerked me suddenly alert, sent claws of terror ripping at my quivering nerves, and I began to scream too. For I had realized that the woman was my sweetheart, was dearer to me than life itself. And yet I could not remember who she was!

But my screams had caused her tormentors to turn toward the door of my cell. One of them cursed me, and I saw that he was a lean, stooped man with a black beard. His companion was dressed in a black gown and a hood like an ancient hangman. Now they left the girl and came toward me.

They paused in the doorway, stared at me curiously, and the bearded man said, "What's wrong with you, Bluebeard?"

"I'm not Bluebeard," I rasped, and cursed him.

He laughed. "Who are you then?" he asked.

The harsh oaths sputtered to silence on my lips. I couldn't answer. Cold horror jelled my blood. Who was I? I stared at my questioner with dumb hatred. Under the shadow of his black hat I could see nothing but the yellow pin-points of light that crawled in his eyes. Was this man the devil himself, that he could paralyze

not only speech but thought with the burning currents of his diabolical eyes?

"You see," the fiend spoke to his hooded helper, "he has already lost his own identity. But his other soul, the soul that will
replace the old one, is not yet fully born. We must melt his soul
again in the cauldron of pain and shape it to our Purpose."

Melted in the cauldron of pain! Merciful God! I knew now
what that meant. I looked down, saw the thing that encased my
foot and leg. It was an iron boot reaching to within a few inches of
my knee, and now the hangman had knelt beside me, had picked
up a hammer and a wooden wedge.

The hair on my scalp began to crawl, and the sickness clutched
again at my stomach. I began to writhe against the straight-jacket.
But it held my arms pinioned fast, and outside of it were ropes
binding me securely to the heavy chair in which I sat.

I couldn't escape; there was not the remotest chance, and I
knew it. And now the frightful torture was beginning again. I felt
the wedge thrust in between the iron boot and my leg. The hammer began to tap. I shut my eyes, clamped my teeth down on my
tongue. My jaw muscles quivered. Tap, tap, tap! went the hammer,
driving the wedge deeper, crushing the bones of my leg and foot
like a vise. I reared up against the ropes with a spasmodic jerk, fell
back, weak and dizzy with the fearful pain that coursed up from
the crushed bones of my leg and shot in flame-like flashes through
my boiling veins, burned into scarified nerves, until my whole
body was one terrific ache, and each tap of the hammer was like
an ice pick jabbing at my temples . . .

I had sworn not to cry out, but as the wedge went deeper and
the pain of pinched pulverized flesh was swallowed up in the in-
tenser agony of cracking bones, a bloody froth gathered on my
lips, and animal-like groans were forced from my lungs by the
convulsive jerking of my diaphragm.

Tap . . . tap . . . tap!

The world was reeling. Blinding flashes of fire spread round
me, seemed to be sucked into my lungs, seemed to be eating at my
disintegrating vitals. I began to pound my head against the wooden
back of the chair, praying for death, swift and merciful to blot me
out. But death wouldn't come, though my entire body seemed
swollen now until it was one monstrous boil puffed to the bursting
point with internal heat. I whimpered then, blubbered, sobbed,
wailed sickly. There was no longer strength enough in me for a
scream.

And then I heard the voice speaking, and my senses seemed to clutch at it, cling to it, mad for any distraction from the eating pain.

"Think of nothing but what I am saying," the voice intoned. "Fasten your mind on it; it will carry you out of the pain, out of yourself. You are Giles de Rais. Your soul is the soul of Giles de Rais, the son of Guy de Montmorency-Laval, the adopted son of Jeanne de Rais. Though born in the fifteenth century, your soul is still alive, has been resurrected in a new body. For a while that will seem strange. Then you will be accustomed to it. You know the life you have lived; you know the ruling passion that sways you—your love for blood, your ecstasy at shedding it, the intoxication of secret murder and secret torture. In the dungeon of your castle were the bones of one hundred and forty of your victims whose cries for mercy were sweet in your ears, and whom you slaughtered with joy. Already, in your new incarnation you have done one murder. You will do others. A whole city teeming with potential victims awaits you. Go among them as a wolf, sate your gnawing fierce hunger . . ."

Tap . . . tap . . . tap!

I could still hear the hammer forcing the wedge a little deeper, a little deeper. But I no longer felt the pain. The soft currents of the voice were bearing my consciousness away. Presently the voice itself faded, became confused, indistinguishable from my own thoughts. And presently my thoughts themselves ceased.

I awoke with a start, sat up abruptly, stared about me. I seemed to be in the same narrow room, but I was on a bed. There was a dresser with a mirror in the room and a candle shed its wan radiance over the scene. I was fully dressed, even to my coat, and I was listening intently. It seemed to me that a voice had said, "Get up; it is time to go."

I flung my legs off the bed. A sharp pain shot up from my left ankle to my thigh. I winced, touched the leg gingerly with a finger. It was swollen, sore. But I was able to move the foot, the toes. I got up, tested it with my weight, took a few steps and stopped before the dresser. I drew back with a start. A strange apparition confronted me in the glass—a face that was haggard, lean, sinister and with a black fringe of whiskers running down the jawbone to a pointed beard, and a black mustache curling down from the upper lip to meet it.

But I didn't have time to puzzle that out. The door had opened behind me and I turned to see the hooded hangman standing in its embrasure. My first impulse was to cower away from him like a dog that has been whipped. Then I seemed to understand that he would not torture me any more.

"It is time to go," he said.

I stood still while he came up to me, fastened a blindfold over my eyes. Then a cane was thrust into my hand, a hat placed on my head, and taking my arm, the hangman led me out. "The cane," he told me, "contains a thin steel sword-blade. You will need it."

I felt the cold air as we came outside. Then I was pushed into a car. The car sped away. I sat there in utter darkness, leaning on my cane. My mind seemed a total blank. Finally the car stopped.

"Do you know who you are," asked a voice from the front seat.

"I am Giles de Rais," I answered automatically.

"Do you know what you must do?"

"Yes, I know." The answer surprised me even then.

The car door was opened; I was helped out. I stood there dumbly, heard the motor of the car roar as it shot away. Then I removed the blindfold from my eyes.

I was standing at the west end of the viaduct. It was night again. Behind me gleamed the lights of the business district; ahead and to my left was the street on which my apartment house stood. My apartment? That did not seem entirely clear. Then I remembered; it was the apartment of the man whose body I now occupied. He was a different sort of person from me—a law-abiding fellow whom I now regarded with contempt. But at last I had got the upper hand of him, after living hidden in his blood and brain for all these years Now I, Giles de Rais, was master!

That thought warmed me with a savage feverish glow. I knew now what it was that I had to do. There was a murdered boy hidden in the bath room. He must be concealed. And I must have another victim—tonight!

I began to walk, limping, but with quick, nervous strides. My cane tapped on the pavement. There was a sword inside that one, a strong keen blade, ready to my purpose. I passed lighted houses, staring at them with a feverish, furtive hunger. I was a lean wolf who had strayed into a peaceful sheep fold. I was a hungry wolf with the smell of blood and the bleat of victims tantalizing my mind. Once a child ran across a yard, stumbled up the steps of a house. My whole frame quivered; it was all I could do to keep on moving. The thirst for blood was hot in my throat.

A sort of drunken savagery was mounting in my veins. I was impatient. I wanted to gloat over the hidden corpse of my victim, I wanted to capture another. I was in the middle of the block next to the one in which I live when I stopped suddenly like a hunter who sights game. Under the bleary street lamp at the corner, a woman had paused, was staring at the houses across the street. She was young, with a small trim figure outlined by her dark coat, and under a small black hat her dark hair gleamed like carved ebony. A strange excitement shook me. I saw myself grasping the coils of that black hair, jerking her head back so that the soft curve of a throat was exposed, drawing the keen blade of my sword across that curving whiteness!

The woman moved on. I followed at a safe distance, breathing hoarsely, watching her with feverish eyes. And then, in the shadow of some shrubs in front of my apartment house, she stopped.

I stopped too. Then, with a furtive movement the woman darted across the yard, crept into the shadows and made her way toward my window!

Astonished, I hurried forward, got behind the shrubs where she had stood. What could it mean? The woman had stopped at my window, seemed to be fishing for the latch to the screen. I felt my muscles tighten with alarm. She had managed to open the screen, was crawling into my room!

A hot wave of alarm swept over me. I thought of the ghastly cadaver that lay behind the locked door. The woman must be a police spy, creeping in to find the proof of my guilt!

Limping quickly across the lighted space, I gained the shadows of the building, stole along softly to the window and peered in. The woman's shape was a dim silhouette in the doorway that led into the front room. Now, with slow, exploring steps, she went on.

I lifted myself over the sill, careful to make no sound, careful not to let my injured leg drag or knock against the wall. I lowered myself to the floor in the shadow of the bed, crawled along on hands and knees to the door through which the woman had passed, and there straightened up and stood flattened against the wall. I was throbbing now with a crazy fit of hatred and bloodlust. Here was a victim ready for my uses, and the fact that she was a spy would make the murder doubly sweet!

I stiffened. The woman was coming back with slow, groping steps. I would seize her, bind and gag her before she could cry out. Then I would take my time about killing her.

She was in the doorway now. Another soft step and she was in the room. She hadn't seen me! I sprang.

My arms went around her from behind; one hand reached up and clamped across her mouth, stifling the cry that came gurgling from her throat. A hot wave of madness misted my mind. She struggled in my arms like a bird caught in the coils of a snake. I threw her across the bed, still holding one hand tight against her lips, and reached for a sheet with which to gag and bind her. But with a sudden jerk she threw her head free and one short scream ripped through the silent darkness.

But that was all. My fingers closed quickly on her throat. My head was throbbing now, pulsing with the hot currents of my mania. I wanted to save her, to torture her with the cruel sword blade, but once my fingers had buried themselves in the soft flesh of her throat I couldn't turn loose! I felt her body shake and quiver, felt it stiffen finally with a spasm and go limp. I drew my hands away quickly. But she was already silent and motionless.

I felt that I had cheated myself. Her death had been too swift. I limped back to the door where I had left my cane leaning. I gave the handle a sharp twist and a pull; the long thin blade flashed out. In two strides I was back at the bed. I raised the sword in my right hand, seized her black tresses in my left and yanked to lift her head. But instead of what I expected, the hair came away in my hand!

I paused, puzzled. The woman had been wearing a wig. In the dim light from the window I could see the tangled mass of lighter hair that had been beneath it. Strange! Curiosity stung me and I went to the window and pulled down the shade. Then I closed the door into the next room, switched on the light and turned back to the bed. I took two faltering steps and stopped. The sword fell from my hand to the floor. My limbs had begun to shake with an ague of horror.

The horror came on me before I understood the reason. Understanding came gradually to my crazed mind. There lay the woman, her pale lovely face staring up from its bed of yellow hair, and I knew that that face was familiar to me, was dearer to me than life itself. And I had murdered her!

But who was she, and who was I? I was certainly no longer Giles de Rais. A fearful sickness had seized me; cold sweat stood out on my skin; the strength that I had felt an instant before was draining from my body like blood from a severed artery. Then, in a blinding flash that stunned me like a bolt of lightning, the whole hideous disguise that had masked my soul fell away, and I knew— knew the unspeakable horror of what I had done.

I knew then that I was Guy Deray, that I had been temporarily transformed into a monster, and that I was now myself again. And the woman I had murdered was Frances Mormar!

CHAPTER SEVEN

THE THIEF OF SOULS

THE AGONY THAT GRIPPED ME then cannot be conveyed in words. The physical torment I had suffered was nothing compared with it. The anguish of the damned wracked my cringing soul as I bent in terror above the woman I loved, praying in silent, mad despair that she might be still alive. But I knew that it was a futile hope. Even before I had pressed the mirror to her lips and brought it away untouched by the faintest moisture of breathing, I knew that the utmost horror had been reached, and I had decided what to do.

When I knew that she was dead I didn't hesitate an instant. The agony that convulsed me was too great to endure. I could not bear to think on it another second. I was like a man whose body is wrapped in sheets of flame. I wanted death, wanted it instantly!

I picked up the sword from the floor and stumbled into the next room. In a swift flash my mind had assembled the details of my suicide. I knelt on the divan. I braced the hilt of the sword against the cushions and placed the point against an interstice between my ribs—just above the heart. A forward lunge and that would be all!

"God in heaven, forgive me!" I choked and threw myself forward.

But the sword point barely penetrated my flesh. Something was dragging me back, something soft yet strangling, that had coiled about my throat, choking off the scream that died to a harsh rattle. I heard voices then, but I could not make out the words. Some tremendous force jerked me to the floor, flung me face down with a stunning shock. Then hands were working over me, tying my arms and legs, forcing a gag into my mouth and binding it fast about my head. Then I was carried into the next room and flung face-down on the bed beside Frances.

I lay perfectly still, too stunned at first to think. And then I began to listen to the voices.

"You see," said one voice, "you can't be sure about them. He went through with the first part of it all right. But when he saw who the girl was it shocked him back to his original character. We'd better have let him kill himself, I think."

"But it worked with the others," the second voice protested. "The difficulty, of course, is that we are using three different forces—the pain that shocks the nervous system and jars the ego loose, the hypnotic suggestion which creates the new personality, and the *dhatura* which numbs the brain, inhibits the normal impulses, fogs the memory and makes the mind pliant and obedient. The problem is to get the right amount of each. I think in his case we should have used more of the drug."

Dhatura! I knew of that strange Indian drug and it explained many things to me now. It explained what had been wrong with me that first night when I had lain paralyzed and seen the face at the window and had listened to the fiends' hypnotic words. My whiskey had been drugged! It explained too the loss of memory which had made me fall so readily into the delusion that I was Giles de Rais. But obviously the fiendish alchemy had not completely succeeded with me. And now . . .?

"Since we can't absolutely depend on it," the first voice was saying, "I think we'd better kill him and get the rest of our program over with tonight. Deray is liable to realize when he regains consciousness that he didn't really commit the murder of the boy, that you suggested all the details to his mind through hypnotism, and his remorse at having killed his sweetheart is liable to drive him to a confession that will expose us. I think this test has proved that your process of transformation will work on only certain types . . ."

The light was suddenly snapped off. They were moving into the other room. The rest of their talk drifted to me muffled and fragmentary. But I caught the gist of it. They were planning to set the apartment house afire. They would start it in the basement after saturating all walls they could get to with turpentine. They intended to burn me alive with the body of Frances!

It wasn't the thought of being burned alive that electrified me then. I had passed the point where fear of death or physical suffering could move me. Frances was dead—dead by my own hands— and I no longer wanted to live. But an acute and harrowing torment clutched my mind when I realized that the fiends were within a few feet of me and that I would be forced to die without being able to unmask them. I knew their awful secret, but I would have to carry it into death with me and leave them free to go on with their ghastly crime.

I heard the door into the hallway close. They had gone out! God in heaven! if I could only free myself! But how? My hands were tied behind me; my ankles were tied together; my mouth was gagged so that I could not make the faintest sound. And in a few minutes the flames would be leaping up from below, licking into the turpentine-saturated walls.

Wild prayers shrieked in my tormented brain. "God, God," I prayed, "if there is a God, show your power now, I don't ask for my life; I don't want it. But give me a chance to rid the world of those fiends!"

I can't say that I expected a miracle to happen; I didn't really have that much faith. But when I suddenly felt the cloth that was tightly stretched across my mouth begin to loosen, it seemed a direct answer to my desperate prayers. Then the cloth was snatched away. I spat the gag from my mouth and lifted my head.

Did I expect to see an angel sent down from heaven to free me? I did see one anyhow. The angel was Frances and she was sitting up and her hands were busy with the bonds that held my wrists.

"Frances," I gasped, "Oh, my darling. . . You're not dead!"

"I was almost dead with fear," she whispered, working frantically to untie the knots. "But I didn't know that it was you, Guy, and of course you didn't know me since those fiends had disguised me too—with that wig and all—before they turned me loose. But when you attacked me in the dark, strangled me, I saw that my only chance was to pretend that I was dead. I faked the spasm and then lay and held my breath until you were convinced that I was dead. I didn't know who you were until I heard them talking just now . . ."

"Hurry, hurry," I whispered. "You've got to get me loose before they come back."

The last knot came free; my hands were loose and we both attacked the bonds that held my ankles. Now they too were free! I stood up, grasped Frances by the shoulder. "Crawl out through the window!" I said huskily. "Phone the police. I'll try to keep them from escaping before the police get here."

Frances ran to the window. I stumbled to the wall switch, snapped off the light, opened the door and stepped into the front room. Then I froze stiff. The door into the hall had opened and closed swiftly and a dark figure had passed inside. I knew that he was standing there, gun in hand, waiting for me to move!

God, but there was agony in that moment! To be so near victory and then to be cheated by that narrow margin! I turned frozen eyes toward the dim outline of the divan. I could not see the sword, but I knew approximately where it was. I bunched my muscles for a leap. Then he fired.

Like a striking serpent, the tongue of yellow flame leaped toward me in the dark and I felt the slug whistle past my ear. But I had already ducked, lunged for the divan, was groping frantically for the handle of the long, sharp blade.

Again the gun blasted the silence, but the shots went too high, and in the next instant I had staggered up, was springing like a tiger toward the spot where the yellow streaks of fire had blazed.

They blazed again. Something struck my left shoulder a sharp blow, stung like lancing fire. But the impetus of my rush carried me on. The point of the blade struck something; my weight forced it forward. There was a hoarse scream of pain. The pistol exploded again but the flares leaped ceiling-ward and the next instant the sword was ripped from my hand by the collapse of the body in which it was buried.

I almost fainted then, but I fought to keep myself erect, staggered to the wall, switched on the light. Then I turned and the horror that rose and broke like a wave over me found voice in the wild and desperate cry that shrilled from my lips.

For the man who lay on the floor with the blade of my sword buried in his heart was Herman Tyrone!

Then the door opened and I spun about. Frances was standing there. "Frances," I gasped hoarsely, "it was a ghastly mistake! It was dark, I couldn't see . . ."

I paused. Why didn't she say something? She looked at him and smiled bitterly. "No, Guy," she said softly, "it's not a mistake. Look at the pocket of his coat there. Isn't that a black wig and beard sticking out? Herman Tyrone was the fiend! He was careful to camouflage his voice, but once, there in the torture room, his beard fell off . . ."

"Then," I interrupted, "you weren't so strongly affected as I, I suppose?"

"I pretended to be completely subdued," she said. "He thought he had succeeded perfectly with me. He had commanded me to come here when he turned me loose. I didn't know why, but I did want to find you to tell you what I had discovered; so I fought to keep my sanity, and succeeded, at least partially. But of course I didn't know you when you attacked me. That horrid beard glued to your face fooled me even after you had turned on the light—"

She stopped. The wail of a police siren knifed through the night, whined to silence in front of the house. Hungrily I gathered Frances in my arms, and despite the repulsive beard, she pressed her warm lips against mine.

The next moment the door was flung open and we could see the bluecoats pounding into the already smoking hallway.

They caught the man in the basement who was kindling the fire. He was Sam Wembly. At first he was stubborn and refused to talk. But about sixteen hours of grilling broke him down. He saw that the jig was up and told everything, and not, I think without a certain defiant pride that went with him to the gallows.

It was he who had first lured Tyrone into the gambling racket. Under the protection of the old administration the two of them had cashed in profitably on a string of slot machines and other gambling devices. Then the smash had come—the election of new city officials. All of their savings had been spent trying to beat the new candidates. Tyrone had even stolen library funds to keep Wembly's paper going, but to no avail.

It was then that Tyrone, overwhelmed with defeat, crazed with the fear of exposure, had evolved his hellish scheme. He and Wembly would stage a reign of terror in the city. This would divert the threatening investigation of his own defalcations, and would throw the public into a panic which he hoped would result in the overthrow of the new officials. He had planned, however, to have them murdered outright if this did not succeed.

The chief problem, of course, in such a scheme was how to get the necessary agents to carry on the hellish business. They had no available money to hire assassins. That was where Tyrone's "reincarnation" scheme came in. He was a scholar and a student of abnormal psychology and he had worked out the process by which, through hypnotism, torture and drugs, the weird prototypes of dead monsters could be created. The Hindu's temple they had found a convenient place to single out the types they needed, minds already prepared by the Swami's teachings. The Swami himself had been unaware of his part in the crime.

Tyrone's reason for choosing Frances and me among his victims was that he was afraid that sooner or later one of us would penetrate his secret. But we were the stumbling blocks in his scheme, for our minds had not yielded to his sway as completely as the neurotic wrecks he usually chose.

The secret torture chamber was in the basement of Wembly's printing plant. The poor wretches found there by the police were taken to asylums. Frances and I were the only victims who escaped a permanent mental derangement, and even at that we were left with mental scars that took longer to heal than the results of physical torture and bullets.

But happiness had a lot to do with our eventual permanent recovery. I am now the City Librarian, having stepped into Tyrone's former job, and Frances is no longer the librarian's secretary, but his wife.

RAMBLE HOUSE's

HARRY STEPHEN KEELER WEBWORK MYSTERIES

(RH) indicates the title is available ONLY in the **RAMBLE HOUSE** edition

The Ace of Spades Murder
The Affair of the Bottled Deuce (RH)
The Amazing Web
The Barking Clock
Behind That Mask
The Book with the Orange Leaves
The Bottle with the Green Wax Seal
The Box from Japan
The Case of the Canny Killer
The Case of the Crazy Corpse (RH)
The Case of the Flying Hands (RH)
The Case of the Ivory Arrow
The Case of the Jeweled Ragpicker
The Case of the Lavender Gripsack
The Case of the Mysterious Moll
The Case of the 16 Beans
The Case of the Transparent Nude (RH)
The Case of the Transposed Legs
The Case of the Two-Headed Idiot (RH)
The Case of the Two Strange Ladies
The Circus Stealers (RH)
Cleopatra's Tears
A Copy of Beowulf (RH)
The Crimson Cube (RH)
The Face of the Man From Saturn
Find the Clock
The Five Silver Buddhas
The 4th King
The Gallows Waits, My Lord! (RH)
The Green Jade Hand
Finger! Finger!
Hangman's Nights (RH)
I, Chameleon (RH)
I Killed Lincoln at 10:13! (RH)
The Iron Ring
The Man Who Changed His Skin (RH)
The Man with the Crimson Box
The Man with the Magic Eardrums
The Man with the Wooden Spectacles
The Marceau Case
The Matilda Hunter Murder
The Monocled Monster

The Murder of London Lew
The Murdered Mathematician
The Mysterious Card (RH)
The Mysterious Ivory Ball of Wong Shing Li (RH)
The Mystery of the Fiddling Cracksman
The Peacock Fan
The Photo of Lady X (RH)
The Portrait of Jirjohn Cobb
Report on Vanessa Hewstone (RH)
Riddle of the Travelling Skull
Riddle of the Wooden Parrakeet (RH)
The Scarlet Mummy (RH)
The Search for X-Y-Z
The Sharkskin Book
Sing Sing Nights
The Six From Nowhere (RH)
The Skull of the Waltzing Clown
The Spectacles of Mr. Cagliostro
Stand By—London Calling!
The Steeltown Strangler
The Stolen Gravestone (RH)
Strange Journey (RH)
The Strange Will
The Straw Hat Murders (RH)
The Street of 1000 Eyes (RH)
Thieves' Nights
Three Novellos (RH)
The Tiger Snake
The Trap (RH)
Vagabond Nights (Defrauded Yeggman)
Vagabond Nights 2 (10 Hours)
The Vanishing Gold Truck
The Voice of the Seven Sparrows
The Washington Square Enigma
When Thief Meets Thief
The White Circle (RH)
The Wonderful Scheme of Mr. Christopher Thorne
X. Jones—of Scotland Yard
Y. Cheung, Business Detective

Keeler Related Works

A To Izzard: A Harry Stephen Keeler Companion by Fender Tucker — Articles and stories about Harry, by Harry, and in his style. Included is a compleat bibliography.

Wild About Harry: Reviews of Keeler Novels — Edited by Richard Polt & Fender Tucker — 22 reviews of works by Harry Stephen Keeler from *Keeler News*. A perfect introduction to the author.

The Keeler Keyhole Collection: Annotated newsletter rants from Harry Stephen Keeler, edited by Francis M. Nevins. Over 400 pages of incredibly personal Keeleriana.

Fakealoo — Pastiches of the style of Harry Stephen Keeler by selected demented members of the HSK Society. Updated every year with the new winner.

RAMBLE HOUSE's OTHER LOONS

The End of It All and Other Stories — Ed Gorman's latest short story collection

Six Dancing Tuatara Press Books — *Beast or Man?* by Sean M'Guire; *The Whistling Ancestors* by Richard E. Goddard; *The Shadow on the House, Sorcerer's Chessmen* and *The Wizard of Berner's Abbey* by Mark Hansom, *The Trail of the Cloven Hoof* by Arlton Eadie and *The Border Line* by Walter S. Masterman. With introductions by John Pelan. Many more to come!

Death Leaves No Card — One of the most unusual murdered-in-the-tub mysteries you'll ever read. By Miles Burton.

The Dumpling — Political murder from 1907 by Coulson Kernahan

Victims & Villains — Intriguing Sherlockiana from Derham Groves

Ultra-Boiled — 23 gut-wrenching tales by our Man in Brooklyn, Gary Lovisi. Yow!

Shadows' Edge — Two early novels by Wade Wright: *Shadows Don't Bleed* and *The Sharp Edge*.

Evidence in Blue — 1938 mystery by E. Charles Vivian

The Case of the Little Green Men — Mack Reynolds wrote this love song to sci-fi fans back in 1951 and it's now back in print.

Hell Fire and **Savage Highway** — Two new hard-boiled novels by Jack Moskovitz, who developed his style writing sleaze back in the 70s. No one writes like Jack.

Researching American-Made Toy Soldiers — A 276-page collection of a lifetime of articles by toy soldier expert Richard O'Brien

Strands of the Web: Short Stories of Harry Stephen Keeler — Edited and Introduced by Fred Cleaver

Through the Looking Glass — Lewis Carroll wrote it; Gavin L. O'Keefe illustrated it.

The Sam McCain Novels — Ed Gorman's terrific series includes *The Day the Music Died, Wake Up Little Susie* and *Will You Still Love Me Tomorrow?*

A Shot Rang Out — Three decades of reviews from Jon Breen

Mysterious Martin, the Master of Murder — Two versions of a strange 1912 novel by Tod Robbins about a man who writes books that can kill.

Dago Red — 22 tales of dark suspense by Bill Pronzini

Two Robert Randisi Novels — *No Exit to Brooklyn* and *The Dead of Brooklyn*. The first two Nick Delvecchio novels.

The Night Remembers — A 1991 Jack Walsh mystery from Ed Gorman

Rough Cut & New, Improved Murder — Ed Gorman's first two novels

Hollywood Dreams — A novel of the Depression by Richard O'Brien

Seven Gelett Burgess Novels — *The Master of Mysteries, The White Cat, Two O'Clock Courage, Ladies in Boxes, Find the Woman, The Heart Line, The Picaroons*

The Organ Reader — A huge compilation of just about everything published in the 1971-1972 radical bay-area newspaper, *THE ORGAN*.

A Clear Path to Cross — Sharon Knowles short mystery stories by Ed Lynskey

Old Times' Sake — Short stories by James Reasoner from Mike Shayne Magazine

Freaks and Fantasies — Eerie tales by Tod Robbins, collaborator of Tod Browning on the film FREAKS.

Seven Jim Harmon Double Novels — *Vixen Hollow/Celluloid Scandal, The Man Who Made Maniacs/Silent Siren, Ape Rape/Wanton Witch, Sex Burns Like Fire/Twist Session, Sudden Lust/Passion Strip, Sin Unlimited/Harlot Master, Twilight Girls/Sex Institution*. Written in the early 60s.

Marblehead: A Novel of H.P. Lovecraft — A long-lost masterpiece from Richard A. Lupoff. Published for the first time!

The Compleat Ova Hamlet — Parodies of SF authors by Richard A. Lupoff – A brand new edition with more stories and more illustrations by Trina Robbins.

The Secret Adventures of Sherlock Holmes — Three Sherlockian pastiches by the Brooklyn author/publisher, Gary Lovisi.

The Universal Holmes — Richard A. Lupoff's 2007 collection of five Holmesian pastiches and a recipe for giant rat stew.

Four Joel Townsley Rogers Novels — By the author of *The Red Right Hand: Once In a Red Moon, Lady With the Dice, The Stopped Clock, Never Leave My Bed*

Two Joel Townsley Rogers Story Collections — Night of Horror and Killing Time

Twenty Norman Berrow Novels — *The Bishop's Sword, Ghost House, Don't Go Out After Dark, Claws of the Cougar, The Smokers of Hashish, The Secret Dancer, Don't Jump Mr. Boland!, The Footprints of Satan, Fingers for Ransom, The Three Tiers of Fantasy, The Spaniard's Thumb, The Eleventh Plague, Words Have Wings, One Thrilling Night, The Lady's in Danger, It Howls at Night, The Terror in the Fog, Oil Under the Window, Murder in the Melody, The Singing Room*

The N. R. De Mexico Novels — Robert Bragg presents *Marijuana Girl, Madman on a Drum, Private Chauffeur* in one volume.

Four Chelsea Quinn Yarbro Novels featuring Charlie Moon — *Ogilvie, Tallant and Moon, Music When the Sweet Voice Dies, Poisonous Fruit* and *Dead Mice*

Five Walter S. Masterman Mysteries — *The Green Toad, The Flying Beast, The Yellow Mistletoe, The Wrong Verdict* and *The Perjured Alibi*. Fantastic impossible plots.

Two Hake Talbot Novels — *Rim of the Pit, The Hangman's Handyman*. Classic locked room mysteries.

Two Alexander Laing Novels — *The Motives of Nicholas Holtz* and *Dr. Scarlett*, stories of medical mayhem and intrigue from the 30s.

Four David Hume Novels — *Corpses Never Argue, Cemetery First Stop, Make Way for the Mourners, Eternity Here I Come*, and more to come.

Three Wade Wright Novels — *Echo of Fear, Death At Nostalgia Street* and *It Leads to Murder*, with more to come!

Eight Rupert Penny Novels — *Policeman's Holiday, Policeman's Evidence, Lucky Policeman, Policeman in Armour, Sealed Room Murder, Sweet Poison, The Talkative Policeman, She had to Have Gas* and *Cut and Run* (by Martin Tanner.)

Five Jack Mann Novels — Strange murder in the English countryside. *Gees' First Case, Nightmare Farm, Grey Shapes, The Ninth Life, The Glass Too Many*.

Seven Max Afford Novels — *Owl of Darkness, Death's Mannikins, Blood on His Hands, The Dead Are Blind, The Sheep and the Wolves, Sinners in Paradise* and *Two Locked Room Mysteries and a Ripping Yarn* by one of Australia's finest novelists.

Five Joseph Shallit Novels — *The Case of the Billion Dollar Body, Lady Don't Die on My Doorstep, Kiss the Killer, Yell Bloody Murder, Take Your Last Look*. One of America's best 50's authors.

Two Crimson Clown Novels — By Johnston McCulley, author of the Zorro novels, *The Crimson Clown* and *The Crimson Clown Again*.

The Best of 10-Story Book — edited by Chris Mikul, over 35 stories from the literary magazine Harry Stephen Keeler edited.

A Young Man's Heart — A forgotten early classic by Cornell Woolrich

The Anthony Boucher Chronicles — edited by Francis M. Nevins
Book reviews by Anthony Boucher written for the *San Francisco Chronicle*, 1942 – 1947. Essential and fascinating reading.

Muddled Mind: Complete Works of Ed Wood, Jr. — David Hayes and Hayden Davis deconstruct the life and works of a mad genius.

Gadsby — A lipogram (a novel without the letter E). Ernest Vincent Wright's last work, published in 1939 right before his death.

My First Time: The One Experience You Never Forget — Michael Birchwood — 64 true first-person narratives of how they lost it.

A Roland Daniel Double: The Signal and The Return of Wu Fang — Classic thrillers from the 30s

Murder in Shawnee — Two novels of the Alleghenies by John Douglas: *Shawnee Alley Fire* and *Haunts*.

Deep Space and other Stories — A collection of SF gems by Richard A. Lupoff

Blood Moon — The first of the Robert Payne series by Ed Gorman

The Time Armada — Fox B. Holden's 1953 SF gem.

Black River Falls — Suspense from the master, Ed Gorman

Sideslip — 1968 SF masterpiece by Ted White and Dave Van Arnam

The Triune Man — Mindscrambling science fiction from Richard A. Lupoff

Detective Duff Unravels It — Episodic mysteries by Harvey O'Higgins

Automaton — Brilliant treatise on robotics: 1928-style! By H. Stafford Hatfield

The Incredible Adventures of Rowland Hern — Rousing 1928 impossible crimes by Nicholas Olde.

Slammer Days — Two full-length prison memoirs: *Men into Beasts* (1952) by George Sylvester Viereck and *Home Away From Home* (1962) by Jack Woodford

Murder in Black and White — 1931 classic tennis whodunit by Evelyn Elder

Killer's Caress — Cary Moran's 1936 hardboiled thriller

The Golden Dagger — 1951 Scotland Yard yarn by E. R. Punshon

A Smell of Smoke — 1951 English countryside thriller by Miles Burton

Ruled By Radio — 1925 futuristic novel by Robert L. Hadfield & Frank E. Farncombe

Murder in Silk — A 1937 Yellow Peril novel of the silk trade by Ralph Trevor

The Case of the Withered Hand — 1936 potboiler by John G. Brandon

Finger-prints Never Lie — A 1939 classic detective novel by John G. Brandon

Inclination to Murder — 1966 thriller by New Zealand's Harriet Hunter

Invaders from the Dark — Classic werewolf tale from Greye La Spina

Fatal Accident — Murder by automobile, a 1936 mystery by Cecil M. Wills

The Devil Drives — A prison and lost treasure novel by Virgil Markham

Dr. Odin — Douglas Newton's 1933 potboiler comes back to life.

The Chinese Jar Mystery — Murder in the manor by John Stephen Strange, 1934

The Julius Caesar Murder Case — A classic 1935 re-telling of the assassination by Wallace Irwin that's much more fun than the Shakespeare version

West Texas War and Other Western Stories — by Gary Lovisi

The Contested Earth and Other SF Stories — A never-before published space opera and seven short stories by Jim Harmon.

Tales of the Macabre and Ordinary — Modern twisted horror by Chris Mikul, author of the *Bizarrism* series.

The Gold Star Line — Seaboard adventure from L.T. Reade and Robert Eustace.

The Werewolf vs the Vampire Woman — Hard to believe ultraviolence by either Arthur M. Scarm or Arthur M. Scram.

Black Hogan Strikes Again — Australia's Peter Renwick pens a tale of the outback.

Don Diablo: Book of a Lost Film — Two-volume treatment of a western by Paul Landres, with diagrams. Intro by Francis M. Nevins.

The Charlie Chaplin Murder Mystery — Movie hijinks by Wes D. Gehring

The Koky Comics — A collection of all of the 1978-1981 Sunday and daily comic strips by Richard O'Brien and Mort Gerberg, in two volumes.

Suzy — Another collection of comic strips from Richard O'Brien and Bob Vojtko

Dime Novels: Ramble House's 10-Cent Books — *Knife in the Dark* by Robert Leslie Bellem, *Hot Lead* and *Song of Death* by Ed Earl Repp, *A Hashish House in New York* by H.H. Kane, and five more.

Blood in a Snap — The *Finnegan's Wake* of the 21st century, by Jim Weiler

Stakeout on Millennium Drive — Award-winning Indianapolis Noir — Ian Woollen.

Dope Tales #1 — Two dope-riddled classics; *Dope Runners* by Gerald Grantham and *Death Takes the Joystick* by Phillip Condé.

Dope Tales #2 — Two more narco-classics; *The Invisible Hand* by Rex Dark and *The Smokers of Hashish* by Norman Berrow.

Dope Tales #3 — Two enchanting novels of opium by the master, Sax Rohmer. *Dope* and *The Yellow Claw*.

Tenebrae — Ernest G. Henham's 1898 horror tale brought back.

The Singular Problem of the Stygian House-Boat — Two classic tales by John Kendrick Bangs about the denizens of Hades.

Tiresias — Psychotic modern horror novel by Jonathan M. Sweet.

The One After Snelling — Kickass modern noir from Richard O'Brien.

The Sign of the Scorpion — 1935 Edmund Snell tale of oriental evil.

The House of the Vampire — 1907 poetic thriller by George S. Viereck.

An Angel in the Street — Modern hardboiled noir by Peter Genovese.

The Devil's Mistress — Scottish gothic tale by J. W. Brodie-Innes.

The Lord of Terror — 1925 mystery with master-criminal, Fantômas.

The Lady of the Terraces — 1925 adventure by E. Charles Vivian.

My Deadly Angel — 1955 Cold War drama by John Chelton

Prose Bowl — Futuristic satire — Bill Pronzini & Barry N. Malzberg .

Satan's Den Exposed — True crime in Truth or Consequences New Mexico — Award-winning journalism by the *Desert Journal*.

The Amorous Intrigues & Adventures of Aaron Burr — by Anonymous — Hot historical action.

I Stole $16,000,000 — A true story by cracksman Herbert E. Wilson.

The Black Dark Murders — Vintage 50s college murder yarn by Milt Ozaki, writing as Robert O. Saber.

Sex Slave — Potboiler of lust in the days of Cleopatra — Dion Leclerq.

You'll Die Laughing — Bruce Elliott's 1945 novel of murder at a practical joker's English countryside manor.

The Private Journal & Diary of John H. Surratt — The memoirs of the man who conspired to assassinate President Lincoln.

Dead Man Talks Too Much — Hollywood boozer by Weed Dickenson

Red Light — History of legal prostitution in Shreveport Louisiana by Eric Brock. Includes wonderful photos of the houses and the ladies.

A Snark Selection — Lewis Carroll's *The Hunting of the Snark* with two Snarkian chapters by Harry Stephen Keeler — Illustrated by Gavin L. O'Keefe.

Ripped from the Headlines! — The Jack the Ripper story as told in the newspaper articles in the *New York* and *London Times*.

Geronimo — S. M. Barrett's 1905 autobiography of a noble American.

The White Peril in the Far East — Sidney Lewis Gulick's 1905 indictment of the West and assurance that Japan would never attack the U.S.

The Compleat Calhoon — All of Fender Tucker's works: Includes *Totah Six-Pack, Weed, Women and Song* and *Tales from the Tower,* plus a CD of all of his songs.

Totah Six-Pack — Just Fender Tucker's six tales about Farmington in one sleek volume.

RAMBLE HOUSE
Fender Tucker, Prop. Gavin L. O'Keefe, Graphics
www.ramblehouse.com   fender@ramblehouse.com
228-826-1783 10329 Sheephead Drive, Vancleave MS 39565

Made in the USA
Las Vegas, NV
15 September 2023